Operation Firethorn

(OCI Series, Book 2)

by

Richard Bergeron

ISBN: 0-9893543-3-4
ISBN-13: 978-0-9893543-3-2

Other works by Richard Bergeron

Needle on the Haystack (OCI Series, Book 1)

Where Did the Sunrise Go? (Poetry)

Three Acadian Generations: The First Bergeron d'Amboises in the Americas
(Family History), which can be found at:
http://www.acadian.org/bergeron.html

Also see my blog: http://bergeron-damboise.blogspot.com/

NOTE

If you want more information (and some "extras") about this book and other
books in the "OCI Series," please go to: richard-bergeron.weebly.com

Thanks ever so much for looking this book up on Amazon.com
and writing a review.

DEDICATION

This book is dedicated to my wife, Barbara, who encouraged me to write. She edited the story many times to make it immeasurably better. Also dedicated to my early readers, primarily Barry Kleider, who provided invaluable feedback.

ACKNOWLEDGMENTS

Many thanks to the following:

My wife Barbara for her encouragement, her patience and her great ability as an editor/continuity editor.
Barry Kleider for the professional photographs.
Barry and his wife Kate for teaching me a bit about diving and for reading the manuscript to try to find my mistakes when writing about the divers in the story. They also served as editor and pre-publication readers.
Martin Daniels for serving as another pre-publication reader.
Bart Palamaro of Indie Author Support for creating the new cover for *Needle on the Haystack* (OCI Series, Book 1) and the original cover for this book, *Operation Firethorn* (OCI Series, Book 2).
The American Indian people of Minnesota for showing remarkable patience with an outsider trying to learn from them.
African Americans, Latinos/Chicanos/Spanish-speaking people, and Asian people of many backgrounds for their patience along the same lines.
European Americans who helped me understand some of their unique traditions.
The following people for supporting me and teaching me how to write better: fellow aspiring writers in writing clubs and in creative writing classes at the University of Minnesota and The Loft of Minneapolis.
George and Bev Roberts for the opportunity to hold readings at Homewood Studios in North Minneapolis.

Special thanks go to the fine editors I had in the workplace, especially Coventry at Control Data Corporation and Ray at MECC/The Learning Company.

CONTENTS

Introduction

Dear Reader,

My situation was unusual during the events described herein. The Navy sent me to Great Lakes Naval Training Center to go through Fire Control Technician (FT) schools. This would allow my engineering degree to better match the technical requirements in the fleet.

The Navy school system begins with a Class "A" school, a basic training program, which I had to attend because it was the Navy's first step for someone who never had any technical training and I had to look like a novice to make future assignments more credible. We had loads of homework in that course. Because I was in this school, I could not play a very active role in the case that our OCI team was working on. Rena Skye was actually center stage this time, more so than when the two of us were a team, which I wrote about in *Needle on the Haystack*.

When I completed "A" School, I was assigned training on a specific weapons control system in a "C" school. Everything in that training used classified information, so we couldn't take any materials out of the building. Thus we had no homework. As a result, Rena could send me to some remote locations on weekends and I could do some work on the case.

I continued to write the record of our work. Rena did a remarkable job of providing the details of many events and I spent many hours interviewing the more active members of the team, both as events happened and shortly after we closed the case. I had some long conversations with Glenn Oliver and Chaské Hunter. And I was even able to interview Leonid Mazursky, who had worked with the criminal leader. In this way, I was able to fill in and correct a great number of details. I could not have reported this case so completely without their help.

Eric Matthews

Prologue

A Major Midwestern City

Loki sat in his secret office in the center of a mansion. Leonid Mazursky, his personal assistant, brought him another vodka martini, which Loki nursed as he fondled the red and yellow rose in his lapel. He looked out into the living room through one of the two-way mirrors. Watched his people. Smiled at some of their antics. Waited.

His active mind jumped to the choice of his code name: Loki. Most people remembered Loki as the ancient Norse god who played the role of the vindictive trickster. But he was much more. The Norse Loki was an agent of necessary change.

And Loki did, indeed, intend to change the world.

The phone on the small table next to his easy chair rang. Leonid answered the call. "Yes?"

Loki looked at the Longines on his left wrist. The time was eleven o'clock in the evening. Leonid listened for a moment, then handed the phone to his leader.

"Speak," Loki commanded.

The man on the other end of the line talked for a moment.

"So the truck has crossed into Illinois. Do it," Loki ordered and hung up. He sat back and congratulated himself and his team. This would be a major accomplishment.

1. Murders on a Rural Highway

Chicago

I looked around the Red Arrow Jazz Club. The crowd was large. The smoke was so thick that I didn't need to light a cigarette of my own. I watched through the haze as the band laid down their instruments for a break. The musicians were a mixture of Negroes and whites, as was the audience. The jazz was great. Dixieland. I loved it.

My name is Eric Matthews. I'm a full lieutenant in the U.S. Navy. I work for the Office of Criminal Investigation or OCI. I thought back over the last eight months when I was part of an investigation led by Captain Rena Skye, who now sat next to me. We busted a drug ring in the Norfolk-Virginia Beach area.

Tonight we were enjoying the band at the Red Arrow. The place was famous far beyond Chicago. Its diamond-shaped napkins carried its printed message: "Greetings from the Red Arrow Jazz Club ... where Dixieland Jass is immortalized!" Franz Jackson and the Original Jass All-Stars were tonight's musicians. But this band didn't limit itself to Dixieland; their repertoire also included traditional jazz, straight instrumental jazz and what might be called saxophone jazz. The band was so good that they'd played at this club for seven years, since 1955.

The others in our party tonight were Jennifer Powers and Glenn Oliver, two more members of our team in the Norfolk investigation. Because the band was on break, conversation was possible. "If you know where to go in Chicago," I laughed, "you can find some truly good jazz!"

Rena nodded and raised her glass. "Here's to Glenn who found the Red Arrow!"

Glenn wasn't just a fan of Jazz - he was a fanatic. Jennie leaned over and kissed the man being toasted. He raised his drink in acknowledgment of the accolades and sipped from it. It was obvious that the slim and shapely Jennie adored him and that he returned the favor. The four of us were here on well-deserved "R and R," resting, relaxing and enjoying ourselves.

"So, here's to good jazz!" Jennie said. She lifted her whiskey and her bottle of beer, one in each hand. Saluting her date with a raised shot glass, she slammed down the bourbon before taking a swig of brew.

Glenn stared at her and laughed through his heavy mustache.

"Where did you learn to drink like that?" I asked her.

"My great-grandfather," Jennie said proudly. "He was born in the 1850s as a slave. After the Civil War he left Texas. He later joined the buffalo soldiers and fought Indians. After the Apaches were defeated, he quit the army and became a cowboy in Arizona. You know, he lived to be over a hundred years old. And he swore it was the whiskey he drank every night that did it. So he taught me how to drink when I turned sixteen."

"Sixteen?" I asked.

Oliver laughed heartily. "Yeah. I guess he followed his own law."

The band returned and got ready for another set. The music started up again. Rena leaned to my ear and said: "Come on, Eric, let's dance."

We never left the dance floor during the whole set. We showed off our fancy footwork to the fast songs, such as "Clarinet Marmalade" and "Mr. Banjo Man." We returned to our moving embrace during "Red Arrow Blues," "Mack the Knife," and other slow tunes, when I buried my face in her shoulder length auburn hair. When the band took its next break, we returned to the table with Jennie and Glenn.

Rena looked at her friend and asked: "Didn't you two dance?"

Jennie looked at Rena as if she were crazy. "You didn't see us out there?"

Glenn tried to control his laughter. "Lady, they weren't able to see anythin' 'cept themselves. I haven't seen folks so wrapped up in each other in a month o' Sundays!"

"Yeah," Jennie replied, grinning. "Must be true love."

The band returned and began to tune up for their next set.

"Be back soon," I said and found the head. All the stalls were empty. I entered the last one, nearest the wall.

Moments later I looked up sharply. Two men had entered the head. They were speaking Russian.

"Все направо, это происходит сегодня. Для получения более подробной информации...."

I was very surprised that these guys were speaking Russian so openly, considering what they were saying. People generally don't talk like they did if they don't want to get themselves killed. Maybe they were totally convinced that they were alone, or that nobody would understand them. But I'm fluent in that language and grew more curious as they talked. I lifted my feet up and put them against the door. I didn't want these guys to see my shoes and stop talking. A short time later, a couple more men came in. The Russians spoke a few sentences in English then stopped talking. I guess they left because I didn't hear any Russian after that. But what I already heard was intriguing.

I was soon with my friends again. I gazed out over the crowd, hoping to catch sight of the Russian speakers. I saw two men going out the door. I made my way to the exit as fast as I could, but the packed bodies of the crowd slowed me down. By the time I reached the parking area, I saw the flash of a long arrow-shaped car turning onto the street and then it was gone. I didn't have time to note its license plate number. But I did identify it as a white '62 Cadillac with a black top. I returned to our table.

I must have looked worried. Or puzzled.

"What's wrong, Eric?" Rena asked as softly as she could with the band playing.

I leaned over to talk directly into her ear. "I overheard two guys in the head talking in Russian."

"Lots of people in this city speak other languages."

"But they don't say what these guys said...."

The music ended and the band adjusted their instruments for the next song.

"What did they say?" Rena asked quietly.

"I'll tell you on the way home." Then I said loud enough for all to hear: "I can't stay out much later. I have to be back at the barracks early in the morning. Weekend duty, you know. Got to love it, it's so much fun."

"You know why you're still playing enlisted man, even here?" Rena asked in my ear, so nobody away from our table could overhear her.

"Sure, I understand," I said quietly. Then I spoke up so everyone at the table to hear. "I wish I could spend the whole weekend with all of you. But I can't." I finished my beer and turned to Rena. "If you want to stay here with them, can I borrow your car to go back to Lakes?"

"She can stay if she wants," Oliver offered. "We can take her back."

"No, Eric's right," Rena replied. She reached out and took my hand. "Come on, let's go home."

We got into the car and Rena maneuvered until we reached the road heading to Great Lakes. "So, what's so secret about the conversation you overheard?"

"The first guy said: 'All right, it happens tonight. The truck is leaving Saint Louis shortly. For more information, you can check with Loki tomorrow. He's at his house.' The other guy answered: 'Who is doing the job?' And the first guy told him: 'Sasha. He's so good that these stupid Americans will never find out who did this job. Or that anything is even missing.' At that moment, two other guys came into the head, but the second guy replied in English as if he were a businessman: 'Very good. We can do business. Keep in touch. Now, I must go on to other work. I will be at my office.'" I shook my head. "I have no idea what it all means. I don't even know what they looked like or where they were sitting," I said. "And I saw some guys leaving." I told her of the car I'd seen pulling out of the parking area. "But that's not evidence. All we can do is report this and let the brass do their thing."

"Crap," she said. "I have a gut feeling we'd save ourselves a lot of trouble if we could follow them."

"Ever hear of a guy named Loki?" I asked.

"No. But you know how my intuitions are," Rena replied. "And right now they're screaming at me."

"Those guys must have felt pretty comfortable. Pretty safe," I observed.

"Or they figured even if someone else was there," Rena laughed, " we're all such stupid Americans, that nobody here would ever be able to understand them."

Rena was silent for quite a while as she drove. "At least we know a couple names. Loki and Sasha. I sure wish we could follow them."

As we traveled, both of us thought about what I overheard.

*   *   *   *

North Chicago

Rena and I returned to our rented apartment in North Chicago. But she wouldn't let me get to sleep right away. We finished a great night in bed. Now, glowing in the aftermath of our lovemaking, she laid her head on my chest. "Mmmm, that might make up for you being on duty all weekend."

"We'll get through it," I chuckled. I held her tightly.

"This is much nicer than when we first met."

"Sure is. Back then, I hurt a lot."

"So did I," she said. "I ached when you left me every time we met."

I was transferred from Great Lakes to Norfolk, where we first met. I served as an undercover operative on the destroyer USS *Hestek*. There, I worked on the deck force, not in any technical position, but the Navy was making it up to me now by putting me through schools so I could work in the skilled technical rating of Fire Control Technician. I'd be working with all the equipment used to control shipboard gunfire or missile shots.

It turned out that Rena was my contact with OCI in Norfolk. She and I had fallen for each other almost the minute we met.

Her original duty station was in California but she was now assigned to the OCI office at Great Lakes at the same time I was sent there to go to school. Neither one of us could figure out why they also transferred her to "Lakes." Perhaps someone had an intuition that she should be there. For whatever reason. At any rate, this let us be together. We shared an off-base apartment in North Chicago, a mile or so from the northernmost gate of the naval base.

Rena snuggled closer to me, if that was possible, nestled her head against my chest, closed her eyes and whispered. "I want to stay like this until dawn."

"You don't want to...?" I asked.

"Are you ready to go again already?"

I grinned. Rolled over to face her. Leaned in to kiss her. "Sure...."

The telephone rang. "Don't answer it," I urged. "They can wait."

It rang again.

"You know I can't do that. What if they need me for a case?" Rena asked.

"You're busy helping me get ready for tomorrow?" I suggested.

"I wish I could." She turned on the bedside lamp and picked up the receiver before the next ring. "Here."

"This is Norfolk Central. Please hold. Commander Blount wants to speak with you."

Rena frowned as she cradled the phone on her shoulder and sat up on the edge of the bed. Blount was a thousand miles away, where the time was 0300. Still, she pulled her robe over her shoulders.

"Captain Skye?"

The woman Marine recognized the voice of her boss. "Yes, sir. What's up?"

"A Navy truck was highjacked and two drivers murdered in central Illinois. We need you to work the site."

"Isn't this out of our jurisdiction?"

"OCI Great Lakes office is short of people right now, let alone trained criminologists. And you're there, working for Commander Fasano."

"Have you notified him that you're assigning me to the case?"

"He called me as soon as they got the report about the highjacking and murders, and asked if he could use you on this case. I said 'yes.' Fasano was ecstatic."

"All right, sir. What arrangements did you make?"

"Go to the Great Lakes office. There's a huge tarmac, a parking lot, nearby. A helo will take you from there down to Glenview Naval Air Station. There's a plane there to fly you south to the town of Highland, near the scene of the crime. The Illinois State Police will take you to the site."

"Any special orders?"

"No. Just do a good evaluation. Make your report to the Lakes office and you have permission from me to follow through on the case for them if they need you. If it's something serious, I'll send you more help. And if you go outside the Great Lakes area, let me know. I'll clear you to get whatever you need wherever you go."

"Yes, sir. I'll do that and keep you up to date."

"I wouldn't expect anything else, Captain. Get going. They're waiting for you."

"Wait a minute, Commander. I have some other information that might be relevant. Eric overheard a somewhat ominous sounding conversation earlier tonight concerning some truck drivers...." She gave her boss all the details of the exchange I'd heard and translated.

"Thanks. That may bear some relationship to this case. By the way," Blount added. "The Highway Patrol reported minimal damage to the truck. The driver-side window and the front windshield were shot out. I'll have Great Lakes Central get someone over to fix the glass. And get some new drivers. Better get going, now."

*   *   *   *

Central Illinois

Rena Skye looked out the window of the small plane flying her from Glenview Naval Air Station to Highland in central Illinois. She couldn't see much in the dark so she let her mind wander. She thought back over her previous assignment. She was a trained criminologist. She impressed the right people. They promoted her to field coordinator and moved her from California to Norfolk. She led a large team of Office of Criminal Investigation operatives to bust a huge Norfolk drug ring.

She was lucky. They permitted her to bring in a number of people she'd worked with before, including her closest friend, Jennie Powers. The others assigned to the project proved to be superb operatives. Skye leaned back and smiled as she thought about her crew. One of the people assigned to the Norfolk drug ring investigation was me, Eric Matthews.

Another new person was Glenn Oliver. He and Jennie were attracted to each other as soon as they met. And then there was Chaské Hunter and Ruth Gardner. This bunch had generated more than the average number of loving couples.

Skye shifted so that she leaned against the bulkhead. She straightened her Marine Corps uniform. Let her thoughts drift some more. For all the good memories of Norfolk, there were some bad ones as well. One agent, Brandon Lunch, came with a huge Saint Bernard whose name was Tango because, as a puppy, whenever Brandon opened a beer, the dog danced around on his hind legs until he got some of the drink he loved so much. Toward the end of the Norfolk investigation, the drug ring caught Lunch snooping around and killed him. Brandon was a great advisor and a good investigator. Rena would miss him.

She inherited Tango. She left him with me, jokingly ordering him to guard me well while she was gone.

Skye wondered about this next job. Would it be as big as the Norfolk investigation? In a way, she hoped so. It would be a good opportunity to work with the old group again.

Rena was tired and there would be a lot of work ahead of her. She forced herself to doze off for a while.

The light plane landed in Highland, Illinois, shortly after dawn.

Skye walked toward the small airstrip's building. An Illinois State Trooper stepped outside as she approached the building.

"Captain Rena Skye?" the trooper asked.

"Yes."

"How do you do, ma'am? I'm Trooper Jack Temple." He held out his hand, which she shook. "Good, firm handshake. I like that. *Semper fi* and all that. Glad to have you on this case, ma'am. I hear you're a crackerjack criminologist."

"You were in the Corps?"

"Yes, ma'am. From '51 through '55. Spent two years in Korea."

"Well, Mr. Temple. Please call me Skye or use my given name, Rena. All that 'ma'am' stuff makes me feel old. It's protocol in the service, but you're no longer military and I'm not so gung-ho, either."

"All right, Rena," he smiled. "My patrol car is around that corner there." He led her to an already visibly used 1962 Chevrolet. She got into the front passenger seat. As soon as he reached US 40, Temple turned on the lights and siren, and stepped on the accelerator.

Before long, Skye saw a couple more state police cruisers, one on either side of the highway. She could see a flatbed tractor-trailer rig some distance in front of the nearest police car. They pulled up behind the closest car.

"Thank you, Jack. That was much faster than I expected."

"Yes, ma'am, uh, Captain. That's why we had you fly into Highland, 'cause it was so close. These troopers will take care of you now. I have to get back to my own stretch of the road. Good luck with your investigation."

Rena stepped out of the cruiser, adjusted her skirt and jacket. She stayed on the edge of the highway as she approached the two waiting patrolmen.

"A woman? They sent us a skirt to do a man's job?" one of the troopers muttered. Skye heard him but didn't say anything.

"Shut up. If she's here from OCI, she's good," the other officer said in a low voice, giving his partner a disapproving look. He turned to Skye. "Captain, they radioed that you landed and were on your way. This is Trooper Tony Swann and I'm Trooper Max Baxter." They shook hands all around. Swann seemed to shake her hand only because he was required to.

"So, what do we have here?" she asked.

"Tony and I were traveling down this stretch of Highway 40. It was nearly oh-two-thirty. I slowed down a bit to negotiate the curving road here. This semi was parked on the side of the road like this." He motioned to the flatbed they stood next to. Its cargo was completely covered by a large tarpaulin.

"We thought the drivers might have a problem, so I turned on the flashing lights as I pulled over and parked. We broke out the flashlights and looked around."

Baxter gave her a complete rundown of what they concluded when they inspected the area. "Everything is still as it was when we examined the scene. When we found this man, I felt the jugular. He was still warm, but there wasn't any pulse. We concluded that the second driver tried to run up that ridge there. Tire tracks and footprints indicated that another vehicle pulled up in front of the semi. Guys from that car must have shot the second driver. We found him up there, still alive."

"Did he say anything?" Skye asked.

"All he said was: 'Thick accent.' Then he collapsed. That driver had his wallet on him. He was a boy named Jerome Hassler."

"Boy? How young was he?"

"Sorry. He was a Negro. Twenty-nine years old. He had a Class A operator's license from Missouri. Lived in Saint Louis." The trooper took a deep breath. "We could see that a small car of some sort pulled up behind the semi. There are footprints back there of the man we think killed the trucker. And somebody dropped a handkerchief that had a capital 'C' embroidered on one corner. The crime photographer arrived an hour later. And he had the message that we should guard the site until you got here from the Office of Criminal Investigation."

"All right. May I look around for myself now?" Skye asked.

Baxter nodded slowly. "It's your site, now, ma'am. We've been told to do whatever we can to support you. And the photos should be here for you within...." He looked at his watch. "Within an hour or so, I'd say. You'll get a complete set as soon as they get here."

Skye nodded. She walked slowly along the road. The truck was completely on the shoulder. So were the tire tracks of the car that had pulled up behind it. She stopped to examine its tracks. "Trooper Baxter, this had to be a sports car. Or a Volkswagen. But I think the footprints where the driver stepped out wouldn't have twisted the way they did and dug so deeply into the dirt unless he was getting out of a very low vehicle. So I think it was a sports car."

She continued toward the flatbed. Baxter trailed behind her. The footprints showed that the shooter had stopped for a while, near the front of his car, before approaching the trucker. This is where he dropped the handkerchief. Skye mentally measured the distance from this point to the trucker's body; it was about ten paces. She stooped to examine the handkerchief more closely then turned to ask the trooper: "Did your folks get photos of this *in situ*?"

"Yes," he replied.

"So I can pick it up now and examine it more closely?"

"Yes, ma'am."

She picked the fabric up with a pen and looked it over. There were tire tracks on it. The monogram looked like a "C." She thought of the Russian conversation overheard in Chicago. Someone with the Russian name of Sasha did this job. She thought of the Russian initials she'd seen for the USSR: CCCP. So she knew the Russian "S" looked like the English "C."

Frowning and shaking her head, she continued. Stopped to examine some of the plaster casts of the tire tracks that Trooper Swann had poured and left in place for her.

She walked over to the truck driver's body. His footprints showed that he left the cab, walked to the rear, stood behind the trailer, got shot, and dropped to his knees. He then fell forward onto the pavement. He landed face down, with his right arm tucked under his chest. Skye stood still for a long minute, inspecting the scene.

The driver was dressed in a baseball cap, plaid flannel shirt, dungarees, and engineering boots. His back had two exit wounds, both relatively small. The back of his head had another bullet hole in it. "So…," Skye muttered, "he didn't die from the first two shots.

She squatted down and rolled the left side of his body over far enough to observe the two entrance wounds. He had a number of small cuts on the left side of his face, most likely from the window glass when it was shot out. Part of the right side of his face was missing due to the exit of the third shot. Even so, Skye could get a good idea what the driver looked like: stocky, heavy jowled, balding, a short haircut but not a crew cut. He bore a slight resemblance to Winston Churchill. Not a lot, but close enough that she noticed.

She turned to the state trooper. "You say you found no identification on him at all?"

"No. Nothing in his pockets or above his visor or on the dashboard. No paperwork for him anywhere," Baxter replied. "The other guy had complete IDs and driver's license. Photos of his family. This one didn't even have a wallet on him."

"He had one. Someone took it. Look at the left back pocket of his dungarees."

"Dungarees?"

"His blue jeans. There's a worn square on the outside of the pocket, an outline where he sat on his billfold."

The trooper frowned. "I wonder why someone would take his whole wallet?"

"So do I. He had to have papers to drive legally. And as far as I know, truckers are very careful about having them with them on the job. Maybe someone was trying to keep us from finding out who this guy was.... They might have known each other and the killer was trying to keep the connection between them secret. Or he had a lot of cash and they were robbing him."

"So why would they take the whole wallet? Why not just the money?" Baxter asked.

"I don't know.... But I do know that Navy records will have all his ID information on file."

"So you think the other driver, the guy on the knoll up there with all his identification, you think he didn't know who the killer was?"

"If that was the reason for taking this man's wallet, then evidently Hassler didn't know any of the people who stopped the truck. Or they weren't worried about it if he did. Lot of questions here to be answered." Skye shook her head. "Have you retrieved any bullets yet?"

"No, Captain. We were told not to touch anything, to let you do your work your own way. And the coroner is on the way. He'll standby until you give the word to take the bodies in."

"All right, thanks." She stared at the body. She frowned. She had rolled the body over enough to see the bullet holes in his chest. She realized that she should have examined the whole front of the man's body. She looked up at the trooper. "Baxter, you got a bunch of photos of the body too?"

"Absolutely. I think we took twice as many pictures as we needed to. And now I'm guessing you want to turn him all the way over."

"You're right."

"Go ahead. We have photos from every angle possible."

"Good." She rolled the body all the way over, so that he lay on his back. His right arm moved a bit. His right index finger was raw and bloody.

"Trooper Baxter, do you have a camera here with you?"

"Yes, I do, Captain. A civilian thirty-five millimeter thing."

"Good. We won't have to call the photo unit back. Look here." She pointed to the spot where the trucker's finger had rested on the pavement. "It looks like he rubbed his finger on the concrete to make it bleed. Then he wrote something here in his own blood. We need to take a picture of it."

"I'll get my camera and be right back."

She gazed at the writing. "Looks like a six and a zero and the start of something else. Maybe a 'C.' Or the start of another zero...."

Baxter returned with his camera. Skye pointed to the writing. "Get a few shots from different angles, please. I want to be sure we get some good clear pictures of this."

"What does it mean? That writing?"

She shook her head. "I don't know."

She stood up. Mentally measured the height of the driver's chest wounds. They seemed to be level with the bottom of the flatbed. She looked under it but there was too much shadow to see anything. She turned to face Baxter and pointed to the place where the bullet exited the driver's face and hit the pavement. "That bullet smashed into the pavement. It won't tell us much except for its caliber. Let's put it in an evidence bag anyway. Just looking at it, I think it's a .38 caliber...."

"I agree."

"It certainly wasn't a .45, or bigger chunks of his back and face would be ripped out. The lab will tell us for sure." She stood up and walked to the rear end of the flatbed. After looking around for a few minutes, she made a note to herself to have the OCI lab try to retrieve the remains of the bullets under the bed of the trailer.

Skye continued along the driver's side of the semi. The driver's door was still open. She pulled herself up into the cab. She examined the shattered side and front windows for a couple minutes then looked around. The cab was clean but lived in, some wax paper sandwich wrappings and a couple half-filled Royal Crown Cola bottles in a wooden holder on the center of the seat. A folded newspaper, opened to the comics page, sat on the dashboard under shards of window glass. She shook off the glass so she could examine the paper. The under side of the paper had a crossword puzzle. Someone had filled in fourteen words. None included either 60 across or down. The clues for those two words were "Arctic footwear" and "Ann Lee's furniture."

"Snowshoes and Shaker," Skye mumbled. "Neither makes sense as a clue written in blood by a dying man...."

She tossed the paper back onto the dashboard: the lab would inspect the cab thoroughly. She hopped back down to the road and continued her walk-around. She followed the automobile tracks in front of the cab until they led back onto the concrete highway, then she cut over to the grass alongside the shoulder.

Skye was almost to the passenger door, which was still open, when she noticed the trampled grass leading up a knoll alongside the highway. She pointed to it. "Is that where the other driver ran?"

"Yes, ma'am. He's forty yards or so into the prairie grass. Up on the knoll there."

She went to the second body and examined it, also turning it over to inspect his other side. She returned to the truck after a few minutes and continued her examination. When she got to the right front corner of the trailer, she lifted her skirt above her knees and climbed onto the flatbed. After looking around for a few minutes, she pulled a small flashlight out of her purse. The rope tying down the tarpaulin had been left untied. Skye held the loose corner up as high as she could without straining, and played her flashlight beam back around the darkness under the tarp. Two missile bodies were strapped to the deck of the flatbed and rested in special wooden forms to keep them in place. The missiles pointed to the rear, their throats facing the cab of the truck. Neither missile had any interior components in place. "Empty missile bodies. One of a Terrier and one of a Talos...."

"Pardon me?" Trooper Baxter asked.

"Talking to myself," she replied. She squatted down and played the flashlight beam over the under sides of the missiles. Then she moved the beam around the inside of the missiles. "There's nothing in the bodies of the missiles. They're completely empty...."

Skye hopped down from the trailer and straightened her skirt. "It doesn't look like anything has been touched except for this corner of the tarp," she said to the patrolman as she returned to the back of the truck. She twirled a strand of her hair while she looked down at the footprints leading from the passenger side of the sports car. "Look at those footprints. This guy got out of the passenger seat and came up here without stopping. He untied the tarp, as if he were coming here for something specific." She paused for a moment. "I wonder what it was. Couldn't have been too big.... Oh, well, let's continue."

She worked her way back where the sports car had parked. She noticed some slightly deeper impressions of the car's tires. She leaned over them and moved all around the impressions to carefully view them from different angles. Biting her bottom lip, she nodded, stood up straight and completed her examination.

She retraced her steps along the short grass next to the shoulder, sweeping her feet back and forth. She made a number of passes, going farther away from the highway each time. Three times she turned to see how far from the road she was, then continued searching. Finally, shaking her head she returned to where the police officers waited.

"They must have used a revolver. Or they policed their brass. There are no shell casings anywhere."

She turned and watched a glass repair truck pull up behind the rearmost State Police cruiser.

"Gentlemen, would you be so kind as to let the coroner know he can take the bodies in for examination? And we can go around and pick up the plaster casts. Do we have packing materials and boxes to put them in?"

"Right here, ma'am. Have you determined a sequence of events?" Baxter smiled. "I'm wondering if I picked up every clue you did."

"We have two cars and a flatbed semi. It looks like the car that parked in front drove up alongside the cab and forced it to pull over by shooting out the driver's window. The shooter would have to be on the passenger side, so there were at least two people in that car. It pulled over in front of the truck as it stopped.

"The other car, some kind of sports car, pulled onto the shoulder behind the truck and waited. Then it pulled up and waited again as the truck came to a stop. It finally came a little closer to the completely stopped flatbed. We can tell it stopped where it did at those places because the tire prints are somewhat deeper where he engaged the clutch to move forward each time.

"The driver and passenger of the sports car got out of their vehicle. The semi driver got out and walked back to ask what they wanted. I would guess

21

that the sports car driver shot the trucker while the passenger in the sports car climbed onto the trailer and untied the right front flap of the tarpaulin.

"I would guess that the killer had the handkerchief in the same pocket as his pistol. I think he dropped it about the time he shot the truck driver, probably when he pulled the gun out of his pocket. And it looks like it fell off to the side a bit."

"How do you know that?" Baxter asked.

"The handkerchief isn't far from the front of the sports car. The trucker's footprints came nowhere near it. It had to belong to the shooter, whose footprints indicate that he paused there for a moment. It fell to the side a bit. I think the shooter never realized he'd dropped it. The sports car ran over it when they drove away. The shooter may have stopped and shot, then stepped up to inspect the body. For whatever reason he definitely wanted the trucker dead. So he shot him in the head to be sure.

"Meanwhile, the other semi driver panicked when he heard the gunshots, jumped out of the passenger side of the cab and tried to run away. From what I saw of the footprints, both men in the front car got out and shot. They put three shots in the other driver's back as he ran. These shooters must have been superb marksmen to hit so precisely at that distance. And in the dark, too, though the stars may have outlined the trucker when he reached to top of the ridge. Or they sprayed the area with bullets until they saw their target fall.

"Then they all got into their cars and departed, the sports car driving over a few footprints and the handkerchief as it did so."

"Well! You are good," Baxter admitted. "We caught most of the points you mentioned, but we didn't catch the deeper tire prints that indicated the starting and stopping. We missed the analysis of the sports car driver's footprints. We were going strictly on the shortness of the car's wheelbase. And we didn't see the message under the trucker."

At that moment, the coroner arrived, with an ambulance right behind. The official stepped out of his car. He handed a package to Trooper Baxter. "Your photo unit asked me to bring these to you."

"They're for her," he said, pointing to the Marine officer. "That's Captain Skye of the Navy's Office of Criminal Investigation."

The new arrival turned to Skye. "Captain, I'm John Cranston, Bond County coroner. I'm glad to meet you. Here are your photos of the crime scene."

"Thank you, Mr. Cranston. I need your coroner's reports on these two decedents as soon as you can get them to me. Will you send them by courier to the OCI Lab at Great Lakes?"

"Certainly, Captain. Anything to help our boys in uniform. Uh, and the ladies, too."""

"Thanks." She grinned, then turned to the troopers again. "Trooper Baxter, you may tell the repairmen they can go ahead and replace the glass on the cab. And the Navy is sending down a couple new drivers. They should be here quite soon. We have jurisdiction in this case because the murdered men were employees of the Navy. Please direct the replacement drivers to drive this rig up to the OCI Lab at Great Lakes."

"They know where it's located?"

"They should, but...." Skye wrote a telephone number on a page at the back of her notepad, tore off the paper and handed it to the patrolman. "If they don't, have them call that number collect to get directions. Then you'll have this rig off the side of the road and back on the highway."

"Thank you, ma'am!"

"And please have the relief drivers bring me the photos we took of the bloody writing on the pavement. Or you can just send me the roll of undeveloped film. We can always develop the photos at our lab."

The coroner's people loaded up the bodies and they headed for the coroner's office and lab.

Trooper Baxter took Skye back to the airport, where her plane was waiting to take her home. As she flew back to Great Lakes, she thought over the crime scene. She sat looking out the window, mulling over her many unanswered questions.

2. Illegal Aircraft

South Dakota

When we were on our last case, a third couple formed among Rena Skye's OCI operatives. Ruth Gardner felt that she was responsible for the deaths of two men during the investigation of the drug ring. Rodney Hunter, known to all of us as "Chaské," felt something special for this disconsolate white woman because of his own problems after fighting in Korea. He agreed to take her home with him while on leave after the drug-ring case was over. So she went with him to his reservation to heal.

Chaské borrowed his brother's 1951 Chevrolet pickup truck. He and Ruth drove south on the local roads twisting through the spectacular badlands area of the Pine Ridge Indian Reservation. They now sat at a campfire not far from the site of the so-called Battle of Wounded Knee.

As they sat by the fire after eating supper, Chaské explained some of his people's history and told of their lands. This beautiful raw land awed Ruth. Her companion's description of it, and of the Great Plains surrounding it was a fitting portrayal of the homeland of his warm and graceful but unbelievably tough people.

Ruth told us about this trip when she returned to Great Lakes. She described the stars at night, how the small campfire didn't diminish them at all. Far away from bright human lights, they were stunning and she felt very close to a power she had not known before. She said it was the beginning of her healing.

Chaské described the Milky Way as the road people travel when they die. He explained that the spur that branches off and ends after a short distance, that is where people lose their way if they haven't lived a good life. Such people fall off the end. They come back, go through another life and try again to be a good human being. He reassured her that she didn't kill the two guys on the last case. But the men who died might need to repeat their lives. As Chaské put it, the drug pusher needed to learn how to behave better and the user to try to find a better way to stand up like a real human being. This fork in the heavenly highway was not a judgment against evil people, but often a place to let people grow up by returning and living a better life.

They talked about how Lakota people prayed and the ceremonies they performed. Many were prayers in themselves: Greeting the rising sun, the vision quest, the sweat lodge and the sun dance.

They talked about the massacre at Wounded Knee, and what a warrior was in Lakota life: not a killer, but someone who takes care of his people, helps to feed the hungry, adopts orphans, honors the elders. Indians will fight for their land and their people. They'll fight with a vengeance when they have to. But a real warrior fights only when it's absolutely necessary. Sometimes a warrior had to kill, but he had no love of killing. He still doesn't.

Ruth expressed a desire to go through a sweat lodge to heal from the deaths she had been part of. Chaské agreed to take her to one the next night.

In the morning Ruth prayed with Chaské smoking the pipe at dawn. The smoke was to carry one's prayers to *Wakan Tanka*, the Great Mystery, God. Ruth prayed for forgiveness and healing.

They headed for home after breakfast. On the way they spotted an unmarked plane, a Cessna 170 or 172 with no registration numbers, flying over new ICBM silos being built. This was an area that was off limits for civilian planes. Chaské pulled the truck onto the shoulder of the highway. He had a camera and a telescopic lens, so they got a number of good photos of the illegal aircraft.

As soon as they got home, Chaské called Commander Fasano at the OCI office in Great Lakes. He described what they'd seen. Fasano mentioned there had been other unauthorized flights around the new missile silos in the Dakotas lately. He told Chaské to call the U.S. Air Force Criminal Investigation Division. This was CID's problem.

Chaské hung up. He sat thinking. Something about unmarked planes, illegal flights, the Air Force, and Indian country didn't fit together very well for him. He got up and walked outside.

They talked about whether he was going to call CID or not, then he took Ruth to the sweat lodge.

3. Confusion and Bloody Ghosts

Great Lakes

Rena got back to Great Lakes about 1230, mere minutes before the officer's mess closed, so she stopped and ate lunch. Then she went to her Great Lakes OCI office. They had assigned Janice McCluskey, YN2, as her personal yeoman and assistant staff person, and the aide was there, even though it was Saturday.

Skye took out the photos that the Illinois State Patrol gave her. She looked over them quickly, and then she examined them again, looking for details she may have missed. Unanswered questions raced through her head. Who were the Russian speakers in the Red Arrow Jazz Club? Where did they work? Who was "Loki?" Where was his house? Who was Sasha? Where did he come from? Was that his handkerchief on the site? If not, whose was it? If it was, why was he so careless as to leave it there? Who was the primary truck driver? Why was his identification missing? Was it possible that he'd simply dropped it somewhere? Or did the killer take it for some reason? Why was the truck was carrying used, empty Navy missile airframes? There was nothing in them that was a security risk at all; so why did they force the truck off the road? Why would anyone, even Russians, be so concerned about spent, empty missile airframes as to stop a truck and kill the drivers? She couldn't even guess at the answers. The only questions easily answered were the truck's origin and its destination.

Meanwhile, Tango and I waited at home. I think the dog was almost as anxious for Rena's return as I was. I checked the time. It was 1430. Either the call she got in the middle of the night was tremendously serious and she was

26

still at the crime scene, or she was back and had to check in with the OCI office here. I wanted to run over to see if she was there and find out what her trip was all about. But I wasn't supposed to be seen going in and out of the OCI office. It wasn't the people in the office that were the problem. Quite a few already knew me because I worked there before I was assigned to the *Hestek*. But I was undercover and would probably stay that way. That was my job now. I had to keep up appearances. The brass were afraid someone from outside our office might see me enter the OCI office, which might blow that cover. So I sat at home and waited for a phone call. Or for Rena to come home. Whichever happened first.

I mulled over my newest duty assignment to study at the Fire Control Technician Class "A" School. I would start tomorrow to learn about the equipment that controlled gunfire aboard ship. Thanks to my background in electronics, I'd be able to race through much of the course.

About 1530 I got tired of waiting. I took Tango out for a short walk before I changed into civilian "work" clothes and pocketed my secondary ID, which described me as a civil servant working on electronic equipment. Then I visited my beloved. When I walked into Rena's office, her head was lowered, like she was looking into the shallow box of items on her desk.

"Hi, Rena! What's all this?"

Her head jerked up. "Eric!" She shook her head as if trying to clear it. She laughed softly. "I'm afraid you caught me napping. I'm pretty tired."

"You get any sleep at all?"

"Some. But I was thinking too much about the case to sleep."

I sat in one of the office chairs. "I got tired of waiting. Wondered what was going on. So I came over to keep you company for a while." I pointed to the box she'd opened. "Can you bring me up to date? What is all this?"

"Two truck drivers were killed. Their cargo was two spent missile airframes. Nothing inside of them. There seems to have been something under the tarp that covered them because one corner was untied and lifted up. But we have no idea what was of interest under there."

"One of the Russians I overheard said we wouldn't even realize something was missing. These guys may have retrieved whatever it was we'd never miss."

"Could be. The state cops sent this box to me, through the OCI lab here. The lab is examining the truck itself and the dummy missiles right now. But I don't see anything here that tells us what the Russians retrieved. It must have been real important, though, for them to kill the two drivers."

I watched her go through all those items in the box for half an hour. She explained what the items were as she checked them out.

On top of everything else were five bullets. The two from under the flatbed were so crushed up that they were useless. Two more were somewhat deformed when they hit the second driver who had tried to run away. The fifth bullet, shot through the primary driver's head and into the pavement was also misshapen. They were all .38 caliber. Somehow the lab determined that one shot that hit the driver in the chest was not damaged much, but then it hit metal under the flatbed and became too smashed to provide much information about the gun. The bullet from the other chest shot entered the chest cavity without damaging any bones, went through the lung, and hit ribs when exiting. Then it must have tumbled before hitting the flatbed. So it was also damaged, but only on one side. It still had fairly well defined rifling marks on the other side. It could be in good enough shape to link the shooter to the crime. If the shooter could be found. If he still had the gun.

Next came another copy of the police photographs and those that Trooper Baxter took of the letters written in the driver's blood.

I looked over all these items but wasn't allowed to spend a lot of time in the office. I kissed Rena goodbye.

"See you later. I'd like to look over all this more carefully."

"OK. Later.... Oh, by the way, here's a gift for you." She held out a key. I frowned. "It's a key to the fire door. Because you're so well known here...."

"You mean they haven't forgotten me?"

"Not at all. They'll let you come here and help if you ever have the time. But you have to be so discrete that you shouldn't ever come in the main door again." She laughed softly. "You have to sneak in the back way. And you can't let anyone see you entering the stairway back there either."

"Okay." I took the key. I kissed her good-bye again. As I walked out, she was frowning as she looked through her shipment once more.

A half hour later, Rena was interrupted by a voice asking: "Captain Skye?"

She looked up. A stranger stood in front of her. She had no idea how he had gotten through security without them notifying her. "Yes?"

"My name is Roger Crane. I'm one of the drivers who brought that flatbed semi here from central Illinois."

"Well, thank you." Skye looked around. A security officer stood at the door. He nodded. She looked back to the trucker. "What can I do for you?"

"Sorry I took so long to get up here, but I had to get some lunch and then getting through your security took some time." He held out the newspaper section she'd seen at the crime scene. It was folded to show comics on one side and a crossword puzzle on the other. "We found this in the cab. Don't know if it's going to help.... It was on the truck driver's dashboard. And folded exackly that way. I heard you people could get clues from almost anything, so I thought I'd better get it to you. I don't know if it'll be any help or not. Good Luck."

Skye took it and stared at the paper for a while, but she didn't see anything that was meaningful to her. "You try to work on the crossword?"

The driver grinned. "No, ma'am. Tommy, the other driver, was goin' to but I told him that might destroy evidence. He put his pencil away real quick. We didn't change any of it. That's the way it was when we first noticed it."

Skye nodded. "Good. We might be able to get something from it. Thanks." She dropped the newspaper onto her desk.

"No, problem. Well, I better go now. Gotta get back to Saint Louis."

Skye held up her right hand. "Wait one, please."

"Yes, ma'am?"

"I'm curious. When would the driver have time to work the crossword puzzle while driving?"

"Oh, when they pulled into a rest stop. Or when the other driver was driving."

"Thanks." She paused for a moment. "Another question. Do you have any idea where the semi came from or where it was going?"

"I saw the manifesto in the truck. I guess you'll have it soon. I couldn't bring it up here with me, so I copied the info on it." He pulled a paper out of his shirt pocket. "It was from California. A place with a strange name. Port Hew-neem, or something like that."

Skye nodded. "I know the place. It's pronounced Wye-NEE-mee."

The driver nodded. "Yes, ma'am. I wouldn't have come up with that pronunciation. I never drove in that part of the country. Anyway, this truck was headed to Washington, D.C. My boss told me to drive it there, but you had us bring it up here instead."

"Where were you supposed to deliver it in D.C.?"

"Let me look." He pulled another paper from his shirt pocket. "Says here, the Navy Museum, located in the Navy Yard."

Skye nodded. "May I see that?"

He handed the job sheet to her. She copied down all the information on it and handed it back to the driver.

"One more question. Did you know the drivers who were killed?"

"Yes, ma'am. We were all members of the same union, the same local."

"What were their names?" She asked.

"The back-up driver was Jerry Hassler. He was a Negro guy. The main driver was Don Jennings."

"Did they drive it in from California?"

"Oh, no, ma'am. They take these military cross-country loads in three steps. From the west coast to Billings or Denver or Santa Fe. Then into the Midwest somewhere. I think this load came through Denver, but I'm not sure."

"So Saint Louis was where Hassler and Jennings started from?"

"Yes, ma'am."

She paused a moment, thinking. "Did Jennings carry a lot of cash around with him?"

The man laughed. "Never. He usually had enough to buy meals and snacks. Sometimes a beer. Or he'd borrow a little from us. He was always doin' that. Then he'd dip into his pile at home and pay us back the next day. Or as soon as he was back in town and could get to his money. I think his wife watched over their money pretty close."

"So he was married…."

"Sure was. Pretty happily, too. They got along really well. They were a great couple."

"So…, someone wouldn't steal his wallet to get his money."

The driver frowned. "Nah, wouldn't be much there. Why do you ask that?"

"Just checking for some details of the case." She paused, then asked: "Jennings and his wife live in Saint Louis?"

"That's right. Not far from where I live."

"Maybe you can answer some other questions I have."

"I'll try…."

"What hobbies did the two drivers have? Did they play cards? Chess?"

"Oh, let's see. Jennings was kind of a crossword fanatic. And he was real close to his two kids. Took 'em everywhere, did all kinds of things with 'em. And he liked to play poker. Hassler, on the other hand, liked to play bridge, would you believe? And chess. He graduated college from Tuskegee University with a mechanical engineering degree. Very well educated, but very down to earth. He loved bein' with people. All kindsa people. We're gonna miss both of 'em. Please catch whoever killed them.

"We will certainly try. Thank you, Roger, you may have sped up our investigation a little. Thank you very much."

She motioned for the security officer at the door to escort the driver back out. She picked up the telephone and called Commander Brian Fasano, her OCI boss at Great Lakes. Since it was Sunday, she had to call him at home. A woman answered, his wife or daughter. Rena introduced herself: "Hi! This is Captain Skye at Commander Fasano's office. May I speak to the commander?"

"Certainly. One moment, please."

She heard his voice within seconds. "Fasano speaking. Skye?"

"Yes, sir. I need your help."

"Whatever I can do, just ask."

"The truck whose drivers were killed near Highland was on its way to the Navy Museum in the Navy Yard in Washington. It came from California, Port Hueneme. I need to know what its business was. And I'd like to confirm its origin. And also to confirm that these drivers picked up the job in Saint Louis. Then we can go where it came from and begin a serious investigation. Also, I got the names of the two truck drivers who were killed. Don Jennings was the driver killed at the rear of the trailer. Jerry Hassler was the man who tried to run. Can you get me some information on them?"

"I'll try. I'll get back to you as soon as I can."

Commander Fasano called back in less than a half hour. "I lucked out. Even though it's Sunday, I was able to persuade the watch at the Navy Museum to give me the phone number of the future curator. That truck carried some empty Talos and Terrier airframes for an exhibit of Naval anti-aircraft capabilities."

"Where did they get the missiles from, sir?"

"Port Hueneme, California. The truck was starting the final third of its trip. One set of drivers took it from Hueneme to Denver. A second set drove the rig from Denver to Saint Louis. The third pair of drivers had started the final leg." Skye didn't say anything; she sat there thinking. Fasano continued: "What are you going to do next?"

"I want to send someone to help the guys in California talk to the people who loaded the truck. And nose around. See what else we can discover."

"I'll set up a flight for you. Are you going yourself?"

"That's what I'm planning right now."

"How soon do you want to leave?"

"Sometime in the next couple days. Let me digest the information I have so far and I'll get back to you about when I want to go out west. Is that all right?"

"I'll get things set up. Let me know when you want to leave."

"Yes, sir. Thank you. Any info on the drivers yet?"

"Not yet. I'll let you know when we get something."

Rena returned to her examination of all the items piled on her desk. She saw all the pieces but had no idea how they fit together. She was intrigued by the photos of the driver's body and the "60c" that he wrote in his own blood on the road. That writing was mystifying. Rubbing his finger on the road until it bled must have been excruciating. It must have been so important to him that he could ignore the pain of being shot and the pain of rubbing his finger raw. What kind of presence of mind did he have to do that while he was dying? And what did it mean, "60c" or whatever it was?

Rena decided she needed some new eyes, some new perspectives. She picked up the phone and dialed the number she had for Chaské and Ruth. She wanted them back at Great Lakes. Then she might be able to go home and get some rest.

*　　*　　*　　*

The unknowns of this case whirled around and around in Rena's head. So she went into the office around 0400. She plopped down into her chair and stared at the items on her desk as she nursed her first cup of coffee.

She picked up one photo at a time and gazed at it. The truck from every angle. The drivers. The missile airframes. The "6-0-c," or whatever it was, written in blood on the road. She still didn't see how the pieces fit together. The driver rubbed his finger on the road until it bled. Nobody would go through such self-torture unless it was extremely important.

She got another cup of coffee. Returned to her desk. Reviewed how the sequence of events would fit the footprints and the tire tracks, some of which overran others.

The truck started out in Port Hueneme, not far up the coast from Los Angeles. It was taking spent missile bodies to the Navy Museum in Washington. The truck's license plates and registration showed that it came from California.

The driver victims in Illinois were from Saint Louis. Or at least nearby, because they picked up the rig in Saint Louis. Hassler's driver's license was from Missouri. Skye wondered if all this suggested that the killer was from the same area.

The drivers could be from almost anywhere, but Rena felt the killer knew Jennings. Why else would the he take all of the driver's identification. It certainly seemed that someone didn't want authorities to know where the driver was from, or who he was, for fear of snooping around the killer's home area. Or maybe it was something else that she couldn't connect yet. It would only take a day or two to get more info from the Navy. But that still wouldn't answer all the questions she had. Rena shook her head. For all she knew, Jennings may have been part of the plot involving the truck and its missile frames…. But she really doubted that.

She stayed awake by drinking six cups of coffee in a row.

Rena's intuition was reliable more often than not. This had been the opinion of her co-workers and supervisors in California, long before she was picked to be the team leader on the drug-ring case in Norfolk. On this case, she believed the killers of the truckers were headquartered in Saint Louis. She surmised that from the conversation I overheard at the Arrow Club. But because we were in Chicago at the time and had overheard the Russians talking there, they may also have a presence in that city. Two big cities. Skye had no idea where to begin looking.

She twisted her hair around her finger. Her mind jumped all over the place. Central Illinois. Port Hueneme, California. Washington, D.C. And Fasano had told her about Chaské's sighting of the illegal flight in South Dakota. Were they all connected? And exactly what did the driver write on the concrete? What did it mean?

She made a trip to the head, then got another cup of coffee.

She mulled over how to investigate this case. She sat at her desk and let her thoughts roam freely. She looked asleep. But after a half hour, she nodded. She recalled the old saying that it was easier to apologize than to get permission. She decided to reserve her old team for undercover operations and use local agents as much as possible for open investigations.

All the coffee forced her to visit the head again. Then she got still another cup. When she returned to her desk, her phone was ringing. It was 0930. She plopped down into her chair and sighed. She clenched her jaw and thought: *What now?* She picked up the receiver and answered: "Captain Rena Skye."

"Commander Blount here." He sounded more tired than she had ever heard him. He took a deep breath. "FYI, we have another problem. Sailors on watch at the New London Submarine Base reported strange sightings. Bubbles in the waters of the Thames River."

"And they called you directly?"

"Yes. Lieutenant Commander Scott Morgan is the security officer there. We went to college together. Been good friends ever since. He called me when the reports began coming in."

"Do they think they're seeing divers?"

"Possibly. Stolichek is already on the way. And I was able to get in touch with Leonard Ford. He'd been running along the Appalachian Trail in New Hampshire for a week or so. I called his mother and she passed on the message that I wanted to talk to him. As it turned out, he'd spent the night at Profile Lake, where the Old Man of the Mountain is."

"Isn't that New Hampshire's symbol?"

"Yes. Ford ran the ten miles down to Lincoln early this morning. He said he knew he'd been out of touch for a long time and needed to check in with his mother, which he did. I told him about the bubble trails. And that observers also saw strange shapes in the middle of the river."

"They only have visual sightings to go on?"

"Of course. I'm sure they'd love to ping their sonars but it's against naval regulations to use active sonar in port." He chuckled. "If there are snoopers in those waters one good ping would deafen them. Or kill them. But we can't do it. No matter how much we might want to."

"Why would you even want to? That's pretty drastic," Rena said.

"One of the Polaris boats was loading a new version of missiles into its tubes." Blount took a deep breath. "That made having snooping divers around there a very touchy situation. So I asked for Ford to help us because he's a diver and can get much closer to any transgressors. His boss, Commander Mason Cott in Newport, Rhode Island, released him to work with me. Well, to make a long story short, his mother and his brother delivered his car to him, so now he's also on the way to New London. He's part of your team now. He'll call you when he gets to the sub base."

"Did you report all this to the admiral?"

"Of course!"

"And then you called me directly...?"

"Remember, you report to Commander Fasano only because you're on temporary assignment to Great Lakes. You actually still work for me."

Rena sat in silence, thinking.

"Rena, are you still there?"

"Yeah," she said slowly. "I understand my chain of command." She paused. "But I don't like the feel of the situation we're in...."

"I don't understand. What don't you like? The strange events in New London? I already sent Stolichek in. And Ford's on his way."

"Right now, one location isn't what's bothering me. It's the fact that this is the third thing in a couple days. It doesn't feel right at all."

"Third thing? There are the murdered truck drivers and the sightings in New London. What's the third thing?"

"Commander Fasano told me that Chaské Hunter reported seeing an unregistered small aircraft flying around new ICBM silos in South Dakota."

"Oh, yes. Fasano mentioned something about that. I thought he turned that over to Air Force CID."

"Mister Fasano told him to do so. But if I know Chaské, he won't."

"Why not?"

"It's right in the middle of Indian country and he'll figure CID doesn't know enough about the area to effectively investigate. But that's one problem location on top of another. Add the fact that the flatbed truck came from

California. It was going to the Washington, D.C. The drivers were killed in Illinois. Now we have problems in Connecticut and South Dakota. Three serious incidents involving five geographical locations."

"Do you think they're all related?"

"Yes, sir. I have no idea how. Or why. But my intuition is telling me that they are." She paused. "Commander, can I officially call my team from Norfolk together again? We were pretty good at brainstorming."

"Not yet. You might be onto something, but we'll have to wait until we're more certain. How's the truck investigation going?"

"I'm planning on going out to California to interview people."

"Don't. Use the folks already out there. People not on your old team. You stay unseen and make sure all of your old group also remain invisible."

"Pardon me, sir?"

"I'll keep your idea of calling your old team together again in the back of my mind because it fits in with something all the OCI commanders are talking about. We think these events are strange, too. And we're conferring with the admiral. When you need to investigate anything publicly or question anyone, use local people. Don't use any of your old team."

"Why not?"

"Be patient. We're working on an idea."

"And you can't tell me anything more, right? Top secret?"

Blount paused before he replied. "Kind of. I'll have more information soon. Hang in there, Captain."

Skye hung up the phone slowly. She thought about the undercover aspects of "her" team, how effective they had been. Now they were no longer together. If only she could gather them all together again, what a unique force they'd be.

But Blount had limited her to use local agents. She wondered why?

She reached for her phone and placed a call to OCI San Diego. She asked for Tony Alvarez or Daniel Han. She got the former. She filled him in on all the details she could. "So, get some local operatives in Hueneme or Mugu to investigate the missile storage and shipping areas. But don't limit the search to those places. Go wherever the trail leads. And we have orders from Commander Blount that you and Han and the rest of our old team, all of you stay out of sight. Let locals do the visible work."

"Okay, Captain. Should we go up there ourselves?"

"You can if you want to, Tony. But stay invisible."

"Do we have enough people here already? What if I need to do some extensive undercover work in a couple places at once?"

"Use the local people. And you already have Daniel Han," Rena said. "I will get you some more help. How about Oliver, Tuttle and Alban?"

"Sounds good. The extra people will help on stakeouts and such. Thanks."

"And there's a man on loan from OCI Great Lakes who I'm going to send out there. A young guy named Dirk Fladeboe. I'm going to send him as a seaman apprentice right out of boot camp here to work in the shipping area. He'll keep an eye on the whole operation and report back to me, but I'd like you to watch over him, if you can. If he gets in trouble, bail him out. Okay?"

"Will do," Tony agreed.

"Do you want me to notify the others of their new assignments?"

"Yeah. I think you should," Alvarez said. "Tuttle and Alban are Navy. It would be best if the orders come from you."

"Okay. I'll let them know. I'm going to stay in the shadows, too," Rena said. "When you guys start working, keep me informed every step of the way. But remember, our guys all have to be invisible. Local operatives who can be visible must do all the interviews. Got it?"

"Got it. We'll do the job right," Alvarez reassured her.

"I know you will, Tony. Thanks." After hanging up, Skye phoned Fasano to have him replace her with Oliver on the scheduled flight to California. Then she called Tuttle, Alban and Oliver, and their commanders, to get them on the way to their new jobs.

*   *   *   *

Skye tried to organize what she knew of the activities in the five locations. She arranged the photos and other items on the crime scene. She made notes about the drivers, the Navy Museum, the license information about the truck, anything else they had learned from all the sources. Then she added what she knew of the incidents in South Dakota and Connecticut. She wrote these notes on sheets of paper torn into quarters. Then she laid them out on her desk with the photos and other items so she could look at all of them with one sweep of her eyes. She sat there, trying to soak it all up, letting it all bubble in her mind, giving her intuition a chance to go to work. But that wasn't happening....

When I arrived there, she seemed mesmerized by it all. "Rena?"

She jumped, startled.

"Oh, hi Eric!"

"I'm sorry. Were you dozing off?"

"No. Thinking. Reflecting. Trying to let my intuition make sense out of it all. I lost track of.... What time is it, anyway?"

"A little after 1630."

"What?" she squawked. "Already? Oh, God, it seems like I sat down a minute ago to look over these things, but that was hours ago."

"You come up with anything?" I asked.

"No," she sighed. "And I do need a break."

"Well, that's why I'm here. Us two. Dinner. And a movie. Remember? The landlord is watching Tango and we're all set to go...."

"Yeah," Rena nodded. She straightened up her desk by making one big pile of all the items in front of her, all the photos, reports, and the newspaper section with the comics. She paused for a moment to study the crossword again as she twirled her hair, then shook her head in frustration. She took all the materials from her desktop and dumped them into a desk drawer, locked it, and stood up. "Okay," she said. "Let's get out of here. Did you drive over?" I nodded. "Let's go."

We both drove home so we wouldn't have to leave a car on the base. While home we changed into civvies. We drove over to a nice little café in North Chicago, well away from the strip where all the local watering holes were. We didn't want to share our conversations with a bunch of drunken sailors, or even any one on the way to that condition.

We sat quietly while we waited for our waitress to get our drinks. I looked at this beautiful woman, this slim woman with auburn shoulder-length hair, stunning figure, dimples in both cheeks when she smiled.

"What're you staring at?" she laughed self-consciously.

"The goddess sitting across the table from me."

"Goddess, huh?"

"Yes, definitely."

Our drinks arrived. The waitress took our food order and left again. "You were a hundred percent engrossed in your work this afternoon."

"Yeah."

"So what's going on?" I asked as I lit a cigarette.

"That's what bothers me. I have no idea. Yet." She sipped her rum and coke. "Somehow, all the events fit together. I can feel it in by gut."

"What events?"

She looked around the restaurant, then shook her head. "Too classified to talk about here. I'll tell you when we get home."

"You've piqued my curiosity. Can't you tell me anything now?"

"There are suddenly a lot of pieces to this whole mess. All over the country: Connecticut, Illinois, Missouri, South Dakota, California.... But no one part seems to fit with any other part. And it's all happening at the same time. My intuition tells me everything is connected somehow. But I sure can't see how."

"You going to ask for our old team to be reactivated?"

She looked at me and smiled. "Great minds think alike. I already asked. But they won't do it." She took a deep breath and another sip of her drink. "What's playing at the movies tonight?"

"Mainside is showing 'State Fair' with Pat Boone, Bobby Darin and Ann-Margret. Hospitalside is showing 'Splendor in the Grass' starring Natalie Wood and Warren Beatty."

Rena stared into empty space for a moment longer and suddenly looked up. "Huh? What were you saying?"

I repeated my last statement.

She stared into nothing again.

"Is there a problem, Rena?"

"No. No, it's not you, Eric. Let's go home."

"No movie?"

"No. This thing is hanging over my head, I'm tired as hell, and I'm not sure I could keep my mind on the movie enough to enjoy it. Let's go home...."

When we got home, Rena sat and stared into space again. I was worried. These events were getting to her in ways I hadn't seen before. "What're you thinking about now?"

"I was going to go to California to direct the investigation. But now I'm sending Glenn Oliver, Hillory Tuttle and Robert Alban to help Tony Alvarez and Daniel Han, who are already out there. They can use local agents to find out who packed the truck." I must have had a questioning look on my face. "Blount ordered me to keep our old team invisible."

I nodded. "Are they going to do any stakeouts?"

"Don't know. Why?"

I held out the small 25x30 telescope I bought in New York City while tracking down my drug user on the USS *Hestek*. "It's easy to carry around, only five-and-a-half-inches long when it's collapsed. Give this to Glenn to take out there. Whoever needs it most can use it. It might come in handy."

"That's a good idea, but I'm going to save me a trip that would take most of the night. Instead, I'll tell the California crew to go buy one or two of those out there and keep them at the office when they're not using them."

She reached for the phone. Dialed a number. "Sheridan?" That was one of the yeomen at the OCI office. "Captain Skye here. Don't let Glenn Oliver's flight take off from Glenview until I talk with him." She listened to Sheridan for a moment. "No. Have him call me at home before he gets on the plane. Also, Oliver is flying out to Point Mugu. So call Mugu and have them get him a car to use.... Okay, thanks." She hung up the phone.

"Okay, Now we can sit and wait for Glenn to call."

"I can think of something more fun to do...."

She snuggled up to me, with a twinkle in her eyes. "All right. But don't get angry when we get interrupted."

*   *   *   *

I was in the OCI office with Rena, drinking my morning coffee. Ruth walked in and greeted us.

"So, how was your trip?" Skye asked.

Ruth smiled. "Great in some respects. I went through a sweat lodge ceremony and that was great. The folks there were very accepting and gave me a lot of support. But we had some troubling incidents, too."

"Like what?"

"Chaské and I had some pretty heavy conversations. He was in the Army during the Korean War...."

"Yeah, we knew that," Rena said.

"He was very deeply affected by all the bloodshed. When I asked him about his experiences, he broke his silence by whispering: 'I don't ever... want to go through anything... like that again. I don't ever... want to have to kill again.' Then he was quiet for another long spell, before he said he prayed with the sacred pipe every day. And he goes through the sweat lodge whenever he can. He said he still needs to cleanse himself every so often of all the blood he spilled. His war experiences haunt him. A lot.

"Then we had to stop to put gas in the truck. The first station we stopped at, the attendant rushed out and pointed down the road, shouting 'Get outa here! We don't serve no prairie niggers here!'

"Chaské left without comment and drove on to the next gas station. The attendants there were even less friendly. One of them pointed a rifle at Chaské. Two other men stood next to him, with evil grins on their faces. 'What you doin' with a white woman, Injun?' the guy with the rifle asked. 'You messin' aroun' with a white woman? Mebbe we oughta jus' string you up here an' now.'"

"Nice guys," I commented.

"Yeah. I thought he was going to open fire any minute. I couldn't think of anything else to do, so I blurted out: 'I'm his sister!' They didn't want to believe that, so I invented a story about us being from different fathers and the same mother, that my father was white. The response was 'Oh, so yer Pop was jus' getting' a little o' that red meat, huh?'"

39

Ruth hesitated for a second. She swallowed hard. "I couldn't believe the racism. I told them, 'I don't know what my Dad's reasoning was. I can't help what my parents did. Right now me and my brother, all we want is to get back home. And we need some gas to do it.' I fluttered my eyelids at him and asked:. 'Would you be nice enough to sell us some?' After thinking it over a while, he agreed to. The other guys tried to talk him out of that. He did sell us some gas. But no full service. We'd have to check our own oil and water. Then he charged us twice as much as the pump read and we had to pay it or he was going to shoot out our tires. Chaské paid.

"When we were back on the road, Chaské angrily said: 'Welcome to the Mississippi of the north.' He said Indians put up with this every day and we were lucky to get out of there alive."

Tears came to Ruth's eyes as she continued. "I mentally compared those guys with the Hunter family's welcome. They made me feel right at home when we arrived." She wiped her tears away.

"We rode in silence for a while before I asked him: 'If white people treat Indians that way, why do you still go into the military? Why do you volunteer to fight for the United States after what our government did to your people? And what white folks still do to them?'

"Chaské shrugged his shoulders and said many Indians fight to protect their lands and way of life, not to help the U.S. And as bad as our government has been to Indians, they had no doubt that it could be worse. I asked again about his experience in Korea. What it was like."

"He didn't answer me for a long time. Then, almost in a whisper, he said it was appalling. Guys died or were chopped up so bad they wished they'd died. He paused. 'The horror doesn't leave,' he said. 'Not ever. Those of us who were there are all haunted by our bloody ghosts.' Two guys from his unit committed suicide. One jumped off the Golden Gate Bridge when they returned. The other one shot himself in the head before they even left Korea. Chaské said those images never left him either. He mentioned years of nightmares and drug and alcohol abuse. All he wanted to do was forget. But he couldn't."

"I knew he had some addiction problems," Rena said softly. "Did he say how he overcame them?"

"Yes. When I asked, he grew silent like he was searching deep inside himself and remained quiet for a long time. Then he said it was the Indian religion. The prayers, and sweats, and sun dance. And he believes that now he has a purpose: try to make a good life and help others make a good life. But," Ruth took a deep breath, "he may be over the drugs and alcohol, but he still has some very deep scars there."

"All right. I'll keep that in mind," Rena said. "Now down to present business. Is he going to call the Air Force CID about that plane?"

"I doubt it. When I left, he said he was going to start calling family and friends to watch for the plane. It sounded like he was going to set up his own network to track down the illegal pilot."

"Wouldn't the Air Force radars have already detected any illegal flights?" Rena asked.

"I wondered about that, too, but Chaské said the plane's altitude was probably too low for the radars to see it. So...."

Rena simply heaved a big sigh.

4. Motives

North Chicago

Rena waited up for Glenn to call her. She stressed the orders to stay out of the limelight. And she told him to have Alvarez get a number of telescopes like mine for the operators to use. He liked the idea; both of them knew I'd used my telescope to good effect on the Norfolk drug case.

When she hung up she flopped down on the bed. She answered me brusquely when I asked what Glenn said. Then she was quiet. I figured she was already out, so I rolled over went to asleep.

But she didn't sleep. She told me later she could only think about the case's overload of information. She was gone by the time the alarm woke me up at 0600.

During the day, she dozed on and off at her desk. Every time she woke up, the piles around her reminded her of the case. Then she'd doze again. Her phone suddenly brought her to full consciousness. She noted the time, 0830, as she answered it. "OCI, Captain Rena Skye speaking."

"Captain, this is Gary Shottness, one of the special agents who works for Commander Fasano. He had me trying to find what information I could about the truck drivers who were killed. Thought you'd like to hear about it first, then I can fill Fasano in."

Rena sat up straight. "Go ahead Gary. I'm all ears."

"The primary driver was a man named Donald Jennings."

"Yeah, I already found out his name...."

"He held a Class A commercial license from Missouri. Had an address in Kansas City...."

"Kansas City? Not Saint Louis?"

"Yep. K.C. The one in Missouri."

"But he picked up the truck in Saint Louis...."

"Correct."

"Hmmm. You have anything on Jerome Hassler, the other driver?"

"Not yet. But we're working on him, too."

"Okay. It seems Jennings was killed first. And they wanted to be sure he was dead. Thus the coup-de-grace shot to the head. So, see if you can get more data on him. Family stuff, activities outside of work, hobbies, hang outs, all that good stuff."

"Will do, Captain."

Skye hung up the phone thinking: *this case gets weirder and weirder*.

Rena got another call later in the day from Tony Alvarez. He notified her that he'd arrived in Port Hueneme from San Diego, and reported in to Lieutenant Commander Jackson Bohn. Because the sailors OCI were interested in seemed to be stationed at Port Hueneme, Bohn provided office space. It had a number of empty desks and a place for secure meetings.

Alvarez filled Commander Bohn in concerning the Illinois murders, the old, spent missile frames and their origin at Hueneme. The Commander asked why someone would kill two drivers over such missile frames.

Alvarez said he replied: "That's the strange thing. The missile bodies were intact. Nothing seemed disturbed. Nothing at all. Now, the imagination can suggest any number of things. And they were headed for a museum. My best guess is that there was something special about that shipment but it was gone by the time we got to the site of the crime. So my mind runs wild around everything from vengeance to espionage to sabotage to lover's quarrels to God knows what. But we need a secure environment here so we can investigate suspects in this area. And we may need to borrow some of your people in the future to help out."

Bohn promised to spare a person or two when the investigation needed them. He also agreed to provide a couple police band radios on a U. S. government security band. One transceiver would be placed in the borrowed conference room and the other in a car supplied by the local office.

* * * *

Great Lakes

Skye returned to her desk after a head call and a refill of her coffee cup. She answered her ringing phone.

"Gary Shottness here again. I have some more information for you."

"Great." She grabbed a pen and some paper. "What do you have?"

"I tried to get everything I could on Don Jennings, the truck driver. I ran a complete check of Kansas City, Missouri. Residences. Hangouts. Girlfriends. I got his whole history. Up to a point. I'll send a written report to you. But Jennings hasn't lived in Kansas City for a year or so. Nobody knows where he moved to. And I checked with the post office there. He never left a forwarding address."

"Crap," Skye groaned. "What do we do now? Any ideas?"

"Nope. The ball's back in your court. You might want to look around Saint Louis where he picked up the truck...."

"That's a lot of city to go into blind, Gary. But I'll think on it. Thanks." She hung up and sat back for a while wondering about Jennings. Finally she visited Commander Fasano to get some additional help. He loaned her a couple of civilian operatives, Steven Montaigne and Sheila Dempsey.

They showed up soon after she got back to her desk. "Wow! That was fast. Ready to get to work?" Both nodded. "All right. Dempsey, here is the phone number of Daniel Han and Tony Alvarez in California. Please contact them and let them know Glenn Oliver is on the way. He'll arrive at Mugu at the time written there. And also, Robert Alban and Hillory Tuttle will report in as soon as they arrive. Tell them you'll be their contact with me. If they have something hot you can shuttle their call to me."

"Yes, ma'am." She took the paper from Skye and turned to go to the desk she'd been assigned.

"Sheila?"

She turned back. "Yes ma'am?"

"You look disappointed. What's wrong?"

Dempsey looked like she didn't quite know what to say. She smiled self-consciously. "Well... uh... Captain, I was hoping for something meatier."

Skye nodded. "That'll happen soon enough. Right now I need help handling this mess. Then you can do some telephone research on the two dead truck drivers, their trucking company, any loose ends you can find. Okay?"

Dempsey smiled, "Yes, ma'am. I'll do what I can."

Skye turned to the other agent. "Okay, Montaigne, you ready to travel?"

He nodded. "I keep a bag packed at home just for that reason. Where am I going and what do you want me to do?"

"Saint Louis, Missouri. Try to track down anyone who knew the truck drivers. Girlfriends, neighbors, parents, anyone. Other truck drivers in the pool and at their union shop. Whoever you can find. Interview them and find out

44

everything you can. Everything," she grinned. "Write a book for me. We know almost nothing about these guys. Anything you find out will help us."

"You got it, Captain."

"Another thing." Skye reached into a pile of papers and extracted a photograph of the crossword puzzle. "This was in the comics section of the paper the truck drivers had in the cab. I'd like to verify that Jennings was the driver who was hooked on the crossword puzzles. But I also want as much other information as you can find on both of them, especially Jennings. I want more about his likes and dislikes than that he did crosswords and played poker. I can't imagine that was all he ever dud in his spare time."

"No problem. How soon do you want me to get back to you."

"Make it reasonable. I'd like a couple days, but take a week or longer if you have to."

"Will do. And I'll call in every day to let you know what's happening."

"Call when you have information to pass on. Be careful and good luck."

*   *   *   *

Skye sat staring into thin air, wondering what Montaigne would find. What if he hit a dead end? Where would they look then? She shuffled through the papers and photos on her desk again, wondering what it all meant. The phone interrupted her. It was Jack Barstow, one of the OCI lab staff. He wanted her to come down to look at something.

When she got there, he gave her a complete set of photographs. He pointed out the writing in blood. Then the handkerchief with the monogrammed "C."

Then he showed her the plaster casts of the tire marks. "Interesting, aren't they?" Barstow asked. "The car behind the truck had what looks to me to be rare, exotic tires. But then, I'm no expert. Right now, I would guess it was a sports car of some type. We're tracking down the possible makes and models that used those tires."

"I figured it was a sports car. Let me know when you identify it."

"Certainly." Then Barstow grinned. "Okay, now for what I think is the big news." He picked up a flashlight, motioned for Skye to follow. He walked over to the flatbed trailer with the missile bodies still strapped down. He climbed onto the flatbed then helped her up. "Look here."

He aimed the flashlight beam into the inside of the first missile. "What do you see in there?"

Skye looked carefully. "Nothing. It's clean as a whistle."

"Right." He sidled over to the other missile body and shined the light into it.

"What about here?"

Rena looked. She shook her head. "Nothing there, either."

Barstow put the flashlight against the rim of the missile's mouth and shined it onto a spot on the opposite inside part of the body. "And now?"

Skye looked. She moved her head around a bit. Frowned. "What *is* that?"

Barstow smiled. "To me, it looked like some kind of sticky residue. Notice the size of the outline?"

"Yeah," Rena said. "Somewhat larger than a piece of paper."

"About the size of a notebook?"

"What the hell is this all about, Jack?"

"Well," Barstow said, "I scraped off a small amount without ruining the outline you can see in there and I analyzed it. It's tape residue."

"Tape…?"

He nodded. "Yeah. It's even still a bit sticky. Whatever was taped there was somewhat large, a report or even a small book, lots of tape, so it was relatively heavy. In fact, the empty space is large enough to have held a three-ring binder. Something was there and taken away.

"We also found fingerprints on the missile body. From what I saw of all those photos, one of the killers walked up to this part of the trailer, opened the tarp there and returned. Without doing anything else, so far as I can determine. I think there were some papers in there. I think that was what the killers were after."

"Thanks," Skye said. "At least now we can look for something that's missing."

Skye's phone was ringing when she got back to her desk.

"Rena? Alvarez here. Glenn got to Hueneme safely. And we bought a couple little telescopes, like the one Eric had."

"Great. Eric found his pretty useful. Any other news?"

"Glenn reminded me that you wanted us to stay out of sight."

"Right."

"Okay," Alvarez said. "I've already made arrangements for a couple agents from out here to do the active questioning of the crew that put the missile bodies on the truck. Hope I didn't overstep…."

"Not at all. I like having smart people on the team. Thanks, Tony. Anything else?"

"I talked with a Lieutenant j-g Bruce Porter, the officer in charge of the missile records room here in Port Hueneme. This is where they keep all the files on the missile research efforts that take place out here."

"So what did you two talk about?" Skye asked.

"It seems that plans for new missiles called Super-Terrier and Super-Talos were stolen. I have one of the guys out here looking deeper into it."

"How could you tell they were stolen?"

"The contents in the file drawer were mixed up. The Super-Terrier papers were in the Super-Talos folder and vice versa. A couple days earlier, they were in their correct folders."

"Who had access between then and the time you saw them?"

"One man that we know of," Alvarez replied. " But Porter said he was the guy who noticed and reported the switch."

"How did Lieutenant Porter get your name and phone number?"

"He said he called the OCI office here and asked for someone investigating the Illinois truck murders."

"I hope your cover wasn't compromised."

"He assured me it wasn't, and agreed to keep us top secret."

"So, was there any suggestion why the files were in the wrong folders?"

"On a whim, I asked if they have one of those new copying machines around his office. They do. They use it to provide copies of documents needed by a select group of authorized people. I think someone copied some items and put the papers back, but they returned them into the wrong file folders."

"Are there any suspects? Who's authorized to look in there? Who's able to get into that cabinet? Who knows the combination to the padlock?"

"Whoa! Slow down. Porter let me call in a fingerprinting crew. Then he gave me a list of people with access to the record room. And we're already interested in one of the guys on the list."

"Your news fits with something the lab here found," Skye commented. "Something about the size of a three-ring binder was taped to the inside of one of the missile bodies on the truck. I'd guess that's where those plans wound up. Looks like we have a motive for the murders."

"You think we stumbled across some spies?"

"Yeah, that occurred to me. So we may have some serious work to do. Anything else on your end?"

"Nope."

"Okay. Call me if you find anything new. Later."

Skye hung up the phone and went to get an afternoon snack. She took it back to her desk. When she'd eaten half of it, Chaské called in a report.

"I called a bunch of friends and relatives and I'm having them watch all over North and South Dakota, Nebraska and Iowa."

"What are they looking for?"

"The plane that was poking around the missile silos."

"I thought you were going to hand that over to the Air Force."

"Well, they didn't seem very sincere. So I thought I'd get some friends out to find this guy."

"No surprise there. You're so stubborn, Chaské."

"When something needs to get done, I see that it gets done. Anyway, I've got about twenty-five people scanning the sky for a plane with no markings."

"Any reports yet."

"Nope. I'll let you know as soon as we find anything out."

"Please do."

Skye returned to the pile of information on her desk. She looked up as a messenger from the lab came up to her desk. They'd evaluated the tape residue inside the missile body. It was left by a commercial brand of tape available through the Navy supply system. Whoever put it there had used a lot of tape. They'd secured a large document, a report or a book but it could have been a packaged bundle, too.

The lab was also trying to match the fingerprints on the missile body. They were starting with local and California police and FBI files.

*   *   *   *

Skye got a call from Commander Blount in Norfolk. "Rena, I have some good news for you."

"I need some. Trying to fit all the pieces together on these crimes doesn't seem to be getting me anywhere. What's up, Commander?"

"Moments ago, the Admiral gave us the approval to create our special undercover team."

"That's great, sir! What're our limits?"

"I'm the CO. Our HQ is here in Norfolk. You're the field coordinator, kind of like my Executive Officer. Everything we do is undercover. No open operations, interrogations, nothing like that at all, ever. The admiral notified all OCI offices this morning that they are to provide your team all the help you need to run an operation."

"I would expect that you or the admiral need to approve an operation before we can do anything."

"Correct. You already have our permission to do whatever you need to for the present investigations. If something else pops up, contact me so I can decide whether it becomes one of your ops or not. As of now, your people can investigate the truck driver murders, the missile silo trespassing, and the suspicious activities in New London."

"Okay, Commander. Can I tell my old team they're special now? And what about those not yet involved in the three existing investigations?"

"Yes, tell them. Place the others at strategic locations so you can cover whatever pops up. And you can transfer personnel to reinforce agents on an active case. You can make those decisions on your own, Major."

Skye frowned. Was Blount getting senile? She was a Marine Corps Captain. "Uh, I'm not a major, sir. I'm a...."

"You're a major now. That was one of the reasons for the delay in getting your team approved. The admiral got your advancement through Congress in record time. Your date of advancement will be the fifteenth of this month."

"This is such a surprise. I wasn't due for advancement for a while yet."

"Well, everyone from your old CO all the way up through Congress, felt you deserved it. Congratulations."

"I can't wait to tell.... Uh, Commander?"

"Yes?" Skye heard the smile in her boss's voice. "Is there a problem?"

"Well, I guess that's what I'm asking. Sort of...."

"Don't worry. Your relationship with Matthews began well before this advancement. Besides, I hear he's being looked at by the review board right now, so he may make lieutenant commander soon. That's top secret. Right?"

"Oh, absolutely, sir. I didn't hear a thing about Eric."

"Okay. Get to work notifying and organizing your crew. And figuring out what's going on at those three locations. Good luck, Major Skye. If there's any way I can help, let me know. Even if it's in the middle of the night."

"Aye, aye, sir."

Skye hung up the phone. She began calling her team members back east and worked her way west.

"First, something strange happened here earlier," Alvarez interrupted her when she called him. "I was notified that the OCI office here got special orders to give us all the help they could. Even if they don't see how it fits in with what they think we're doing."

"That's related to why I'm calling you now. Those orders were issued this morning." Skye explained the team's new special status. "Have you picked up on any suspicious people yet?"

"No. But this morning the Commanding Officer visited me. He was very helpful," Alvarez said. "He brought the officer in charge of the loading area with him, so we could find out who loaded the missiles onto the flatbed. We got the names of everyone having anything to do with missile preparation, movement, the whole operation. Then we got some locals to interview the packing crew. Three seamen were on duty when that truck was loaded up:

Walter Barron, Russell Dillard and Luis Castaneda. And the third class Missile Tech in charge is a Gary Blaine. He finalized the shipment."

"Any of them seem more suspicious than the others?"

"No. No one seems to know why the truck would have been stopped, let alone get the drivers killed. We decided to track all four of them for a while."

"OK. And go back to personnel," Skye suggested. "Get the names of every person having anything to do with this shipment's preparation and movement, even if they didn't help pack it the day it was shipped. Investigate everyone who works in the area. Let me know as soon as you find out if anything else was stolen from there."

"By the way," Alvarez said. "Dirk Fladeboe reported to the missile prep area at Hueneme as a seaman apprentice. He established himself as a quiet type of guy. He talks when someone speaks to him or when he has to ask or say something to get his job done. And that's it. Real quiet type. Right now his job is cleanup and running errands because he's acting like a guy right out of boot camp and unschooled. He noticed another quiet person in the group, Gary Blaine, who doesn't joke around with the others or participate in any after-hours events. Blaine was noticeably unfriendly with a couple of other men. The relationship between Blaine and a Bob Hansard was downright icy."

When the phone conversation ended, Skye called a meeting with her local group to tell them they were special. Then she turned to Sheila Dempsey and said: "I mentioned I'd have some more interesting work soon."

"What do you need?" Dempsey smiled.

"Would you please check the financial records of all of the missile shipping facility crew at Port Hueneme?"

"Sure! I'll start to look from here immediately. But I think it we should have some local California agents check with the banks out west."

"Good idea. I'll tell Alvarez to have folks check the banks out there."

"Any idea where I should start from here?" Dempsey asked.

"Perhaps get in touch with BuPers and research the home towns and the places where the missile crew in Port Hueneme have been stationed before now. Then track down the names of all the banks in each location and see if any of these guys have accounts there. Get all their data."

"Will do, Captain." She turned to go back to her desk.

"Oh, one other thing. Try to find out if any non-Navy customers have deposits from the Navy. Or from sailors. And also if any of the California missile crew received payments from someone other than the Navy."

"I'll get right on it."

"Thanks." The other woman left. Skye called Tony Alvarez again.

"Gee, we haven't talked in ages!" Alvarez laughed. "What's new?"

"The folks here are looking for financial records of everyone from the missile shipping facility. Checking out their hometowns and previous places where they were stationed. But we need your help, too. Have some of your local people out there look into the local bank records of everyone in the loading area. Without raising any suspicions."

"Are you looking for anything special?"

"No. We're fishing. We don't know who is up to what, so look for whatever doesn't feel right, even a tiny bit."

"All right. I'll get some folks snooping around into all the bank records."

"Don't limit yourself to checking out suspects. Look into everyone in the shipping group and anyone else you think might be suspicious, even if they don't work in shipping."

"All right. We'll see what we can find. Anything else?"

"Yes. Get everyone's photo. All of the missile loading crew. But also everybody who enters or leaves any suspect location. Keep them on file in case we need to broadcast the pictures later."

"Think we're going to have a major manhunt?" Alvarez asked.

"I don't know. Let's be prepared," Skye said.

"Will do. Anything more?"

"You have anything in mind?"

"Why stick with financials? How about police and court records?"

"You think someone out there has a record?"

"I don't know. Being prepared, like you said."

"Okay. Look for criminal records, too. Anything else?"

"That's all I can think of right now."

"All right. Talk later. Bye."

After hanging up the phone, Rena had Dempsey add court and police records to her search list. Then she returned and once again straightened out her desktop. She ran across the comics and crossword puzzle page from the semi cab. She put it aside for future analysis. Then she looked over the photos from the murder site. She shuffled through them, trying to analyze the bloody message—"60" or "600" or "60c"—whatever it was Jennings wrote on the pavement. She paused, wondering what that writing meant.

And she glared to the crossword puzzle. "My intuition is screaming at me," she groaned. "All this fits together, but I can't see how...."

She frowned and twirled her hair. "This is one piece of a much larger puzzle. Truck drivers get killed over something in an empty anti-aircraft missile body. Chaské sees illegal flights over ICBM silos in South Dakota.

Some of which aren't even done yet. And then there's the New London's bubble tracks. Wait a minute! There are Polaris ICBMs on some of those submarines! Does all this tie into American missile capabilities? But those surface-to-air-missiles on the truck were old enough to be museum pieces. And they're not ICBMs. Still, I wonder…. We have to be sure we're covering all our bases. I better put some more people to work."

Skye called many of her old team members and assigned them to snoop around every naval base she could think of.

She sat at her desk, thinking. The Navy Museum in Washington, D.C., wasn't even open yet. It would be the single museum in the country that provided a historical overview of the Navy. The exhibits would emphasize naval heroes and battles, but also peacetime contributions in exploration, diplomacy, space flight, navigation and humanitarian services. The Navy was gathering items from many places to create this museum. The empty bodies of the two anti-aircraft missiles on the truck were part of that effort.

Once again, Skye paged through the pile of material on her desk. There was a lot of information. Her intuition wasn't helping her fit it all together. She looked up at the ceiling, thinking, as I walked in through the fire door. She noticed me right away.

"So, what has the genius criminologist figured out?" I asked.

"Hi, Eric! I haven't figured out much. You're out of school already? And in civvies?"

"We were planning on going out to dinner…," I said.

"It's that late already?" She sighed and began to put away her papers. When she was done, she turned to me, smiling. "Eric," she said softly, with a twinkle in her eye. "I have some interesting news."

"Oh, what's up?"

"They're advancing me to the rank of major."

"Wow! Congratulations!" I bent down and kissed her. Then something clicked in my mind and I stood there with my mouth half open. "Uhhh…," I said, barely breathing, "How does this affect the rules against fraternization and all that, as far as we're concerned?"

"Guess." Rena cocked her head and smiled.

"From the look on your face, I'd say we're all right."

"Yep. Commander Blount said not to worry about it. Our relationship began before my advancement, while we were both the same rank."

"You still look worried. How come?"

"I don't know." She closed and locked her desk drawers. "I guess the big question would be about us when you're undercover as an enlisted man and

I'm a major. Now, that's a big difference in rank."

"Well, let's worry about that when I get back into the fleet as a seaman."

"Yeah, we do have a few weeks before anything changes." She stood up and put her arm through mine. "Lets go get some supper."

5. *Suspicious Behavior*

California

Alvarez reported to Skye at Great Lakes. He reiterated the problem with the secure missile records room, the problem Lieutenant Porter had called him in to examine, then he said: "I had a meeting with our fingerprint technician. He examined the file folders, the cabinet and the combination lock."

"He find anything?"

"The prints of the lead petty officer in shipping. Gary Blaine."

"And he's authorized to go into those file cabinets, right?"

"Yes. He was on the access-permitted list Lieutenant Porter gave me."

"When was the last time Porter knew for certain those files were the way they should be?" Skye asked.

"He told me a day or so before the flatbed left with the missile bodies...."

"Anyone else know he made the list he gave you?"

"He said no," Alvarez replied. "Said he'd keep this as quiet as possible."

"Tony, have the local operatives interview the forklift operators, the packers of the truck, every person at that facility."

"They're already on it."

"Good work. Confirm the names of the drivers to Denver and the ones going to St. Louis. Continue trying to gather all the local bank records of all the sailors at the missile shipping facility and those truck drivers ASAP."

"Okay, now for the interesting news," Alvarez said. "Last night Han followed Gary Blaine off the base. Robert Hansard went with him, though he stayed in the car."

"Where did they go? And I thought those two weren't on friendly terms."

"They drove out into Oxnard, to a somewhat isolated house. Blaine went in. Hansard stayed in the car. Daniel drove on a little way, switched off the car lights, turned around, and pulled onto the shoulder to watch. Our little telescope was quite helpful. Blaine turned on a few first floor lights. Nothing else happened for a while. After a few minutes, a light came on in the attic."

"In the attic?" Rena asked. 'What was Blaine doing in the attic?"

"Don't know. The light stayed on up there for about fifteen minutes. Then he left the house very soon after that."

"And Hansard stayed in the car the whole time?"

"Yep," Alvarez replied.

"What do you make of it?"

"We're stumped. But Daniel thought we should go in there and check out the interior of this place when Blaine isn't there."

"Good idea. Do it. But be sure you have an exit strategy when you're there."

"Think we might be followed?"

"I don't know. Just be prepared."

"Okay. Also, Daniel thinks we should look for others who might be involved. Friends. Friends of friends. Even people from other departments. Sounds like a good idea to me," Alvarez said. "What do you think?"

"I like it," she replied. "And find out who owns the house Blaine went to."

"We already have the address of the place. I'll get right on that, too," Tony promised. "Anything else?"

"Yes. Do you have the names of everyone in the missile prep area yet?"

"Yeah. Their CO delivered the list to me late yesterday afternoon."

"Can you give me the info now? Names, rates and ratings of everyone there?" Skye picked up a pencil and pulled a pad of paper over.

Alvarez read off the information from his list. "That's it, I think. Do you have fourteen names there?"

Rena counted the names on her list. "Yes I do. Thanks, Tony. Be careful and don't let your folks get caught doing the snooping."

"Of course not, boss. I do want to keep my job, you know."

"Yeah. Talk to you later." Skye hung up. Then her eyes lit up. "Ahh," she said to herself. "There's something else I should do. McCluskey?"

"Yes, ma'am?" the yeoman replied.

"Would you place a call to D.C. for me? To NavPers Disbursing?"

The yeoman nodded. She picked up the phone and dialed the Great Lakes base operator to set up the long distance call. She hung up and turned to Skye to report: "All the outgoing lines are busy right now, Captain. The operator said she'd make the connection and call you back, all right?"

"Okay, thanks."

Five minutes later, NavPers called back. Rena gave them the list Alvarez had provided and asked them to send her the financial records for all of the sailors on the list. This would let her know what kind of legal income they had. NavPers Disbursing agreed to send her the information by the end of the day.

*   *   *   *

That night Gary Blaine returned to the house he'd visited before. Alvarez and Han followed. They drove a quarter mile beyond the place, turned around, and parked. Blaine spent almost twenty minutes there. The routine was the same: lights on downstairs, then in the attic for about fifteen minutes. This appeared to be an important location. It seemed that Blaine came here on a regular basis. He turned on exactly the same lights each time.

The agents waited a half hour after their suspect drove off.

During this time, Han inspected the house with the telescope. He made mental notes concerning the placement of windows and the blind spots that people inside the house couldn't see.

"Okay, Daniel. Up and at 'em," Alvarez said. He checked his watch. It was 2330.

"Anything special you want to know?"

"Check out the interior, especially the attic. I'm most interested to find out what he's doing up there."

"On my way," Han replied. He got out of the car, crossed the road and took a route that brought him to the side of the house. He dashed onto the front porch, picked the lock, entered the building, and closed the door.

"I sure hope he locked it again…," Alvarez said to himself. Then he waited in the car to pick up Han when he was done.

Han turned on his flashlight and looked around the living room of the house. It had the typical furniture: a couch, a hassock, a couple easy chairs, a television set. There was a thin carpet on the floor, covering the center of the room. It didn't go all the way to the walls. Daniel could see the old floorboards around the edges. They creaked as he walked across the room.

He looked behind every door he saw until he found the stairs going up to the attic. The steps creaked under his feet.

As Alvarez sat in the car waiting, he mulled over the information he received earlier. The personnel list Lieutenant Porter gave him included the man Han followed to this house earlier. And the fingerprint technician already found a good print and matched it to this man's files. Gary Blaine had definitely handled the Super-Terrier and Super-Talos files.

By now Han was in the attic. Tony caught a reflection of the flashlight every so often, but Daniel was careful about not letting light go through the window. Tony watched with the little telescope. This was a standard stakeout. Boring. And the minutes dragged by.

Then Alvarez sat up, startled.

Blaine unexpectedly drove into the driveway.

"Daniel, get the hell out of there however you can. *Now!*" Alvarez whispered to himself. He checked his watch. It was almost midnight.

6. New London Suspect

Connecticut

Ford called Skye and reported in. He and Stolichek had checked in with the security office at the New London Sub Base a few days earlier. Lieutenant Commander Scott Morgan, the security officer, assigned them desks and gave them all the available details of the sightings out at the piers.

A couple watchstanders had noticed bubbles in the waters of the Thames River. The events were not random, but streams of bubbles traveling more or less in a straight line. It looked very much like there were divers under the water. All agreed these events warranted investigation because of the top-secret nuclear-powered Polaris subs stationed at the base.

Morgan offered to provide more men on the piers, supply them with night-vision binoculars, and loan some small craft to the OCI guys so they could watch the area from across the river. Ford swam out on the river that night to get a feel for the area: what the river felt like; what a diver would feel and see in the water; and to get ready for better conditions when they occurred. He sent Stolichek to watch from an island across the river. Ford himself swam a bit downstream on the same side of the Thames.

It was very dark and difficult to see anything in the water, even on the surface. It was one day brighter than the quarter moon, raining all the time, and cold. But they'd keep trying. On their second night out, Stolichek thought he saw a diver's head, first in the middle of the Thames, then behind a Polaris submarine, and again in the middle of the river. From its movements, George thought the diver was heading downstream. They decided to expand their search farther toward the coast in the next few days.

They also met Special Agent Justin Thein, who had coordinated some other agents out on the piers to watch from the submarine side of the river.

The next time out, Ford and Stolichek settled in down river from the submarine base. It was raining again and the visibility was low. Ford said that was why he had to go out and look around for himself. But it was hopeless. He couldn't see a thing. The wind roughened the water's surface. The rain refused to let up. There could have been divers all over the place, but their bubbles would have been invisible, thanks to the plopping raindrops. And the forecast predicted rain all night. So they decided to go in, warm up with hot coffee, damn the weather, and report to Rena.

*   *   *   *

Thein came in later than the other two. He'd been standing at the end of one of the piers in the rain. He was almost as miserable as Ford and Stolichek.

He'd watched for an hour or so when a sailor approached him.

"Who are you?" the man asked. "And whatcha lookin' for?"

The OCI agent showed the sailor his identification. "I'm Justin Thein from the Office of Criminal Investigation. I'm keeping an eye out."

"For what? Somethin' in the river?"

"Yep."

"Whaddaya think's in the river?" the sailor asked.

"Don't know. We thought we saw bubbles."

"Like divers, maybe?"

Thein looked at the other man. "My turn to ask you questions. Who are you and where are you stationed?"

"Me? I'm Jeff Masters. Jefferson Masters, ETR2. I'm on that boat, there." He pointed to the sub moored at the closest berth.

Thein made a note of the submarine's hull number. "Well, we aren't sure if there's anything to the reports or not, but with all the nukey boats around here, we don't want to take any chances."

"Got it." Masters stood and watched the river. After a few minutes of silence, he returned to his boat. Thein decided to check the man out.

The next day, during standard work hours, Thein placed a call to the Navy Bureau of Personnel. A Wave answered the phone. "BuPers Enlisted Records. Marcia Carlson, YN1, speaking."

"This is Justin Thein, OCI Special Agent. I need to check the record of a sailor at the New London Sub Base. Can you help me out?"

"The normal procedure is to have base or ship command order them for you and we'll send them out within a week or so."

"I'm working a highly classified case and I'm in a pretty big hurry. Can we expedite this? It would be great if you could look through this man's service jacket and tell me what it says."

The Wave paused. Thein heard her explain the situation to someone else. As soon as she said "OCI" the other person replied and Carlson spoke again. She asked for, and got, his OCI special access code. "Mr. Thein, the fastest way to do this is for you to give me the person's name, rate or rank, service number and duty station. I will retrieve the service jacket and call you back."

Justin had gathered all appropriate information before calling. "All right. The man's name is Jefferson Davis Masters. Service number 549-20-64. His rate is ETR2. He's stationed on the submarine USS *George H. Thomas*."

"Let me repeat it back to you. Jefferson Davis Masters, ETR2, 549-20-64, on the USS *George H. Thomas*."

"That's correct."

"And what's your phone number there, Agent Thein? This could take until tomorrow some time. If you're not at your phone, I can leave a message with whoever answers for you and you can call me back as soon as possible."

He told her his number. "Thanks, Carlson. I appreciate your help. Talk to you soon."

The agent spent the afternoon completing paperwork. He would eat supper, grab a quick nap, and go out to the piers again to watch for divers. He was getting up to leave when his phone rang. "Thein, here."

"Carlson here, at NavPers. I'm looking at Masters' file now. Is there anything specific you're looking for?"

"Does anything specific stand out?"

"Yes. He's a good sailor. His lowest quarterly mark is a three point six. He has a top-secret clearance, no, wait, he has a crypto clearance since he began repairing that kind of equipment. He has six and a half years of service, and he was recommended for advancement to first class. He took the test and will be advanced in a month, on May fifteenth. It looks like he will also get his first Good Conduct Medal soon afterward. I don't see anything bad in his record."

"How about comments on his quarterlies."

"Wait one." Thein could hear pages flipping. "Comments range from 'Excellent technician' to 'Exemplary petty officer, often volunteers, helps co-workers with their studies and submarine qualifications efforts' and 'Extremely conscious of security.' And he had a commendation Captains Mast for quote extremely conscientious performance end quote."

"So there's nothing bad in his whole record?"

"If there is, I don't see it. Why are you investigating him?"

"He was snooping around and asking questions while I was doing my job. The comments about him being so security conscious and his commendation answer the questions I had about him."

"Anything else I can help you with?" Carlson asked.

"No, I think we've covered all I need to know. Thank you for your help."

"It's a pleasure," she laughed. "For all the queries we get about people in trouble, this man is refreshing."

Thein hung up the phone and got his supper. As he stood on the pier that night, he decided to further investigate Jefferson Masters.

The next morning, he made an appointment with the captain of the USS *George H. Thomas*. He walked across the brow at the time set for the meeting. A man with the rank of Commander stood waiting.

"Captain Miller?" Thein asked.

"Yes. Mr. Thein?"

The OCI agent nodded. He started to pull out his badge but the officer shook his head. "Wait until we get to my cabin." The captain motioned toward a hatch. "Let's go below. Please follow me."

They went through the hatch and down a thin ladder, wound their way through the boat's crowded spaces. When they got to the captain's cabin, Miller sat at his desk. "Please show me your credentials now." Thein showed his badge. The officer nodded. "So, what can I do for you?"

"I need some information about one of your crew, Captain."

"Who are you interested in?"

"Jefferson Masters. What can you tell me about him?" Thein asked.

"He is an exceptional sailor. Does his work quickly and efficiently. He was recommended for advancement to first class petty officer, which he made. His advancement is pretty fast for any rating, though not unusual for electronics technicians, missile techs and a few others." The commanding officer hesitated. "And he is a fanatic about security."

"More so than normal? More so than others on board?"

"Yes."

"Any idea why?"

"Yes. His brother is stationed on an aircraft carrier. One of their nuclear weapons technicians committed suicide a year ago." Miller's eyes showed a touch of fear. "And the guy painted a message on one of the A-bombs."

Thein frowned. "What was the message?"

The officer took a deep breath. "'I could have blown you all to hell.'"

"Good Lord!"

Miller nodded. "Yeah. It made my hair stand on end when I heard about it. It shook up Masters' brother. And Masters, too."

"Is that when he became so security conscious?"

"He was always careful to do his job well and keep classified material secure. But, yes, he kicked it up quite a few notches a year ago."

Thein rose to go. "Thank you, Captain. I appreciate your input."

"No problem. Glad to help. Here, let me show you the way out."

7. Escape

California

"Come on Daniel. Find some way out of there," Alvarez whispered urgently. He turned on the car's motor but not its lights. He held his foot on the brake and put the transmission in gear.

Blaine unlocked the front door and entered the house.

Han heard the floor creaking. He frowned as he stood up. He wondered who was downstairs. Then he noticed a billfold on the table next to the radio equipment.

He didn't wait to hear the stairs to the attic start creaking, but walked to the front of the attic as quickly and quietly as he could.

Outside, Alvarez was still chanting to himself, almost praying. "Come on Daniel. Get out of there *now*!"

Then he saw Han open the attic's front window and climb out onto the porch roof. Daniel closed the window behind him and dropped flat onto the roof. He was almost invisible in the dark.

Minutes later Blaine came out of the house, locking the door behind him. He patted his back pocket, evidently to be sure his wallet was in its normal place, and walked to his vehicle. He backed out of the driveway and drove off.

"Daniel, you are a very smart man," Alvarez said softly.

Han watched the car disappear from view before he slid to the side of the porch in slow motion. He selected a spot where it would be hard to see him from anywhere else in the neighborhood. Alvarez inched the car forward, still without any lights on. Han slid over the side of the porch. Held on with his hands so he had a shorter distance to fall. Dropped down to the ground. He ran for the road, staying in the dark areas he had mentally mapped out. Tony pulled up at the same instant that Daniel reached the car. Han jumped into the car while it was still moving. Alvarez moved a couple houses down the road before he turned the car lights on.

Han leaned back in the seat, trying to catch his breath. "Man, that was too close! I'm sure he didn't catch sight of me. Hope I didn't leave any traces I was there. Otherwise, he's gone and this end of the investigation is over."

"See anything interesting in there?" Alvarez asked as he sped up and headed for the base.

"Nothing on the main floor. But lots of radio equipment in the attic." He pulled a small camera out from his pants pocket. "I did get a few photos of the equipment, the dial settings, whatever I could before he returned."

"You know what kind of radio equipment he has up there?"

"Yeah. Ham radio. I had an uncle who was into that. Talked to people all over the world. And I noticed a pretty tall antenna rising behind the trees in the back yard here. You can't see it from the road, but I could see it from the rear attic window. This guy is talking to someone pretty far away. But you know what I think is odd?"

"What?"

"All the dials were set to zero."

"Why is that so strange?"

"I don't know for sure, Tony. But my uncle would hardly ever change the radio dials when he shut down. This guy here is paranoid or something, setting everything to zero the way he does."

"Wonder if he does it all the time."

"You want me to go back regularly and see?"

"Yeah, I think we should. But we have to prepare for it better," Alvarez said. "I can get his working hours from his officers. Spend a week or so observing when he comes to the house, then go back in when you're pretty sure he won't be there. The safest time should be his duty days."

"Then find out what days he has duty."

"Will do, Daniel. And another thing. We should get some short wave sets of our own in place so we can intercept their signals and the responses they get. That's going to become more important as this investigation goes on."

"I agree," Han said.

"Good. I'll check it out with Captain Skye."

8. *Going Nowhere Fast*

Great Lakes

Rena sat at her desk planning for the bank account search. She determined which agents would examine the records of each person who had anything to do with the missile shipment from Port Hueneme, those who had packed the truck, the truck drivers, and everyone in between.

I watched her out of the corner of my eye. It was Saturday and I was at an empty desk eating donuts, drinking coffee and smoking cigarettes. We got to the office early because Ford and Stolichek came in from watching the Thames River around sunrise. They knew Rena wouldn't be in the office then, so they ate breakfast before they called.

I got more coffee. I tried to wake up enough to do the homework for my FT training. It had been pretty easy so far because I was already an electronics engineer. But I didn't let them know it. In fact, school was too easy. I fell asleep during the first afternoon's lecture.

Ford phoned from the New London Sub base around 0800 our time.

"Anything to report?" Skye asked. Of course I couldn't hear what Len was saying. Rena listened, then said: "Sounds like you have to expand the area you're watching. Get some observers farther down river to see what the shadow is." Another pause. "Good. Let me know what you find, Len."

She hung up. I sat there with raised eyebrows. "Observers on both sides of the Thames saw bubble trails in the water," she said. "And George spotted a shadow out on the river, which might be a boat. The bubble trail that people saw appeared to be going toward it. Nobody spotted any divers."

Nodding, I returned to my studies. Rena returned to work. When lunchtime drew near, I packed up and asked: "You have to wait for more reports?"

She nodded. "I expect to hear from Alvarez. And I hope Hunter calls."

"Okay. I'm going home for lunch. What time do you expect to get out of here? I'll fix some supper for us."

"Don't know. I'll call. You can come over and pick me up."

"Will do." I got ready to leave.

"Here, Eric, I made this up for you." She handed me a copy of a crossword puzzle. "They found this in the cab of the flatbed. You're a crossword nut. How about seeing if you can solve this one? See if you can find anything significant in it. Pay special attention to the area around box six or sixty. Okay?"

"You think the message in blood is connected to the crossword?"

"I'm not sure." She shook her head. "But I'm playing a hunch. We don't want to leave any stone unturned. Try it and see what you can see."

"Okay. Can I do the puzzle instead of fixing supper?"

"Sure, if you're willing to pay for dinner at a restaurant," she grinned.

"Hmm, I'll have to think about that."

When I got home Tango needed to go out, so I took him for a walk. It's challenging to go out with a horse disguised as a dog and try to keep him down to a walk. After we got home, I studied a while, then turned to the crossword.

I spent an hour working on the puzzle. It wasn't as easy as I first thought it would be. Nothing special leapt out at me. About 1630 I put the puzzle aside and started to make supper. Tango stood on his hind legs to watch. When Rena called for me to pick her up, I put the half finished dinner in the cold oven out of the dog's reach.

As soon as Rena got into the car I noticed she had gold oak leaf clusters on her collar instead of her captain's double silver bars. "You put your major's collar devices on early?"

"Commander Fasano did, right before he left for home." She grinned. "Then he shook my hand, congratulated me, and ordered me to go out and celebrate. I get to wear them legitimately tomorrow. You start supper yet?"

"Yeah. We can go home, put it in the fridge, and go out for dinner, drinks, dancing, and then home for…."

"Hmmm," she grinned. "I wonder what you want to do when we get home. Sounds like a wonderful evening. Let's do it."

Rena brought me up to date while we waited for dinner. "Alvarez called." She looked around our area of the restaurant. Satisfied that nobody was very close, she quietly gave me the details of their conversation. "The local people interviewed the man in charge of loading the flatbed. They didn't find anything unusual about the shipment or the loading."

"Did the guy make any comment at all about the shipment?" I asked.

"Tony said he acted quite innocent, asking, 'Why would anyone want to stop it and kill the drivers?'"

"Good question," I said. "This guy didn't seem nervous or worried about OCI questioning him?"

"He seemed very much at ease. But I still ordered Alvarez to set up a watch on him."

"And you're going after the financial data of everyone involved?" I asked.

"Yes, as soon as the banks open Monday morning," Rena replied. "Tony'll call again when he has something new to report."

"Chaské didn't call in?"

Rena shook her head. "He's a real loner and won't call unless he has something definite to report. Besides, he might be out in the countryside where there aren't many phones. You get any of the crossword done?"

"Yeah, some."

"Anything pop out at you?"

"Nothing at all."

She stared at her plate for a few seconds, then mumbled to herself. "This case is going nowhere fast." Finally, she blew a kiss to me, smiled and said: "Let's drink and dance and go home to do you know what."

After we were done with the first round of "you know what" and were sitting in bed smoking, a thought popped into my head. "Rena?"

"Hmmm?"

"I just thought of something...."

"Yes," she said in a very affirmative tone.

"Huh? 'Yes' what?"

"Yes, let's do it again."

"That thought's always with me. But I wasn't thinking of sex."

She turned and hit me in the arm. "What else would you be thinking of at a time like this?"

"I remembered all the crossword puzzle answers get printed a day later. We could call the paper in Saint Louis and get a copy of the next day's paper so we can examine it already done."

She looked at me with such a look of surprise.... "Why'd you think of that now?"

I shrugged. "Who knows how my mind works?"

"Yeah, I haven't figured that out yet."

I grinned. "I've been playing with the puzzle a good part of the day. It's tougher than I expected."

"Afraid you won't get it done correctly?"

"No. I'm sure I can solve it. But I want to be certain you're convinced we have the correct answers."

"I'll trust you. Finish the puzzle."

"All right. Thanks for your confidence."

"Tomorrow," she said.

"Huh?"

"Finish the puzzle tomorrow. Not tonight."

"Well, all right. If that's how you want it. Then we can try to find a clue at six or sixty across or down."

"You're kind of smart after all. But I have all the confidence in the world you can get the job done right."

I grinned. "Now...," I reached for her again. "Come here. I'll show you how I can get another job done right. Again."

9. *New Input, New Suspect*

Great Lakes

Next morning, Justin Thein called Skye from New London to request enough underwater cameras to put behind each sub's fantail. He also asked for motion sensor cameras to put on the piers. They had some of each but needed more for complete coverage. Rena agreed to try to get the equipment.

*   *   *   *

"Hi, Rena!" Tony Alvarez greeted when Skye answered her phone. "I have some new information for you about the finances of the people here."

"Great! I hope it's useful."

"You get to decide. Most people here have no bank accounts. A few people have both savings and checking. Most of their pay goes in. And a little extra. Don't know where the extra comes from, but it's so small, I don't think it's any kind of payoff. Two of the three are married and the third is engaged. So the description of better financial planning fits more with those facts."

"Part time jobs? Wives and fiancée working?"

"Don't know. Couldn't find anything. But there were two real surprises. First, Blaine's bank accounts looked clean. He puts most of his pay into a checking account and pays the same exact bills each month."

"Interesting. But I still feel he's the person who stole the records and taped them inside the missile," Skye said. "What's the other surprise?"

"Robert Hansard's bank records showed some large sums of money were put into his savings account."

"He works alongside Blaine, right?" Skye asked.

"Correct."

"And they can't stand each other?"

"The best we've been able to find out."

"Could be a show." Rena said. "Did the money appear regularly?"

"Every quarter," Alvarez replied.

"How much?"

"Anywhere from a couple hundred to a thousand every three months."

"Almost sounds like an annuity of some sort," she mused. "Is it an inheritance, paid on a regular basis? Did the bank indicate where those payments came from?"

"No. There was, however, a consistent account number associated with the payments," Alvarez explained.

"Account number? That could indicate they from another bank. Or some other kind of financial institution."

"We'll keep investigating and try to find out," Alvarez promised. "I'm not so sure this is money for espionage. I'd think a spy's pay would be more than a grand or less each quarter. Also, he wasn't the guy who broke into the records. We found Blaine's fingerprints there, not Hansard's. So what's with Hansard?"

"I still think Blaine's the one we're looking for. But even if Hansard isn't a guilty party, there's a question about him now and I'd like an answer. See what you can find out, Tony. Right now Hansard presents the biggest question mark in my mind. Have some of your guys follow Hansard. And a couple others watch Blaine and the house. And get photos. Photos, photos, more photos. Same as in Norfolk. Get pictures of everyone at any suspect location. And keep them on file in case we need to send them somewhere."

"Will do," Alvarez said.

After she hung up, she sat thinking for a long time. "My intuition tells me our guilty man is Blaine. But where the hell is his payoff? It could be in an off-shore account…," she mumbled. "You can bet he's not doing this for nothing. And *why* is he doing it? What the hell is his motive?"

"Dempsey!" Skye called. "I have a special job for you."

"Sure, Major. What do you need?"

"Round up Lieutenants Powers, Gardner and Jaf, and have them report to me. As a group. I want all of you here at once."

"Yes, ma'am. Right away."

Dempsey and the three waves were soon gathered around Skye's desk. "Okay, ladies, take this list of names." Skye pointed to copies of the names Alvarez gave her. "They're all part of the missile handling group out in

California. We want to find out as much possible about their finances. Pay, bank accounts, investments, etcetera. Questions?"

"Any idea how we go about this?" Ruth asked.

"We use our imaginations. We try a thousand things. Something will come through," Jennie replied.

"I heard about a couple other groups who're also searching for this kind of information. Great Lakes people, folks out in California." Laura commented. "Any special reason we're duplicating their efforts?"

"Every person sees an event with different eyes. Same principle as interrogating a witness to a crime. Everyone comes up with different information. Some of it is contradictory. Some is corroborative. All of it is from a different perspective. When you put it all together, you often get some pretty decent results. That principle is good enough reason to duplicate efforts."

"Yes, ma'am."

"All right," Skye said. "Let's get busy."

*   *   *   *

California

Alvarez called Rena and told her that the California team decided that while Tuttle followed Blaine, Han wanted to watch some of the other guys. Those from the loading docks and the vehicle pool. The receiving group. Records and disbursing, too. He wanted to see what they were doing. Daniel wasn't convinced the only guys involved in this operation were Hansard and Blaine. He persuaded Alvarez to let him check out others, as long as Tuttle didn't have to watch Blaine's house by himself.

Han also continued to watch the house in Oxnard. The next night a man in a dark jacket showed up. A large brim hat kept his face hidden. He entered the house. Turned on some lights downstairs. A few moments later, he turned on lights in the attic. Han could see signs of him through the windows above the porch. He saw the man's shadow move around a little, then nothing. But the attic lights stayed on.

Finally, the man turned off the lights. Han picked up his camera and prepared to take pictures. He got very lucky. The man came out onto the porch, into the light of the moon. He took off his hat to scratch his scalp.

Daniel opened the camera lens to let in enough light for night photos without a flash. He snapped four quick shots, then sat back in the car seat. This person was not one of the guys in the missile prep and packing area. Han prayed that he got some good pictures because he did not know this man's name and would need a good photo to identify him.

10. Another Suspect

Great Lakes

"I found where the missile packing group's extra money was coming from," Laura Jaf reported. "One of the sailors, Rick Wilson, has a part-time job. He picks up and delivers television sets for a TV repair shop."

"Who else has an extra job?" Rena asked.

"Juan Garcia, married with two children, has a second job as a waiter."

"And the third person with extra income?"

Ruth answered this time. "Randy Johnson's wife, Carolyn, does some artwork, caricature drawings, down on the beach. And so we're able to explain all the extra money."

"Good work, you two. Thanks," Skye said. "Sheila?"

"I got confirmation of all three part-time jobs from the IRS. They have W-2 forms for them."

"How'd you get IRS data? I'm pretty sure that's illegal."

"I have an aunt who used to work for the IRS," Sheila grinned. "She still has a number of good friends there. And she says if she doesn't push for too much info, like dollar amounts, she can get some data on a promise not to spread the information all over the country."

Rena shook her head in disbelief. "You gals constantly surprise me. Okay, Jennie, you have anything to report?"

"You better believe it. Robert Hansard's quarterly payments come from Switzerland."

"How did you find *that* out?"

"From a friend who works at my bank," Powers explained.

73

"And isn't that illegal?"

"Honey, ask me no questions and I'll tell you no lies."

"Did you help Sheila and Laura and Ruth find their information?"

"No. They did their own work their own ways."

"All right. Back to Hansard. Does he report his extra income to the IRS?"

Sheila answered: "There are checks at tax time to the IRS and the amounts fit what taxes he would have to pay on that amount of money."

"So it looks legal."

"So far. But it sure would be nice to verify where his quarterly payments came from and why the amounts varied."

"I agree. But I don't know how we can find those details." Skye sighed. "Okay, ladies. See what else you can find on the rest of the crew out there."

Skye reported this new information to Commander Fasano. Late in the afternoon, he called her into his office. "After your report this morning, something occurred to me so I checked some connections I used to have. They're still available. I think I can help your financial investigation."

"How so, sir?"

"Would you welcome a Swiss Bank Account search?" he grinned.

"An actual search of where Hansard's payments are coming from? Well, certainly. But, how could we arrange that?"

"That's classified. Don't breathe a word of this to anyone else."

"No, sir. I won't."

"I'm going to ask them to look for payments to American sailors. And I need your personal help. I need some names to check. More people than Hansard, like we're doing a broader search."

"I'll send you a complete list and update you if we find other people involved. You can choose however many you want to have them look into."

"Thank you, Major. I appreciate your cooperation."

"I appreciate your willingness to take this chance of being discovered."

"I'll be waiting for your information."

"Yes, sir."

*　*　*　*

California

Daniel Han requested Security to send him a complete set of identification pictures of the whole missile shipping crew. When he got them, he sat down to try to identify the floppy hat man. He examined each photo, one at a time. He took his time, looked intently. Compared them to the pictures he developed from the film he took at the Oxnard house. But it was difficult to connect the pictures he took in the dark with official security photos.

When he was almost at the bottom of the pile, he stopped. Frowned. Glanced from one of his photos of the floppy hat man to the official picture. Back and forth. Breathed a sigh of relief.

"That's him!" Han announced. "One of the forklift guys who loaded the packaged missiles onto the truck and strapped them down on the flatbed!"

Alvarez looked over his shoulder. "So, what's his name?"

"Roy Villand."

"Okay. I'll tell Fladeboe to watch him carefully."

* * * *

The same day, OCI San Diego sent two ham radio sets and scanners to Alvarez at Port Hueneme. Alban and Han obtained a geodetic survey map of the area and identified Blaine's house on it. Oliver, who had an Electrical Engineering degree from Tuskegee, calculated where the best places would be to set up the ham radios to triangulate signals from both Blaine's house and from back east, from whoever Blaine was sending signals to. OCI suspected the target area would be Saint Louis. Other indicators also suggested the same location. But everybody wanted proof.

They positioned one of their radios north of Port Hueneme in the town of Chrisman. The equipment was in a delivery van where agents could work unseen. They located the second radio set in another van at Mugu. Each van had police radios and short wave sets using security scramblers. Daniel watched the house.

They were able to go into action that night. Han notified the radio crews when Blaine entered the Oxnard house. Everyone was ready to do his job.

Ten minutes later they found the local transmissions. Transmit. Silence. Transmit. Silence. Transmit. Silence. There were other transmissions all over the bandwidth. But none seemed to come from the Midwest. There were no discernible responses to Blaine's messages. In a matter of minutes, the scanners on the OCI receivers detected fifty-three transmissions other than Blaine's. None of them began when Blaine's transmission stopped or ended when he began to send messages again.

They heard their suspect clear as a bell. But he seemed to speak in some kind of code. It wasn't another language. It sounds like nonsense, gibberish.

Alvarez had them keep trying. He was more interested in finding the other end of the conversation than in understanding what they're saying. They needed to find out who Blaine was reporting to.

The second scanner team was also not able to detect any responses to Blaine's transmissions. He transmitted then waited a while before transmitting again. Sometimes he waited for a considerable period. It looked like he was talking to someone, but they couldn't detect any responses.

Both teams noticed the same thing. Oliver wondered: "How does he know he can or should send his next message?"

They found signals from all over, even overseas, but the timing was off. It was impossible to connect one to the other.

Glenn thought the station responding to Blaine was using a different frequency to do so. But they didn't know what it was and their scanners couldn't seem to find it.

*   *   *   *

Fladeboe called Rena from Port Hueneme.

"What's up, Dirk?"

"I had a strange little encounter with Gary Blaine. Thought you should know. It might click with other data you have."

"What happened?"

"At lunch, I sat down at a spot off to the side of the mess hall. I wound up across from Blaine. Nobody said a word until the other people at the table finished and left. It seemed like Blaine was in a blue funk, not as observant as he was earlier.

"I commented on his mood. When I questioned him about this, he was very vague. Tears appeared in his eyes but he blinked them away. He got up without finishing his lunch. Told me to mind my own business. He said he could handle it himself, and walked away."

"What do you make of it?" Rena asked.

"I have no idea. But he seemed pretty upset."

11. Little Horse

South Dakota

Skye returned from getting coffee and had to hurry to answer her phone. Chaské's soft voice greeted her. "Hi, boss!"

"Chaské! What's happening with you?"

"I'm with my brother Troy and my cousin Ray Takini. Our network of friends and relatives guided us to track down the unmarked plane."

"You found it?"

"Oh, yeah. After we followed the sightings for a while, we began to see the plane. Then one evening when we were close to the Nebraska border, we sat around watchin' Ray overcook a coupla rabbits he shot. The plane flew right over our heads. So climbed into Troy's pick-up and ate as we traveled. We moved a little more than five miles and camped until we saw the plane again."

"And the small steps enabled you to follow it?" Rena asked.

"Yeah. We traveled short distances each day. It was a bit slow, but we could see that guy each time he flew. Then one day we saw him, and he seemed to rise up from the ground. It looked like he had taken off moments before."

"Did he?"

"Yeah. We found his private airfield. Close to the village of Oxbow. Not far from the town of Alliance. That's in the far northwestern corner of Nebraska. The airfield's on a buffalo ranch. Basically, it's a long stretch of well-cut grass with fields on one end and a big barn on the other. When we first saw it, the main barn door was still open and we could see the Cessna inside.

"There's a grove of trees about a quarter mile from one side of the strip. We

77

set up an observation post in those woods an' stayed under cover until we saw the plane take off. There's also a grassy knoll with a few trees on the other side of the airfield. And there's a lot of prairie grass, real tall stuff, where we can hide if we're real careful.

"We remained in the trees, in case there were still people in the house who could spot us. The ranch house was an older two-storey building, nicely painted and well kept. The residents obviously didn't want to attract too much attention.

"We decided we'd take turns standin' watch. And one of us could go into Alliance every coupla days to make a report to you.

"As we watched the house, we noticed two other people lived there, other than the pilot. One was a stocky man who did somethin' in the barn every coupla days. He stayed there for a while, but didn't came out with anything either. No tools, no feed, nothing. Whenever he went into the barn, a light appeared up in the loft and went out shortly before he left the building. He never took anything in with him. The other person was a middle-aged woman. She seems to be the housekeeper. The pilot himself didn't leave the house except to prep his plane and fly it.

"Then the other day, Troy went into Oxbow for some supplies. He talked to some folks in the store and found out the name of the pilot was John Little Horse. It sounds like it's an Indian name, but none of us remembers ever meetin' or hearin' of any Indians with that name."

"All right, Chaské. Keep watch on him and try to find out what he's doing, if he's photographing the ICBM silos or what."

"Will do, Rena. And we'll keep you up to date."

13. Compromised

Connecticut

The phone rang as Skye entered her office. Ford called to report what he and Stolichek had seen around the New London Submarine Base. "At first, all we saw was bubble trails in the river, nothing else. We assumed a diver like him would use a boat as a base of operations, so we moved farther down river each night to try to find it.

"Justin Thein came up with the idea to ask the captain of the *George H. Thomas* to have his crew use their sonar equipment in listening mode to try to find the diver and follow him by listening to the sounds of his breathing apparatus underwater. We carried updated geodetic survey maps of the river valley and a walkie-talkie the captain of the *Thomas* gave us.

"Stolichek did see a head pop up out of the water. The *Thomas's* sonar heard the diver breathing and his air bubbles flowing from his mask. They followed the sounds until they ended.

"The sub sent George the bearing where the diver's noise ended. He looked there with his binoculars and noticed a small shadow on the water. It seemed to be a rowboat. I slipped into the water and swam out there to investigate. It was indeed a rowboat, with a small outboard motor. A man sat in it, holding a flashlight. He seemed to be writing down notes. Then he started the motor and headed down river.

"The next night we moved even farther down river in hopes of seeing where the little boat came from. After waiting a long time, we heard the muffled sound of a larger boat working its way upriver. It stopped near the opposite bank from us. It looked like a small cabin cruiser.

"I heard the small outboard motor head upriver. Then I headed for the cabin cruiser. I lifted myself up on the gunwales to investigate this boat. It had radio equipment, but that was about all I could make out in the dark.

"When the other diver returned, I saw a man in a wet suit with air tanks on his back. He climbed into the larger craft and got into regular clothes. I returned to where I left George."

"How big was the cabin cruiser?" Rena asked.

"Thirty-five feet or so. He anchors it and takes the little outboard upriver. Then he leaves the outboard anchored when he dives and snoops around."

"Where do you think he went when he left the area?" Rena asked.

"I don't know. He might have a place down river. Or a marina. Or a boat yard. Whatever."

Skye was silent for a while. "Next time you guys go out, try to get even farther down river."

"You want one of us to watch the subs and piers alone?"

"Oh, no. Get some other operatives to watch the river where you've been. You two are a good team. Go down river together to see where the diver goes after he gets back into the cabin cruiser. Okay?"

"Yep. The OCI office here has been very helpful. We'll get a few more guys on it and track down that small craft."

"Let me know how it works out."

* * * *

Ford and Stolichek moved to a new position closer to Long Island Sound. They sat on the riverbank again, watching and waiting. The night was clear but it was a bit breezy, the wind varying from eight to fifteen miles an hour.

"The office sure got the radio equipment into place fast," Ford observed.

"Yeah," Stolichek agreed. "It's nice to have quality help, isn't it?"

"Sure is." Ford unwrapped another candy bar. "We're going to get some good info tonight."

"I hope so."

"Quite an effort," Ford said. "But you and I are supposed to get far enough apart so we can triangulate the cabin cruiser's location and match our sightings up with the electronics."

"You better get out there, then."

"I'm on the way." Ford climbed into the motorized rubber raft the OCI office provided and headed farther down river.

The diver didn't show up.

*　　*　　*　　*

There was a soupy fog over the Thames River. Even so, Ford prepared himself to go out. Stolichek thought he was crazy. How could anyone see anything in this pea soup? But Ford insisted.

Around 0100, they heard the cabin cruiser's motor. It slowed down then became silent. The fog helped the transmission of sound, so they heard the soft splash of an anchor being let into the water. Ford swam in the direction of the sounds. After a while, he made out the shape of the cabin cruiser with the small rowboat behind it. They were close enough to the shore where the diver could drop anchor in the shallow waters.

The shadow of a man pulled the small outboard up to the stern of the cabin cruiser and then slipped over the rear gunwale into the smaller craft. He stayed low in the small boat. He started the outboard motor, which laboriously pushed the rowboat upriver toward the submarine base.

Ford swam all the way around the cabin cruiser and under it. The craft was diesel powered. Ford could see the twin screws under the fantail and the exhaust pipes on the stern. Then he unclipped a small waterproofed flashlight from his belt and turned it on. He lifted his mask up to his forehead and put the small flashlight in his mouth. He made another trip around the boat, this time lifting himself up from the water like a gymnast, hands on the gunwales. He kept far enough away from the deck so he didn't leave any telltale wet spots. The flashlight reflected off the glass of the portholes, so it was sometimes difficult to see the inside of the craft very clearly, but he saw enough to make some educated guesses.

He was able to make out and memorize the registration number on the hull. His final examination was from the stern. There was a ladder on the back. And a name, *Mermaid II.*

Ford pulled himself up to deck level, then pushed himself farther up, keeping the rail at his waist. He walked his hands sideways to look into the cockpit and the cabin as best as he could.

It looked like the boat could sleep four people. It had a good radio set. It had radar. It was seaworthy, if the waves weren't too high. Nothing seemed out of place. Nothing was left lying around. But the radio set was enticing. When Ford spotted a few towels on one of the bench seats, a plan sprang into his mind. He kept himself as high as he could on the stern's ladder. Stayed there until most of the water dripped off his body. Then he boarded the boat.

He shielded the flashlight as he headed to the radio set and memorized the dial settings. He saw some papers but didn't read them for fear of getting them wet, which would be a sure giveaway that a stranger had been aboard. He knew he would remember every little detail of what he saw. As a member of the Underwater Demolition Teams, the "frogmen," he did more than blow up obstructions or targets. It had often been more important to gather intelligence. For those jobs they selected guys with phenomenal memory capabilities. Ford's was exceptional.

He picked up one of the towels. Wiped up the water from his footprints as he returned to the stern. He straddled the gunwale, folded the towel the way he'd found it, and with a flip of his hand, tossed it back onto the seat where he found it.

He entered the water. Swam away from the side of the boat a short distance. Turned to face the craft, which he could still see through the fog. Barely. He treaded water, watched and listened.

Not long afterwards, the small boat with the outboard motor returned. It pulled up alongside the cabin cruiser. The spy diver got into the cabin cruiser then pulled on the small craft's bow line and tied it to a cleat on the stern of the larger boat. The diver then turned toward the cabin.

The man took off his mask and tanks, then shed his wet suit. Ford breathed a little easier. He hoped the water the spy splashed around would hide any of the intruder's drippings on the deck. Now in his skivvies, the spy picked up a towel and started to dry his face. He looked at the towel, frowned, and snarled something in Russian.

Ford had no idea what the man had said, but his voice sounded quite irritated. Ford quietly dog-paddled closer to the boat. He heard the Russian fling the towel onto another seat. Saw the shadow lean over and stand up with another towel. He watched the man dry off his hands, face, and hair, grumbling all the time.

The Russian put on a pair of trousers and a shirt, then started the engine of the cabin cruiser. The vessel turned, luckily away from Ford. It headed down river and out to sea. Or to Long Island.

Ford swam back to shore where he re-oriented himself. Soon Stolichek was helping him out of the water.

*   *   *   *

Ford and Stolichek returned to OCI headquarters around dawn. They had a lot of help out there that night. A tremendous amount of radio tracking equipment was put in place. They had a number of "fishing boats" on Long Island Sound.

And they had a couple submarines at work, too, to triangulate the sounds underwater, thanks to Justin Thein's idea of using passive sonar, putting the equipment in listening mode. And they had visual observers all along the shore of the Thames in Connecticut and in "fishing boats" off the coast of Long Island. They used every possible way of triangulating the sources of the signals on both ends of the transmissions. They even got some photos from high altitude aircraft.

They put all their data together and plotted the observations on a map.

"So, did all of this provide anything concrete?" Skye asked Stolichek when he called in.

"We got an idea where the boat's signals were going. The northern end of Long Island. Triangulation points coincide with the cabin cruiser. They got plenty of pictures and Len identified it as the one he visited."

"Are you sure the cabin cruiser you're watching is the one sending the signals?" Rena asked.

"Oh, yes. Triangulation pinpointed it very accurately, right where the Thames River enters Long Island Sound. Len saw the diver leave, climb into the rowboat with the small outboard motor and go upriver. Later, the others tracked the returning diver. Until they picked up the signals to Long Island."

"Why did they quit then?"

"It was almost sunrise and they didn't want to give themselves away."

"What's next from your point of view, George?"

"Now that we have the boat's registration number, we have to expedite finding the owner. And we have to find who the cabin cruiser is talking to on Long Island."

"I agree," Skye said. "And I'd suggest you get your fishing boats along the coast of Long Island to find where the it docks."

"Will do. Len wants to talk to you now."

"All right. Put him on."

"Hi, Rena," Len greeted. "When I climbed onto the cabin cruiser, I got the frequency settings they were using." He recited a sequence of numbers. "Also, the boat's name is *Mermaid II*. And I got its registration number, too." He gave her the number.

"I'll start people checking it out."

"By the way," Ford said, "does Eric happen to be around? I need him to translate something."

I happened to be in the office for a cup of coffee before school started.

"He's right here." She handed me the phone.

"What's up, Len?" I asked.

"I need a translation of something I overheard last night. My accent is probably off, but I remember the sounds. Ready?"

"Sure."

"'Nee cheh go nee kog da nye vih sih kha yet ve toy vlazh nos tee.' What's it mean?"

I laughed. "Where'd you hear that?"

"The spy on the cabin cruiser said it when he returned after I was there. He picked up a towel, got irritated, tossed it halfway across the boat and said those words. What do they mean?"

I laughed again. "They mean 'nothing ever dries in this humidity.' Not real important."

"Actually, it is. He blamed the humidity for the damp towel and didn't suspect I'd been there."

"Why would he suspect that?" I asked.

"Because I used the same towel to wipe up my wet footprints when I left the boat after examining his equipment."

"So you lucked out," I laughed. "Here's Rena. She wants to talk to you some more."

Rena twirled her hair for a moment. "Len, here's what I'd like you to do. Follow up on my intuition. See what this guy does with his radio. When he returns to his boat, does he report in? Who does he talk to? Where is the other party located? Set up triangulation points. Find out what he's doing."

"Yeah, I know. We're trying," Ford said.

"I'll contact the OCI office in New London and have them get anything you'll need. I'll even pay for it out of my budget."

Ford laughed. "George has been listening in as we talked. He wants to know, since you have such a large budget, can you give him a pay raise to make up for his discomfort?"

"Tell him he doesn't know what suffering is. No pay raises until we're done here. Talk to you later, Len."

"Thanks, boss. Later."

As soon as Rena hung up, she kissed me goodbye. I left for school. Then she turned and shouted: "Sheila! I need you to track down some information!"

* * * *

Skye left her desk to get a fresh cup of coffee. When she returned, there was a message for her: "Call Blount ASAP. Fasano."

She frowned. This wasn't normal procedure. Could this case get any worse?

She picked up the phone and called her boss. "You wanted me to get in touch immediately, sir?"

"Yes. Go to the Communications Center there. I'll call you in five minutes."

"What's this about, Commander."

"Five minutes." He hung up.

She made her way to the Comm Center. Poked the secret code into the buttons on the lock. Entered the room and made sure the door closed after her. The remainder of the five minutes seemed to crawl. Finally, the phone rang.

"Here," the crypto radioman chief petty officer answered. He paused to listen for a couple seconds, said "Aye aye, sir." Then he turned, gave the handset to Skye, and addressed his crew. "OK, folks, we have orders to vacate the room for a short time. Take a break."

Skye waited until everyone was gone. She made sure the door was closed and locked. She lifted the handset. "Skye here."

"This is top secret and you have to, first, be very careful, and second, come up with some way to work around this."

"This sounds bad, Commander. What's happening?"

"The CIA met with the Admiral a short time ago and he called me immediately. Also on the secret line. We got a report from an American mole in Moscow, one of our spies. Loki was a little nervous."

"Eric heard that name in the rest room at the Jazz Club."

"Right. The Russians have a report of OCI creating a special super-secret investigating unit." He paused for effect. "To investigate the murders of two truck drivers in Illinois."

Skye gasped. "But we got created only a week or so ago. This means...."

"Yes," Blount said. "You've been compromised. They know about our group."

Rena shook her head at the handset. "It's more serious than that, sir. It means we have a spy *inside* our group. How else could they know this fast? My intuition...."

"Yes?"

She sighed. "My intuition failed me on this one, sir."

14. Bits of Positive News

Great Lakes

Commander Fasano stopped off at Skye's desk.

"Morning, sir!" Skye greeted. "What can I do for you this morning?"

"I just got a call from Switzerland."

"Good news. I hope?"

"Sort of. Our oh-eight-hundred here is sixteen hundred there. My contact was wrapping up some work and called me before he left for home. He did agree to look for payments to American sailors in California, but couldn't promise anything specific."

"Great! I hope he finds something for us."

"I gave him your list. He said he would stay in touch. We'll see."

"Thank you, sir."

Rena sat deep in thought. Our group was compromised. The Russians knew about us. And the best solid information we had seemed to be a sighting of a small boat on a foggy river in Connecticut. She was somewhat at a loss for what we should do until we got more solid information. And it still seemed none of the clues fit. We got nothing new back from Switzerland. It felt like the case had ground to a halt. All we could do was watch and wait. There was some slow progress in California, North Dakota, and Connecticut. But not much. Living proof of the Navy's unofficial motto: Hurry up and wait.

*   *   *   *

After Fasano departed, Rena left me a message through the FT school

86

office. So I dropped in to see her during lunchtime.

"What do you need?" I asked.

"A lunch partner."

"How do we do that? You're dressed in your officer's uniform and I'm in my enlisted's."

"We can go to the gedunk. They serve hamburgers, hot dogs, fries, that kind of stuff."

"Okay," I agreed. "We'll look like an officer with one of her people."

So we went to the gedunk, which is the Navy slang for a combination ice cream parlor and hamburger joint. I got a cheeseburger and Rena got a plain hamburger. We both got fries and a chocolate malt. We found an out of the way table so we could talk and not be overheard.

She watched me eat for a while before she laughed and said: "You explained to me about wrapping your free arm around your tray to keep it level. You think you're still at sea? You know that table isn't moving under your lunch...."

I chuckled. "It's become a habit. The *Hestek* rolled and pitched so much I got into the habit to keep your tray level pretty quickly. I have no idea how long it'll stick with me...."

"I'm glad they don't send women to sea." She took a few more bites of her food. "Please go over the crossword puzzle with a fine-toothed comb. I'm frustrated at trying to figure out what '60c,' or whatever it is, means. They don't use anything with a "c" in it. But my intuition is screaming to me that it has something to do with the puzzle. Right now I'm stumped. And furthermore...."

"Yes?"

"Tony Alvarez is using some short wave radio sets installed in their cars out in California to track down who the suspects are transmitting to and track down where their bosses are. And Ford and Stolichek also found short wave radio gear on the suspect diver's boat. This is frustrating, too. How many people will we need in order to track down all the communications of these people?"

I nodded. "Sorry, but I'm glad my job is to learn strange new pieces of equipment. I do not envy you your job right now."

When I returned to school, I snuck glances at the crossword the all afternoon. Nothing clicked. I wondered if we were looking at the whole thing wrong.

*   *   *   *

"Major Skye, this is Commander Fasano. I have some information from Switzerland."

"Good news, sir? Helpful?"

"They haven't found anything yet. They're still looking."

"Nuts," Skye commented

"Don't despair. There are layers of security they still might have to work through. There was nothing obvious out in the open."

"So we wait."

"Right."

"Okay. Thanks, Commander."

Skye was despondent. She and Fasano had been coming in earlier than normal, hoping to get some enlightening information from overseas. But the negative report they got was not helpful.

"Hurry up and wait," Skye mumbled as she stared at the pile of papers and photographs on her desk. "I never did like to do that."

* * * *

I completed my crash course at Fire Control Technician A School on Friday. When our graduation ceremony was over, I stopped off to see Rena. "Let's take some time off," I suggested. "The Chicago Symphony is playing Beethoven's Sixth this evening. I got a couple tickets cheap from a classmate who can't make it. Let's go listen."

"I can't, Eric. There are too many questions still unanswered here."

"Come on, Rena. You can't live in this office. We need some time together, too, to relax and be with each other."

She stood up. "I know, Eric. But I can't. And the Sixth is such a beautiful piece of work…. I wouldn't want you to miss it. Especially when you got cheap tickets. Why don't you go without me?"

"That's no fun."

"I'm sorry." She stood, eyes downcast. Thinking. "How about if I find someone else to go with you?"

"You have anyone in mind?" I asked.

"How about… Jennie?"

Jennie had been in our home numerous times. And the three of us, or the four of us when Glenn was around, had always had a great time.

Looking back on this now, I don't know what came over me. But I was stunned at Rena's suggestion. Suddenly I had to personally confront the core of the issue of race relations in America and to overcome a racism I didn't even know I had. And I had to do it in seconds. A white guy and a Negro woman together on a date?

Rena read my mind. "Eric! Why the hesitancy? You've been out in public with Jennie before…."

"But she was with her boyfriend. Not me." I stood there, staring at the floor, thinking of what some of the consequences could be from people seeing a white man with a Negro woman.

But I couldn't refuse to take Rena's best friend to the symphony. I swallowed hard. Heart pounding, I nodded and said: "All right. Give her a call and see if she'll go with me."

She said she would.

So Jennie and I went to the concert in Chicago. The worst thing that happened was one couple got up and moved away from us. The music was magnificent. We enjoyed each other's company, to the point where we went out for a drink afterward. We selected to a place on the South Side, a Negro neighborhood. Nobody there even gave us a second look.

* * * *

Skye pessimistically reached out to answer the phone again. "Here."

"My, aren't you the glum one!" a familiar voice said. He laughed. "Is this the new OCI protocol?"

"No, sir, Commander Fasano! Sorry, sir. I was tired and down in the dumps and…. Sorry. I…."

"No problem, Major. I got some news very early this morning. It may help rouse you a bit. If nothing else, it will prove to be interesting."

"I need some good news, sir."

"Try this on for size. Records show a California missile technician with sudden large amounts of money in a Swiss bank account. Quarterly."

"Is it Gary Blaine?"

"No. It's Robert Hansard. Pronounced 'ahn-sarr' over there. It turns out it he inherited a large sum of money from an aunt who lived in Switzerland. Thus the Swiss account. Rules for the release of the funds were written into her will. He got a lump sum and a bunch of stock investments. So the amount he gets depends on how the stock market behaves. Hansard receives, quarterly, two percent of the value of the fund plus the stock dividends. If the account makes more money, he receives more money. Kind of like a variable interest rate."

"So he's legit."

"It certainly looks like it."

"Well, pardon my attitude, Commander, but, *crap!*"

That night, Rena and I celebrated my graduation by going over to Rockford in civilian clothes and dining out. She actually let go of the job for a few hours. We had a wonderful time. Even danced after dinner.

15. Playbills & Murderers

Great Lakes

Skye sat thinking about Steven Montaigne. She hadn't heard from him for quite a while. She wondered what he was doing, what he would find, how soon he would report. What if Saint Louis was a dead end? Where would they look then?

Later, in the evening, Montaigne decided to call Skye before going out to supper. She wasn't in her office so he called her home number. I answered the phone.

"Hello."

"This is Steven Montaigne in Missouri. May I speak to Captain Skye?"

I recognized the voice. "Sure. But she's a major now, Steven. Hold on a minute."

Montaigne heard Skye's voice within seconds. "Hi, Rena. Steven here." He chuckled. "In Hannibal, Missouri."

"Why are you in Hannibal?"

"You suspected the killers were in Saint Louis, so I'm keeping away from anyone who might find me suspicious. I'm being cautious. Sightseeing. Up here I can play like a tourist. Visit all the Mark Twain sites."

"So what do you have for me?"

"First, I found out what union local Don Jennings and Jerry Hassler belonged to. I found their union hall. One day, after work I followed a couple of the drivers from there to their favorite bar. I stood outside and took the time to finish my cigarette, not because I couldn't smoke in the bar—which would be ridiculous—but because I didn't want to give anyone the idea I'd followed them. I wanted information, not suspicion.

"I overheard a couple of the drivers talking about the two dead men. They almost held a memorial there over their beers. I got some interesting information. I sat on an empty stool a couple places farther down. Ordered a beer. Listened to the buzz around me. These guys, Greg and Dave, knew and liked Jennings and Hassler. I got to talking with them. Dave was the man who let Jennings' wife know what happened. Then he took her over to her sister's place.

"Jennings, the primary driver, was the guy who worked the crossword puzzles. He was a fanatic about them. He did crosswords when sitting and waiting or standing in line. Others would read a book or shoot the breeze. He'd work on a crossword."

"I've heard a little bit about that," Rena said. "Anything else?"

"Yes. He liked to play poker a lot. But his favorite hobby was acting. He was an actor in a community theater."

"Was he in a play now?"

"Yeah. This is interesting, and maybe important. He was in a play called *Winston, Franklin, and Joe*."

"Oh-kaay. What role did he play?"

"Winston Churchill," Montaigne replied.

"Makes sense. He did look a bit like Churchill. Who played the other roles?"

"I found the Savoy Theater. The playbill listed all the main actors. I don't know if the names will mean anything too you, but perhaps you should note them in case they become important in the future."

"Okay. Let me have them."

"Arkady Badurov and John Crystal are the names of the other two actors. They still hadn't come up with a replacement for Donald Jennings."

"All right. We know Jennings played the part of Churchill. And I would bet Badurov would play a Russian. That leaves Crystal."

"The janitor there let me in the stage door and gave me the information. You're right, Arkady Badurov does play Stalin. John Crystal plays Roosevelt. And he gave me other pieces of information that might be important."

"Like what?" Skye asked.

"Crystal is kind of uppity. An upper class type. He even sounds a bit like FDR. Badurov is perfect for the part of Stalin. He is Russian and has a Russian accent."

"Thanks, Steven. This information is good to know."

"Anything else you need?" Montaigne asked.

"You know, it might help if we uncovered more about Crystal and Badurov. Where they live. How they live. Whether or not they liked Jennings. What their other habits and hobbies are. Let's try to flesh them out, okay?"

"You got it, Rena. I'll get on it right away. I'll start with Badurov. Follow him around. See what I can dig up on him."

"Let me know when you find anything," Rena said.

"Will do."

* * * *

Rena told me what Montaigne had discovered, what play Jennings had been in, who the other actors were and the roles they played. As soon as she told me this information, we looked at each other, slapped our foreheads and made a mad dash for the crossword puzzle.

"Check out anyplace on the puzzle with a six in its location," I said.

"Sixty across, the clue is 'Arctic Footwear.' You know the answer?"

"'Snowshoes,'" I replied. "Doesn't seem meaningful. What's the clue for sixty down?"

"'Ann Lee's furniture.' Wouldn't that be 'Shaker'?"

"It fits,'" I said. "It means nothing to me."

"Okay, what's six across?" she asked.

"Six across? I thought the driver wrote sixty-C. How do you get a six in either direction?" I stopped short. Raised my hand, finger pointing in the air. "Wait a minute. Sixty. Sixdy. Six-D.... What's the clue for six-down?"

"Soviet leader at Yalta. Stalin!" Rena yelped. "Stalin! What I thought was 'six-zero-c' written in blood was the beginning of 'six down.' In capital letters. From a shaky, pain-affected hand. The killer is the Russian actor in that play! Someone Jennings knew. So Badurov took all of Jennings ID, thinking nobody would know...." Rena stopped short. "Oh my God! I have to warn Montaigne. He's going to investigate the killer more closely!" Then she simply sat there, wringing her hands.

"Aren't you going to call him and warn him?" I asked.

"I can't." Her lower lip fluttered. Her voice trembled as she answered: "He doesn't have a stable address or phone number. I'll have to wait until he calls me before I can warn him."

16. California Houses

California

"Hey, boss. I have some news." Alvarez said over the phone.

"What's up, Tony?" Skye asked.

"Commander Jackson Bohn here has a number of good friends helping him dig up information for us. He heard about our search for the owners of the house we're interested in and he called a friend who's in the real estate business. He got us the name of the owner of those two houses. It's Roy Villand. The floppy hat man Daniel just identified. And there's more. Villand owns two other houses. And there's a co-owner, some import-export company in Chicago named New Horizon Imports."

*　　*　　*　　*

Alvarez happened to be in the conference room, when Glenn called via the police band radio in the car.

"Leader, this is Golf. I'm followin' Blaine," Oliver reported. "But he didn't go to his house in Oxnard. He went to another house in a very residential neighborhood over in Camarillo. Want me to keep watch on him?"

"Yes. Watch him every time he leaves the base. We need to figure out what these guys are doing all the time. When you return, we can do a debriefing."

"Will do. Out."

Oliver got out of the car to look around. The house had a driveway going to a garage in the back. The neighboring house on next door was dark. It had a driveway running parallel to and ten feet away from Blaine's.

94

He half-ran up the driveway, to the neighbor's garage and back. He was in the rear of the property long enough to see a set of back stairs on Blaine's house, leading up to what he guessed would be an upstairs apartment. He returned to the car, wondering why Blaine had a second home. He took out one of the little telescopes they'd bought in imitation of the one I bought in New York. He could see most of the living room through the front windows. He noted the address.

A light came on upstairs. Blaine came to the front window. He had a beer, but didn't seem to be drinking it. Merely holding it. He looked quite distraught. He shook his head a number of times. He glanced up in the air. It looked like he took a number of deep breaths and sighed. Oliver couldn't be sure, but Blaine's body seemed to shake a few times as if he were sobbing. He stood there like that way for a long time. After a while, he retreated farther into the room and Glenn could no longer see him.

"I'd sure like to know what's botherin' him so much," Oliver mumbled as he started the car, put it in gear and drove off. "Leader this is Golf. Over."

Han answered this time. "Go ahead, Glenn. What's up?"

"I have another address to check out for ownership. If it isn't one of our guys, check the rental records, too." He recited the house's address and description.

"Hold on a minute," Alvarez said. "All right, I'm back. It's one of the addresses Commander Bohn gave me. Ray Villand owns that house."

*　　*　　*　　*

The two OCI ham radio vans returned to the Port Hueneme office. The agents reported to Alvarez.

"We found nothin' new," Oliver said despondently.

"Yeah. Try as we might," said Tuttle, "we couldn't determine which signals were responding to the local messages."

"We even pointed our antennas in the exact direction of Saint Louis. Nothing clicked."

"We found the signals going out." Tuttle said. "Then there was a pause. Then they sent another transmission. Then another pause. The length of the pauses varied."

Oliver took a deep breath. "So how do y'all think Blaine knows when to transmit again? Does he get some kind of go ahead signal?"

"We don't even know if he's receiving transmissions in return," Tuttle added. "Or at what frequency."

95

"Also," Oliver added, "we've been listenin' to their messages, too. It sounds like a bunch of gibberish. I speak Swahili, Hindi and some Afrikaans. Bud speaks Portuguese, Italian and some Gaelic. And this doesn't sound like anything we've ever heard."

"Is it an Asian language? Or Russian?" Alvarez suggested with raised eyebrows.

Bud Tuttle shook his head. "We thought about that. But we've both been around enough to recognize Japanese and the tonal languages of China. It's none of them. And it is *not* Russian. It's gibberish. We're stumped."

"Okay. Go get some rest," Alvarez suggested. "We have to figure out something else to do. Right now, we're going nowhere fast."

* * * *

Tony Alvarez called a meeting of the Hueneme team. Dirk Fladeboe was excused because he was deep undercover in the missile-shipping department.

"The way I see it," Han said, "I have two jobs to do. First, I have to follow Gary Blaine to determine his routine. Take photos. The other job is to go inside the house on a regular basis and check the status of the radio equipment. Try to determine the transmit and receive frequencies...."

"We found his transmit frequencies...," Glenn observed.

"True," Han said. "But we haven't discovered who he's talking to. Once we have that information, we can start listening in to his messages."

"I agree. But later we may have more for you to do," Alvarez said.

"We already found out some important information. Blaine goes up into his attic regularly. He goes into the house and the lights come on in the attic at the same time on a regular schedule. He seems to send out radio signals every few days."

"I've been thinkin' 'bout the signals we already picked up," Glenn said.

"What about them?" Alvarez asked.

"We can detect whenever he's doin' his thing. But the way he pauses between transmissions is kinda strange."

"Why?"

"He waits different lengths of time. There's no regularity there. No system. And I been wonderin' why."

"Come to any conclusions?"

Glenn nodded. "I think he's waitin' for the other guy to quit talkin'."

"So why don't we hear the other guy?"

"Because," he paused for effect. "The other guy is answerin' on another frequency. And we don't know what it is. And since it's not comin' from the house, we haven't picked it up."

"So what can we do, Glenn?"

"Get more scanners. Scan outward in four different directions from Blaine's house. Whenever we pick up another frequency from somewhere else, we check to see if it meshes with his transmissions. Time the frequencies to see if they fit two people talkin' to each other."

"I thought we've been doing...."

"Yeah. But we c'n determine whether or not he's talkin' to Saint Louis. I suggest we scan for signals from north-north-east, east-north-east, east-south-east and south-south-east. We have to find out where the other end of his conversations is."

"Another thing is weird," Han said. "We've listened to some of Blaine's transmissions. Everything we hear is in some strange sounding foreign language. Or it's some kind of strange code."

"Record those conversations and let's see if we can crack the code," Alvarez ordered. "And I'll get some more scanners and set them up in vans so we can move them around."

17. Arkady Badurov

Great Lakes

"Hi, Rena! Steven here."

"Hi! How's it going down in Saint Louis?"

"Kind of difficult, but that may be my fault. Friday I bought a ticket to the stage production of *Winston, Franklin and Joe*. I enjoyed the play a lot. The story was a good one and the actors were exceptional, even though this was community theater.

"I had researched the physical and personality characteristics of Stalin, and during the play I studied Arkady Badurov's features and how he portrayed his character. Like the real Stalin, Badurov is short, no taller than five and a half feet. He bears a remarkable resemblance to the real Stalin. His hair was brushed back and he had the dictator's bushy mustache. Either had smallpox or the make-up people did a phenomenal job, because he had a pockmarked face. They also faked Stalin's shortened left arm and stiffened elbow, which was the result of a carriage accident in the dictator's earlier years. But they couldn't do much about the shriveled hand. Badurov kept it hidden away most of the time as Stalin had done."

"And his acting was good?"

"Oh, yes. Badurov gave his character charm and politeness around the other statesmen. But he presented a sharp contrast when he was with his own people, exhibiting the dictator's notorious impatience, intolerance of other's views, and lack of self-control."

"So why do you think your difficulty down there might be your fault?"

Montaigne sighed. "When the play was over, I tried to rush to the stage door so I could follow Badurov. But the crowd impeded me, so I wasn't able to get out of the theater fast enough to catch the actor leaving.

"The next evening, I stood outside the stage door for two hours, but the actor didn't came out. I saw most of the other cast leave but not the Russian. It dawned on me Badurov must have run like hell out the stage door as soon as the final bows were over."

"Was there another showing on Sunday?"

"Yes, a matinee. This time I parked back some distance from the stage door of the Savoy, a half hour before the play ended. I turned off the engine and waited. I also scrunched down to stay out of sight as much as possible. I tried to make my car look like it was a vehicle parked in the alley."

"Did it work?" Rena asked.

"Well, yes and no. Another car came through the alley ten minutes before the play ended. It pulled right up to the door. But I didn't notice the driver keeping his engine idling. Badurov rushed out, ran out, in fact, and hopped into the car, which sped off. I hurried to start my car, but by the time I got out of the alley, I couldn't see any other cars. Now I'll have to wait until next weekend for another performance."

"Well, live and learn, Steven. Let me know what happens next week. Meanwhile, I need to warn you. Be careful around this guy. We think he may be the killer. So he could be extremely dangerous."

"Wait a minute. From the briefings I got up there at Lakes, I thought the killer dropped a handkerchief with a 'C' on it, the Russian letter 'ess'...."

"Yes he did."

"Wouldn't that indicate the killer's name begins with an 'S'?"

"Yes...," Rena said, realizing where the logic was taking them.

"So, there's no 'ess' in Arkady Badurov's name. So he can't be the killer, Rena. The pieces don't fit."

"You may be right," she sighed. "But you be extra careful, anyway. We have other indications that say this actor is the killer. But what you pointed out proves there's too much here we don't understand."

"I will be careful," Montaigne reassured her.

18. Moving to Long Island

Connecticut

The Connecticut night was clear. Ford and Stolichek again called for aerial surveillance and alerted the "fishing boats." But, again, the cabin cruiser did not make an appearance.

Stolichek called Skye in the morning to let her know about the dead end.

"Dead end? Not exactly," Rena said.

"What do you mean?"

"We got a report back from the boat's registration number."

George was ecstatic. "Wonderful! Where's it from?"

"Get ready," Skye warned.

"Uh-oh. Already I think I'm not going to like this. Where's it from?"

"Not New York, like we thought," Rena said.

"Where, then?"

"Would you believe... Chicago?"

"Chicago? So how did it get out here?" Stolichek asked.

"I can imagine, but it won't answer *why* it's out there," Skye said.

"What do you mean?"

"It had to go through the Saint Lawrence Seaway. You know it opened in 1959 and vessels of all sizes can go between even the farthest of the Great Lakes to the Atlantic Ocean...."

"You're funny," Stolichek said. "I could have figured that out myself."

"Or it could have been towed out there by the company that owns it."

"Company?"

"Yeah," Skye replied. "Something called New Horizon Import Company, headquartered in Chicago."

"This case gets weirder and weirder every day."

"Tell me about it."

*   *   *   *

It was another bright, clear night in Connecticut; the moon was not long past full.

Stolichek and Ford positioned themselves very close to where the spy diver had anchored his cabin cruiser before. They prepared their camera with a strong telescopic lens. They were very happy when the spy diver showed up. They were able to get photos of him changing into his wet suit and climbing into the rowboat with the small outboard motor. Remembering Skye's request to get lots of photos, they used a whole roll of film for these pictures. Then they reloaded the camera in preparation for the diver's return.

They didn't work alone. Security had also spread the "fishing boats" and a few high-flying aerial-surveillance helicopters all along the river and around a large area of Long Island Sound. They wanted more coverage but they didn't dare overdo it and take the chance of the spies becoming suspicious. They were trying to do everything they could to follow this guy home. Everyone used cameras with strong telescopic lenses and very fast film, so there would be no flashbulbs involved.

All the preparation paid off. The fishing boats looked very innocent. The helos were quite high and at some distance and they were using infrared film.

Ford and Stolichek documented the spy diver climbing back into the cabin cruiser. They also got photos that proved the identity of the boat and its registration.

The OCI crews tracked the boat all the way to Long Island. They noted the dock where the boat tied up and the house that the diver entered: a house located about three miles northeast of Orient, New York. Stolichek and Ford later found the location on a geodetic survey map. The house was located in a wooded area east of Pettys Bight and west of Mulford Point.

*   *   *   *

Meanwhile, the Air Force security at Cape Canaveral called the OCI office in Washington, DC, and asked for help. They reported seeing signs of divers in the restricted waters off the cape. But they didn't have any experienced diver units themselves. The suspected divers were at the southern end of the facility, in the Navy's Polaris Missile area.

The person taking the Air Force request called Commander Blount at OCI Norfolk and gave him the information from the Cape. He asked Blount to send a diver to Florida because the people at the Cape were quite anxious about this situation. The fact that the Navy was going to have some critical test launches in the area increased their concern.

Blount promised to help. He contacted Major Rena Skye at once. That afternoon he had Skye transfer Ford from New London to Canaveral.

*   *   *   *

When Skye heard about the house on Long Island, she sent Morgan Delano out to team up with George Stolichek and help watch the people there. Ford was already on the way to Cape Canaveral. Justin Thein and others from the New London OCI office stayed on watch around the New London Naval Base and on the Thames River out to Long Island Sound.

Stolichek and Delano sailed in one of the "fishing boats," towing a rubber raft behind them. They stayed well out from shore until very late at night. Then they rowed the rubber raft to a location on Pettys Bight. They beached the raft at a clearing on the eastern side of the woods where the house was located.

They noticed a grass landing strip as they walked inland toward a stand of woods. There was a path from the airfield through the woods, going toward the house where the cabin cruiser had tied up. The house was in the middle of a large yard with woods all around it. They checked out the whole area.

And they were careful not to attract any attention. As Del commented: "We don't want to wake up any dogs or guards. I'm too bee-yoo-tee-ful to be hurt by these guys."

Stolichek had a hard time controlling his laughter.

Even so, the two men were able to step through last year's fallen leaves without making much noise. They walked from one end of the grove to the other. The docked cabin cruiser was at the back of the house, to the north. A long driveway from the main road came through the woods south of the house, and circled around at the front door.

They decided Delano would stay on watch while Stolichek went back to report what they'd found.

*   *   *   *

In the following days, the New London OCI office relocated all of the "fishing boats" to Long Island Sound. Every one of them had ham and police radio equipment. They listened to transmissions from the "Orient House" in the woods. They took photos of every action the spy diver did. Watched everything from Long Island Sound while Stolichek and Delano watched the house from the woods.

A man and a woman lived in the house. The diver almost seemed like a guest. And there were guards. With one single dog.

*　　*　　*　　*

Stolichek slid silently through the woods surrounding the "Orient House" and arrived to relieve Delano about 0100. Del was right where they agreed for the watch change location. Everything was quiet. The two men talked in whispers. George commented that the people they were watching weren't stupid and they might examine the area on a regular basis. Thus the OCI agents tried to be extra careful not to leave tracks or other indications they'd been there. And they should establish a few back-up spots to meet and relieve the watch.

Del suggested renting a place to sleep and eat nearby. He thought there should be a number of places for rent in the area, because it was so recreational. And they could use the north end of the landing strip, near Long Island Sound, as long as they kept a low profile and made sure the relief times were when people wouldn't be watching.

Stolichek liked the idea of renting a place. Del would begin scouting around the next day. But Del was also worried about the dog smelling them and giving them away to the guard. As he put it he was "too precious a guy to be a doggie snack."

George wondered how they could stop the dog from finding them.

"Well, they don't let him run loose very often. So that's in our favor," Del said. Then he grinned. "But I already thought of a solution. I'll let you know about it later, George."

19. Slow Progress

Great Lakes

I began my class on the Mark 37 gunfire control system, abbreviated "GFCS Mk. 37."

That evening I was home alone with Tango. Rena was still at the office trying to unravel the mystery, trying to make sense of all the clues.

I played with the dog for a while. I talked to him as we played. "I'll be able to do this a lot more now. All of C school uses classified material, so we can't take anything home to study. There's no homework. And when Rena's so busy with the case, what else can I do?"

When my supper was ready, I sat down and ate, then spent some time typing, writing, and trying to get the details of this case written down.

*   *   *   *

Commander Fasano called Skye into his office. As she entered the room, he said: "Close the door, please."

Skye did so, frowning. "What's up, sir?"

"I have some news. But first, where are all the locations you're working on this case?"

"Port Hueneme, California. The skies over South Dakota and a buffalo ranch in Nebraska. New London submarine base and a house in Orient, New York, way out on Long Island. Our diver is at Cape Canaveral. Why?"

"Any red flags around Canaveral?"

"No, sir. Air Force security down there reported possible divers. Heads

104

popping up in the surf. But that's it. I sent Len Ford, our diver, down to watch the area. But I'm not sure he's even there yet. He hasn't reported anything."

"Here, read this." He handed her a typed news release from the radio room.

> 25 April 1962, 16:50 GMT. Launch Platform: SSBN 609 SAM HOUSTON. Launch Vehicle: Polaris A2. LV Configuration: Polaris A2PE-1. Test mission. Agency: USN. Apogee: 600 mi. ETR Launch Area just off the coast of Canaveral: Longitude: -79.0000 deg., Latitude: 28.5000 deg.

Rena looked up. "The newest Polaris worked."

Fasano was smiling. He nodded. "Not a hitch."

"What does this mean for us?" she asked.

"Nothing. Or a whole lot. Who knows? It seems all of your areas of investigation have something to do with our newest missile capabilities...."

"Even Hueneme and those old missile bodies?"

"Mmmm hmmm. Hueneme is helping with plans for what they're calling Super-Terrier and Super-Talos."

"Yes, sir. I knew that."

"They want to make two combinations of anti-aircraft and anti-missile missiles. Some hope they'll be able to knock out an enemy ICBM in mid-flight. We don't know for sure how those old missiles fit into the picture, but they might, considering the records in California seem to have been compromised."

"So everything we're looking into may have something to do with our long range missile capacity. Or the defense against the same from an enemy."

"Right. And since we're running new Polaris tests from the submarines themselves, I expect we're going to get more action around Canaveral, too. Let Ford know about all these connections and the submarine tests. Over a secure phone line. Tell him to keep an especially sharp eye out for other divers. It's one thing to see divers' bubble trails in a river. It's an different animal if the divers are in the ocean."

"Anything else you want me to do, sir?"

"Basic planning and preparation. Get ready. Determine who else you want to send to the Cape and get them off any other jobs you have them on. Just in case we need to build up our group in Florida."

"Aye, aye, sir. I'll get on it immediately."

*　　*　　*　　*

Rena placed a call to a Norfolk phone number. The receptionist there answered. "Federal Bureau of Investigation."

Skye frowned. The number she dialed should have taken her straight to a friend's desk. "I'm trying to reach Evan Dawes...."

"Would you identify yourself, please?"

"I'm Major Rena Skye of the Navy's Office of Criminal Investigation. I need to contact Agent Dawes for him to be my FBI liaison on a case."

"Mr. Dawes was transferred out of Norfolk on another assignment."

"Where was he sent?"

"I'm sorry, Major. I don't have the authority to release that information. I hope you understand that I'm simply obeying orders."

"Does Agent Dawes have a replacement there who I could talk to?"

"Yes, Henry Bridges. I'll transfer your call to his desk. Please wait."

"Thank you."

While she waited she thought back to the news Commander Blount had told her a short time ago. *The Russians know about us. We have a spy in our midst who told Moscow about our group.... I don't know who that spy is, but he or she is right here in the middle of us or the Russians wouldn't have found out about us.*

A minute later, a voice brought Skye back to the present. "FBI, Agent Henry Bridges. How can I help you?"

"Mr. Bridges, I'm Major Rena Skye of the Navy's Office of Criminal Investigation. We are trying to track down some information on a John Little Horse of Oxbow, Nebraska, which is near Alliance. We hope you can provide some info for us."

"I'll sure try, Major. Give me your phone number so I can get back to you."

"It might help for you folks to know," Skye added, "this guy flies a Cessna 172 with no registration markings on the plane. And he's flying it over new ICBM silos in South Dakota."

"Got it. Thanks. I'll do what I can for you, Major."

*   *   *   *

Skye pulled out her geodetic survey maps. Stolichek had given her the complete description of the land around the house in Orient, New York. She found the house on her map.

"Sheila!" she called out to her yeoman.

"Yes, major?" Dempsey answered.

"I need your help...."

The young ensign came over to Skye's desk. "What's up, ma'am?"

"I need the phone number for the post office in Orient, New York."

"Sure, major. I'll get right on it."

Fifteen minutes later Dempsey placed a piece of paper on her boss's desk. "There's the phone number you asked for."

"Thanks." Skye dialed the number. She got the postmaster on the line. "Hi! I'm Major Rena Skye of the U. S. Navy's Office of Criminal Investigation. I'm in charge of investigating a major case for the Navy. If I ask you for some information would you keep my request secret?"

"Sure, major. No problem. How can I help?"

"I need to know the address of a specific house. It's on the north shore of Long Island, a bit west of Pettys Bight. It's next door to a grass airfield and it's surrounded by woods."

"Yes, I know the place." He gave her the address.

"Thank you very much. I appreciate your help."

"No problem, major. Glad I could help."

After she hung up the phone, Skye sat back and thought. *How great it would be to have Chaské here to do the research we need. I think I'll call him back. I need to know who owns the property on Long Island that Del and George are watching. And I think Chaské can be a lot of help on some other searches. Meanwhile....* "Janice!"

"Yes, major?"

"I have a job here."

"Yes, ma'am."

"Get some of the Waves to help you. Here's an address. I need to know who owns the property."

"Okay. We'll track it down for you."

"Thanks."

20. Transfers

Cape Canaveral

Leonard Ford reported in to Rena shortly after he arrived in the town of Port Canaveral.

"So you're all settled in down there?"

"Yeah. I rented a car, got a motel room and reported to the Cape Canaveral Air Force Station. To their security boss, a Special Agent Steven Tramora."

"Will you be able to get along with him?"

"I think so. At first he had a hard time believing we suspected the Russians were watching everything going on at the Navy end of the Cape. Until I explained what we'd found in Connecticut and on Long Island and told him about the scuba divers.

"I told him we thought the Russians were trying to find out about our ICBM capabilities in order to have a better idea about what they'd need to do or adjust if they can find and duplicate the Navy's planned anti-missile capabilities. Then he asked me how we planned to counter these guys."

"What did you tell him?" Skye asked.

"I told him we didn't plan to counter them at all, but to find them and arrest them. To help us do so, I asked his permission to watch the Navy's area of the Cape, to watch the beach and restricted waters at night."

"Tramora asked if I planned on working alone. I told him we didn't have any other divers, but others would cover my back. He promised to give us all the help he could, starting with as many walkie-talkies as I would need."

"So it sounds like you're all set up there."

"I do believe so."

"What else do you need from me?"

"Don't know yet. Let me scout out the area and see. I'll let you know as soon as I can."

*   *   *   *

That night Ford watched over the southern part of Cape Canaveral from shore. He saw nothing unusual. The lights in this part of the base were aimed to illuminate the crews preparing missiles for tests. Not much light reached where he was. His eyes grew somewhat accustomed to the darkness and he didn't notice anybody outside the gantry areas. He looked around the area where he stood, close to Launch Complex 29, the Polaris Missile test site. He saw nobody on the beach or in the water. But the darkness was like ink; the new moon was a little more than a week away.

It seemed like the U.S. space program was also very dark and dreary. An Air Force Minuteman shot failed on launch the day before. Earlier, NASA had a successful Saturn test—all hundred and twenty three seconds of it. I seemed that very few such failures and minor successes ever reached the American public. In comparison, the spectacular Russian successes made headlines: the first artificial satellite Sputnik, a live dog in orbit, and then putting a human, Yuri Gagarin, into earth orbit. The public didn't hear much about Russian failures. And the U.S. had trailed the Russians for a long time.

Ford burrowed into a stand of brush next to the launch site, a location where he could watch the beach. He sat in his wet suit, his oxygen tanks on his back. His mask hung from his neck. His fins lay at his feet, ready to be put on at a moment's notice. He swept the waters with his binoculars. All he saw was the normal surf of the Atlantic.

He'd brought a thermos bottle of very strong coffee. He settled it in the bushes for future use.

He swept the area with his binoculars every five minutes or so. The fourth or fifth sweep, he thought he saw a diver in the water. The guy didn't get close enough to the shore to be in the white surf. He disappeared in the troughs behind the ocean swells.

Even if Ford was certain a diver was out there, he couldn't follow him underwater at night. He'd lost sight of the guy anyway. Or else his eyes were playing tricks on him. He was still tired from travelling....

He sat there watching the ocean for two and a quarter hours. The surf rolled in. It conveyed tranquility. Peace. Its calm cadence was mesmerizing.

Ford dozed off.

He woke up with a start and quickly scanned the waterfront. He thought he saw a diver's head in the water off shore again. He tried to clarify his vision by rubbing his eyes. The dark spot in the restricted waters was still there. Without a doubt, it was a head in the water, beyond the breaking surf. Ford reached for his fins and put them on his feet. When he looked up, the head was no longer there. He scanned the area with his binoculars but couldn't find the diver again.

He sat on the beach until his eyelids drooped again. He stood up. Stretched. Ran his binoculars over the Atlantic. There was no sign of anything in the water, but the swells and troughs made it difficult to determine if anyone was there or not.

He reached for his thermos of coffee. Stood up and swept the water again with the binoculars. He started walking parallel to the water line.

The area was empty. Almost desolate. There were quite a few lights some distance away, but they were all shining toward the inside spaces of the gantries. It looked like NASA, Air Force or Army crews were preparing for an upcoming missile shot.

*   *   *   *

Rena wanted to find out how Ford was doing, but to get in touch with him, she would have to leave her phone numbers at the Canaveral security office and wait for him to get back to her. So she left a message for him to call her as soon as he checked in.

"Hello?"

"Rena? This is Len. You have a different number now?"

"Hi! Thanks for calling back this early. I was expecting you to call quite a bit later. This is my home number. So don't call me here too often."

"All right. I'll won't call after midnight, I promise," Ford laughed. "I checked in a bit early at the security office, then watched the shoreline last night. Don't have a phone out there on the beach. What's up?"

"I have some news for you. I don't know how much the office there is telling you. It's NASA, Army and Air Force and this is about the Navy."

"I heard about some tests from the other armed forces. The U.S. Ranger spacecraft crash-landed on the Moon. What's the Navy's story?"

"Yesterday the USS *Sam Houston* test launched one of the new Polaris A2 missiles in the Eastern Test Range off Cape Canaveral. The missile's apogee was six hundred miles in altitude."

"If it reached that height, I gather the launch was successful?"

"Yes. Thought you'd like to know. Have you seen any activity there yet?"

"As a matter of fact, I did see a diver's head in the water, but he didn't come close enough to be in the surf. Then I lost sight of him. It's hard to see people in the water at night unless they're in the surf."

"How are you going to find these guys so far out?"

"Haven't thought it all the way through yet. If I go out there, too, it would be easy to miss something so low in the water while I'm bobbing around on the surface."

"Would it help to get you a boat to use?"

"Right now I can't see a real good reason for it. Maybe in the future."

"How about someone to work with you? I can send Everett Cobbe down there to help. He's a first looie in the Marine Corps. He worked with us on the drug ring case in Norfolk. The two of you can try to track the spy diver from his entry into the water to where he watches from."

"I'm willing to try that. But I don't even know what he'd be watching. This diver can't swim out to the Test Range. It's way too far out. And he might get a missile up his ass if he's in the wrong spot. I was hoping he'd come ashore to take pictures of the loading docks or the gantries where they'd be during the pre-launch period. Anyway, yes, I'd love to have Cobbe's help. A third person would help, too. Then we can hash this whole thing out as a team."

"All right. I'll see who else I can come up with. And I'll work at you getting a small craft of some sort. A coxswain, too. So we'll give you a team of four.... Hold on, a minute." Ford could hear her talking to me. "Eric says I should try to get a transfer for a second class bos'n's mate named Al Cisco. Says he knew him on the USS *Hestek* and he can be trusted. He can serve as your coxswain. Do you have a spot where I can tell them to meet you?"

Ford thought for a moment. "Yes. The Royal Baby's Bar and Grill, between the Canaveral Barge Canal and Bennett Causeway. Any cabbie can find it. Let me know when he'll arrive and I'll be sure to eat there that night."

"Great. I'll cut Cobbe's transfer orders immediately."

The next day, Rena was also able to get OCI Great Lakes to transfer Ryan Murray, a civilian intelligence specialist to Canaveral to help out. And she got Commander Blount in Norfolk to arrange a transfer for Al Cisco. Blount also arranged the transfer of Andrew Hagen, a Marine helicopter pilot.

*   *   *   *

Rena decided to take a quick field trip to Cape Canaveral to see what else she might be able to do for the growing OCI crew there.

In an efficiency just short of a miracle, Everett Cobbe arrived at Cape

Canaveral in one day. He met Ford and Rena at the Royal Baby's Bar and Grill, where they ate supper. Ford seemed to pay a lot of attention to their waitress, who was not only very efficient and attentive to their needs, but very good looking.

All agreed their meals were excellent.

As she cleared some of the dishes off the table, the waitress gave Ford an appreciative, almost a come-hither, glance. She had pitch-black hair, dark flashing almost almond-shaped eyes and a deep tan complexion. Her lips were neither full nor thin. Her cheekbones were prominent but not Asian. Ford mumbled what sounded like "She's stunning!" He gave her a big smile. He wanted to talk with her, but she was working and, regrettably, the OCI people also had work to do.

Rena sat back and listened; this was Ford's show.

"What we doing tonight?" Cobbe asked. "You need me right away?"

"Afraid so. You can sleep in tomorrow."

"No sweat," Cobbe grinned. "The Corps trained me to stay awake. What do you need?"

"Let's take a gamble." Ford pulled out a piece of paper and a pencil. He drew a rough map of the area, the Air Force Station, Cape Canaveral where missiles were launched, the Canaveral Barge Canal, a fishing-charter area and a marina in Port Canaveral, which he thought might be the diver's starting point.

"Any of these areas might be our diver's starting point. Or maybe not." Ford paused. "I didn't see any boats when I thought I saw the diver in the waters off the missile launch area. He could be starting anywhere along the Barge Canal. Port Canaveral is the closest town to the open ocean. The missile base is to the north of where the canal meets the ocean. So it could be a short swim if he enters the water near here." He pointed to the canal opening at the ocean.

"You want me to go out there and watch?"

"Yeah, I'd like you to."

"What should I be looking for, specifically?"

"Best case, a diver going into the water, either from land or from a boat. Next best, a diver on the surface heading out to sea or coming back in. Third, a trail of bubbles from such a diver. Or a guy in a boat in the middle of the night. You may or may not see diving equipment in the boat. Have a camera handy?"

"Yeah. In my bags. I'll unpack it before tonight. Where do I sleep?"

"Come on. I'll take you to my place. It's at a local motel. You can stay there, too."

"Won't you be too crowded?"

"Rena's already going to be sleeping on the floor. You can grab another piece of the floor. We'll get an apartment when we know where to move to."

Skye accompanied Ford out to the Cape. They batted around some ideas for finding out who this spy diver was and tracking him down. By the time they came in, Rena had the beginning of a plan in her mind.

*   *   *   *

Meanwhile, on the USS *Hestek* (DD-856), a personnelman named Don Huber tracked down Cisco. "Hey, Al. Looks like you're getting off the Old Haystack."

"What are you talking about?"

"I have your orders right here. Orders for a Cisco, Albert, N-M-N, BM2. See?"

Cisco took the sheet of paper the personnelman held out. "So, where are they sending me?"

"It looks like Cape Canaveral," Huber replied.

"What's going on? Why would they send me there?"

"I have no idea. To be honest, I didn't even think Cape Canaveral would have billets for bos'n mates there."

"What's the *Navy* got at Canaveral?"

"Some kind of missile testing facility."

"When am I supposed to show up down there?"

"Four days from now. Oh-eight-hundred on one May, 1962."

"Four days! That's hardly enough to pack up and travel down there," Cisco protested. "And why would they even want me?"

"Maybe they need someone who knows boats, or how to care for metalwork," the personnelman grinned, "or can tie good knots, or can paint real pretty, or can do any of that other bos'n stuff."

"Oh, you're funny, Don. Real funny."

"Yeah. Somebody's got to keep a sense of humor in this outfit. You aren't due for shore duty, are you?"

"Not by a long shot."

Cisco hit the rack wondering about his orders. Fell asleep wondering about them. Woke up in the middle of the night wondering. Thought of something in his past. His recent past. A novel. Something about a spy. That was it! *The Secret Agent* by Joseph Conrad.

He grinned. Nodded. At least he knew who was behind this. The new assignment might be fun....

He went back to sleep.

*   *   *   *

We got this story from the FBI man involved some time after these events. This is where it fits chronologically.

A maid in the Sand Dollar Inn, located in Cape Canaveral, Florida, called the FBI. After some initial questions, they decided to send an agent to interview the her.

"What is your name, miss?"

"Maria Holland, sir."

"Okay, Maria. Tell me what you saw."

"I do not know, really. The guest did not use his 'Do Not Disturb' sign on the doorknob. I entered his room to clean it. He shouted at me to get out."

"Did he do anything else?" the agent asked, wondering why the Bureau sent him down to Florida for this.

"He acted crazy, grabbing some papers he had on the bed and almost kind of hiding them."

"Could you tell what was on the papers?"

She shook her head. "No. I did not see them clearly enough to tell."

"So what made you so suspicious of him?"

She shrugged her shoulders. "I have worked here for many years and seen many people. Even military men who visited Cape Canaveral. But I never saw anyone act the way this man did. I just got a very strange feeling about him."

"Do you know this guest's name?" he asked.

She shook her head. "No, sir."

"What is his room number?"

"312."

"Thank you. Now, I need to know if he changes his behavior or if he gets ready to check out. Will you let me know if he does either of those?"

"Yes, sir."

"Thank you, Maria."

The FBI agent checked with the hotel management. Maria Holland had worked there for fourteen years. She had a good relationship with her employers and she returned their trust and friendship with vigilance. She was solid and trustworthy. The agent decided she might indeed have stumbled across some suspicious behavior. *I think I will look a little more closely into this man. A maid with so much experience might be able to detect something out of the ordinary.*

21. Small Steps Forward

California

Since the school I was in now didn't permit materials to leave the building, we had no homework and I was free to go out to California the same weekend that Rena visited Cape Canaveral. The crew out there was going to try to get Gary Blaine's receiver frequencies and had designed an elaborate scheme to do so: interrupt the spy in the middle of his radio work and sneak in to take a look at his equipment. I was to go with the team to observe.

We waited in the OCI office for Alban to report from Blaine's house in Oxnard. Alvarez picked up the microphone to the police radio set on his desk as soon as he heard Robert's voice. "This is Leader. Go ahead."

"Our friend has arrived. Over."

"What's he doing now?"

Alban chuckled into the microphone of the police radio in the car. "He's cleaning up the garbage I threw on the porch. It's going to delay him a while, but you better get here as fast as you can."

"We're on the way." Alvarez turned to the other two agents in the office. "Daniel, your idea gets tested tonight. You have all the printed materials?"

"Bud has them."

"Tuttle, you remember what you're supposed to do?"

"I'm ready, Tony. And I have the props right here to support me."

"Let's go then."

The four of us dashed outside and got into the car. Alvarez broke most speed limits to get to the suspect house as fast as he could. Blaine was already there; the attic light was on. Alvarez breathed a sigh of relief. Now, if we were able to pull this off....

Alvarez stopped the car a short distance away from Blaine's house. Tuttle, Han and I got out of the car. Tony drove down a short distance. Turned around. Parked on the shoulder with his lights out. We approached the house from an angle where Han knew we couldn't be seen from inside. Alban stayed in his car as another lookout.

The Tuttle and Han approached the front porch through the shadows. Han, dressed all in black, climbed up onto Tuttle's shoulder. The latter stood up straight, holding Han's ankles. Tuttle tapped his friend's ankle with his fingertips three times. On the final tap he pushed up with all his strength.

At the same time, Han threw his arms up. He grabbed the edge of the porch roof. Swung himself sideways. Reached out with one foot and placed it on the roof. He leveraged himself over the edge. Rolled himself up the incline a little. Then he lay quietly, catching his breath while Tuttle and I dashed back to the street.

Tuttle reached inside his shirt and pulled out a sheaf of papers. Then we walked along the road toward the sidewalk going to Blaine's house.

Han stood, stooped over. He approached the attic window and peeked in. He tried to open the window a little. The lock was still unlatched from his earlier escape from the building. He smiled and gave us a thumbs up. Blaine was already on the radio. Daniel sat down on the porch roof so he could watch from the corner of the window. Then he waited for us to do our thing.

Tuttle and I walked up to the door. Han later told us Blaine jumped when Tuttle knocked. Looked around. Tuttle knocked again. Blaine said something into his ham radio microphone, then took off his earphones and started to go downstairs to answer the door. He stopped, returned to his radio and turned a dial, then headed downstairs. As soon as he was gone for a minute, Han slid the attic window open and went into the room.

Blaine opened the door.

"Hello, sir," Tuttle said. "My name is Hector Trimble. This is Charles Swanson. We're collecting money for the American Cancer Society."

"I'm not interested," Blaine said. He began to close the door.

Tuttle stuck his foot in the way. "But sir, all your neighbors have given. See?" He held out the sheaf of official looking papers, filled with the names, addresses and donations of everyone on one side of the neighborhood. He waved the papers in front of Blaine's face. "See? Everyone's giving to help find a cure for cancer. It's a terrible disease, you know."

"How much do you want?"

"Whatever you can afford, sir. We'd greatly appreciate whatever you could donate."

Blaine heaved a great sigh as he reached into his pocket. He looked at the bills he pulled out. Selected a five. "Here, take this and go away."

"Oh, thank you! Now what's the name I should put down for you?"

"Blaine, Gary."

"Thank you, Mr. Blaine Gary."

"No! Gary is the first name and Blaine is the last name."

"Oh! So sorry, sir. And how do you spell your last name?"

Blaine rolled his eyes in exasperation. "B-L-A-I-N-E."

Tuttle repeated each letter in turn. Then he held out the paper on which he had been writing.

"And is this your correct address?"

The other man looked. Nodded. "Yes, it is. Now are we done?"

"One more thing, sir. This is a tax-deductible donation. Let me make out a receipt you can use when you fill out your taxes."

Blaine waited impatiently. Accepted the receipt. "Are we done now?"

"Yes, sir. And thank you very much for your generous donation." Tuttle completed his sentence to a closed door. We returned to the street. Turned to go in the correct direction for the sequence of names we'd shown our most recent donor. When we got into the shadows we crossed the street and waited.

By now, Han was back on the porch roof. He looked around, slipped over the side, and hung from the edge by his hands for a moment. When he let go, landed on the grass. He turned, bent over to make himself as small as possible. He ran to the street at the same angle to the house he'd used to get there.

Alvarez rolled the car up with the engine idling. Han jumped in while the car still moved so no brake lights would give away its presence. Tuttle and I returned the same way.

"So," Alvarez said. "Did it work?"

"Yes and no," Han scowled. "I verified his transmitter frequency. Got nothing on his receiver frequency. These guys are smart. As Glenn suggested, they might be using different frequencies for each direction they send their information. Before he headed downstairs, it looked like Blaine turned his receiver frequency dial back to zero. It was on zero when I got inside."

"Nuts! Anyway, good work, guys. Those geodetic survey maps and the county tax rolls sure came in handy to give us the information to fill in on your Cancer Society form. Great work!"

"Yeah," Daniel said. "Now all we have to do is find out what frequency these guys are receiving on. Let's go home and get some sleep."

*   *   *   *

Oliver agreed with the transmitter frequency setting Han found in the Oxnard house. They had no frequency for the receiver. They installed newer scanning equipment in their vans so they could search for the frequency.

The next day, they intercepted Blaine's messages. Halfway through the sequence the scanners picked up a message coming from another location. It seemed to "handshake" with Blaine's transmissions. The timing matched the times when Blaine was not transmitting.

One of the teams detected a very weak response signal. They told everyone else what the receiver frequency was. The question was raised why the signal being sent to Oxnard was so weak. Glenn explained that the timing matched, but the signal was not coming from Saint Louis. He guided the scanner teams to position their antennas. The signal got stronger and stronger as they turned the antennas to the northeast. Then the signal got weaker.

Glenn asked each van for the bearing of their strongest signal. He pulled out a map of the U.S. and plotted lines from the locations of the two vans in the directions of their strongest signal. The lines crossed in a remote section of Idaho.

"Idaho?" Oliver asked. "Why the hell're they transmittin' from Idaho?"

Later in the day, Alvarez called Commander Bohn and arranged for two more radio vans to be created. They would need more such vehicles to nail down the suspects' transmissions. They would use short wave radio sets with security scramblers to communicate with each other and with Port Hueneme.

Alvarez also asked for more people to help track the signals. He got Tomas Morelos, Terry Halvorson, Charlie Williams and Rupert Townes, all members of the Norfolk drug bust crew. Everyone arrived within a day. But Alvarez had to pay a price for the people who transferred in: Daniel Han was ordered to catch the next flight to Ellsworth Air Force Base outside Rapid City, South Dakota, and meet up with Chaské Hunter.

Morelos and Halvorson took one van to Nyssa in east central Oregon. Williams and Townes made up the other team. They had orders to go to Bozeman, Montana.

*   *   *   *

Alvarez and Oliver worked with the scanner vans on alternate days. When he wasn't working, Glenn followed Gary Blaine. After a few times going to the Oxnard house, the suspect returned to the Camarillo house again. The OCI agent parked across the street where he could see into the front windows but also get a decent view down Blaine's driveway.

Blaine headed upstairs right away, where Oliver had seen him the last time he was at this house. But this time, the suspect didn't seem so despondent. He paced back and forth a bit. Looked out the window as if he were waiting for someone to arrive. About 2300 another car pulled into the driveway and parked close to the back stairs. Blaine closed the shades to the front windows.

A man got out of the car. He went up the back way to the second-floor apartment. A couple more lights came on upstairs.

Oliver decided to remain where he was until the new arrival left. He left his window open to hear noises. He dozed through the night.

The newcomer stayed until dawn. Blaine departed early enough to get to the missile preparation area on time. The newcomer left a half hour later.

Well, young men, Oliver thought. *That looked a bit more familiar than just good friends. If you are homosexuals, then welcome to the ranks of the feared, the hated and the spat upon. Us Negro folks have been there for a long, long time. I hope you all survive it.*

Oliver started his car and drove back to the base.

*   *   *   *

Meanwhile, the OCI agents in the two additional radio-tracking vans drove overnight to their destinations. They pulled to the side of the road, set up their equipment and waited. The next day, Alvarez called them on the high-security ham radio sets when Blaine began broadcasting. After the suspect finished, the teams reported the directions the responses came from. Alvarez plotted them on Oliver's U.S. Map. The lines crossed at a place named Kit Fox Butte, Idaho.

After everything seemed to quiet down, the short wave in the OCI office blared again. Alvarez rushed to his radio set and answered. The teams had continued to listen after Blaine's message was received and acknowledged. The receiving party in Idaho then began transmitting again. The person in Kit Fox Butte spoke the same gibberish as Blaine, with slight variations, almost like he was forwarding Blaine's message to someone else. The two locations seemed to have a conversation for a while. The scanner teams got a bearing on the next location. They gave Alvarez the bearings.

Oliver plotted the new bearings. The next day Alvarez gave the vans new locations to go to, one of them to Salt Lake City, Utah, and the other to Pierre, South Dakota. He told them to start moving right away and get set up as soon as possible.

Operation Firethorn

22. Agent Down

Nebraska

The OCI team watched the buffalo ranch practically twenty-four hours a day. On the days that Little Horse made a flight, the stocky man would come out first, check the plane's oil, fill the fuel tanks, and perform some other preparations for flight. When he returned to the house, the pilot, John Little Horse, came out of the house and took off. When he returned, he parked the plane in front of the barn doors. The aide came out on a tractor, connected a hitch to the Cessna 170's rear wheel, and pulled it into the barn. Then he would close and lock the barn door and return to the house.

Some time later, the aide would return to the barn. The light in the haymow would come on for about fifteen minutes. When the light went out, the aide would leave the building again, locking it up once more.

*   *   *   *

"Skye here."

"Hi, boss!" a soft voice responded.

"Chaské! What's happening with you guys?"

"Nothing real exciting. We spend our time watchin' John Little Horse. He flies off every two or three days, is gone for hours, and returns near dusk. We keep the airfield and the ranch house under constant observation. There are two helpers on the ranch, a cook and a man who works in the barn where the plane is stored. He also keeps the airfield well mowed. We take photos any time anybody moves."

"It's tedious and boring work. But there's a feelin' in the camp that one day somethin's gonna happen to break the case open. Or you'll give the order to take this guy down. Until then, as they say in the Navy, we hurry up and wait."

Chaské took a deep breath before he continued. "We got us a motel room in a decent sized town nearby, name of Alliance. We're usin' it as a communication base. I'm callin' you from there now."

"Do you need any more help?" Skye asked.

"I already called for four more of my friends and relatives to come here. I think we're okay. Why?"

"I'm sending you someone from California who has been very active in tracking down the ham radio signals out there. I'd like him to see if this Little Horse is one of the people relaying those messages. Or if he might be doing more."

"You mean, like sending the information he collects somewhere else?"

"Right."

"Sounds good. Who're you sending us?"

"Daniel Han."

"Glad to have him. When will he get here? I'll drive up to Ellsworth Air Force Base and pick him up."

"Let's say two days from now. Then I'll have time to get some radio equipment for you guys, too."

"I'll be there waitin'."

When Chaské returned from Alliance, he found his cousin Ken Eagle Trapper, and friends Amos, Bobby Big Bear, and Frank Lightnings had arrived to help.

Chaské clued in the newcomers as to the job they'd be doing. Ken and Amos brought cars with them, so Chaské set up a schedule for the car owners to go into Alliance and make the telephone reports to Great Lakes and to buy food for the gang, already cooked so they wouldn't have to light any fires the folks at the ranch could see. He would give them money for the food and the gas. He also described how everyone would take turns, two at a time, watching the ranch, taking pictures if anything interesting happened.

Amos asked who the suspect was. When he was told the man's name was John Little Horse, he commented that the name sounded Indian. Ray insisted he was not. "I watched him with our little telescope," he said. "Little Horse doesn't look like an Indian. Doesn't walk like an Indian. Doesn't move or gesture like an Indian, or look at the sky for eagles or nothin'. He's not one of us. We don't know what or who the hell he is. All we know is he makes illegal flights over restricted areas, over the new missile silos up north."

*   *   *   *

Chaské drove up to Ellsworth Air Force Base near Rapid City, South Dakota, to pick up Daniel Han, who helped him load a bunch of ham radio equipment onto the truck. They pulled into the OCI camp in Nebraska well after dark. The newcomer was introduced to everyone in the camp but all he could see were shadows of people. No campfire was allowed.

"Sit yerself down," a voice invited.

"Hungry? Have some supper," another person said.

"Here y'are, Dan," a third man declared as he put a plate in Han's hands. "There's a spoon on the plate, there, and more food where this came from. Welcome to the group here."

"Thanks." The new arrival took the spoon and filled his mouth. It was store-bought potato salad but it tasted pretty good. He felt so comfortable with this reception he didn't even tell them he preferred being called "Daniel." "Dan" was okay with these guys.

"Let's see who we're talking to." A soft light appeared for a few seconds. "Ho! Where you from?"

"San Francisco," Han replied around a mouthful of salami.

"No. I mean where are you *from*?"

There was confusion in Han's voice as he answered. "I just told you...."

Chaské chuckled. "He's askin' what tribe you're from."

"I'm not Indian. I'm Chinese." Han wondered if this was going to make a difference here.

"Yeah, I figured you either for Asian or Indian. Some of our folks have eyes like yours."

Another voice asked softly: "Chinese communist?"

Daniel could hear the teasing in the question. "Of course not."

"Good. I had to fight them Chinese communists in Korea," the voice chuckled.

"My family came here from China over a hundred twenty years ago," Han said. "They really didn't want to leave home, but they did welcome the employment here."

"What kind of work did they do?"

"They helped build the railroad out west."

"Ah! Sided with the conquerors, eh?" The words sounded even more teasing than before.

"I guess," Han answered. "Most Chinese who came here were kidnapped. I

124

don't think they knew what the railroad was doing to Indians. And they were almost slave labor themselves. Believe me, they didn't enjoy that! The family stories say that they wanted to get away from that kind of work and build a better life. If they had a choice, I think they would have rather run a laundry or a restaurant or do something else on the coast." He paused.

Nobody spoke. Not even Chaské; this was kind of a rite of passage and he wouldn't interfere unless it was necessary.

Han continued. "They didn't have much choice. And they sure didn't like working with people who called them 'Chink' and spit on them."

The silence continued for about five seconds. Then Ray Takini said: "No sweat, man. That's past history. Glad to have you with us."

He offered his hand. Han could feel the acceptance and the darkness didn't feel quite so dense. He vaguely saw Ray's hand in front of him. He put his plate down and reached out to accept his new friend's reception.

"Welcome to our little group," Ray said, grabbing a large thermos. "Have a cup of coffee."

Chaské chuckled. "You've been accepted, Daniel. If you aren't offered coffee in an Indian home, you better run. Quick. So, now you know you're indeed accepted here by these guys."

"Good," Han said with a smile nobody saw. "I was beginning to wonder, there, for a while."

"I hear the teasin' in your voice," Ray said. "You're gonna fit right in with this bunch of skins."

"Isn't that an insulting name for Indians?" Daniel asked.

"Not if it's said by an Indian to another Indian."

"Wow!" Chaské said. "Daniel, you got accepted fast."

"Thanks, guys. Now what are we doing here?"

Chaské filled him in. "So we know what this guy is doin' and we think we know why. But we're stumped why he's using an Indian sounding name. John Little Horse. None of us know any family with such a name, and Indian folks at least know about each other's names. So we watch twenty-four hours a day and wait. Take pictures of whatever they're doing around the ranch house there. And we all take turns watching."

They slept, everyone taking his turn on watch. They spent the next day, Sunday, watching, sitting around, and discussing what to do next....

*　　*　　*　　*

John Little Horse came out of the ranch house, double-checked his aide's preparations on his plane, got in it and took off.

Chaské and Daniel waited for an hour or so to be sure he didn't return and that the helping hand wasn't going to go into the barn. Then they walked to the barn from an angle that put the house out of sight, so someone looking out of the residence wouldn't be able to see them. They were going to investigate what else was in the barn, especially in the hay loft.

They entered the ground floor and looked around. There was nothing out of the ordinary. All they could see were items relating to the animals and the farm: tools, hay, the tractor, the mower, and other such items.

Han tapped Chaské on the arm and pointed to a ladder going up to a loft, then climbed up to investigate. He saw a ham radio set in one corner. He returned to the top of the ladder and motioned Chaské up. The latter moved over to examine the equipment while Han scooted around to the back of the set to see how everything was hooked up.

Chaské heard a footstep behind him. As he turned, the stocky ranch hand swung a three-foot length of two-by-four. Chaské's left arm erupted in searing pain. His arm deflected the two-by-four upward. His head exploded in agony and he saw stars. Then he lost consciousness....

23. Watching the Marina

Cape Canaveral

During the day, Everett Cobbe watched the marina in the town of Cape Canaveral. Sometimes he observed from outside the fence, as if he were admiring the boats tied up there. Sometimes he would buy a sandwich, some potato chips, and a bottle of soda pop, then go over to the marina and watch, like he was spending his lunch hour there, dreaming of owning a big boat.

He saw a number of thirty- to forty-foot cabin cruisers, but he couldn't identify any of them as a boat he'd seen traveling along the Barge Canal very early one morning. But he continued to watch.

He did this for a week. Then he saw a young man who resembled a person he'd seen on a boat going through the canal at night. There was a somewhat younger woman with him on one of the boats. Both wore black wetsuits. The man adjusted the tanks, mask and regulator the woman was wearing. Then she jumped into the water, feet first. She stayed down for about ten minutes. When she surfaced, the guy reached down and pulled her out of the water. Cobbe thought it was strange that people were diving inside the marina.

When the caretaker passed nearby Cobbe called out to him: "Hey, Mac, you let people scuba dive inside the marina?"

"What're you talking about?"

Cobbe pointed to the young couple. "Those folks over there in the wetsuits. Isn't she diving?"

The marina guy looked where Cobbe was pointing. He grinned. "Oh, them! He's teaching her how to dive. Later, he'll take her out to open water for more complete instruction. He has them start their lessons here."

"So, he's a professional scuba instructor?"

"Yeah. He makes his living by taking folks out from this marina. Been doing that five or six years, now. You up for learning to dive?"

Cobbe shook his head. "Nah. Don't think so. I'd get claustrophobic with everything wrapped around my face."

The caretaker laughed. "You don't know what you're missing, man. It's a real thrill down there."

"I'll take your word for it. But I'll still stay up here where the air I breathe has some breeze to it." They talked a little more. Then Cobbe got into his car, looked around one last time and drove off.

24. Down But Not Out

Nebraska

Daniel heard the two-by-four smack Chaské and heard his friend fall to the floor. He came out from behind the equipment. Looked at the assailant and said: "Wrong move there, mister!"

The man swung again. It seemed obvious that he hoped to do the same kind of damage to this second stranger.

Han stepped toward the ranch hand's body, inside the swinging arm. His back took all the power away from the assailant's attack. The two-by-four wrapped around Han's lower rib cage without hurting him. He whirled, arm raised to the horizontal. He stepped back just a little. His elbow connected with the side of the man's face.

The attacker began to fall.

But the karate Han learned taught him not to stop until he was certain he was out of danger. He drove his left fist into the man's chest.

The ranch hand's body was still dropping. Han drove his right-fist directly into the man's face. The assailant crashed to the floor.

Han knelt on one knee to examine his attacker. The man's right cheekbone was smashed, his sternum was caved in and his face was mush. Daniel checked for a pulse. There was none. He searched the body and found a driver's license. The document listed the man's name as George Denison. Han took the man's wallet; he would send it on to Skye so she could track down the man's real information. Then he left to get some help from the rest of the OCI team.

Chaské woke up slowly. He had intense pain in his upper left arm and a searing headache, which was so bad he had trouble sitting up. It reminded him of the time he'd gotten a spinal tap to dull the pain during a medical test. He was told to stay horizontal for an hour. But he was too impatient. When he sat up too soon, he almost fainted and had to lay flat for quite a while longer.

Han returned and bandaged Hunter's head. Gave him four aspirins. Chaské sat up with difficulty. He tried to stand up and almost lost consciousness again.

"Sit down, damn it. Sit!" Han commanded. "You're hurt. Take your time. We'll do our best to help."

Troy, Ray, Amos and Ken climbed to the loft, one by one. Troy stooped next to his brother. He looked up to Han with questioning eyes.

"We have to get him to a doctor immediately," Han said. "How about you and Ray help him to the ground floor."

Troy rummaged around and found a heavy rope. He brought it back to Chaské and Ray. Daniel helped them run the rope around Chaské body under his arms. He tied it behind his friend's back.

Han stood up. He motioned to the others. "You guys bury the dead man some place where he won't be found by humans or animals."

"Isn't that illegal?" Amos asked.

Han shrugged. "He attacked us. And he's part of some clandestine operation."

"Are you sure?"

Chaské looked through his pain as he was being lowered to the ground floor. "Yes," he said between gasps. "An unmarked plane. Flying over restricted areas taking photos. I'm sure. Go bury him."

Han examined the ham radio in the loft. The dials were not turned back to zero. He copied all the dial positions. Then he looked around the area. Set a few objects back into place, the same as they were when he first came up. He looked down from the top of the ladder. Chaské was safely on the ground. "Hey, guys!" he called. "Send up the rope so I can put it back. We want to leave as little evidence as possible that we were here."

Ray coiled the rope then climbed the ladder to give it to Daniel.

Han put it back how he found it, then climbed down the ladder. He picked up the phone in the barn to try to contact Rena.

"She's not here, right now," said the yeoman.

Daniel was frustrated. "When will she be back?"

"I don't know, sir."

"Tonight?"

"I don't know. Can I take a message?"

"No. I'll try again later." He hung up the phone and turned to the Indians. "All right. Now we have to get Chaské some medical help. If nothing else, we

130

need to be sure his arm and head are okay. Especially his head. I don't think his arm is broken but we can't be certain And he might have a concussion."

"Is there a doctor around here?" Troy asked. "An emergency room?"

"No," Han said. "We can't have any civilian records. We'll go up north to Ellsworth Air Force Base."

"I'll go with you," Troy said. "I want to be sure my brother's all right."

"Then have Amos go to the motel and call Major Skye. And here," he held out the identification he'd taken from the assailant. "Give her all the information on this guy. See if she can get a good, true ID on him. And here are the frequency dial settings I copied. Give these figures to her also."

"Listen," Chaské said softly. He continued between shallow breaths. "Amos, first call Bobby Drum in Pine Ridge and tell 'im we'll be makin' our way up U.S. 385 toward Hot Springs and Custer. Tell him we're comin' up in Troy's old pickup and he should meet us and drive us to Ellsworth."

Amos nodded. "I'll get the messages out, Chaské."

*   *   *   *

Daniel Han and Troy Hunter met Bobby Drum where U.S. 385 met U.S. 18 from Pine Ridge. Bobby had the nice comfortable extended van he and his family used on the powwow circuit. They got Chaské to lie down in the back and raced north to get emergency medical help at Ellsworth Air Force Base, ten miles northeast of Rapid City. The medical staff took the patient in for examination. Three hours later a doctor came out to make his report.

"Troy Hunter? I'm Doctor Hanson. We've finished examining your brother. X-rays, various other tests, the whole shebang. I'm happy to report that Rodney has no major problems."

"Rodney?" Han asked.

Troy grinned. "That's Chaské's given name. Chaské is a Lakota name for the first-born son." He returned his attention to the doctor. "So, how bad off is he?"

"His arm is all black and blue and has a slight crack in the bone. And he has a very slight concussion."

"Can he return to work?"

"Not yet," the doctor said. "Give him a chance to heal. Three or four days' rest. Then we'll run another battery of tests. We do not want to play games with possible brain injuries. We'll see how he is in a few days. Are there others who can stand in for him?"

"Yes. We have a whole team on site," Han said.

"Good. I want him to rest here. We can put him up for a few days, but I want to be sure his symptoms don't get any worse. If he improves, then I think he can leave here. We'll see."

Later, Han got through to Skye from Ellsworth. "Rena, this is Daniel."

"Hi! How's it going out there?"

"Sweet and sour. You know Chaské got hurt, right?"

"Yes. Amos Counts Coup called me. How bad is it?"

"Bad enough. The doctor here wants him to stay in the hospital for three or four days before running a set of pre-release tests. Chaské has a small crack in his left humerus. And a possible concussion, which is the major issue."

"But it's not horribly serious, right? Is he conscious?"

"Oh, yes, ma'am. He was awake throughout the trip from Nebraska to Ellsworth. But he was only partially alert."

"Then he has orders to rest and obey the doctors."

"I'll pass that on, ma'am. So Amos got through to you...."

"Yes. He told me about the person you killed in a fight. You must throw one nasty set of punches, Daniel."

"I was taught not to quit until I know I've won. How about the frequencies we saw on the ham radio setup at Little Horse's ranch?"

"I got those, too. That radio may be the set at the Oxbow location Alvarez's roving radio detection crews found. And the frequency you gave me for Little Horse's transmitter is the same as Oxnard."

"How big an operation do you think we're looking at?"

"Big and growing. But that's my problem. Don't worry about it."

"Aye, aye, ma'am. Rank has its privileges."

"God, what a wise-ass. Anyway, tell Chaské to obey the doctors and rest. I'd like you to go back and work the buffalo ranch with Chaské's people. Get as much as you can. Photos, photos, photos."

"You got it, Major."

Daniel visited Chaské and passed on Rena's orders. "You stay here and obey the doctors' orders. If they want you to stay longer, Major Skye says to do it."

"Crap," Chaské mumbled, screwing up his face.

"What's the matter?"

"I wanted to do somethin'."

"I can do it for you. Tell me what you want done and I'll do it."

Chaské looked Daniel in the eye. "All right. I'll give you precise directions. Here's the job for you to do...."

Operation Firethorn

25. Bos'n's Mates and Boats

Cape Canaveral

I was studying the Mark 25 gunfire control radar and pretty well had the circuits down cold. So Rena wanted me to meet Al Cisco in Florida and introduce him when he arrived to join Ford's crew. I served with Al on the *USS Hestek* and this might ease the transition for him.

Cisco was told to dress in civilian clothes and to meet his contacts at the Royal Baby's Bar and Grill, on the far end of the outside patio. He showed up while I was on a trip to the head. He didn't recognize anyone there and nobody approached him. So he sat at a corner table with his back to the wall. Ordered a cup of coffee. Pulled out a book from his back pocket and started to read.

When I came out of the head, I noticed Al on the patio. The rest of the team was lounging around the corner, watching the unfolding scene. Ford was already going over to greet the newcomer. I hung back and watched with the crew. Cisco looked surprised by the muscular man with a well-trimmed mustache who slid uninvited into a chair across his table. Len pointed to the book Cisco was reading and grinned. "What kind of tome do you have there?"

"What?" the bos'n's mate asked, taken aback at the abruptness of the other man's question. He looked around the establishment, but he saw nothing out of the ordinary.

"Let's get some food. I'm hungry," Ford said. He waved to get the attention of a waitress. He turned to Cisco. "You hungry?"

The waitress arrived. She was a beautiful young woman, maybe mixed race. The man who had flagged her down seemed to know her, at least a little bit.

"You want to order?"

"Sure," Ford said. "Steak and eggs, hash browns."

"Anything else?" the waitress asked.

"Not for now."

"'For now,' huh? That fits more with what I've seen you eat before," she grinned, then turned to Cisco. "How about you?"

"Why not? I'd like a T-bone and a baked potato, butter but no sour cream." He held up his coffee cup. "And a refill."

The waitress nodded and took the orders back to the cook.

Cisco turned to Ford. "Who are you, anyway?"

"I'm sorry. I thought you were expecting me to show up."

"I *am* expecting someone. How do you know who I am?"

"Okay. First, I assume you are Al Cisco...."

The bos'n's mate nodded. "Yes."

"Good. Glad to meet you, Al. I'm Leonard Ford. Call me Len." He spoke very softly. "I'm part of the team Eric Matthews is on. He described you quite accurately: tall, crew cut blond hair, very observant. I imagine you've already spotted the rest of our team. He said you'd be reading a book. A big one. He called it a 'tome.' I saw you reading, though nothing looking like a tome, but reading nonetheless. So I put two and two together and came up with you."

Cisco smiled and nodded. "Sounds like a description Mr. Matthews would give. I don't see him here. Where is he?"

Ford turned and looked around. "He went into the head. Should be back any minute." I stepped out into the open. "Ah, there he is!"

I walked over to their corner. Cisco looked up and smiled. "Hi, Mr. Matthews! I suspected this transfer had something to do with you."

I grinned back and nodded, then said: "How you doing, Al? And drop the 'mister' crap. On this team, we're not that formal. We have too much other important stuff to do than to mouth all those Navy niceties."

Cisco looked at me in surprise. "What have I gotten myself into?"

"What do you know already?" Ford asked.

"Nothing. I received a surprise set of orders to Cape Canaveral. When I checked in at the Navy office there, they gave me directions to meet some people at this location. So here I am."

"Okay, here's the skinny. We need your help on our present project. And if you're willing, we may want you to stay on our team."

"Your..., Eric's...?"

"Same difference. We're pretty secure here but don't mention any organization names. Ahhh, our food is here...."

The waitress brought their meals over. After everything was arranged on the table, Ford cut a bite of steak. Dunked it in the egg yolk, popped it into his mouth. Talked around his food. "Actually…" he swallowed, "It's Major Rena Skye's team. By the way, she's Eric's girlfriend now. The Norfolk drug job is over and she's divorced from her ex-husband. Her team is a special undercover group reporting to Commander Ronald Blount in Norfolk. Now, let's introduce you to the other guys." He motioned for all of the team to come over.

Ford cut another chunk of meat. While he chewed, we pulled an adjacent table over to make enough room for all of us. We'd already ordered food and we brought it with us. I greeted the newcomer: "So, Al, How're you doing?"

He offered his hand, which I shook. "Pretty good, Mister…."

"Hey! We're a working team. Just call me Eric."

"That's fine with me."

"Okay, guys," Len interrupted. "Introduce yourselves to everyone else. Round robin, everyone. Everett, why don't you start?"

"I'm first lieutenant Everett Cobbe. I did a number of jobs on the last case, winding up at Punk's Bar for the takedown. I'm a Marine; I'll do any job you give me."

"Andy Hagen. Second Lieutenant, USMC. I'm a helo pilot."

"Ryan Murray, civilian. My specialty is intelligence gathering and I have exceptional night vision. So I guess I can go up with you at night, Andy, if you need another pair of eyes."

Hagen nodded. "Glad to have you, if Len gives the okay."

"My name is Richard Morris," the Negro said. "You can call me Rick. I'm a third class engineman in the Navy. And I'm not sure why they ordered me to be with this group."

"Al, you're next," Ford said.

"Al Cisco, bos'n's mate second. I worked with Mister, uh… Eric on the *Hestek*. And I also don't know why I'm here."

I turned to the other guys. "Al is way too modest. He kept his mouth shut when he deduced that I was on some kind of an undercover mission. He likes to sit around reading and watching people. Filing away every little piece of information in his head. Putting it all together when it's important. And he's a man of action when action is needed. He saved my life when a drug lord was shooting at me. Killed the guy. He took his .45 out of the holster, loaded the chamber, aimed at the man's heart, steady as a rock, all the while asking the OOD for permission to shoot. The instant he got it, the shot was on its way. Al has a lot he can give us."

"What kind of books do you read?" Morris asked. "Spy stories?"

"Seldom," Cisco replied. "I read a lot of philosophy, some psychology, many of the classics, and science."

"What kind of science?" Hagen asked.

"I don't have much of a math background, but I love reading about modern physics. George Gamow. Cosmology, astronomy, physics. He wrote a great book called *One, Two, Three ... Infinity*. And I like Isaac Asimov."

"The science fiction writer?" Murray asked. "I like him, too."

"Oh, he wrote a lot more than science fiction. Like a book titled *Of Time and Space and Other Things*. And many, many books on astronomy, physics, chemistry. And a whole bunch of other topics."

"So you're going to solve all the mysteries of the universe?" Ford grinned.

Cisco shook his head. "Nope. Just using my brain. I love learning."

Ford waved his hand in front of him. "Don't take me wrong. I admire people who read like you." He took the final bite of his dinner. "Most of the time, I'm too busy diving, eating or trying to stay in shape to read so much."

It seemed I wasn't needed to introduce Al to the crew. They were doing quite well on their own. Most sailors do and I should have realized it before I made this trip. Still, it was good to see him again.

"So what's my job here?" Cisco asked.

Ford swallowed the last of his food. Pursed his lips. "Well, whatever you can do to catch bad guys. Here's what we're up against...." He spent the next five minutes quietly filling his team in on what he knew of the spy ring. "So we're a small part of a big operation. And we have a lot of territory to cover. Look...." He pulled out a drawing of the area south of the cape and east of the canal. "I'll watch from Canaveral itself, here. Everett Cobbe can continue watching the Canaveral Barge Canal. Andy Hagen and Ryan Murray will watch from a helo in this area north of where the canal meets the ocean, out here over the water. Al Cisco and Rick Morris will be south of there, out beyond the beach, patrolling in a whaleboat...."

"Can we get a fifty-foot launch, instead?" Cisco asked. "We could maneuver better with a more powerful boat."

"Hmm, a cabin cruiser would fit in better with the boat traffic around here than a Navy fifty-footer," Cobbe said.

"Wouldn't a cabin cruiser be pretty expensive?"

"Not necessarily," Cobbe replied. "I'm hanging around one of the larger marinas. There might be some reasonably priced boats for rent."

Ford nodded. "I'll get you some funding."

Cisco and I did get a chance to shoot the shit over a couple of beers later.

*   *   *   *

The OCI team watched the water every night. Nobody saw any trace of the spy diver. Even along the Canaveral Barge Canal, Cobbe saw nothing.

Ford called a meeting of the team.

"I'd guess the diver isn't swimming down the canal. If so, he'd have to go the full length of the channel through Canaveral City. I saw his tanks, and I don't think they're big enough to last on such a long round trip. He has to be taking a boat out and then going into the water somewhere out there."

"So what can we do?"

"Hagen and Murray should continue sweeping the waters off shore from the helo."

"How about the boat?" Cobbe asked.

Ford nodded. "We got the funding for it. But we have to be frugal."

"How frugal? I have my eye on a twenty-five-footer. Cisco and I already looked at it."

"It's in good shape," Cisco said. "And the rental price is reasonable."

"How much is it?" Ford asked. Cobbe named the price. "No problem. That's in our range. But see if you can get him down a little bit."

"I think we could," Cisco said. "I'm sure I can find some problems to warrant a reduction."

"Are there problems with it? You said it was in good shape."

"It is. But I have a good eye when it comes to boats. I can make a big thing out of any small defect that couldn't hurt us."

Ford chuckled. "Great. Here's a check. Already signed. You can fill in the name of the owner and the amount."

"This is your account," Cobbe observed.

"Yes. We have to cover our tracks. The renter can't know it's for the Navy."

"Gotcha," Cobbe said. "We'll get it tomorrow."

"Then we can re-name it," Cisco added.

"The owner will let you do that?"

"Yeah. As long as we change it back to its original name when we return it."

"What're you going to name it?"

Cisco grinned. "I was going to name it the *Pequod* after the ship in *Moby Dick*. We are, after all, chasing a whale, of sorts. But the whale sank the *Pequod*. And I don't want to jinx our operation. So then I thought of another great sea story, *Two Years Before the Mast* by Richard Henry Dana. He was an

138

inspiration for Melville. He sailed to California on the *Pilgrim* and returned on the *Alert*. The latter name is more appropriate."

"So it is," Ford agreed. "Let's name it the *Alert II*. Which is what we need to be to catch this guy. Now, everyone has walkie-talkies?" Everyone nodded except Hagen. "I know Ryan will have one in the helo. Andy, can you tune into our frequency on the helo's radios?"

Hagen nodded. "No problem."

Ford continued: "Here are the code names we're going to use. I'll be 'Alpha,' the Helo will be 'Hotel,' Cobbe will be 'Bravo,' short for Barge Canal, and the cabin cruiser will be 'Charlie,' short for Cisco. Use 'Echo' when you want to address everybody. Understood?" Everyone nodded again. "So, let's get a bit of rest and get out there tonight and track this guy down."

Cobbe visited the marina again, looking for clues to the spy diver. This time, he entered through the gate. Walked around the piers themselves. Examined each boat with care.

The marina manager came out. "This is private property," he said. "Members only. I thought you understood that. What're you doing in here?"

"Shopping."

"Huh?"

"Yeah. I'm in the market to rent a boat and checking out some of the nice ones I see to get an idea of what's around."

"All right, but be careful. People don't trust folks just walking around looking over their expensive boats."

"I'm trustworthy."

"And why should I believe you?"

"Let's go to your office."

They entered the office. Cobbe showed the manager his OCI ID.

"Well, glad to meet you, Mr. Cobbe. My name is Joe McHenry. You may have noticed a couple private owners do have their boats up for rent. You might want to talk to them."

"Thanks. I already have one in mind. But right now I'm just watching boats, owners and traffic."

"How long do you need to stick around here?"

"All night. And I may need to return on an irregular basis. There will be nights when I have to sit here and watch the canal."

"Okay." McHenry reached into a drawer. Pulled out something. Handed it to Cobbe. "Here's a key to the gate. Now you have access to the marina whenever you need it."

Cobbe returned to the piers. Kept looking around. One boat—a thirty-foot cabin cruiser—made an impression on him. There was something familiar about it, something he felt he should know. It was very similar to the description Ford had provided of the boat used at New London and Long Island Sound. He looked for the name on its fantail. It was called *Mermaid II*.

*   *   *   *

Cobbe rented the nice little 25-foot cabin cruiser he'd been eying. Then Al Cisco and Rick Morris took it out on the ocean, south of the outlet of the Canaveral Barge Canal, to get used to how it handled.

Everett Cobbe watched the Barge Canal. He was dressed in black to fit in with the darkness of the night. He walked along the bank of the canal for no specific reason. But he was a Marine and thought of this operation as a battle. Therefore, some additional reconnoitering was in order. He didn't find anything new to help the investigation.

There were no boats in the canal. There were no boats out on the water at all. So he watched and waited.

26. Essence of Skunk

Long Island

In order to get a first-hand feel for the situation at Orient, Long Island, Rena took another trip. Our guys were quite concerned about the guard dog there. The owners did keep it chained up. Even so, it refused to stop trying to get loose and run to Delano and Stolichek's hiding places. The owner was getting more and more suspicious.

The OCI agents moved their primary watch post a quarter mile toward the road. When the wind shifted, the dog changed the direction it was interested in. Stolichek didn't know what to do about the animal's constant interest in their location. If the guards decided to bring the dog over to investigate….

Rena happened to be there a couple days later, when Delano relieved Stolichek for their watch on the house. He was carrying a spray bottle.

"What do you have there?" Stolichek asked.

"My dog-proofing kit."

"What do you mean? What's in the bottle?"

"I have a friend in Conneticut who's a veternarian. Name o' Jack. His specialty is de-skunking tha little animals people wanta keep as pets, so they don't get all stunk-up, ya know?"

"So what's in the bottle?"

"Jack extracts the skunk oil and sells it to people who may need pertection against wild animals. Hunters and campers and such folks, ya know?"

"You mean to tell me…?"

"Yeah. A very strong deterrent to dogs. I call it essence of skunk."

"And we're supposed to use…?"

141

"Sure. Doggy comes around. Ya spray 'im in the face. Doggy goes away. It's that easy."

Rena had a difficult time stopping herself from laughing out loud.

"I don't know if I want to be around that stuff. Skunk oil is foul," Stolichek said.

"Well, ya either take it 'n' use it if ya need to, or ya become a doggie treat. Yer choice."

"Yeah.... I'll have to think about it. You find a place nearby to stay?"

"Certainly. There's all kinds of small homes 'round here fer tourists, people wantin' to come here 'n' get away from tha city, ya know?"

"Where's the place you found?"

"In Orient proper. It's a one-room economy thing, ya know? I can almost walk over there ta go ta sleep. An' I c'n eat there, too. A hotplate comes with it."

"Wonder if I should think about doing the same thing."

"What're ya talkin' about? There's room there fer both of us. Here's the address and directions, and a key." He handed the items to George. "Go there and sleep." He paused and looked around. "So, anything happenin' here?"

"No. It's pretty quiet. The diver took the boat out but he's not back yet."

"All right. I'll greet 'im when he returns. Go get some shut-eye." Stolichek chuckled, waved, and headed for the rented room. Del turned to Skye. "Okay, Rena. Ya want me ta show you tha whole layout here?"

"Sure. Give me a better idea of what you're up against."

"Follow me." He took her all the way around to the other side of the house. Then he pointed out the dock. "An' there's where tha diver fella parks 'is boat. If we're anywhere in the northern half of tha property, we c'n hear 'im when 'e pulls in."

"This is an awful lot of territory for two people to watch," Skye said, "especially when you have to take turns in order to get some rest."

"Ya got that right, lady."

"Most of the time you watch from the woods on the other side, right?"

"Yeah. It's where the landing strip is an' we want ta be sure we see whoever comes in that way."

"You want some more help?" Rena asked. "At least a couple more guys to watch from this side?"

"Wouldn't turn 'em down, ya know?"

"And I'll be sure the 'fishing boats' continue watching from the Sound."

"We'll take whatever ya c'n offer."

*   *   *   *

Rena stayed with Delano when he returned to the rented room. And she went back out on watch with him. They picked their way through the post-midnight darkness, going to the rendezvous in the woods to assume the watch. When they found George, Del sniffed the air and whispered loudly: "Gawd! You get sprayed by a skunk?"

"No," Stolichek growled.

"Their dog come around?"

"No."

"Then, why tha strong skunk smell?"

"I'm not going to tell you."

"Aww, you can tell me." Del stuck his face into his friend's face so he could see him in the dark. He shook his head in disbelief. "Nah, I don' believe it. You sprayed *yourself*?"

"Yeah," Stolichek mumbled.

"So what tha fu…, pardon my French. Why'd ya do that? Nah, *how'd* ya do that?"

"An owl. Behind my right shoulder. On a branch. I thought someone was starting to ask 'Who are you?' I was real nervous and jumpy. I had the spray bottle in my left hand. I turned to the right to spray, but I flung my right hand around and it was still too high when I squeezed the sprayer." He paused for a long second. "I wound up spraying my hand."

"Ya know, this is kinda difficult to imagine." It was everything Del could do to control his urge to laugh. And Rena had shoved her jacket sleeve in her mouth to keep quiet. Del continued: "Why doncha ya show me? Re-enact tha scene."

"You want me to spray myself again?"

Del shrugged his shoulders. "I'd kinda like ta see how ya did it, ya know?"

"Go to hell, Del. I'm not going to spray myself again. One time was bad enough."

"Aw, gee. I'm only tryin' ta imagine what happened…."

Stolichek changed the topic of the conversation: "Does this wash off?"

"Yeah." Del paused. "Kinda."

"What do you mean, 'kind of'?" Stolichek demanded.

"How long ago ya spray yerself?"

"About ten minutes ago."

"Oh, man. Go back ta tha boat. But don' get into it. Get inta the water 'n' wash off. That's fer starters. Then wash yerself with vinegar."

"I don't have any vinegar. Where the hell am I supposed to get vinegar around here?" Stolichek asked.

"You don't have any vinegar?" Del asked incredulously.

"No. Do you?"

"O' course! Got me a little bottle in my pocket. You think I'd even be around essence of skunk without bein' prepared?"

"So let me use *your* vinegar!"

"Oh, sure," Del said sarcastically. "An' what would I use if that there animal came out to make like I was a doggie treat? An' I had ta use the skunk essence. Ya do have some left, doncha?"

"Of course! You brought us a quart of the damned stuff."

"Awright. So what if I then got some of it on myself. I'd be shit outa luck 'cause you used all my vinegar. Uh-uh. You take yer little rubber boat over to Conneticut there. It might help ta trail yer hand in the water alla way across. I don't think tha sharks'd try to eat sumthin' smellin' like a skunk. When ya get across the sound, stop at tha nearest store and buy some o' yer own vinegar. It cuts tha skunk oil pretty good. Or you can try tomata juice. I heard that works pretty good, too."

"You won't let me use your vinegar?"

"Nope. Gotta save it fer me. Just in case."

"Jeez, some friend you are." Stolichek turned and started to walk toward the rubber raft.

"Hey!" Del whispered loudly. "I didn't spray you! And gimme that! I gotta have it to pertect myself here, ya know?"

Stolichek threw the skunk spray bottle behind his feet as he walked away, grumbling. "Find it in the dark. Hope you spray yourself."

Rena returned to Great Lakes with a tale to rival any sea story ever told.

*　　*　　*　　*

"Major Skye, we're still seeing bubbles in the Thames River," Justin Thein reported. "There are still divers here. Right around the fantails of the submarines."

"Are those underwater cameras working?"

"They're working, but we get murky pictures. We can see tanks, hoses, mouthpiece, fins, and the guy's body. But they're too cloudy to identify this guy's equipment. And we're getting nothing on the above-water cameras. Nothing except bubbles."

"I'll try to get some other divers in the area. If for no other reason than to check for possible sabotage. As long as the spy diver is around. I'll keep you posted."

Skye pressed the cradle button on her phone, released it, waited for the dial tone and called Commander Blount. "Commander, we have a problem. Remember the other day when you wondered about having enough people to cover this job?"

"Yes. What's happened since then?"

"We have enough bodies. But not with the necessary skills."

"We already gave you another Russian speaker. Where else are we weak?"

"Divers. There are still all kinds of diver bubble trails around the subs in New London. And Justin Thein's cameras do work, but…."

"Not clear enough?"

"The surface ones see nothing but bubbles. And the underwater ones see a guy in a full wet suit, including a mask. But they're so murky they can't even identify his equipment. We're getting nothing from them."

"So what do you want to do?"

"Well, sir, I can think of a couple actions. We don't need divers to try to track him. We've already followed the diver back to his base of operations on Long Island. What I'm concerned about now is sabotage. We can put anti-diver nets around the sub base, but they'd be very expensive. And almost impossible to be sure no diver could get through them. But what if we could get three or four divers out there each night to meet this guy and scare him away…?"

"It's worth a try. I'll see if I can persuade Commanders Mason Cott of OCI Newport and Scott Morgan, the New London security officer, to come up with a bunch of divers we can borrow. Good enough?"

"Thank you sir. Let's hope that works."

* * * *

Stolichek called Skye a few days after she returned to Lakes.

"Hi, George! You get your skunk oil dilemma resolved?"

He chuckled. "Oh, yeah. But I think I have something more important to report."

"What?"

"Well, nothing exciting was happening around here. I watched the house from the woods and all was quiet. Until about 0300.

"I heard the loud droning behind me. I turned and made my way toward sound, toward the landing strip. I stayed close enough to the path but still in the dark woods. I sure didn't want someone coming down that path to see me.

"I walked until I came to the edge of the trees, a few feet away from the runway. It had lights along the sides, which we had not noticed before. It was a miracle we hadn't tripped over them. They were lit now to show the plane where the safe runway was. A small plane taxied to a spot very near the beginning of the path.

"A man with a flashlight got out of the aircraft. He walked through the plane's landing lights just before they were turned off. He was of average height. He had short hair. In the dark, I couldn't tell what color his hair was. He was clean-shaven. I wanted to take a photo of him, but the click of the camera might have alerted him. Then he walked down the path toward the house.

"I stood still, trying to decide if I should follow the man or not. Then the pilot got out of the aircraft to examine its tires and flight surfaces. He played a flashlight over the plane. As I watched, it seemed that something was wrong. Then it hit me. The aircraft was unmarked. It had no registration number on it. I began taking as many photos of the plane as I could. An hour later the visitor returned from the house. I got a few pictures of him, too, but from a rather long distance. I hope it's not too long for easy identification. I continued taking photos all during the plane's takeoff."

"Great job, George. Get those photos over to the New London office and have them send them to me by courier."

"Will do, ma'am."

When we received the photos, we recognized the plane. It looked like the same one in Nebraska.

27. Another Agent Down

Great Lakes

Skye's phone rang again. "God, doesn't this thing ever stop? My job has become one of answering this damned telephone!"

She picked up the receiver. "Major Skye here."

"I'm Jimmy Cranston, Chief of Police in Saint Louis, Missouri. Does a man named Steven Montaigne work for you?"

"Yes. Why do you ask?"

"We found him unconscious in an alley down here last night. He's still alive. Barely. He was very badly beaten. He still had his wallet, money and identification, so we don't believe the motive was robbery. And that's how we knew he worked for the Office of Criminal Investigation."

"How bad is his condition?"

"He's still unconscious and the doctor says he's lucky to be alive. Three broken ribs. A broken arm. A cracked skull and a concussion."

"Oh, God…. Where is he?" she asked.

"We took him to Saint Alexius Hospital, then called you folks."

"How soon can we bring him back here? We have a very good hospital at Great Lakes, and we'd prefer to…."

"His attending physician is a Doctor Louis Morgan at Saint Alexius," the police chief interrupted. "He wants to wait until Mr. Montaigne wakes up and they can do an evaluation of the damage when he's conscious. They'll let you know when that happens."

"I'm sorry, Chief. I can't allow him to wait so long. I want him back here immediately."

"I'll let you and Doctor Morgan hash that out. Here's his phone number."

Skye worked out arrangements with the doctor. The Navy would send a medical helicopter to Saint Louis to bring Montaigne back right away.

*   *   *   *

Skye's phone rang again.

"Major Rena Skye."

"Commander Blount here. I got to thinking over the weekend. How much more of all this counter-spy work can your group handle? I was wondering if you have enough people."

"Oh, we have plenty of people. We have help from all the local offices. And as one area of investigation closes down, I'm moving operatives around. I moved Han from California to Nebraska. Moved Stolichek from New London to Long Island. Moved Delano to help him there. A couple guys from New London are on their way to Long Island to help Stolichek and Delano. Then I moved Ford to Canaveral and I sent Cobbe down there with him."

"All right. As long as you feel you can cover all the places."

"Yes, sir. I think we have as good coverage as we had in Norfolk. But the locations we have to watch are spread out all across the country."

"But if you ever wind up short, you will let me know immediately, won't you? This is too important not to. We can get you more people if you need them. Okay?"

"Yes, sir. Thank you."

*   *   *   *

Skye glanced over her desk for at least the tenth time today. All she saw was piles of paper representing unknowns. Strange events in California, South Dakota, Nebraska, Connecticut, Long Island, Cape Canaveral, Saint Louis, and maybe Chicago. It didn't seem to end.

She had no idea if or how these locations were connected. No idea where this was leading them. Photos of dead truck drivers. What looked like "60c" written in blood, but which they now knew was the beginning of "6 DOWN." Diver bubble trails in the Thames River near New London. Unmarked aircraft.

She glanced over her desk. She caught sight of the crossword puzzle from the murder scene. And the photos of the driver's hand in on the road. "Oh, yes," she sighed. "Who is the 'Stalin' he was trying to tell us about?"

She thought of Brandon Lunch who was murdered by the drug gang on her last case in Norfolk, Virginia. *Oh, how I wish Brandon was still alive*, she thought. *I miss him dearly. At least I have a reminder of him.* She dropped her hand down to scratch Tango behind his ears, but the big Saint Bernard wasn't there either. They wouldn't let her bring him on the Naval Base.

She sighed. *Brandon and I were able to bounce ideas around productively. But then I'm able to do that with Chaské..., and with Eric, too. And he's right here with me. But he's so busy with school....* She stifled a sob. *But I'm way too busy with this damned case. And I live with him. We must spend more time together.*

She glanced at her watch. It was 1630. She needed some rest. A change of pace. She knew I would be going home from school in a short time. She picked up the phone and called the FT school office, leaving a message for me to call her back.

When I did so, she drawled: "Eric? How about...?" She paused. "Meet me at the office as soon as you can get over here."

"Problem?"

"No. The usual thousand unanswered questions. I just need a break."

"What do you want to do?"

"Let's take a walk along the lake. Then go out to dinner."

So we took a slow walk along the lakefront, on the road below the cliff behind the FT school. Arm in arm. Then we drove some distance north of the base, to a restaurant we knew about in the small town of Zion, where there weren't many sailors. When we got home, she grabbed me, hugged me, kissed me like she hadn't done in a long time. "We haven't done this right for too long. Please accept my apology for not paying enough attention to you."

"You talk too much," I said, returning her kiss.

She responded with an intensity of lovemaking greater than anything she showed since those truck drivers were killed and she took over this case.

*　　*　　*　　*

My weekend was free and I promised to mull this whole mess over. Saturday produced no new perspectives. We needed a rest. We came onto the base to eat Sunday brunch but couldn't park in our normal place, across the street from Barracks 501, the FT student barracks. The huge parking lot there was being used for the annual Great Lakes Sports Car Rally. We parked on the other side of the tarmac where all the observers and the waiting sports cars parked.

The whole area was full of cars and spectators. This wasn't a long-distance road rally, but a timed run of a circuit laid out on the tarmac with orange cones.

One car at a time ran the course. A timekeeper flagged the cars to start and clicked the stopwatch when the driver crossed the finish line. Any cones knocked over deducted points.

All kinds of cars were participating: Corvettes. Older Thunderbirds – the real sports car 'Birds. Karmann Ghias. Morettis. There was even a Jaguar XKE, a Maserati, and a Ferrari, expensive cars owned by officers or very senior enlisted men.

We ate brunch. The rally was still going on when we came back out, so we watched for a while. Rena stood there frowning and twirling her hair. Something popped into my mind. "Didn't you say one of the cars at the murder site was a sports car?"

She nodded.

"Did you get any dimensions of it?"

"We got the wheel to wheel width and the length between front and back wheels."

"I wonder how much variation there is between all these makes and models."

She pulled my head down to her and kissed me. "I love you. Come on."

We walked over to a guy with a clipboard. He wasn't the timekeeper but checked new arrivals in and took down their information.

"Pardon me." Rena said. "Can we talk a bit?"

"I'm pretty busy right now. Can it wait?"

"Will you answer one question for me?"

"If it's a short question…."

"Yes or no: if I gave you some dimensions of a car's wheel base, could you identify the make and model?"

"Not me. But I know a mechanic…."

Rena handed him a card. "Please have him contact me. Or visit me."

The rally handler looked at the card. Raised his eyebrows. "OCI, huh?"

Rena nodded.

"I'll try to get him over to your office tomorrow."

"Good enough for me. Thanks."

He waved his hand and returned to work.

28. Tracking Radio Signals

California

Out west, the radio signal tracking teams waited in Salt Lake City, and in Pierre, South Dakota. Each team brought an extra ham radio set so they could listen to the transmissions from one location and look for a response signal from somewhere else.

When the California folks let them know Blaine was transmitting, they kept one antenna on Kit Fox Butte, Idaho, and began to sweep the horizon for replies. Within five minutes they'd picked up another set of bearings.

This time the responses looked like they were coming from a hamlet named Oxbow, Nebraska. Alvarez was stumped. They had already been running all over the country, so he gave the teams directions to places where they could pick up the next set of signals from almost anywhere: Oklahoma City and Council Bluffs, Iowa.

*   *   *   *

The next time Blaine transmitted, they kept one antenna on Oxbow, Nebraska, and swept the horizon for appropriate responses. They picked up still another set of messages. This time they came from even farther down south, a place called Prairie Dog Flats, in Texas.

Alvarez thought the next step should be to Saint Louis. Or it could be New Orleans or Atlanta. Alvarez had one team remain in Oklahoma City. He sent the other team to Springfield, Illinois.

29. Meanwhile, Back at the Ranch

Nebraska

The OCI crew at the buffalo ranch had a new problem. The team members who stayed in Nebraska hurried to dispose of George Denison, John Little Horse's aide. They took his body a mile or so down the highway, carried it a quarter mile into some woods and buried it. They did this while Little Horse was still out flying.

When Little Horse landed, he positioned the plane in front of the barn door, as he normally did. But his aide was not waiting as was usual. The pilot went into the house to look for him, then came back outside and searched all around the house and barn. Not finding his aide, Little Horse began to expand his search area, gradually circling around the ranch buildings.

When the OCI team realized what that the pilot was expanding his search area, they quickly backed off. When the spy went behind the barn, they ruffled up the grass and leaves where they'd been to make it look like nobody had ever been there. Then they moved their post back and broke out their high magnification binoculars to watch the ranch. Little Horse looked for Denison for nearly an hour before he returned to the barn. He connected the tractor to the plane and pulled it out of the open landing field. After closing the large barn doors, he went up to the hayloft. He stood in the second-floor doorway and looked around for a while. He was obviously very puzzled. He moved back into the loft, probably to make a radio report to his superiors. A short time later he returned to the house with a worried look on his face.

*   *   *   *

The next day, a different plane landed at the buffalo ranch.

Two men got out. They went into the house for fifteen or twenty minutes before they came back outside and began a thorough search of the area. The OCI team backed off to a wooded hill about a mile from the house. They watched the searchers diligently.

As the new arrivals expanded their search they approached the wooded hill where the OCI team was. The team pulled completely off the ranch property. They mostly stayed in the motel room, but did a number of drive-by inspections of the ranch until the new plane was gone for a few days.

They did roam along the boundaries of the ranch with binoculars strapped around their necks. If questioned, they planned on saying they were bird watching. The searchers never approached them, though they continued to examine the area in great detail for three days. Han and the Indians concluded that these guys were looking for the missing ranch hand.

The extra guys finally seemed to leave the area. At least the OCI team didn't see them for a few days. But now, before Little Horse took off, he went around the perimeter of the airfield and some of the adjacent territory to examine the area. Daniel found a new lookout post, farther away than the group had originally been, but where they could still see the house, the barn, and the plane when it took off and landed.

*　*　*　*

The hospital at Ellsworth Air Force Base released Chaské on his promise to remain inactive, to not do a thing except rest for a while. He called the office of the motel in Alliance and left a message for the OCI crew to contact him at the hospital. He was lucky. Amos Counts Coup came into Alliance to make a report to Rena and buy some food for the team. He got the message and called Chaské early that same evening.

Daniel came up to Ellsworth that night to pick up Chaské. They met David Morrison in Rapid City. He brought two sets of radio detection equipment from Great Lakes for them. As soon as they transferred the equipment to Daniel's car, Morrison returned to Great Lakes. Chaské and Daniel traveled back to the buffalo ranch in northern Nebraska. They got a good night's sleep, then began to set up their new radio detection equipment.

Daniel thought they should place the new scanners to see if Little Horse got a response from the direction of Saint Louis when he sent out his messages. Chaské liked the idea. Some of the other Indians manned the scanners. As

Chaské pointed out, "None of us live in a city. There are times we don't have a telephone handy. So a lot of us have some other way to call for emergency help. Many of us grew up with short wave."

But Little Horse wasn't talking to Saint Louis.

The next morning Chaské called Rena.

"Chaské! How are you doing?"

"The docs let me go as long as I promised to rest another four days. So I'm back at the ranch."

"But not doing anything that could hurt you, I hope."

"Nope. I'm doin' important activities like sittin' and watchin' the house. And comin' into Alliance to make these calls. Seems that's goin' to be my job for a while."

"So what do you see when you're sitting and watching?"

"Yesterday Little Horse sent out some short-wave messages. We got a pretty strong readin' on the people responding to him."

"Where were the responders?"

"Copy these figures down." Chaské named the bearings where the responders had been. "Those are relative to our location. But they're to our northwest!"

"Doesn't sound right. Hang on. I'm going to plot them on my map here." There was silence on the line for a minute and a half. "Interesting. It looks like he's calling into Oxbow, Nebraska.... And Alvarez's short wave teams have already detected Oxbow relaying signals down to Texas. If they *are* talking to Saint Louis as we suspect, they're sure going about it in a roundabout way...."

"Hmmm. Perhaps you should set up stations all around there now. Monitor the frequencies we've found and confirm their home base is in actually in that city."

"I like that. Meanwhile, you keep monitoring Little Horse. Let me know if you get any different readings." Rena paused for a couple seconds. "Now, I have some news for you. I got a report from the FBI on George Denison, the man who hurt you. As if we needed more proof of who's running this whole operation, the man Daniel killed turned out to be a KGB security agent at the Soviet Union's United Nations office. His real name is Gyorgi Denisov. Let Daniel know. You guys might be on a hit list with them. And warn your friends and relatives so they can go home if they want to."

"Believe me, they'll stay. But who the hell is this John Little Horse?" Chaské demanded

"I'm working on that. But maybe you should be."

Chaské didn't catch the last sentence.

"Also, could you investigate the Cessna aircraft? Look for unmarked un-registered Cessnas. And we do have its serial number."

"How did you get that?"

"When I was in the Army, one of the guys flew a Cessna in his spare time for fun. He had me help look for the serial number to put on his insurance papers. So, when I was at Ellsworth and it looked like I'd be there for a while, I asked Daniel to do me the favor of finding it and told him where to look. He snuck into the barn and got it."

"With the people right there in the house? Wasn't he pushing his luck a bit?"

"Nah. He was careful. Went to the barn from a direction where people in the house couldn't see him. At 0330. Hours after they turned off the last light. And he used a small flashlight to read the numbers. Nothing dangerous. So, would you check out the Cessnas for us? Along with John Little Horse?"

"Isn't this your strong point? Your job?"

"Yeah, but who else do we have who knows Indians and can track people."

"First, the tracking seems to be done. Second, do you trust your friends to do the watching? How about if I transfer another agent in to work with them?"

"Who?"

"How about Wesley Rusk? He and Daniel have worked together on the west coast."

"Can he get along with Indians? Some of my relatives and friends can get a bit testy with outsiders."

"He lives in California now. But he's a Clallam Indian, from Washington state."

"Okay, let's give it a try."

"Fine. I'll send Wes. Then you can leave your friends to watch the house with him and Daniel. You come back here to do your research. And I have other problems you might be able to help me solve."

"You sound tired and worried. What other problems are you talking about?" Chaské asked.

"I'll fill you in when you get here. I don't want to get into it over the phone."

"Okay. When will Wes get here? I'll drive up and meet him at Ellsworth.

"How about meeting him this coming Monday? All right?"

"Will do," Chaské agreed.

"Good. Then do you think you could be ready to get back to Great Lakes and start work here on the following Wednesday or Thursday? I can even get you a military flight to Glenview NAS or Chanute Air Force Base in Rantoul,

Illinois. The latter location is a bit farther, hundred thirty miles or so south of Chicago. Someone can be there to pick you up."

"Sounds good to me. Let me know which of the two I'll be going to. See you soon"

*   *   *   *

The routine in the OCI camp was, well, routine. Somebody always watched the ranch. The flurry of activity after the disappearance of the KGB agent gradually died down, but it was still possible someone could come looking around where OCI had its camp. Thus, the location had to be kept very clean— no garbage, no ashes, definitely no footprints. It took a lot of work to erase every vestige of habitation. But it kept the off-watch people busy doing constructive work.

After a couple days of such intensive cleanup, Chaské had them move to a "base camp" in a different grove of trees a couple miles farther from the ranch house, a place not even on Little Horse's property. The agents limited their activity to the location where they hid out to watch the ranch. This reduced the danger of discovery.

*   *   *   *

The observation crew at the Nebraska buffalo ranch continued its surveillance. John Little Horse flew off every two or three days, was gone for some hours, and returned near dusk. The OCI crew tried to keep the airfield and the ranch house under constant observation. The lone helper on the ranch was the cook, though another man came in each week to keep the airfield well mowed. Little Horse himself took over transmitting the messages from the ranch. The OCI crew took photos any time anybody moved.

Each day after Little Horse flew, the crew drew straws to go into town, call in a report and buy more food.

Like all surveillance, it was tedious and boring. But there was a feeling in the camp that something would soon happen to break the case open. Or orders would come out from Great Lakes to take this guy down.

Until then, as they learned from the Navy slang Chaské had picked up, they hurried up and waited.

Their patience paid off. Their radio tracking pointed to Oxbow and Alvarez's teams tied Oxbow to Prairie Dog Flats, Texas, to Saint Louis. Skye was pleased to hear the news. But she still had questions. She sat at her desk, thinking. *We're able to track the signals going into Saint Louis, but we don't know what they're saying. We have to crack the code used in the radio transmission messages.*

Rena ordered every recording of every message be sent to her office.

*   *   *   *

Daniel drove Chaské up to Ellsworth Air Force Base. Hunter caught a flight to Chanute, south of Chicago, where Rena would meet him. Then Daniel waited for Wesley Rusk to arrive. They drove back to the OCI camp together.

Daniel had been thinking about something for quite a while. The ham radio tracking crews had proven the buffalo ranch was sending radio messages to someone in Saint Louis via the link in Oxbow. Daniel wondered what he might discover inside the ranch house itself. This could be dangerous, but ever since the ranch hand was killed, Little Horse and the housekeeper were the sole inhabitants of the house.

One day, Little Horse took off and the housekeeper left a half hour later to go shopping. Han waited another half hour. He patted his small camera in his pocket. Then he walked up to the back door and picked the lock. Stepped inside and locked the back door behind him, in case the woman returned before he was done. He didn't want an unlocked door to advertise his presence.

He made a quick sweep through the house. Everything looked very normal, except for one room on the second floor. It was locked and required an old fashioned skeleton key. He didn't know how to pick this kind of lock.

He slipped into the adjacent bedroom and looked out the window. There was no porch on that side of the house. No way to get into the locked room. He looked around the bedroom, felt along the tops of all the furniture, looked under the pillows and patted down the bedding. There was nothing under the sheets or in the pillowcases. He looked under the bed and felt all around the bed frame. Nothing. He looked through all the dresser drawers, checking every thing without moving the clothing out of place. Nothing. He examined the closet with the same thoroughness. Patted down everything on hangars. Nothing. Examined the walls of the closet. The rear wall seemed a little bit loose. It might be a door into a locked room. He pushed and pulled on everything he could think of. Nothing happened.

Then he noticed the wooden closet rods all sat in semicircular flanges. He lifted the ends of each rod. One of them clicked when he lifted it and the back wall opened slightly. He pushed the clothing aside and entered the room. As he stepped through the entry, he looked back at the wall that had swung open and noticed a clothes hook on it. It wiggled when he pulled on it and the door mechanism clicked. It was how he could unlock the secret door from the hidden-room side.

It looked like a den. There was a desk and a file cabinet. A small safe was on the floor in a corner. There was also another closet on the other side of the room. It looked like the place had been built to be another bedroom. He walked across the room and entered the closet. It was a darkroom. He recognized the trays, the bottles of chemicals and the line and clips to hang drying prints. There were no prints or negatives in the room.

Han returned to the room. Sat down at the desk and looked through all the drawers. He saw nothing of interest. So why was the room locked? He looked around again. The safe! There must be something in it. He sat down in front of the heavy metal box. Put his ear against the front of the safe. He turned the combination lock in very small increments. Between hearing and feeling, he got the combination in about ten minutes. He pressed down on the handle. The door swung open.

The safe held a pile of photographs. Daniel took them out and looked through them without moving anything out of order. Many were pictures of ICBM silo sites with description of their locations. There were also some papers in Russian. One of them looked official, important. He knew enough to be able to sound out the Russian letters, with some effort. The middle line of the certificate had two words: Ян Коничек. It seemed to be a name.

Han took out his little camera and proceeded to take pictures of the official-looking paper and of every photo he thought looked important. He worked quickly, knowing he was already pushing the time limit for not getting caught. The camera ran out of film.

Han wound the film back into its capsule. Popped open the camera. Put the exposed film into his pocket, took out a new roll and reloaded the camera. Closed the back and wound the film to the first picture. Continued taking photos. When the second roll had been exposed, he put the camera in his pocket. Returned Little Horse's pictures back in the safe the way they had been, then closed and locked the safe.

He got up and exited the way he'd entered. He pulled the back wall shut with the clothes hook. Made sure the closet rod was back in place. Arranged the clothing the way it had been. Stepped through the bedroom, being sure he left no traces of his visit there. Returned downstairs.

When he got to the bottom of the stairway, he heard the back door open. The housekeeper was returning from her shopping. Daniel rushed to the front door and unlocked it. The loud click of the lock being opened alarmed him. He stepped out and did his best to make no noise when he closed the front door. Then he ran around the nearest corner an instant before he heard the front door open again. The woman stepped out onto the concrete steps.

"Is someone out here?" she called.

Daniel held his breath.

The woman shook her head. "I could have sworn I locked the front door before I left. And I do believe I heard some noise from here a moment ago." She stepped down to the walkway in the front of the house. "Is anybody out here?"

30. The End of Secrets

California

While Rena was mulling over where the radio signals were going, the tracking teams waited in Oklahoma City and Springfield, Illinois. When Blaine transmitted again, the radio vans picked up the signals from Prairie Dog Flats, Texas. But the team in Springfield couldn't get a good reading for the origin of the next signal response. They moved their van to the other side of town to try another angle.

A day later, Alvarez let them know, once again, that Blaine was transmitting. This time it worked. Within minutes they reported the positions of the location where the transmissions were going from Prairie Dog Flats.

This time they got a bull's eye. The bearing lines crossed on the south side of Saint Louis, right where Skye thought the spy boss was hiding.

Alvarez had the teams stay where they were to monitor the transmissions. He was curious to see if they were talking to anyone else.

*   *   *   *

Alvarez looked up from his paperwork. Glenn Oliver was listening to an audiotape, rewinding and listening again. Over and over. Then he picked up a pencil and a pad of paper. He listened to a few seconds of audio and stopped. Wrote some words on the paper. Listened to the tape some more. He continued doing this until Alvarez asked: "Glenn, what in the world are you doing?"

"Transcribin' the messages Blaine was transmittin'."

"I thought it was all gibberish."

"Me, too," Oliver grinned. "But the more I listened, the more I thought I could detect some little bits of meaning. Now I want to see it in print."

Alvarez shook his head and returned to his papers. Sometimes it was so difficult to figure these engineer types out. He wondered how Rena could live with me.

An hour later Oliver threw down his pencil and groaned. "Good Lord! How could we not have seen this before?"

"What did you find?"

"Tony, it's so simple it threw us all. Look here." He pointed to a series of words he'd written down: IKOL SIHT SI DRANXO. "When they're sayin' these words, it sounds like gibberish. 'Specially when they're pronouncin' them naturally with variations in the tone of their voice. And sometimes they're pronouncin' the words differently than they would if they were read in reverse."

Alvarez's mouth dropped open. "They're speaking backwards?"

"I think so. Remember the sample I pointed out? What you noticed is if you read the words from left to right, the way they were spoken. But read the individual words from right to left, what do your have as you go right across the line...."

"LOKI... THIS IS... OXNAR.... Well, I'll be...."

"Yep. And they spoke it like a natural language, which helped to hide it. 'Ee-kol, sith see drankso. Loki, this is Oxnard.' And," Oliver continued, "the response from the other end of the radio connection was spoken the same way. DRANXO, OG DAEHA. And they didn't stick with strict English pronunciation. These deliberate mispronunciations served to make the messages even foggier. 'Oxnard, go ahead.' The 'go ahead' is not just backwards talk. They pronounced the second and third words 'awg day-hah' instead of 'ohg deh-huh.' It's ingenious."

"So now we can figure out what they're reporting and the instructions they're getting."

"Right."

"So, what was this message about?"

"Like most of Blaine's messages, it was a simple 'Hi! We're still here and ready to follow orders.' Right now, this bunch is merely maintaining an open contact."

"Glenn, you're a genius."

"No. I wasn't on the ball. It took me way too long to catch on. Better tell Rena about this."

*   *   *   *

"I think Gary Blaine is a homosexual," Alban reported.

Glenn Oliver, sitting at another desk, looked up sharply.

"Why do you think that?" Alvarez asked. "That's a pretty serious charge against a sailor. It can ruin his life."

"We've seen him meet with Villand a few times at the Camarillo house. Villand always came over later and Blaine paces the floor waiting for him. And they seem somewhat tender with each other when they part in the morning."

"We can't convict people on 'seems' and 'somewhats.'"

"Fladeboe also gave me some information about things he's observed. You should talk to him."

Oliver took a deep breath, then announced in a low voice: "I suspected this some time ago."

"So, why didn't you report it?"

"No proof. Just 'seems' and 'somewhats' like Robert reported. Besides," Oliver looked down at his hands for a long moment before speaking again. "I'm a Negro from Georgia. My grandparents were held in a different kind of slavery…."

"But slavery was outlawed during the Civil War! How…?"

"Oh, folks invented all kinds of ways to continue it. My grandparents were sharecroppers."

Alban frowned and shook his head. "What're sharecroppers?"

"Negroes and poor whites that worked a farm for a landowner. The landowner supplied everything they needed to grow the crops. And ran a store so they could get food and clothing on credit."

"Doesn't sound like such a bad deal."

"Doesn't sound like it, no. But the store provided everything at an inflated price. And then the crop came in and it was worth, say, seventy-five percent of what the folks owed. But, under local law, they still had a legal debt and couldn't move away until the debt got paid. But it never did, because the same thing happened the next year and the year after. And the year after that. So they were legally—*legally*—stuck there until they were debt free. But that never happened. Meanwhile, the landowner had almost free labor."

"They ever get out of it, Glenn?" Alvarez asked quietly.

"Yeah. When they died. My father ran away and joined the Army. So he got out of there. And my aunt stayed to care for the grandparents in their old age. When the grandfolks died, one of my uncles came back at night and quote kidnapped end-quote my aunt and moved her to Detroit, where she lives today with her family. When Dad got out of the Army, he never went back. He moved to Atlanta, a big city, where he got married and raised us kids."

"So what does this have to do with Blaine?"

"Bein' a minority in America, and havin' such a history of bigotry in my family's history, I didn't want to bring this man into the open, into the prejudice and hatred I knew he'd get."

"I can empathize with you, Glenn. But Blaine's a prime suspect," Alvarez protested. "This could be relevant!"

"How?" Oliver asked adamantly.

"You ever hear of blackmail?"

"What's that got to....? Oh, Lord, Lord, Lord."

"Right. If somebody knows about this, they can get him to behave in ways he otherwise wouldn't. He may not be a spy. He may simply be protecting himself from someone else who knows and who wants to be able to say he didn't do anything wrong."

"Hansard?"

"Could be," Alvarez nodded. "Or it could be Villand, Daniel's wide-brim hat guy, in which case he could just be setting Blaine up." He took a deep breath. "All right. I think our meeting is over. Now I have to talk to Fladeboe."

He picked up the phone and called the officer in charge of the shipping department where both Blaine and Fladeboe worked. He arranged to meet the undercover agent in a very out-of-the-way neighborhood bar. Alvarez raised his hand when the other man walked in.

"Alvarez," he greeted with a nod.

"Hello, Dirk. We need to talk."

"About what?"

"Robert Alban told me that you have been watching Gary Blaine as I asked you to do."

"I've tried."

"Robert also mentioned that you have observed some behaviors that may indicate a... uh... a relationship of one sort or another between Blaine and Villand."

"Yes.... I don't want to ruin their lives, but...."

"You think they are homosexuals?" Fladeboe nodded. Alvarez continued. "What makes you think this?"

"The way they behave around each other."

"Come on, now. They wouldn't give themselves away publicly."

"Oh no. They haven't. But I can see the little signs."

"Like what?"

"The sly smiles between them. The veiled jokes they laugh at, but which others nearby can't see the humor. Various little motions. Things like that."

"What makes them indications of homosexuality? And how do you know about them that you recognize them?"

Fladeboe swallowed hard. "I'm not queer, if that's what you're asking. But one of my brothers is. I've lived with these indications for a couple decades. I could have recognized the relationship between Villand and Blaine even if they'd been more careful."

31. Han Almost Caught

Nebraska

"Is anybody out here?" the ranch housekeeper called out again.

Daniel headed to the rear of the house as quietly as he could. He got behind the barn an instant before the woman rounded the front corner of the house. He ran away from the barn, keeping it between him and the house. He dropped into the first low spot he found and lay there, trying to catch his breath.

The woman didn't look any further. She re-entered the house. Moments later she came out the back door and began carrying her groceries in.

After ten minutes Daniel got up and made his way back to the OCI camp. Later he called Great Lakes and told Rena about his discovery of the silo photos in the darkroom.

"Get those photos to me as fast as you can."

"They're already in the mail, Rena. Also, I found an official looking paper with what might be a name on it. It might even be the pilot's real name, in Russian...."

"Wait... okay, I have a pencil and paper. What did the words look like?"

"The first word had a backwards 'R' and a small capital 'H.' The second word had a capital 'K' then a small 'O,' another small capital 'H,' a strange looking 'H' with the middle part slanted upwards to the right, a straight-up capital 'Y' with the bottom part straight down the right side instead of down the middle, a small 'E' – backwards '3,' and a small 'K'."

"I got it. Wait a minute. Eric is right here." She paused for a moment. "He says, yes it is a name: Jan Konichek. The first letter is equivalent to our 'Ya' and the upright 'Y' is a 'CH'. Thanks Daniel. I'll get someone on this to search for more information about this guy."

Daniel and Wesley Rusk continued to keep watch on the Little Horse Ranch. They took photos, monitored the movements of the people, and collected every conceivable kind of data. As they watched, Han was mesmerized by the starry night sky. He shook his head and asked: "Man, I've hardly ever seen the stars like that."

"Yeah. It's some view, isn't it?"

"The only other time I've seen them this bright was out at sea. I don't think I'll ever get tired of this spectacle."

"Haven't you ever been out in the country at night?" Rusk asked.

"Nope. This is as good as at sea with lights out condition set."

32. Sharing the Case

Cape Canaveral

It was another boring night at Cape Canaveral. But if the diver showed up again, they were ready for him.

"Echo, this is Alpha," Ford said into his walkie-talkie. "Everyone ready?"

"Bravo, aye," Cobbe replied.

"Charlie, aye," Cisco reported.

"Hotel, aye," said Hagen, the helicopter pilot.

"Echo this is Alpha. Stay awake and keep alert. Out."

Everything was quiet for hours. Ford remained alert, but spent a good bit of time daydreaming about the waitress at the Royal Baby's Bar and Grill.

Then the spy diver appeared.

"Echo, this is Alpha. I have contact. Our guy is coming ashore. Start sweeping. Out."

Hagen lifted the helo off the tarmac on the Air Force Station. He headed south to the eastern end of the Barge Canal, then turned east. He began sweeping back and forth across Canaveral Bight, south of the Cape. Back and forth. After some time, he reported: "Echo, this is Hotel. I see a cabin cruiser in the bight. Alpha, is the contact still ashore?"

"Hotel, that is affirmative."

"Echo, I'm going in for a closer look." He dropped the helo almost to the water. Closed in on the boat. "Echo, we see a cabin cruiser. It's about thirty feet long or so. Ryan is looking at the boat with his gigantic binoculars. I'm shining my spotlight on it. Ryan says the boat is empty. He sees civilian clothes folded up on the cockpit seat. Now I'm going around the boat. Going around it. All right, we see a name on the stern. It's… it's named the *Mermaid II*. Over."

"Echo, Alpha. That's the same boat I saw on the Thames River close to the New London Submarine Base. Over."

"Echo, this is Bravo. I saw it tied up in the marina I've been watching. Out."

"Hotel, Alpha. The contact is back in the water now. He should be arriving at his boat in a while. Back off a bit and let us know when the diver returns. Over."

"Hotel, aye." There was a no conversation for a while. "Echo, Hotel. The diver is back on the *Mermaid*…. Over."

"Hotel, Alpha. Get out of there. Go to a spot over the Air Station near where the canal enters the Atlantic and hover there. When you're convinced the *Mermaid* is heading into the canal, back off and go home."

"Echo, Hotel. I'm pulling away, but we can see the diver. He's getting out of his wetsuit and into street clothes. Over."

"Hotel! This is Alpha. Get the hell out of there! Now! I do not want him to realize we're watching him. Out!"

"Hotel, aye. Out." Hagen took the helo up and headed west, to a point over the inlet near the base's Gate 1.

"Charlie, Alpha. Bring the *Alert* up to a point where you can make out the Atlantic entry to the canal in the distance, but no closer. Let us know when you see the *Mermaid*. Try not to let him see you. Over."

"Alpha, Charlie. How about if I go in past the marina. Make him think I'm going to another docking facility? Over."

"Charlie, Alpha. Not a real good idea. It's not very credible for two boats to be coming home at the same time this late at night. Over."

"Charlie, Alpha. Good point. We will extinguish all lights are and try to stay invisible. Out." There was another long period of silence. "Echo, Charlie. He's entering the canal now. Out."

"Bravo, Alpha. Keep an eye out for him. Try to follow him home after he leaves the Marina. Over."

"Bravo, aye. Out."

"Echo, Alpha. All the rest of us can go home. Get some sleep. Out."

Cobbe sat in his car waiting. The *Mermaid II* pulled into the marina and tied up. The diver secured his equipment. Locked it up. Walked to his car. Using very fast film and a telephoto lens, Cobbe got a good photo of the man.

The diver started to drive. Cobbe followed at a respectable distance. There were very few other cars on the streets. He turned his headlights off for variable amounts of time and then turned them on again. Pulled off the street like he was parking, turned off the lights, and drove back onto the street for a block or so before turning his lights on again. The diver pulled into the driveway of a house in Cocoa Beach about four and a half miles to the south of the Barge Canal. Cobbe continued a little farther and parked. Wrote down the address of the house. There was a building to his right, on the other side of the street from the house. It had stores on the ground floor and a combination of small lofts and office spaces on the second and third floors.

Cobbe saw an "Apartment for Rent" sign on the second floor. He copied the phone number so he could inquire about it. Then he returned to the marina. Found the diver's boat. He noted the registration number so he could track down the owner. Then he returned home and went to sleep.

Unknown to Cobbe, another man followed him from the Cocoa Beach house to the marina. He frowned and muttered to himself: "What the hell are *they* doing here?"

* * * *

The next day Cobbe rented the apartment in Cocoa Beach. Now he could watch the diver's house. He set up a camera to photograph every person who even approached the place. He also had a good set of binoculars so he could collect license numbers and solid descriptions of each person.

Cobbe later had a meeting with Ford. He described the diver and gave Ford the address in Cocoa Beach. Then, while Cobbe set himself up to watch the house there, Ford visited the local post office. After the postmaster checked with the OCI office in Washington, D.C., he gave Ford the name of the person living at the address of the Cocoa Beach house: Allen Dobbins."

A man in the shadows watched Ford come out of the post office building. Made a note in his notebook, then snapped it shut angrily. "First I catch one of them tracking a suspect," he grumbled. "Then watching the house from a rented apartment. Now this. I have to find out what the hell is going on here...."

* * * *

Ford knew he wouldn't get in the water off the Cape. It would be impossible to track anyone under water, because of the darkness of the night. But he continued to wear his black wet suit, in order to make it more difficult for others to see him.

It paid off.

The spy diver came ashore. Took off his fins in the surf. Lifted his mask up to his forehead. Took a notebook and a camera out of a waterproof case. Got them ready. Took some photos. Made some notes. Put his notebook and camera back into his watertight packet. Put his mask back over face and adjusted his regulator. Walked out into the surf. Put his fins back on. Walked into waist-deep water. Sank under the water.

Ford was elated. He'd been able to get a photo of the spy's face while the guy had his mask up on his forehead. He stayed around for an hour or so after the spy left. He wondered why the Russians were putting such effort to spy on the US space program. Or were the missiles all they were interested in? They could be scared of what the U. S. was developing here. The Polaris missile "bases" would be undetectable. Submarines would carry and launch their missiles from underwater. The Russians couldn't know where they would come from, anywhere from the middle of the Atlantic or Pacific. Or from offshore in the Baltic or Black Seas. It would almost be a sure win for America if these missiles had to be fired.

*   *   *   *

Now they knew where the diver, Dobbins, lived. The OCI team established a twenty-four-hour stakeout in the apartment across the street from the Cocoa Beach house. The first morning they watched, Dobbins drove from the Cocoa Beach house to the Sand Dollar Inn. He carried a package with him.

Cobbe followed him with difficulty. The man drove to the parking lot of the hotel. He got out and entered the motel. Cobbe pulled over, watched and waited. The diver came out after a very short time. Without the package. He got in his car and headed back the way he came.

Cobbe entered the hotel to interview the concierge, a middle-aged woman. He asked about the man who had walked out of there a few minutes earlier. After he provided identification, the concierge said the man had her call the guest in Room 312 and tell him he had a visitor. Cobbe asked who the guest in Room 312 was. She said he was a salesman named Douglas Voight. He'd come downstairs and met the visitor in the lobby. They talked for a while then the visitor handed Mr. Voight a package. They spoke a few more words, and the visitor left. As Cobbe turned to leave, the concierge said: "By the way, you're the second man who's here investigating Mr. Voight."

Cobbe thought quickly, then replied: "Oh. I didn't realize my partner got this far in the investigation. I guess I should have checked with him first."

He returned to his rented apartment in the town of Cape Canaveral and phoned Ford to tell him about the diver, the package and Allen Dobbins. He also mentioned someone else was also investigating these guys.

Ford placed a long distance call. "Hi, Rena. We found out the names of two people here involved in gathering information on Canaveral."

"Let me have the names. I'll see what we can dig up."

"The diver's name is Allen Dobbins. The other guy, who claims to be a salesman, calls himself Douglas Voight. And Dobbins passed a package to Voight in the latter's hotel lobby."

"All right. I'll get someone on this to identify who these people are and where they came from. Meanwhile, you guys stay there and try to track who their contacts are, if they have any. Especially, if Voight mails the package Dobbins gave him."

"Then I'll make another visit to Mr. Vinson, the postmaster."

"Correct," she agreed. "Let me know if anything else pops up."

"Oh, by the way, we also have a report that there are others investigating Voight. And maybe Dobbins, too."

"No other information on that? No idea who the other party is?"

"No."

"Keep me updated."

"Of course. Talk to you later."

*　　*　　*　　*

The United States was still trying to catch up to the Soviet Union's missile superiority. The Navy's Polaris seemed to be working well, at least most of the time. But the success stories for other American systems weren't as positive. It had been almost a year since President Kennedy set the goal of reaching the moon by the end of the decade. All of the armed forces, as well as NASA, were anxious to achieve consistent, successful rockets.

Sometimes the goal seemed impossible.

On 9 May 1962 the Army tried to fire a Pershing missile from Launch Complex 30A. It failed to launch.

Out at sea, on the same day, the USS *Sam Houston* tried to launch another Polaris. It, too, failed to launch.

The next day, the Air Force tried to launch a Thor missile from Launch Complex 17B. Another failure to launch.

But on 11 May, people at Cape Canaveral were elated. At ten in the morning, the Air Force was able to launch a Minuteman. And later the same day, a little before 1330, the *Sam Houston* launched another successful Polaris missile shot.

*　　*　　*　　*

Ford left his lodgings and headed for the rented Cocoa Beach apartment. Cobbe rode with him so he could relieve Rick Morris, who was on watch. Ford parked right in front of the apartment building. He noticed a flash of light from somewhere. Looked around. Once again the sunlight flashed off the lens of the OCI agent's binoculars up on the second floor.

"Oh, shit," he said. "I hope it's not too late...."

"What...?" Cobbe asked.

Ford ran inside and up the stairs, Cobbe right on his heels.

The man who had been following Cobbe now sat in his car half a block back. He was taking notes on the OCI activities. He was not very happy about the events taking place.

Ford opened the door to the apartment. A shot rang out.

Someone grunted and swore. "Damn! That was stupid of me."

Ford heard a car screech away. He ran into the front room. The window was open. There was a small hole in the screen. Rick Morris sat on the floor, his back against the wall. Ford rushed to the window. He saw the shooter's car but it rounded a corner before he could get a shot off.

Cobbe tore open Morris' shirt to examine the wound. "You're lucky, man." Cobbe said. "You were moving sideways when he pulled the trigger."

"It's my own fault. I shouldn't have been so close to the window and I should have realized someone could see me."

"That wasn't the problem," Ford said. "You were looking out the window in such a way that the sun was reflecting off the lens of the binoculars. I was rushing up to warn you. Let's get you to a doctor."

"It's merely a flesh wound," Morris insisted.

"It might be," Ford said, "but I want to be sure it doesn't get infected."

"Where are you going to take him?" Cobbe asked.

"There's a medical facility at the Cape Canaveral Air Force Station. We'll take him there."

They all left together. After the doctor cleaned the wound Morris was released. "See?" Morris grinned. "I told you it was no more than a flesh wound."

"Yep. And I believed you. But we play it safe with our people."

When the group returned to the Cocoa Beach apartment, they saw signs of an attempted break in. But the locks held.

*   *   *   *

We got this story later from the agent involved.

The FBI man working around Cape Canaveral walked up to the front desk of the Sand Dollar Inn. His hands rested on the counter, folded over his badge holder. He needed to verify some information, so he asked the receptionist behind the counter: "I'd like some information on one of your guests."

"I'm sorry, sir," she said, "but I can't violate the privacy of a guest."

"This might help you decide." Dawes said quietly. He held up the badge from the surface of the counter, his body shielding it from others behind or alongside him.

The woman looked closely. "What is it you want to know, sir?"

"What is the name of the guest in room 312?"

She looked on her room listing. "Douglas Voight."

"One more thing. I'll be sitting right over there reading the newspaper. When Mr. Voight leaves the hotel, will he turn in his key?"

"Yes, sir. He's supposed to do so. And so far, he has."

"All right. When he turns his back to leave, make some kind of motion or point to him or something to let me know that person is Mr. Voight. Will you do that for me?"

The woman nodded her agreement.

"Thanks," the FBI man said. "Now, is the room next to Voight's empty?"

"No, sir. That room is taken for another four days."

"I need to be in there. Is there any way we can arrange it?"

The woman thought for a few seconds. "I can upgrade the present guest to a better room. You'll be able to move into room 314 tomorrow."

"Thank you very much. How much does the room cost?"

She named the price. He put enough cash down for a week. Signed the papers. Then he turned and strolled over to a table in the lounge area. Picked up a newspaper. Sat in a chair that had a good view of the front desk and began "reading" the paper.

Two hours later a man turned in his room key. This was the third person to do so since the FBI man sat down. The guest turned to walk out the door. The receptionist looked at the agent, nodded her head and pointed to the guest. Mr. Voight was average height. He had short brown hair. No facial hair. His angular face radiated a look of extreme confidence. His body was muscular, well developed, like he worked out at a gym somewhere.

The FBI man folded his newspaper and followed the guest outside. Voight

174

was entering a cab. The agent flagged down another cab. He pulled out his identification. "Follow that cab pulling out now, but be very discrete. I don't want them to know we're following them."

The man did some shopping and returned to the hotel. The FBI agent sat down in the lobby and watched. After Voight caught the elevator to his floor, the receptionist motioned to the FBI man and waved him over to the desk. "Room 314 is now empty and cleaned. Here's your key, sir."

"That was fast. Thank you."

She smiled. "Yes. The previous guest was more than happy to take the upgrade without any additional charge."

He chuckled. "Wouldn't anyone be?"

He took his key, retrieved his luggage from his first room, and took it to his new room. The head of the bed was next to the wall that separated his from Voight's room. He had bought some food. He settled onto his bed with his supper, leaned against the wall and listened with a stethoscope. "If he talks to anybody," he mumbled to himself around a sandwich, "I might be able to get some clue who his contacts are."

*   *   *   *

Maria Holland, the cleaning lady at the Sand Dollar Inn, waited until she saw Douglas Voight leave his room. She waited fifteen minutes before she entered into another room she knew was empty and called the concierge's desk to be sure the guest in room 312 had left the building. He wouldn't let her into the room when he was there and she had to clean it.

Mr. Voight had taken a taxi somewhere.

Maria hung up. She unlocked the room. It was empty. She cleaned the bathroom. Dusted everything. Vacuumed the carpet. She checked the spare blankets and pillows in the closet. They seemed piled higher than in all the other rooms. She looked to see what was under them. She found a briefcase.

Maria frowned. She hadn't run across anyone who hid possessions this way before. Her curiosity won out. She extracted the briefcase. It wasn't locked so she opened it. Inside, she saw a number of thin strips of film, about a half inch wide. She hurried to arrange things back the way they had been.

She checked the closet again to be sure everything was arranged as it was before. It looked like nothing had ever been moved. She backed out of the closet. Closed the door. Wiped the doorknob clean.

This was all very strange. She'd never seen anything like those little rolls of film. And why would Voight try to hide a briefcase with film in it? She cleaned the rest of the room and left.

The next day, Maria did not see the "Do Not Disturb" sign on the doorknob. She didn't know if the man was in his room or not, so she knocked and got ready to enter the room to clean again.

"Who is it?" Voight shouted.

"The maid. Can I come in and clean your room?"

"Go away! My room does not need to be cleaned! Do not bother me again!" he bellowed.

"Yes, sir!" she replied and moved on to the next room.

The same thing happened the following day. Maria wondered about this man. His behavior was not typical. Most people were fanatic about their room's cleanliness. Then there was the briefcase full of the strange little strips of film. The more she thought about all this, the more she suspicious she became. She'd never seen a guest behave this way. She remembered the FBI man who had met with her a short time ago.

She rolled her cleaning cart into an empty room. Made sure nobody was in the hallway. Hurried to Evan Dawes' room and knocked. He opened the door. "Maria!" he whispered. "Come in!"

She reported that she thought something strange was going on in Voight's room.

"What did you see that you thought was odd?" Dawes asked.

"While cleaning the room the other day, I noticed the spare pillow and blanket in the closet were higher than normal. Higher than they should have been for the items stored there. So I checked it out. The guest had put a briefcase under them."

"Is that unusual?"

"I thought it was. It seemed to be hidden. I wondered why. Travelers and businessmen usually have briefcases. I wondered what was so special about this one that he wanted to hide it?"

"Did you look into it?"

She nodded. "There were many rolls of film. Very small. There were striprs of film rolled up. The film was about a half inch wide."

"Microfilm." Dawes thought for a while. "Thank you, Maria. And as I mentioned before, let me know if you see anything else that is different, or if he gets ready to check out."

"Yes, sir. I will do so. And please, sir…?"

"Yes?"

"Please do not to tell the management. They have a rule here that the help is not to spy on the guests. And they might consider this to be spying…."

"Don't worry, Maria. You keep on helping me and I won't tell anyone anything."

The maid seemed to breathe easier.

33. Disappearing Suspects

Great Lakes

Skye stood by her desk, deep in thought. This case progressed in fits and starts. And it had taken on a whole new dimension because of the news Commander Fasano gave her a week ago about the accuracy of the new Polaris missiles and how they changed the balance of power in the Cold War.

"You look lost in some very deep thinking," a soft voice said.

Skye looked up in surprise. "Chaské!"

"Uh huh. You said you wanted me here by now. So here I am. Ready to get to work."

Skye sat down behind her desk. She looked up at the man, grinned and asked: "Have you seen Ruth yet?"

Hunter shook his head. "Haven't found her yet. I may need directions." He took a deep breath. "Gee, what a horseshit situation for a good trackin' Lakota guy to be in."

Skye laughed. "Don't worry. We'll get you two together again. Soon."

"So, why were you so deep in thought?"

"It has to do with our case against these spies. I'll tell you after the information gets de-classified."

Chaské shook his head. "Knowin' the military, that could take decades. Right now I need to know two things."

"Which are?"

"First, what do you want me to start workin' on? And second, where's my woman hidin' out?"

"You're the researcher. I want you to identify Little Horse. Daniel saw a paper with the name Jan Konichek written in Russian letters. Find out who this guy is, where he came from, all the goodies. Identify the Cessna to do it, or forget the Cessna if it turns out you don't need that data to identify the pilot."

"Will do."

"And it's easy to solve your second request." She pointed to a door leading to the Waves' desks. "Right through that door."

The man turned and began to walk in the direction indicated.

"And Chaské?"

He stopped and looked back. "Yeah?"

"Take her home before you start making love to her," she said. "You two can take the rest of the day off. I'll see you both tomorrow."

The next day, Chaské began his work of researching John Little Horse.

*　　*　　*　　*

"Is there a Major Rena Skye here?" the man asked as he entered the OCI office, accompanied by a sentry. The woman looked up, frowning because she didn't recognize him.

"Yes. That's me," Rena replied.

"My name is Barry O'Hearn. I'm a machinist mate on base here, and also an auto mechanic and sports car fanatic. I was given this card by a friend who said you wanted to see me."

"Oh, come on over and sit down."

"How can I help you?" he asked as he sat on the offered chair.

"O'Hearn, we have some sports car information and we'd like to know if you can identify the make, model and year."

"I can try. And please call me Barry."

Skye wrote down a couple numbers. "Okay, Barry. This is the distance between the front and rear wheels. The wheelbase, right?"

O'Hearn nodded.

"And this is the distance between the left and right wheels."

"We call that the track," he explained.

"Given this information, can you identify the car?"

"Are these numbers exact?"

"The wheelbase may be off by an inch or two. I had to work with imprints in the dirt. But the track should be real close."

"I'll try to get you some information. At least I should be able to narrow it down to a two or three makes and models. Let me take these numbers with me and I'll see what I can do."

"Thanks, Barry. Here's my phone number so you won't have to make another trip over here."

"No problem," he said as he stood up. "It's no great distance coming over here. Unless you preferred me to call."

Rena shook her head. "No difference to me. Your choice. I look forward to hearing from you."

*   *   *   *

Rena reached to her desk when the phone began ringing. "Major Skye, this is Commander Fasano. Please come to see me as soon as you can."

"Aye, aye, sir." Skye hung up and headed for her interim boss's office. She wondered about the note of urgency in his voice.

When she entered the room, Fasano motioned for her to shut the door.

"I have some more Polaris news," he said. "This one proves the new version works the way we want it to."

"I thought the previous tests already did."

He grinned. "Not with the kind of bang made in this test. "

"What happened?"

"The USS *Ethan Allen*, SSBN-608, is operating in the Pacific as a unit of Joint Task Force 8 on an operation called 'Operation Frigate-Bird.' On 6 May 1962 it fired a nuclear-armed Polaris missile. While submerged. Its nuclear warhead was detonated over the South Pacific at the end of its programmed flight. They described the shot as hitting the target 'right in the pickle barrel.'"

"So we have a true deterrent to a nuclear war."

Fasano nodded. "Yep. There's no way the Russkies can track a Polaris boat. They can be anywhere in the world. And with the range of the Polaris missile, they can hit any target inside the Soviet Union."

"No wonder they're out to get all the data on our missiles they can," Skye said. "If those Super-Terrier and Super-Talos missiles get made and work this well, then we can even shoot down any ICBMs they launch for retaliation. It would no longer be a situation of mutual assured destruction."

"Yes. Right now, without the anti-missile missiles, if a war starts, both sides lose," Fasano said grimly. "All parties have enough A-bombs to guarantee it. But if we have effective anti-missile weapons and they don't, we can protect ourselves and they get obliterated."

"So bringing this case to a successful close may give us an assured victory if the Russians ever start anything."

"And they're scared to death of such a scenario." Fasano nodded. "I don't like the idea of killing another whole country. But I'd rather do that than see two whole countries disappear. So, let's be sure we get these spies so they don't equalize the playing field."

Skye nodded as she turned to leave. The case her team was working on had taken on a whole new dimension. She slowly walked back to her desk.

*   *   *   *

Chaské interrupted Skye at her desk. "Hey, boss."

"Hi, Chaské. You look like the cat who just ate the canary. What's up?"

"I've been talkin' with the FBI office in Chicago."

"Long conversation?"

"Yeah. We've been talkin' on an' off for a while, now. Here's the report I just got." He chuckled. "It's pretty interesting."

He dropped the report on Rena's desk then turned and walked away, grinning all the time.

Rena picked up the report. It was short, but…. She skimmed through it. Smiled. Re-read it slowly. "So," she mused. "So now we know who John Little Horse is. But we still don't know why he's using an Indian-sounding name…."

Amos Counts Coup later called in a report from Nebraska.

"Hi, Amos!" Skye greeted. "Is Daniel with you today?"

"No. Troy and I made the trip today."

"Okay. I have some interesting news for your whole group. Chaské was able to track down some information about Little Horse. He found the information yesterday."

"What is it?"

"Little Horse is Czechoslovakian."

"That's it?"

"Yeah. But Chaské's still working to get more on him. At least we know where the guy came from. And this may explain why he's working with the Russians."

"How in the world did Chaské find this information? And without finding anything more?"

"He was able to find the guy's application for his pilot's license. It listed his place of birth. Little Horse was born in Moravany, a small town about a hundred twenty five miles southeast of Prague."

"But why does he call himself 'Little Horse'? To make others see him as Indian?"

"We don't know. Yet. Watch him like a hawk."

"How can we watch him when he's out flying?" Amos asked.

"Has he ever taken any luggage with him when he flies?"

"We haven't ever seen him do that."

"Well, if he takes a suitcase with him, stop him immediately," Rena ordered.

"Why not arrest him now?"

"Not yet. We'll let you know when."

"All right. You're the boss. I'll pass on this information to Daniel and we'll wait."

That afternoon, Rena saw Chaské come out of the break room with a cup of coffee. He came over to her desk and halfway sat on one corner of it. Took a sip of coffee. Grinned. "We got lucky. Again."

"What do you mean?"

"Earlier I was gettin' a cup of coffee." He raised his cup for emphasis. "Commander Fasano came in an' we started talkin'. I mentioned we'd found out John Little Horse came here from Czechoslovakia. But we couldn't figure out why he had a name that sounded Indian. I told him my FBI connection didn't know. He said he'd try to find out how we could check that out."

"When was this?"

"About 1300 this afternoon." He took another sip of coffee.

"So it's too soon for him to have anything…."

Chaské smiled. "Not so. He called me in about fifteen minutes ago to tell me something very interesting."

"Which was?"

"One of Fasano's aides has a Czech background. A guy by the name of Jacob Skala. So Fasano asked him if he might know why Little Horse is usin' an Indian-sounding name. Well, Czech family names are similar to American Indian names here. In translation, they can be almost anything: Man Who Hurries, He Slept Standing, He Makes a Fool of Someone. For example, Skala's name means 'Strong as a Rock.'"

"Okay…."

"So Little Horse's real name, his Czech name, could be somethin' like 'Konik' which means pony, or 'Konichek,' Little Horse. Or some other similar derivation."

Rena's eyes opened wide. "It's Konichek."

"How do you know?"

"Daniel saw the name Jan Konichek on a paper inside the ranch house….

*   *   *   *

182

The next day, Alvarez called Skye. "It almost seems that Blaine's bosses know we've cracked their code."

"Why do you say that, Tony?" Rena asked.

"We intercepted a message in spelled out Russian letters, not the backward-English-words code we've seen before. But it was different, and not simply Russian spelling. And, because it was so different from all the other messages we'd heard, this seemed much more important. The more we looked at it and tried to figure it out, the more we thought it was something weird. And I mean weird."

"What do you have, Tony?"

"Blaine's bosses sent a message in what sounds like Russian. None of us know any Russian except some of the numbers, 'yes,' 'no,' and 'Do you speak Russian?' But nobody here can understand even a word of this in the whole message. Do you have a tape recorder and microphone available?"

"Play it for me first. Let me listen to it," Rena suggested. Alvarez did so. "All right, Tony. Call me back in half an hour. I'll get my tape recorder and set it up with a microphone. And I'll try to get Eric in to listen. He speaks Russian."

"Okay, boss."

Alvarez called back in thirty-two minutes.

"You ready, boss?"

"Yes. And Eric is here to listen as well. We're all set up and our recorder is running. Go ahead and play your tape." She pressed the "Record" button on her machine. When Alvarez was done, Skye checked that her recording was complete and clear. "Okay, Tony. We got a good copy. Now we'll analyze it and get back to you as soon as we have something."

"Good enough. Talk to you later."

Skye leaned back and looked at me. "Well, you heard it, Eric. What're they saying?"

I shook my head. "It's a series of Russian letters. But they're not words. It's nonsense. The letters they used did not spell a single Russian word I know. And the other Slavic languages are close enough that I would have recognized *something*. But I didn't understand a thing in the whole message."

"Nothing?"

"Huh-uh. Must be some kind of code...."

"Crap."

"Sorry I couldn't help." I looked at my watch. "But I have to get back to school. I'm late for the end of the break, now."

"All right. Get going."

"See you later." I bent over and kissed her before rushing out.

Skye spent a few minutes wondering what to do next. Then she called Fasano. He promised to try to find someone to help.

Skye wanted an answer to this a little faster, so she called her operational senior, Commander Blount, in Norfolk for help.

"Let me think, here," Blount mused. "There are a lot of Russians in New York City. And my old friend Charlie Skripps is the officer in charge of OCI at the Brooklyn Navy Yard. I'll give him a call and see if he has anyone we can use. If he does, I'll have him call you directly."

Fifteen minutes later Skye got a call from Commander Skripps. "Major Rena Skye?"

"Yes, sir."

"I got a call from Ron Blount a few minutes ago. He wondered if I could help you. What's the situation?"

Skye explained the strange messages Alvarez sent her.

"I don't know any Russian," Skripps said. "But I do know a number of people who do. And one of them has some special capabilities in that language. I will get her to Great Lakes by tomorrow morning."

"Actually, Commander, if you can get her to your phone sometime today, or if you can give me her number, I can play this over the phone for her."

"Good idea, Major. I'll have her here shortly."

An hour and a half later, Skye got a phone call from a woman with a slight accent. "Is this Maychor Rena Skye?"

"Yes it is."

"My name is Senny Rusakova. Commander Skripps asked me to telephone you. He said you had a problem with some Russian languach. How can I help you?"

"Thank you for calling so quickly, Mrs. Rusakova."

"Oh, please chust call me Senny."

"All right, Senny. I'd like to play a tape for you over the phone and see if you can make any sense out of it. We have a Russian speaker in our group here but he couldn't make anything out of this. He said it was all gibberish."

"Play it for me and I will try for you."

Skye played the tape into the phone. When it was finished she asked: "Senny? Could you understand anything in the message?"

The woman's voice was filled with surprise. "Why, yes. I worked in Chermany with the United States Army. We cracked a difficult code there, but later the Soviets quit using it. This messach is the same code they used in

Chermany six years ago. You are lucky they reuse it."

"How can we understand what they're saying?"

"You say you have a Russian speaker on your staff there?"

"Yes we do. A man named Eric Matthews."

"He learned the languach in school?"

"Yes, in college."

"Is he fluent?"

"Possibly. But he's very good."

"All right. Are you ready to write?"

Skye grabbed a pencil and a pad of paper. "Go ahead."

"This is a code," Rusakova explained. "Once you know the key, it is simple. To start, count the number of the Russian letters in the first word. That is the displacement of letters in the Russian alphabet. They use it throughout the messach. If the first letter is a vowel, the displacement is toward earlier letters in the alphabet. If it is a consonant, the displacement is toward later letters in the alphabet."

"Can you give me an example?" Skye asked.

"Yes. The Russian word for 'yes' is 'da.' If 'da' was the first word in the messach, every letter in the messach would be two letters later because the 'Da' has two letters and begins with a consonant the displacement would be to later letters, not earlier. So the word 'da' spelled 'deh-ah,' or D-A in English, would come out 'ee-yeh, or E then a softer E, like with a Y in front of it."

"I think I understand. But we would be receiving the message *after* it was changed. How would we know what the first word would be so we could go back to the words as they were before being shifted?"

Rusakova chuckled. "That is where you need someone who is *very* fluent. It would be best to have a native speaker because this deciphering would be so difficult to someone who learned the languach in a school."

Skye took a deep breath and let it out noisily. "So what can we do now?"

"I wrote down what I heard. Here is my translation: 'Close your operation. Your work is done. Go to Vancouver. Leave tomorrow.' This is what I see right now. I can check it out and call you again to confirm that or to correct it. Is that good for you?"

"Yes, Senny. Thank you. But we might be too late. The tomorrow in that message is today. I will have to try to close the border to British Columbia to stop the people from getting away."

"I wish you good luck, Maychor."

"Thank you. And thanks for your help."

"I am glad I could do so. I hope it works for you."

Skye called Alvarez again. "Tony, have you guys out there been taking photos like crazy, same way I had you do in Norfolk?"

"Sure, boss. You trained us. Why?"

"The message you got that was so scrambled up…. It was an order for the spies at Hueneme to close shop and run to Vancouver. So, get at least two copies of photos of everyone in the missile handling area. Get a Navy flight and fly up to the Canadian border between Seattle and Vancouver right away. We need the guards on both sides of the border to look for whoever goes missing from Hueneme, arrest them and turn them over to us."

"You got it, Rena. I'll get the crew on making copies of the pictures while I arrange a flight from Point Mugu. I'll leave as soon as I can."

"Thanks, Tony. With a little luck, we may catch them at the border. And before you leave," she added, "be sure to notify the RCMP, the CSIS and the CRA. They'll meet you and the fugitive as soon as both parties get to Vancouver, whether by car, air or ship."

"Who are all those groups?" Alvarez asked.

"Various Canadian police forces. The RCMP is the Royal Canadian Mounted Police, the Mounties. The CSIS is the Canadian Security Intelligence Service. And the CRA was the Canada Customs and Revenue Agency."

"Thanks. Gotta go now. We'll talk later when I get back."

Skye said good-bye to a dead phone. She let Commanders Fasano and Blount know about the order to go to Vancouver. Blount agreed to make the calls to the Canadian agencies and had Skye notify Fasano that Norfolk was taking care of it. Two countries were now officially looking for an unknown number of suspects.

Rena was ecstatic at getting two major breakthroughs recently, John Little Horse and the Russian code. She sat back with a grin on her face. She felt pleased with the progress of the case for the first time in a long time. She left for home a little early, showered and got all dolled up.

As soon as I walked in the door, she greeted me with: "Come on. Chop-chop. Get a move on. Get showered, shaved and dressed up. I want you ready to leave here in twenty minutes."

I frowned. "What's up? Where are we going? What kind of dressed up should I get?"

She came over to me, smelling all nice and pretty. Rubbed against me the way I like her to. Whispered in my ear: "Get into your best civvies. We're going somewhere to dine out and dance and then we can come home and play with each other."

I laughed. "I'm ready to do any of those, but all three in the same evening!

186

Gee, I think I've died and gone to heaven."

"Eric, you know you don't have to die to get your heaven from me. Come on, now. Get moving."

"You're all hopped up! What's the celebration for? Did you get that Russian code cracked?"

"Yes. And that's following our breakthrough with Chaské's information on John Little Horse I told you about last night. Now, let's go. We have to drive to this good restaurant I found in Rockford. So," she grinned, "your orders, junior officer, are: Get a move on. Now."

The way she looked and the hunger in her eyes, told me I shouldn't argue. After all, she was the boss. I wore a very happy face as I obeyed.

Since we were both in civilian clothes, and in an out-of-the-way location, we wouldn't be seen by anyone who would wonder about this officer and her "enlisted" lover being together. So we made the best of a rare evening. We ran over to Rockford and ate in a very nice restaurant. The waitress told us about a great club with a very good band that played a variety of music: rock-n-roll, jazz, soft-swaying hold-me-even-closer slow dance tunes, the whole spectrum. We thought nothing of gluing our bodies together on the slow dances, kissing openly, all those great activities.

We dined, and danced and worked off all the calories from dinner. Then we came home and stripped our clothes off and worked those calories off all over again.

*   *   *   *

The next morning, someone came into the office and stood in front of Alvarez's desk. Tony looked up. Fladeboe stood there waiting. "Hi, Dirk. What's happening? You quitting the undercover act?"

"I may have to if what I think is happening," Fladeboe said.

"You don't look too happy."

"Blaine, Hansard and Villand are all missing this morning.."

"I bet this is the result of the order they got from on high, the order to close up and head for Canada. But Hansard, too? I thought we'd determined he wasn't part of this operation…. And Villand is the owner of the houses in Oxnard. Why would he leave his real estate?"

Fladeboe shrugged. "Orders, I guess. Many of us follow orders blindly. All I know for sure is those three guys are not at work today."

"Okay. Thanks, Dirk. What're you going to do now?"

The other man smiled. "Go to Chicago. Major Skye re-assigned me."

"When are you supposed to report there?" Tony asked.

"Tomorrow if possible."

"Do you have a flight scheduled?"

"Yep. 1700 tonight from Mugu."

Alvarez stood up and offered his hand. "Well, thanks for the job you did here and good luck on your new assignment."

Fladeboe shook hands. "Thanks, Tony. Good luck to you guys, too."

Alvarez called Rena to give her the news.

"I expected someone to disappear. But not three people."

"Any news from the Canadian border?"

"Yeah." Skye sounded disappointed. "It looks like we missed them. One of the border guards remembered Villand and his floppy hat passing through on a legitimate passport. Nobody could identify either of the other two."

"Okay," Alvarez said. "I'm going to have my people check out where those guys lived. I want to be sure they're not sick at home."

He sent Han and Tuttle to check on Hansard. The house was empty and there were signs the man had packed his bags. Even his shaving kit was gone. None of his personal effects remained in the barracks, either. Alvarez assumed he'd also run across the border.

Alvarez sent Oliver and Alban to the Camarillo house to check on Blaine. After they jimmied the lock they looked around. No clothing was messed up or out of place. The bath and shaving gear was still in place. They found Gary Blaine in the garage. Hanging from a rafter.

"Come on, Robert. Let's get this poor guy down from there."

They found a note in his pocket. It read: "I can't stand it any more. I never wanted to hurt my country. But Villand and Hansard made me do things I didn't want to do. Stealing security materials so they could give them to someone. They said if I didn't do it he'd tell the Navy I'm queer. I know what that means. Undesirable discharge. And because of that, no good jobs for the rest of my life. This is my only way out."

Oliver heaved a big sigh, tears in his eyes. "I'd like to destroy that note so the Navy will at least send him home like any other guy."

"I don't know. It would be destroying evidence of his crime...."

"I think he's paid enough for crimes he was forced into. Let's give the kid a break. Send him home to be buried proper."

Alban paused for a moment, then nodded, took the note, and set fire to it. He crumpled up the residue to fine ash. "And this way, there's no real proof of his crime. No more than some circumstantial evidence."

Oliver nodded. "Yeah. The kid's had enough grief in his life. We don't need to give him or his family any more in his death. Thanks, Robert."

34. A Room Search

Cape Canaveral

The FBI man who had been watching the OCI team around Canaveral entered his hotel room. He picked up the phone and asked the hotel switchboard to connect him with a long distance operator.

"Good morning. How may I help you?"

He grinned mischievously. "I want to place a long distance call and reverse the charges. Please connect me with...."

He waited for the connection to be made. Then he heard the woman's voice. "Major Skye here."

"Hi, Rena. How are you?"

"I'll be damned. I'm hearing voices from the past. What's up, Evan?"

"Well," Dawes said. "I'm wondering why you guys have the Cape Canaveral area saturated with agents. What's going on?"

"And why would the FBI be interested in that?"

"Because they're starting to get into the way of a case I'm investigating."

"When did you first get down there?"

"About a week ago. We got a call from a maid at the Sand Dollar Inn. She saw a guy who wasn't acting normal and she called us."

"That must be the guy we know as Douglas Voight."

"Yes. His real name is Vasily Zubkin. Anyway, I get down here and I see the place flooded with OCI people. What brought your people down here?"

"We've been following these guys since April. From the New London Submarine Base to a house in Orient, Long Island, to Canaveral. Do you know who the scuba diver down there is? We know him as Allen Dobbins."

"That could be Eduard Pletner. I don't know of any other Russian diver. I'll check him out."

"We have photos of both. We have confirmed identifications. What other news can you give me?"

"One of your operatives got shot yesterday."

"What!?" Skye pause to catch her breath. "Evan, why do you sound so nonchalant about one of my people getting shot up?"

"I didn't say he got shot up," Dawes said. "It was a flesh wound.

"Who was it? Can you describe him to me?"

"He's a Negro. From what I saw, the only Negro agent you have down here."

"That's Rick Morris. He's an intelligence-gathering specialist. How did you know he got shot?"

"I saw him and another OCI guy getting into a car and heading out. I'd guess they were going for medical help. The wounded man was walking. He was laughing and joking with the others. So I figured he wasn't hurt too badly. And, oh, you should train your guys a little better."

"What do you mean?"

"After they left, one of the bad guys tried to break into the place they'd rented to use as an observation post. I scared him away for you. Tell your guys to never leave that kind of place unmanned." Dawes took a deep breath. "Also, the FBI here was able to identify the shooter and the would-be burglar. We're watching them so they don't get away."

They spent a half hour filling each other in on their sides of the investigations.

"You know," Dawes concluded, "OCI is infringing on my investigative domain down here."

"How did you reach that conclusion? We were there a long time before you were."

"Your bailiwick is Navy. When the Russkies moved into this area, the operation expanded way beyond the Navy. All of a sudden it included NASA, the Army, the Air Force. Internal national security. My territory."

They agreed to split the work in Florida.

*   *   *   *

Ford got a call from Skye telling him to gather all the OCI people together and wait for a visitor. Ford, Cobbe, Cisco, Hagen, Morris, and Murray gathered and waited. Dawes showed up.

191

"When I spoke to Major Skye," Dawes began, "we talked about who'd do what on this part of the investigation. Because the Cape Canaveral area includes NASA, Air Force and Army operations as well as Navy, we agreed to split the responsibility for investigating the area."

"What's that mean for us?" Ford asked. The others let him take the lead in what felt like it might be a long question and answer session.

"Skye agreed that I'm the lead here. You guys can investigate any Navy-related operations. But I need to know when you do anything else."

"Like what?"

"Like following a suspect out of the Navy area. Or making an arrest. That includes the diver, now that you have identified him."

"What is the real name of the diver and who is his friend in the Sand Dollar Inn?"

"The diver is Eduard Pletner, a Russian. He calls himself Allen Dobbins here. He is an experienced diver, coming out of the Soviet equivalent of our Underwater Demolition Teams. The FBI has been trying to get him for a couple years," Dawes explained. "The other guy is Douglas Voight. I suspect he's a carrier and someone higher up in this spy ring. His real name is Vasily Zubkin. We believe he is from the KGB, the Soviet secret police."

"Are we... you... going to take these guys down?"

"Eventually. But we want to find out more about them and what they're doing. Like what they're looking for and who they're reporting to."

"We're convinced they're looking for more info on our missile systems."

"Yes. But which ones specifically?" Dawes asked. "That we don't know. And we don't know who they're reporting to, though we do believe their boss is somewhere in the Midwest. Possibly Chicago."

"That's a big city to hide in."

"I agree. Anyway, we're all working together now. Please keep me informed about what you're up to and I'll do the same for you," Dawes promised.

"Should we continue keeping watch of these two guys?" Cobbe asked.

"First, you guys need to move your surveillance location in Cocoa Beach. Once they know where to shoot at you, it's time to move."

"We already have," Ford said.

"I'd like OCI to keep an eye on Pletner, AKA Mr. Dobbins," Dawes continued. "And I need some help watching 'Voight.' I have a hotel room right next to his and listen through the wall with a stethoscope. I'd like some help doing that surveillance as close to a twenty-four-hour-a-day operation as possible. I've also been getting some help from one of the maids at the Sand

Dollar Inn and she may be able to help us some more.

"Also, I need help when these men go out somewhere. I want to watch where they live and when they're gone. Others may try to contact them and we should find out who they are. So let's determine who works where...."

*   *   *   *

Dawes shared his hotel room with Andy Hagen, the helo pilot and with Rick Morris. When the hotel manager realized Morris was also living there, he told Dawes: "Either the Nigra moves out or y'all will have to. Take yer choice."

Dawes was irate. "Don't pull that shit with me!" he commanded. "He's part of my team. He stays with us or we will leave and we'll do everything we can to empty every room here."

"And how would y'all do that?" the manager sneered.

Dawes shrugged. "We could call an exterminator. There are roaches and rats all over the place."

The manager gasped. "That would ruin our business for months."

"You're right. And I'd do it, too. We're here on a police investigation to protect your right to run your business. So we all stay here or nobody does."

"All right. Have it your way," the manager said. He walked away grumbling to himself.

Dawes smiled at his victory, wondering what J. Edgar Hoover would say if he found out about this. His boss wasn't the most willing person to help the cause of integration in the United States.

The next day Voight left his room early and didn't return until late. Andy Hagen was returning from dinner and met him in the elevator. Both were going to the third floor.

"Good evening!" he greeted.

Voight smiled. "Yes it is. It has been a good day all day long."

He had a very slight accent, almost unnoticeable.

"What was so special about it?" Hagen asked.

"Saint Augustine, the oldest city in this country. It was very interesting to visit. I am on vacation here and want to see what there is in this area."

"Where are you from?"

"I'm from Illinois. I plan to go deep-sea fishing later this week. I could not do this in Joliet." They stepped out of the elevator together.

"I hope you have a great time. Catch a big fish! It should be fun."

"I think so." He stopped in front of Room 312. "Good evening to you. Perhaps we shall meet again."

Hagen nodded. As soon as he got into the hotel room he reported his conversation to Dawes. "All right. Since you made contact, you should try to be around whenever he does his tourist bit. Those fishing trips go out pretty early. Right now, I'd say you should read your newspaper in the lobby early every morning."

Hagen agreed.

Dawes then called for help from Ford. "I need help watching the lobby to find out when Voight is going deep sea fishing. Then I want Murray to go into this guy's room and try to evaluate what he has there. Who among your OCI group can pick a lock the best?"

"I'll ask around. And I'll send Murray over right away."

*   *   *   *

Dawes' group at the Sand Dollar Inn kept a close watch on Voight. They kept one man in the lobby at all times. Dawes did bow to the hotel manager's sensitivities by never assigning Morris to the lobby. Whoever was there spent his time reading the complimentary newspaper, doing the crossword, writing letters, and other "normal" lobby activities. Each spent a different length of time so nothing looked regular or planned. They often "changed the watch" by having one man show up early. Both sat for a while doing their activities. Neither man acknowledged the other. Then, at some random period of time, the off-going person would leave.

Hagen was in the lobby when Murray sat down to read the paper.

Both men were there when Voight came down. He turned in his key to the desk. He saw Hagen as he walked toward the front door. He nodded his head in recognition so Hagen said: "Hi! How are you today?"

"Good morning. I am very well, thank you. I am off to go deep-sea fishing!" He sounded like a child with a new toy. Hagen noticed that when he was more excited his slight accent was a bit more noticeable.

"Excited?"

"Yes. Very much so."

"How far out does the fishing boat go?"

"Oh, I think some number of miles," he grinned. "We will try to catch very big fish."

"Well, I wish you good luck. I hope you catch a real trophy."

"Yes, that would be something to show my friends back home," Voight laughed. And he left, very eager to go fishing.

Hagen nodded to Murray. "Tell Dawes. I'm sure he wants to get ready. I'll confirm Voight's fishing trip." He followed the Russian. Came back an hour later. Reported to Dawes. "He went aboard the *Fisher III*. It was full of other people. I'd say seven or eight paying customers. They headed straight out to sea. I could see the boat all the way to the horizon."

"Okay. Let's get to work. Morris, please sit in my room and wait."

Knowing the race situation in this hotel he wondered out loud if Dawes' reasoning was to not let him be seen.

"Not at all. Call Ford and have him send Cobbe or Cisco to sit with the phone. Hagen will call us when the fishing boat's on the way back. When one of those guys shows up, I'd like you to join us in Voight's room next door." A grinning Morris relaxed, willing to baby-sit Dawes' room until relieved.

Hagen returned to the pier to watch for the boat's return.

There was no need to pick the lock. The hotel manager was so happy Dawes did not assign the Negro agent to duty in the lobby that he provided a key.

When they entered Voight's room, Murray carried a box, about a foot in each dimension. He set it down, opened it up, and took out a camera. "This is the newest instant camera made by Polaroid. It's not yet on the market. They said in another year or so. The pictures come out and are developed in minutes all by themselves. Sometimes they aren't as clear as I'd like, but this should help us considerably." The agents searched every inch.

They took photos of every place they searched. He used the "instant" photos to show how the closet was arranged so they could put it back the same way they found it.

Suddenly there was a knock on the door. Everyone froze. The three men drew their weapons and waited, looking at each other, trying to decide what to do next.

35. Still Stumped

Great Lakes

"Hello! Is this Major Rena Skye of the United States Navy's Office of Criminal Investigation?" asked an unfamiliar voice.

"Yes it is...."

"I'm Sergeant Major James Courtland. I'm an inspector in the Border Integrity Program of the Royal Canadian Mounted Police. My office is located in Vancouver, British Columbia. We've been working with the CBSA, the Canadian Border Services Agency, to try to find some individuals for whom your OCI issued an alert. A man named Robert Hansard and another named Roy Villand. Am I speaking to the correct party?"

"Yes you are. How can I help you?"

"I'm calling to bring you up to date on our search."

"Have you found Hansard and Villand?"

He cleared his throat. "Regrettably, no. Not yet. But we have expanded the force assigned to the search. We are watching the whole western border. And searching for them in British Columbia, Yukon, Alberta, Saskatchewan, and large portions of the Northwest Territories."

"Well, please keep me updated, will you?"

"Certainly. And could I ask for a favor?"

"Of course. How can we help?"

"Do you have a set of high quality photographs you could send us? Shots from front, the sides, and at various angles. I know this is a lot to ask, but it could help us tremendously. Can you get all those for us?"

"I don't know if we can get all the angles, but I'll have my people gather what they can. Where should I send them?"

After he gave her his address and fax number, Rena hung up her phone. She sat there and rubbed her eyes. Frowned. Planted her elbows on her desk. Put her head in her hands. Wondered: "Did Hansard and Villand go to Vancouver or was Vancouver a code word for someplace else? It could even be a code for a location in the opposite direction. In Mexico." She moaned. "Can't anything ever be easy?"

Then she called Alvarez to have him fax the desired photos to Vancouver.

* * * *

It was early Sunday Morning. Rena drove me to the FT school barracks because I had the duty. I was in my seaman's uniform. She was in her Marine officer's uniform. "Anyone ever ask you what you, a seaman, are doing with a Marine officer?"

"Yep."

"How do you explain it?" she asked.

"I tell them you're my sister."

"Sister? So you live with your sister?"

"Sure. We have separate bedrooms, don't we?"

She punched my arm. "No! We don't. Unless you want it that way!"

"Not at all, my love. Gotta run, now, or I'll be late." I kissed her cheek and grinned. "Bye, Sis! Thanks for the ride. See you tomorrow."

She drove away, shaking her head.

* * * *

Rena was in her office again, hoping to figure out how all the information about this case fit together. She sat at her desk, twirling her hair, thinking. They were getting signals from every direction. There seemed to be pockets of spies in a network throughout the U.S.

Messages were going to the Saint Louis area from all over the country. They had detected signals from Idaho to Nebraska to Texas. And other signals from Cleveland. And from Atlanta to Memphis. They all seemed to go to Saint Louis.

She had no idea what all these messages were saying. To best evaluate what was going on she needed to see each individual message. She picked up the phone and talked to every local leader she had, or left messages for them. She ordered every recording of every message to be sent to her office.

And then she didn't know what she'd do if they were all in a code OCI didn't know or even if they were in Russian.

* * * *

Rena worked all weekend and she was tired. Hitting her head against a brick wall. Almost burned out. She ambled to the office coffeepot to get her third refill. Commander Fasano was there, also refilling his cup. He took a sip and shook his head. "I drink way too much of this stuff."

"At least it's decent coffee. Not like what you get in the mess hall."

"I agree. How's your case going?"

"We get some progress in fits and starts." She stopped to think for a moment. "I have a single Russian-speaking operative. And that's Eric. But he's busy with school. Would it be possible to get another Russian speaker?"

"Is a woman all right?"

She grinned. "She might be better than a man. There could be places to use her where I couldn't use Eric."

"Good. I think I know of someone who's available. I'll get back to you as soon as I can."

36. A Suspect Travels

Cape Canaveral

Evan Dawes and some of the OCI people were inspecting Voight's hotel room at the Sand Dollar Inn. When they heard a knock on the room's door, all three men drew their weapons and waited for a moment. Dawes motioned for the crew to put their weapons away. "It's probably Maria, the maid."

He opened the door. Looked into the hall and nodded. Then he turned to the crew and grinned. "It's Maria." He turned back to the maid. "Are you here to clean the room?"

She nodded.

"Would you please return later to do this room?"

"Certainly," she whispered.

"Thank you. I'll let you know when we're done here."

The maid nodded and turned to go to the next room.

The OCI crew continued their work. They found Voight's briefcase hidden under the spare blankets in the closet. Murray picked the lock. There were photos and reports about the missiles on the Cape Canaveral launch complexes. They photographed and inventoried everything there. Then they returned all the items, re-locked the briefcase and put it back under the blankets. They put everything else back together so the room looked like it had been when Voight departed.

Hagen, who had remained at the pier until he saw the boat returning, called Dawes's room.

The crew was putting the final touches on Voight's room when the call came in. Cisco came over from the FBI man's room and told them the

Russian's fishing boat was back.

"No problem," Dawes said. "We're pulling out now."

They closed the door behind them. Dawes turned to Murray. "Go find Maria. Tell her we're done and she can return to clean the place. But also tell her she'll have to hurry because he's on the way back."

*   *   *   *

Ford and Cobbe ate supper at the Royal Baby's Bar and Grill. The waitress smiled at Ford. Once again, he inventoried all her good points: pitch-black hair, dark flashing eyes, a deep tan complexion. Her figure wasn't anything to sneeze at, either. She looked Indian to him and he thought she was beautiful. He smiled back. "Hi! Where are you from?"

"Right here, honey. Floridian, born and bred." She tilted her head and examined him a bit more closely. "How 'bout you?"

"Maine and New Hampshire."

"Yankee, huh?"

"Not completely. Part Native."

Ford took a bite of his food.

"Oh?" the waitress said. "Your great-great-great-grandma was a Cherokee princess?"

Ford almost snorted his food through his nose. "Oh, excuse me! Your comment took me by surprise. I'm English, Acadian French and Abnaki. No princesses. Indian folks didn't have princesses."

"I know. I'm also Indian."

"What tribe?"

"Miccosukee. We're a little west of Miami."

"How come you aren't working down there? Aren't you enrolled?"

"Nope. The Miccosukee enroll you if your mother was from the tribe. My father was from there but…." She lowered her voice. "My mother was Negro. Indians and runaway slaves mixed a lot here in the South."

Ford realized the young woman lowered her voice so she wouldn't trip any racist alarms in the room. She wanted to keep her job without causing trouble.

"What's your name?" Ford asked.

"Emily. Emily Mangrove."

"I'm Len Ford." He took a deep breath, hoping for an affirmative answer to his next question. "Would you go out with me, sometime?"

She tilted her head again and looked at him. "You like to dance?"

He nodded.

"What kind?"

"I do rock'n'roll and Indian. Fancy dancing, but as I get older I wind up opting for men's traditional more and more. I have to be in better shape than this for the fancy steps."

She grinned. "You have a date. If you can do it, we can go down home and do some of our dancing. Otherwise we can make the local scene. When you want to get together?"

"Right now my work is taking almost all my time. But I'll try to get through in a week or two. Can I have your phone number?"

"You sure can, honey." She gave it to him with a knowing smile.

Cobbe watched her walk away. He nodded his head. "You may have just hit a home run, Len."

"Hope so. But right now, we better get to work."

There was little or no activity out on the Cape that night. The diver came out; Ford saw him around the launch complexes. Sitting in his hiding place, Ford munched on a box of cookies, and thought: *Dobbins can't be getting much in the dark of the night unless he has very expensive superb German camera and lenses. Even when he's out in a full moon, like tonight. And from what I can see, he doesn't have such equipment. All he'd see anyway were missiles at gantries, fueling. He might watch a blast off from out in the ocean during the day. The missiles at the gantries now don't even have any panels off. Nothing's uncovered. He might check almost every day because he has no idea what the launch schedules are and he feels he might be lucky and stumble onto something.*

Ford shook his head and finished a sandwich, then felt around in his pack for something else. *I must stop all this eating*, he thought. *I know I'm gaining weight. And I'll have to run more than normal through the mountains back home.* He grinned and thought: *Or down in the Everglades somewhere.*

*   *   *   *

Douglas Voight took another trip. Ryan Murray followed him to the place where the tour started. He returned and reported to Dawes. "This time he's going up to Merritt Island Nature Preserve."

"Why is he doing all this touristy stuff?" Hagen asked.

"The twenty-one thousand dollar question." Dawes said drily. "I wish I knew. But all we can do is wait and watch."

"What if he's meeting someone this time?" Rick Morris asked. "I'd think it would be easy to slip away from the crowd...."

201

Murray rubbed his chin. "What if he's handing off bits of intelligence?"

"I can get the helo and follow him," Hagen offered.

"Where is this place? This nature preserve?"

"This side of Oak Hill, west of Mosquito Lagoon. It kind of borders on the NASA Space Center."

"Isn't it too late to follow him now?"

"I don't know. But the helo pad is on the way to there. And all he'd know is there's another aircraft flying around a military base."

"All right. Give it a try."

Hagen rushed out to get his helo going. He returned hours later.

"I could see him at times," Hagen reported. "From what I could tell, he stayed with the crowd. If he passed anything on, it was very stealthy and to someone right next to him."

"So, then, I wonder why the hell he's going to all these places."

"Perhaps he *is* on vacation...."

Dawes shook his head. "I don't believe it. Keep in mind all the photos and descriptions of Cape Canaveral he's storing in his closet. And he's in contact with the diver who takes notes and photos at the Cape. And I can't believe someone in this business goes sightseeing for the hell of it. It must be some part of his plan...."

*   *   *   *

Evan Dawes sat on his hotel room bed, leaning his back against the wall. He was using his stethoscope, ear tips in place and the diaphragm against the wall behind him. He hoped to get some clue as to what Voight was up to.

The FBI agent jumped when there was a soft knock on his door. He ripped the stethoscope off and shoved it under his pillow. Answered the door. Maria, the maid, stood outside, looking up and down the hall. She scampered into the room. Dawes closed the door.

"What's the matter?" he asked.

"I don't want anyone to see me talking to you like this. Or to hear what I'm going to say."

"Why?"

"I could get fired for talking to a guest about another guest. The man in the next room, he's checking out this morning."

"Do you know where he's going?"

"I heard him say something about Chicago."

"To you?"

202

"Oh, no. I was downstairs checking on what rooms were rented during the night. I overheard him talking to the concierge at the front desk. Asking him about flights to Chicago."

"Did he mention where he was going? What hotel. What part of the city."

"No. Not that I heard."

"Okay, thanks."

"Does that help?"

"I don't know. We'll see." He opened the door and looked down the hall in both directions. "You can go. There's nobody in the halls."

Maria hurried out. Dawes returned to his stethoscope. He heard noises like somebody packing. Voight was, indeed, preparing to leave. While he listened, Hagen came in from breakfast. "Andy, listen here for a while. I have to get some things together. He's leaving and I'm going to try to follow him."

Dawes scurried around packing while Hagen listened. "Andy, there are some photos and papers in the dresser drawer, there. One of you guys take them to the police station right away. Have them send those over their facsimile machine to Rena and to the FBI office in Chicago. Have both of them double-check the identities. And see if they can find out where Voight might be going in Chicago...."

"Evan, I heard the door slam shut."

"Main or closet door?"

"It sounded heavy. Must have been the room door."

"Damn! Hope I can get what I'm missing on the way." He closed his suitcase and rushed out the door. He reached the lobby while Voight was at the front desk, holding out his room key.

The concierge took the key and asked: "Well, Mr. Voight, are you going on another sight-seeing trip today."

"No. I need to check out. I must return home today. There is a problem at work for which they need my presence."

Something clicked for Dawes. *So, that's what all the tourist trips were about,* he thought. *Get any watchers used to him going out for a whole day at a time. If we thought he was going on another side trip, he'd be out of our grasp. I'm glad Maria warned us.*

Dawes decided not to check out. There were still the OCI agents in the room; they could do it later. He followed Voight west to the train station in Orlando. The man walked to a ticket window and picked up his reserved ticket. When he left, Dawes went to the same window. Flashed his FBI badge and identification. "What was that guy's name?"

"Douglas Voight," the attendant replied.

"And where was his ticket to?"

"It was a ticket to Chicago."

"Did he happen to say where he would be staying in Chicago?"

"No, sir."

"Okay. Give me a ticket for Chicago on the same train."

The attendant prepared the ticket and handed it through the window. "There you are, sir. Here's the track number and there's the departure time. Have a good trip, sir."

"Thanks." Dawes walked to a row of phones along the wall. He had the operator get him Rena's number.

"Major Skye."

"Hi, Rena. Evan here. I'm taking a train to Chicago to follow one of the guys we were watching around Cape Canaveral. Douglas Voight. Your guys here are going to send you information and photos by police facsimile."

"What're you going to do in Chicago? Do you need any help?"

"I don't know yet. The FBI is there, too, you know."

"Yes, Evan, I know," Skye said. "But the more operatives you have, the better the chance of success."

"You're right. And we have some challenging tasks to do."

"Like what?"

"You'll get photos of Voight and Allen Dobbins. The FBI office in Chicago will also get the photos," Dawes said. "We're going to have to find everything we can about Voight's business up there."

"I'll see what else I can do to help. Stay in touch, Evan."

"Will do, Rena. As soon as I figure out what we need. We'll talk later. Bye." As soon as Dawes hung up he called the Chicago FBI office. "You guys will be getting some photos of a Douglas Voight. He's on his way up there by train. When he arrives, find him and follow him. Check all the hotels. Find where he's going. Where he's going to stay or where he lives. And where he works or who he meets there."

"Will do, Agent Dawes. Are you coming up here, too?"

"Damn right I am. I believe this guy is a Communist spy. I want to get him."

Dawes hung up and walked to the waiting room. While waiting to board the train he noticed the segregated water fountains. One was a stainless steel refrigerated water cooler labeled "Whites Only." The other was a plain porcelain drinking fountain, supplied by a water pipe going to the back of the cooler. The porcelain fountain was labeled "Colored." He thought he knew what would happen if a Negro dared to drink from the "white" fountain. He wondered what would happen if a white drank from the "colored" fountain.

Then he thought how nice and fast police work was when they used the facsimile devices. The facsimile was an optical scanning device. The original was put on a spinning drum with a thin, bright light shining on it. The original reflected the light. The reflections varied in intensity because of the light and dark parts of the document. A sensor detected these variations, converted them to sound, and sent across the phone line.

At the receiving end, the equipment reversed the process. The receiver's drawing device duplicated the original image on a blank sheet of paper, also on a rotating drum. The price of these facsimile devices was very expensive. But the FBI and the larger police departments had a real need of them to transmit instant crime-fighting information across the country when necessary. Much faster than the mail.

Dawes carried his suitcase along the waiting train. He kept far enough back from Voight so it would not be obvious that he was following the man. When Voight got on the train, Dawes waited a while before climbing onto the same car. He turned left into the hallway of the car and passed the washroom. He entered the seating area. Voight faced him, sitting in the middle of the car. Dawes walked past him without making any eye contact. He took a seat to the rear of the car.

He sat back and let himself relax.

He watched the town of Orlando go by as the train pulled out of the station. Soon they were in the countryside. Passing through orange and grapefruit groves. He enjoyed the scenery. There was no reason not to. Voight wasn't going anyplace.

37. Montaigne Wakes Up

Great Lakes

"Major Rena Skye."

A slightly familiar voice spoke into her ear. "Is this the Office of Criminal Investigation of the U. S. Navy?"

"Yes it is. How can I help you?"

"I am Sergeant Major James Courtland, an inspector in the Border Integrity Program of the Royal Canadian Mounted Police. My office is located in Vancouver, British Columbia. We've been working with the Canadian Border Services Agency to try to find two individuals for whom your OCI issued an alert. Men named Robert Hansard and Roy Villand. I believe we spoke earlier about looking for these men."

"Yes we did. I'm the one who requested Canada to look for them. Did you find them?"

"Indeed, we did. Some Mounties found Hansard hiding out in Regina, Saskatchewan, under an alias. The photographs you sent us let us make a positive identification. We are now holding him in Vancouver. I'm curious, what is the man accused of?"

"He is a sailor in the U. S. Navy. We plan to court martial him on a charge of espionage."

"A spy, eh? How soon can you send people here to take charge of him?"

"In a day or so. As early as tomorrow, if we can make good flight connections. What address should I tell my people to go to?"

The Mountie told her.

"And what about Villand?"

206

"Oh, yes. I regret to inform you, Mr. Villand decided to try to run from us. He was in the Canadian Rockies at the time. He drove quite fast and had an accident. He ran off the highway. His car fell about a thousand feet before hitting solid rock. I'm afraid the man died on us, about which I feel terrible."

"What did you do with the body?"

"We have it in a local morgue. We can send it to you if you desire...."

"But he is dead?"

"Yes ma'am. Certifiably."

"Then can you send me a death certificate? And dispose of the body as you would with a John Doe?"

"I can send you a death certificate. But we would prefer to ship the body back to the States. Have you an address to which we could send it?"

"Certainly. Send it to the OCI Laboratory, Great Lakes, Illinois."

"Thank you, ma'am. Do you have any other questions or needs?"

"No thank you, Sergeant Major. Thanks for all your help. I'll get some men to Vancouver as soon as possible to take Hansard into custody."

As soon as their conversation was finished, Rena called Tony.

"OCI, Alvarez speaking."

"Tony, this is Rena. A Mountie inspector in Vancouver by the name of James Courtland called me a few minutes ago. They found Hansard and are holding him for us. How soon can you and Glenn get going to Canada?"

"We'll get the first flight out. Do you think the two of us will be enough?"

"Don't you?"

Alvarez was silent for a few moments. "Yeah, I think we can handle it, as long as we aren't both asleep at the same time. We'll need to watch him like a hawk. We know he'll try to run again if he thinks he can...."

"Sounds good. And give the Mounties a sincere 'Thank you' from OCI."

"Will do. I'll call you as soon as we have him locked up."

"Bring him here, to Lakes. I want him in the brig here, where we have a lot more people to watch him."

"Will do. See you soon."

*   *   *   *

Rena mulled over a possibility. The FBI was involved in this operation now. She wondered if Evan Dawes was going to ask for more OCI help. She wondered who would be best to send to him.

She thought of the great job Steven Montaigne did for her in Saint Louis. But he had been severely beaten some time ago. He'd been in a coma for a long time over at Hospitalside. He wasn't one of her super secret agents. And he wasn't even available yet. The doctors were certain he was going to pull through his present situation. Skye believed she could use him again if and when he was able to work.

And from Tony Alvarez's reports, Dirk Fladeboe had done a very good job undercover in Port Hueneme. She nodded again. She called the appropriate senior officer and persuaded him to send her Fladeboe on TAD, Temporary Additional Duty.

Now, who else could I get? She thought. *Alvarez's radio tracking teams are done tracing the signals all the way to Saint Louis. Maybe he could let one of those guys go.*

She telephoned Tony. The duty yeoman answered. "Is Alvarez back from Canada yet?"

"No, ma'am. He and Oliver are due back in an hour or so."

"Okay. Have him call me as soon as he gets in."

"Yes, ma'am."

Tony called two hours later. "Hi! You got Hansard safely locked up?"

"Definitely. He's in the brig here with a double guard."

"Good job," Rena said. "Now, I need your help on another matter."

"Sure, what can I do for you?"

"Are you guys done with the radio signal tracking?"

"Yeah, I think so."

"Can you send a couple guys to help me here?"

"Sure. I can send Glenn Oliver and Tom Morelos, and I'll have them bring Hansard to you at Lakes. How's that?"

"Sounds good."

"How soon do you need them?"

"ASAP."

"They'll be on the way in a couple hours," Alvarez reassured his boss.

Rena was pleased. Now if Dawes needed them, she would be able to send Fladeboe and one of the others to help.

Meanwhile, she asked Chaské to investigate the location of the New Horizon office and what janitorial service they used in their building. She thought perhaps she could persuade the cleaning company to put a couple of her agents on the cleaning crew. If Dawes needed the help.

*   *   *   *

Skye's phone rang. She sighed and rolled her eyes as she reached out to answer it. "Skye here."

"Are you Major Rena Skye?"

"Yes I am."

"I'm Robert Davis, one of the doctors caring for a Steven Montaigne. We have your name as the contact person for Mr. Montaigne."

"I hope it hasn't changed for the worse...?"

"Oh, no," Davis said. "On the contrary, he woke up a couple days ago."

"Why didn't you contact me then?"

"When people come out of a coma, especially a long one, they come out quite slowly. We've been evaluating his condition all morning. Are you a relative of Mr. Montaigne's?"

"No, I'm his commanding officer. From your calm voice, I'd say Steven's condition is pretty good."

"Certainly. You may visit him if you want to. But please realize, he's going to act a bit out of it and not all there. Given what I've seen the past couple days I think he will improve a lot over time."

"I'll be right over."

Dr. Davis met her outside Montaigne's room. They entered the room together. Skye approached the bed slowly. The patient looked asleep.

"Is he awake?" Skye asked the doctor.

He nodded. "On and off. Which is normal."

Montaigne opened his eyes for a few seconds. "Steven," Rena said, "how *are* you?"

He looked at her through dropping eyelids. "Tired. Been sleeping," he mumbled. "I remember waking up.... Kind of.... They're helping...."

Rena patted his hand. She stood and faced the doctor. "Can we talk outside?"

He nodded and they moved into the hall.

"Can you tell me how soon he'll return to normal?"

"That's impossible to say. People coming out of a long coma have their own schedule. It could be a few days. It could be never. All we can do is wait."

She sighed. "This whole case we're working on is hurry up and wait. I'll return tomorrow. I need to find out every detail of what happened to him."

"I can tell you a little bit. He was beaten quite viciously. And it's my guess, whoever was doing the beating continued after he lost consciousness. Give him time to recover at his own pace. And realize a full recovery may never happen. But even if he does recovery completely, he might have some physical or psychological problems, in any combination. Don't count on any rapid or complete recovery and you may be pleased at the result."

"You don't sound very hopeful."

"Let's call it being cautious. I've seen too many of these cases to be any other way."

38. New Plans

Great Lakes

Rena interviewed Meredith Tarsa, a civilian contract agent sent over by Commander Fasano. This was the result of Rena's request for an additional Russian speaker.

"Meredith, I....

"Please, everyone calls me Merry...."

"Okay. Merry, tell me about your background."

"My parents grew up in Hungary. Because of the Iron Curtain, they also learned to speak Russian. I grew up speaking both languages at home."

"How did you get out of Hungary?"

"We left during the revolution in 1956. My mother, father and two brothers. My parents saw that the Russians and the Hungarian Communists had pulled a lot of guards off the borders to quell the rebellion. They knew it would still be tricky, but we left our house in the middle of the night and left the country."

"So your father didn't think the revolution would be successful?"

"He hoped it would be and we stayed in Austria until it failed completely. Then we moved on."

"How did you get out of the country?"

"We went through a small town on the western border, the Austrian border. My father told anyone who stopped us that we were trying to be safe from the fighting, and we were going to visit relatives in Szombathely until the government could win and we could return home."

"And the police allowed you to do it?"

"Yes. My father's brother actually did live there and Dad had some letters from Uncle Enre. So he could prove he had relatives where we'd be 'safe.'"

"Did you actually go to your uncle's house?"

"Oh yes," she said with a grin. "We picked up their family and continued on to Austria, which was a few kilometers to the west. Both families left Szombathely at two in the morning. We were out of Hungary and safe in a very short time. Then, when the revolution was suppressed, we came to America as refugees. We all changed our names to American names. They renamed me and gave me my nickname. Meredith became my official name when we became citizens. We settled in Saint Louis, Missouri. My family still lives there."

"You learned English very well. I don't hear any accent at all."

"I was young and watched lots of television. I imitated what I heard, too. That's how I practiced. And with a name like mine, nobody ever suspects I'm fluent in two other languages."

"Could be invaluable." Rena paused for a couple seconds. "Are you single?"

Merry hesitated for a second before she replied: "Yes."

Rena noticed a look in the young woman's eyes. She got a distinct impression Merry was lying. So she decided to push the issue a bit. "Why? Why are you still single, a pretty young woman like you?"

Merry shrugged: "I haven't found the right guy yet."

"Good," Rena said. She didn't know why, but her thoughts jumped back to when she first met Laura Jaf in Virginia Beach. Laura gave her the impression of being "uppity," and since then Jennie made comments about Laura's arrogance, her attitude of "her against the world." It turned out to be pretty accurate. Rena did not want to get another operative like Laura. So now was the time for a test. "Would you be willing to take up with a guy if an investigation needed you to?"

"What do you mean by 'take up with'?" Merry looked at her questioningly. "Are you asking about my morals?"

"I guess I'm trying to figure out what I can ask you to do on an investigation other than speak Russian."

"What are you trying to ask me?"

"There may be circumstances where it would be better to assign a single woman. I already have some operatives whose relationships might get hurt if I had to ask them to get close, shall we say, to someone we're investigating. Would you be willing to sleep with a guy if it made success on an assignment easier?"

Meredith swallowed with some difficulty and replied in a low voice: "Yes."

Rena sat and looked at the other woman for a long moment.

"What? Is there a problem?" Merry asked.

"I'm trying to figure out how and where to assign you."

"So, are you hiring me?"

Rena nodded. But she still had doubts.

*　　*　　*　　*

Rena sat down at her desk to begin the day's work. Her eye caught a newspaper headline on another desk:

John Glenn First American in Orbit.

We might be catching up to the Russians. It's about time. I know we have the technical ability.... Well. Back to work.

She glanced over the piles of papers on her desk. She caught sight of the crossword puzzle and the photos of the driver's hand on the road.

"Oh, yes, that thing," she mumbled to herself.

Then her eye caught a diagram she'd drawn hoping to figure out where the spy headquarters were in Saint Louis. They had been able to trace the radio signals to the south side of the city, but had not been able to find the exact location of their origin. They had surrounded St. Louis to search for the address of the location sending and receiving the radio signals. But they didn't get any better results than a location somewhere in a two-block radius.

We might have to try something different, she thought. *But what? I could send someone down to Saint Louis. To do what? To try to find the Russians?*

"Yeah, right," she mumbled. "And how the hell could they do *that*?"

*　　*　　*　　*

Skye's phone rang. *It seems half my job is answering this damned phone...,* she thought. She sighed and reached out to answer it. "Skye here."

It was Dr. Davis. "Steven has been making remarkable progress lately. I think you could come over and interview him. But don't push too much."

When she got to the hospital, Rena tried to reduce the pressure on her agent by asking Montaigne what he remembered. Then she asked a few questions to clarify his responses.

"I was following this guy.... I can't remember his name right now...."

"Arkady Badurov," Rena reminded him.

"Yeah. That's his name. I missed him a few times... when he came out of a theater…. This, as soon as he ran out the stage door… and he got into his car…, I followed him…. But his driver somehow knew I was following them…."

"What makes you say that?"

"Because…." He thought for a minute. "He drove all over town trying to shake me. They made two stops…. The first was at a bar called… let's see, it's name has a bunch of Zs in it…. I don't know…. The second place had a name like it was a winner, but it was a person's name."

Rena thought for a moment. "A name like a winner. Hmmm. Victor?"

"Yeah, that's it. Club Viktor…. But the guy wasn't in the car…. At the second place, the guy was already gone…. He must have gotten out at the first place. So… I returned to the first place. I went in to order a drink.

"The waitress came over and asked me something in Russian…. I told her I was sorry but I didn't speak Russian…. Then the bouncer came over and told me to leave. The place was a private club… and they don't let anyone in unless they are Russian…. Nobody else…. They pushed me right out the door…." He took a deep breath and shook his head. "I'm sorry, Rena…. But I'm so tired I can't continue."

Skye patted his hand. "You did fine, Steven. Just fine."

*　　*　　*　　*

Rena came up with a plan to send people to Saint Louis, though she was concerned about their safety. She suspected the Russians had given Montaigne his severe beating, though she had no corroboration other than logic.

If true, it suggested that any of her male operatives would receive the same treatment if they didn't speak Russian. Then she thought of sending the Waves down there…. The Russian men might be friendlier toward women they could conceive of as targets of their attention. Jennie could stay in the background, watch over them and hopefully get help if needed.

As she drew up her plans for sending the women down there, Rena's mind worked overtime. Her intuition screamed at her about security and the possibility of her people being compromised. One thing in particular bothered her. She was pretty sure of the loyalty of the three waves. But there was a slight chance…. Each one of them had exhibited some kind of a worrisome behavior.

Rena decided it would be best to cover all possibilities. She picked up her phone and dialed the telephone operations office for the Great Lakes Naval Base.

"Base Communications, Brownleigh speaking."

Rena identified herself, then said: "I need to track calls made from Lakes to off-base locations."

"That's a big job. Where would you expect the caller might be?"

Rena sighed. "Well, I wouldn't expect calls to be made from any barracks. Nor from any of three or four work locations. Public phones would be the most likely…."

"So you want us to put a bug on all public telephones on this humongous base?"

"I don't need to bug the phones. I need to track where the calls are going."

"What are you looking for?"

"I want to know about calls from here to off-base locations."

"Any place specifically?"

She thought for a moment. "Yes. In or near Saint Louis, Missouri. Within a hundred mile radius?"

There was silence on the line for a full thirty seconds before Brownleigh replied. "You know, Major Skye, I think I may be able to help you."

"How soon could you have it set up?"

"A few days. I'll let you know when it's done."

"Thanks a million, Mr. Brownleigh."

After she hung up the phone, Rena sat at her desk mulling over the plan she wanted to put into place.

*　　*　　*　　*

The next day, Rena talked with Montaigne again.

Montaigne said he visited the bar that had a bunch of Zs in its name. He tried to order a drink again. He remembered three Russians coming up behind him. Two of them grabbed him by the arms and forced him out the back door.

"One man said: 'We told you to get out of our private club.' A second guy said: 'And we want you to stay out.' The third man, who was standing in front of me, said: 'Yes. We do not like people who follow us all over and put their nose in our business. Now we will be sure you will not be able to return.'

"He hit me in the stomach. When I doubled over in pain, he threw a roundhouse punch to my head. I somewhat remember my head snapping to the side. Then I lost consciousness. The doctors here told me I had been kicked in the ribs, legs and head. They said they could tell from the cracked bones and the black-and-blue marks."

*　　*　　*　　*

Montaigne was released from the hospital. He stopped in at the office. He asked Skye to bring him up to date on the case. After a few hours, they took a coffee break. They met Chaské at the coffee pot.

"Tell me, Chaské," Steven asked. "How did you get this job with OCI?"

Chaské rubbed his forehead as he thought. "After my time in the Army, I dragged myself way down."

"What do you mean?"

"I drank heavily. Used drugs. Cocaine, some heroin."

"Why?"

"If you'd seen the carnage I saw, you would've gone off the deep end, too."

Steven frowned in thought. "But thousands of guys saw events like those. Why didn't they all go bonkers?"

"I don' know. They might not have seen the same kind of slaughter. Maybe they weren't on the front lines as long as I was. I just don't know," Chaské said, shaking his head. "Same as I don't know for sure why I bounced back as fast as I did, while some of the other guys are still institutionalized."

"How were you able to bounce back?"

He explained how the Lakota holy men and the pipe, sweat lodge and sun dance saved him. Gave him a reason to live, a reason to come back to normal. "It's gentle but strong. And the whole family helped. But others beside Lakota folks helped me. An old army buddy worked wonders. An Ojibwe guy, actually, name of Sammy Canoe. He visited me every once in a while through those years. He was the one who persuaded me to turn to the pipe for healin'. Maybe even more than my family did, because he'd been through the same crap I had. He had problems, too, for a while, and his tradition, Midéwewin, saved him."

"So what happened after you got better?"

Chaské smiled. "I got a free college education through the GI Bill. Sammy still had contacts in the military. After I graduated with a degree in sociological research, he told me he'd heard about some jobs in the intelligence community, and one or two of them might be right down my alley. One was. And here I am. How'd you get started in this business?"

"As a kid I always wanted to be a cop," Steven said. "We had enough money to send me to college, where I majored in criminology."

"Sounds like Rena," Chaské observed.

"The rest was a natural progression. I looked for a job. The federal position had better medical and retirement plans. I'd graduated magna cum laude. So I was invited in by OCI and I joined up."

They finished their coffee. Rena looked at Montaigne. "All right, Steven. You're up-to-date now. But you still need more rest. What are you doing here? Go home and rest for a week or two."

"I have nobody at home and I'd go stir crazy. So I thought I'd come here and visit."

"Well, I want you to go home for a few days, at least. Sleep a lot. Sleep is a good healer. When you come back, we'll see what we can give you to do that's not too strenuous."

Chaské nudged him. "She's the boss. Better do what she says."

Montaigne sighed as he stood up. "I guess so. If I watch the soap operas on TV, I'll fall asleep instantly. There's one way to get a lot of rest. See you in a few days."

* * * *

"Hi, Rena."

The woman turned to see Glenn Oliver and Tom Morelos. Both had big smiles on their faces. "We've delivered the traitor."

"Where'd you take him?"

"We asked Commander Fasano where he wanted the guy. He assigned a couple other agents to take him to the brig," Glenn said.

Tom held out a paper attesting to the imprisonment of the spy. "Signed, sealed and delivered. Here's the paperwork."

Skye took the document, looked it over, and filed it in her desk. "Thank you. That was quick work. How'd you two like to stick around here for a while?"

"Sounds good to me," Glenn chuckled. "You might want to ask Jennie if she wants me to…. But I don' know about Tom here."

"Whatever you need me to do, Major."

"I'd like to keep you here for back-up. Just in case…."

"Yes ma'am," Morelos said.

"Great. Take a day or two off. Be back here Monday morning."

"Thank you, boss! Where's Jennie?"

Rena pointed in the direction of the Waves' desks. Glenn raced off, smiling broadly.

"Well," Morelos said. "He might not get much sleep for a while. But I think I'll find a place to stay and catch up on my shut-eye."

Skye pointed again. "Yeoman McCluskey, there, will set you up in the barracks."

When Glenn came back to the office the following Monday, I spent my whole lunch break interviewing him. In fact, I spent my lunch hours all week talking to him, to get the full story on the California operations and the tracking the radio signals. He helped me get a lot of this story right.

*   *   *   *

It was Friday afternoon. I got off school early so I stopped off at the OCI office. I kissed my true love, then slouched in a nearby chair. I was ready to go home for the weekend, or as much of it as Rena's work would let her have.

She sat and stared at the crossword puzzle, which had been buried under papers for way too long and which she'd rediscovered earlier that day. She sat there with a big frown on her face, deep in thought. "I can feel it. This damn puzzle is important," she grumbled. "Why can't I see what it's trying to tell us? And then the driver wrote on the road in his own blood.... We know he was trying to write 6-DOWN. The puzzle answer was 'Stalin.' The solitary common point is the play Jennings was in."

"So far as we know," I commented.

"Yeah. And Montaigne found 'Stalin.' A guy named Arkady Badurov. Now we have to find him, track him down, determine if Badurov is the real killer, and arrest him."

"How're you going to do that?"

"A plan's been running around in my head."

When she stopped talking, I asked: "What're you thinking about doing?"

"I'm not ready yet. Tell you later."

"Okay, let's go home...."

Rena checked her watch: "I can't. Not this early. It's 1500 now and I should go over these things again. You go on. I'll be home as soon as I can."

I grinned. "OK. I'll be waiting...."

She smiled sweetly. "How about with supper."

"I'll take the car. Call me when you want me to pick you up."

At home, I started to make supper. Tango thought I was fixing him some kind of special treat. He stood on his hind legs, front feet against the top of the counter, to "help" me. I had to drag him into the living room to get him out of my way, a pretty vigorous job with a Saint Bernard who doesn't want to move. With a lot of effort and some harsh commands I got him to stay. I had to repeat the process a few times, but I eventually got some supper fixed. Then he stayed away when he tried to smell the food on the stove and realized how hot it was.

When Rena called, I performed my magic trick of stuffing the meal in the oven so the dog couldn't get to it. By the time Rena and I got home, the meal had cooled, but not much. With a bit of re-heating, we enjoyed our supper together.

* * * *

Rena sat thinking about the present situation and the personnel she had available. She wanted to initiate a plan to send the Waves to Saint Louis and have them try to contact the Russian men. She couldn't conceive of horny men doing the same kind of damage to pretty ladies that they did to Montaigne. So they should be safer than he'd been.

But she still had doubts about safety. And about the loyalty of the people she would have to use. She twisted her hair around her fingers as she reviewed her options.

The Russians know about our group. Commander Blount notified me about that recently…. I'm sending my people into grave danger, more than ever since we have a Russian spy in our midst…. And we know they will get violent if they suspect someone is investigating them.

She thought of Laura Jaf's arrogance. Rena had noticed it from their very first meeting in Norfolk. She had no idea what it was about. But it was there. Was she hiding something?

And Rena wondered how committed Ruth Gardner was. She remembered that Ruth wanted to quit when the last case began to get tough, after two people died. Ruth thought the deaths were all her fault. They weren't, but she couldn't see it.

And then Meredith Tarsa's family was from Saint Louis, and originally from Communist Hungary. Right now, this was enough to put some nagging doubt in the back of Skye's mind. And Tarsa spoke fluent Russian. But was she reliable? The thought occurred to Rena that Merry might be the sleeper who had gotten into the intelligence community to wait for the right moment. Merry's shyness further complicated the situation. She seemed to be hiding something during her interview. Was she hiding something about her past? Her loyalties? Rena was almost sorry she'd brought the woman into the group. *Stop this*, she thought. *You needed a handy Russian speaker. And all your doubts are based on circumstantial evidence. Be careful. Watch her, give her a chance to prove or hang herself. Watch her carefully.*

But the Russians know about us….

Then a major factor dawned on Skye. OCI had learned about the mole over a month ago. And Merry had been part of the group for a much shorter period of time. She couldn't have been the mole. Unless she was a second enemy agent come to join the first one….

Skye planned to send the three female operatives on this mission. And she didn't know who she could trust and who she couldn't. She heaved a big sigh. She would send Jennie to act as guardian angel for the other women. Powers was the one woman she knew for certain she could trust. But that would put a very heavy burden on her best friend.

Rena got up from her chair, retrieved three small boxes and began putting together the special items she would give her women for this new assignment. She called her supply petty officer and ordered some special equipment: six walkie-talkies and a backpack.

* * * *

Rena called Jennie Powers into the private conference room in the corner of the OCI office space. "I have a special assignment for you, Jennie. I want your acceptance of it."

"You ought to know by now I'm always at your service, honey."

"Yeah, but this assignment could get dangerous."

"Why? What's so different about this job?"

"I want to send you to Saint Louis to babysit the other three women."

"All right. Been there, done that. Remember Norfolk?"

"Yes, but you weren't so involved with operatives who may not be on your side."

"What do you mean?"

Rena broke her vow of secrecy about the spy in their midst. And she told her friend of her doubts and fears about the other women.

"You didn't ever say anything before about us being infiltrated. How long have you known?"

"Almost a month now."

"What've you been doing about it?"

"For the most part, trying to figure out what to do. How can we find the mole? Even so, I think we need to send people to scout out Saint Louis. We know the killers of the truck drivers are there and we need to get indisputable proof. We need to find the sports car and it's driver. And we believe the leader of all the spy groups we've been following may also be there. We know the neighborhood where these guys are working out of but we haven't been able to pinpoint their exact location. I'm going to give special instructions to each of the women. I think I have it worked out." She explained her plan in detail. "So

220

when I send the ladies to Saint Louis, I'll need you to be mother hen to them again. Are you on board with that?"

"Honey, do you even have to ask?"

"For this job, yes I do. We know these guys are killers. And I won't force you to do this. It has to come from you."

"And if I refuse? Then what're you going to do?"

"I don't know." She looked down at her hands. "I might go myself...."

"Now you're talking like a crazy woman. Get off that crap! Look, you're the commander of this here team. And you can't leave your post and put yourself in danger. You simply can't. You hear me, girl? My God! If anything happened to you this team would fall apart...."

"I don't think so...."

"Then you're too blind to see how important you are. You hear me?"

Rena sat there silently.

"Hey! *Do you hear me?*"

"Yes," Rena whispered.

Jennie took a deep breath. "Yes, I'll go to Saint Louis."

"Thank you." Rena paused. "I want you to take Tango with you. He'll watch your back for you and may come in handy in other ways."

"So, what're you going to have the others do?"

"I'll tell them when I give them their code names and special items."

"What code names?"

"I'm going to tell each of them they are part of a special operation. The names of the operations are Firethorn, Silverbell, and Thunderbush."

"Where'd you get those names?"

"They're names of plants I ran across. They sounded like good secret operation names. Is there a problem with them?"

"No. I'm wondering why give each of them a different name?"

"I hope if there's a leak, somehow the code name will come out and we'll know who the infiltrator is."

"Sounds like a weak plan. What if they tell each other their secret names?"

"I'm going to classify each name as top secret and swear them to secrecy subject to court martial."

"Think it'll work?"

"I don't know. I hope so.... Remember my intuition. Something tells me we'll crack the case wide open here. At what cost, I don't know. But we have to try."

"What are the special items you're going to give them?"

"Each operative will get a barrette with a hollow center along its length."

"What's that for?"

"I don't know…. It was a whim. It could serve as a snorkel device if necessary. But it's one of a number of devices. There's a stiletto pen. Push the clip a special way and a sharp spike pops out instead of the pen. Then there's a two-shot zip gun. They'll also get a bulletproof vest. During World War II, the U.S. developed a vest using Doron Plate, a fiberglass-based laminate. In fact, these vests were used in the Battle of Okinawa. We've taken these and added multiple layers of silk on both sides. Silk was used to stop old slow velocity gunfire and we added silk in hopes of creating an additional bit of protection. And last but not least, each of them will get a walkie-talkie locked on a different frequency."

"Why?" Jennie asked.

So they can't know what the others are saying, what they're reporting."

"So who'll they be talking to?"

"You, of course. You'll get three walkie-talkies. Each one will be set to the frequency of one of the other Waves. That's so you can hear any of the others at any time. I'll also give you a backpack to carry the three units at the same time. And I'll give you all the other objects, too."

"I doubt I'll need them. Now, all three women are getting all of these?"

"Yes."

"So if one of them is the Russian agent, she'll know what the other two have as far as protection and weapons?"

"I can't help it. I'm trying to give one or another of them a slight advantage. Hopefully, the spy won't get around to telling everyone in their organization before one of the women has to use the items. If any one thing helps just a little bit, it's worth it."

"And you're giving all of these to all three of them?"

"Yes. Because I don't know who the infiltrator is. So I have to treat all of them equally. And pray. And rely on you to watch over them. Now, go out there and send them into me here, one at a time. Take this suitcase with you. It has all your devices in it. Don't open it until you're alone."

"Yes, ma'am, aye, aye, roger wilco, and all that stuff. I'm on the way."

Rena met with each operative individually. She assigned code names to each of them. She also gave each of them an alias. Ruth would be known as Rachel Johnson. Laura would assume the name of Linda Martin, and Merry would use Marcia Linner. Chaské, with Steven Montaigne's help, had researched a list of clubs where the Russians hung out: The Izbiza and Club Viktor were on the top of the list. Rena gave the list to the women. They were to find the killers of the truck drivers, Don Jennings and Jerry Hassler. Try to get into the Russians' houses and identify everyone working out of them. And get as much proof as they could find.

39. Children at Orient House

Long Island

It was late Friday afternoon. A Cadillac Coupe de Ville pulled up in front of the Orient house. Morgan Delano watched from the woods.

The guard stepped outside. Glazov and his wife followed. A man and a woman got out of the vehicle. Two children, a boy and a younger girl, followed them.

"Hello, Vladimir," the new arrival greeted. Then he turned to Glazov's wife and bowed. "Greetings, Gana."

The house owner took the other man by the shoulders. "Welcome, Filip. And also to your beautiful wife, Maricha."

"What about us?" the boy asked.

Gana turned to him. "But of course, Maxim. You and Shedra are welcome." She took their hands, smiled at Maricha, and said: "Come, children, let us go and see if the honey cakes are ready."

Shedra danced up and down. "Oh, goody! Honey cakes!"

Glazov steered Filip and Maricha toward the door. "Come, brother, we can join them for tea and cakes."

Later in the afternoon the two children came outside and played with the guard dog, Pavio. They played for an hour and a half, until their mother called them in to get ready for supper. Luckily, the breeze varied from non-existent to blowing away from the house, into Del's face.

The OCI agents watched the whole day. They took good photos and sent them back to the New London Security Office, which duplicated them and provided copies for Great Lakes OCI.

*   *   *   *

Stolichek watched the Orient house, but he was getting exhausted. Twelve hours a day for…. He'd lost track of how many days. He was not paying as close attention to details as he should. And he dozed off way too often. They were supposed to be getting some more people to help, but he had no idea when they'd be available to stand watch.

The back door opened and Stanislov, the guard, let the dog run loose instead of chaining it up as usual. It raced around the yard at the rear of the house. Then it ran to a spot near the woods on the other side of the yard, lifted its leg and urinated on a tree.

Don't come over here, Stolichek thought.

The man picked up a stick and threw it. The dog retrieved it. The man reached to take the stick back, but the animal decided to play tug-of-war instead. At last the guard got the stick in his hand and threw it again. The pair played this way for about ten minutes before the dog lost interest.

A gentle breeze began to blow from behind Stolichek toward the house.

The OCI agent didn't notice the change. But the dog did. It stopped playing, lifted its head, and raced across the yard toward the woods. Stanislov ran after it, shouting for it to heel. But Pavio had picked up the scent and he paid no attention to the command. He ran into the woods, straight for the man hiding there.

*   *   *   *

Pavio headed straight for Stolichek. The agent held his spray bottle of skunk essence in his hand.

The dog raced into the woods. The guard, ran after him, shouting for him to return. The barking dog stopped in the woods, a couple yards from the OCI agent. Stolichek sprayed him with the skunk oil while the guard was still in the yard. Pavio ran back to the guard, yelping.

Stanislov roared with laughter when he thought the dog chased after a skunk and got sprayed. Then he turned angry at having to clean up the animal. He chained it outside with one command: "Stay!"

Pavio couldn't help but stay where he was put. Whimpering, he moved out as far as the chain permitted and watched the location where he'd found the "skunk." He kept pulling against his restraint, trying to get to Stolichek's hiding place.

Stanislov watched the animal. He wondered what made Pavio so insistent on getting back to a skunk. Maks, the other guard, came out and they talked about the situation. They got more and more suspicious as they talked.

"You act very strange," Stanislov said to the dog. "I will investigate those woods later tonight."

Stolichek retreated a bit farther back from the house, even though he wouldn't be able to observe it as well as before.

* * * *

Stolichek checked the time. He still had three hours before his watch was up. He was about to lift his binoculars to examine the house when he heard a small voice to his right.

"What are you doing?" it asked.

He jumped, startled, then calmed himself. He turned to face the young girl. He waved his binoculars in front of himself. "I'm bird watching."

"My brother does that. You're facing the house. Are there birds over there?"

"Some. Swallows and wrens," he answered in as calm a voice as he could. "What's your name?"

"Shedra."

"And how old are you, Shedra?"

"Ten"

"Do you go to school?"

"Uh-huh. We're tutored."

"And what's your favorite subject?"

"Dancing."

"What kind of dancing do you study?"

"Ballet, of course." She performed a couple steps on her tiptoes. "But now, we're visiting our uncle who lives here." Shedra paused and thought for a moment. "What's your name?"

"My name is George."

"And where do you live?"

"In Sag Harbor."

"I never heard of it before. Where is that?"

Stolichek pointed to the south. "It's over there. About halfway across the island."

* * * *

Stolichek and Delano didn't observe the house that nigh because the guards already indicated they planned to search the woods. And they decided it would not be wise to switch their shifts watching the Orient house. Catching one birdwatcher was within the realm of possibility. Catching two different men "looking for birds" would be suspicious and might tip off the Russians they were under surveillance.

It was a smart move. The day after meeting Shedra, her brother showed up. He had a small pair of binoculars around his neck.

"Who are you?" he greeted Stolichek suspiciously.

"My name is George. And what's your name?"

"Maxim. What are you doing here?"

"I'm bird watching."

The boy cocked his head, raised his eyebrows and asked: "And where are you from?"

"I live in Sag Harbor."

"That's the other side of island. Why come here for bird watching?"

"It's not as crowded as the town is. And I'm looking for new birds, ones that I haven't seen before."

"You know this is private property, don't you?"

"The folks back there to the west said it was okay to check out the woods. But I didn't know where the property line was. Guess I'll leave if your uncle doesn't want me here."

"How do you know my uncle owns this place?" Maxim demanded.

"I saw your sister yesterday and she told me." He paused for a moment as if he were thinking something over.

The boy stared at Stolichek for a long moment before saying: "I think you'd better leave the property."

The OCI agent nodded, turned and walked out of the woods. Maxim followed him but stopped at the edge of the trees. Stolichek walked on, without looking back. He walked across the airstrip and around the house on the other side. When he knew he was out of sight, he turned to go back to the place Delano had rented.

"I think we'll have to stay clear of the woods for a while," he suggested.

"Why?" Del asked. Stolichek told his partner about the boy. "An' he was very suspicious?"

"Yeah. Much more so than the girl had been."

"He's older, ya know? And they train 'em young. So whadda we do now?"

Stolichek picked up the phone. "I'm going to report this to Rena."

227

"It's kinda late," Del observed.

"If she's not in the office, Ford gave me her home number. With orders not to call her there after midnight." He contacted the operator and had her place the long distance call to Great Lakes.

"Major Rena Skye."

"Hi Rena. This is George. We have a problem here." He explained the situation to her.

"All right," she sighed. "Take a rest. Don't go anywhere near the place tonight."

"How about tomorrow?"

"Play it by ear. Do your bird watching thing as you cross the field toward the woods. At the first sign the Russians are there, veer away, continue bird watching, and go somewhere else. You go in, not Del. You're the one they've seen before. No sense letting them find out there's more than one of you. We may have to let this place sit unwatched for a while."

"How about some sort of remote watching?"

"Television equipment is way too heavy to put in trees," Skye laughed. "And leaving it on the ground is a dead giveaway. In a day or two, try going in from the Long Island Sound side or something."

"Okay. We'll play it real slow and easy."

"Also," she added. "Do you know what the visitors' car looks like?"

"Yes. We do have some photographs on the way to Lakes. "

"Try to get the license plate number of the car, too. We need to make a firm identification of these people."

"Will do. I'll call back when we have the info." Stolichek hung up the phone, then explained the orders to Delano.

*　　*　　*　　*

After Stolichek finished telling Delano of his meeting with the children the latter said: "I don' like it." He sat and thought for a while. "Hah! I got a plan."

"Uh-oh. What're you thinking of now?"

"I played a bit of a drunk in Norfolk on our last case. Was pretty good at it, too, ya know?"

"So you're going to be a drunk in the woods?" Stolichek asked.

"Nah. On the main road. Back 'n' forth along where their driveway comes out, ya know? I c'n even fall down inta the ditch if they get suspicious. Also, there's a decent stand of trees on the side of Main Road, across from the Orient house. If I havta, I c'n hide in there.

"You have any booze here?"

"Gonna go out 'n' buy some right now. What smells good on a drunk?"

"I don't know. Plain old whiskey, I guess," Stolichek said.

"Yeh. Don't like that. Rather drink good rum or good brandy."

"Well, you can't be a drunken bum with twenty-year-old scotch. Go for some cheap brandy, then."

Delano returned a half hour later. He had a bottle of Christian Brothers Brandy and an empty Everclear bottle, which he began washing out.

"Where'd you get the empty bottle?"

"Store owner gave it to me."

"You tell him what you wanted it for?"

"It was a her. I tol' her I was goin' to a costume party as a drunk. What else could I say? 'Goin' on a stakeout 'n' I havta look tha part'?"

Stolichek laughed. "So why didn't you get some good cognac?"

"That's sippin' stuff, ya know? Too expensive fer tonight." He finished washing the empty bottle. Carefully poured the Christian Brothers into it. "There. Looks cheap, tastes great, ya know?"

And he left. He returned about midnight. He was wet.

Stolichek watched him enter the apartment. Del didn't seem the least bit affected by the brandy. "I was expecting you to get back here drunk as a skunk. Didn't you drink it all?"

"Nah. No need, ya know? They all left the place 'bout ten o'clock, uh, twenty-two-hundred hours. Tha man, his wife and tha two kids, all gone."

"Good. The kids were too nosey and too hard to keep track of. I'm glad they're gone," Stolichek said.

"Me, too."

"How come you're wet?"

"There's this thing called rain, ya know?" Del replied.

"I didn't see or hear any signs of rain."

"No thunder or lightning. Very gentle rain. But ya still get wet." He paused for a moment. "By tha way, I got their license plate number." He wrote down a number and handed it to Stolichek. "Now, ya think it's gonna be okay ta go back there in tha mornin' 'n' watch tha place?"

"I think so. Let's do it. Very carefully."

"Agree. We don' know what them kids told the ay-dults, ya know? Tha guard 'n' his puppy could be lookin' fer us."

"Well, let's be sure we have plenty of your 'essence of skunk.'"

*　　*　　*　　*

229

Saint Louis

Loki sat in his office behind the two-way mirrors. Leonid Mazursky, his personal assistant, brought him a vodka martini. He took an appreciative sip and sighed. "Ah! That is very good."

He took another sip. Let the beverage roll around his tongue. The phone rang. Loki swallowed as Leonid answered the call.

"Hello!" Mazursky was silent for a few seconds. "He is right here."

Loki took the offered phone. "Speak."

"We may have a problem here on Long Island."

"Details?"

"Both children met a man in the nearby woods. He claimed to be a birdwatcher."

"What makes you think he is not?"

"He may have been around here for a while. The guard dog has also behaved strangely recently."

"How so?"

"He raced into the woods. There was definitely something there. But very soon, he ran back strongly smelling like a skunk."

"And why is this strange?"

"We have never seen any sign of skunks before. We have never seen any of those animals. And we have not smelled one before either."

"All right. Search the area carefully. Tonight. With strong torches, flashlights. Permit the dog more freedom to explore when he wants to look among the trees. Let me know immediately if you find anyone."

*   *   *   *

Long Island

The next morning Stolichek took his time going to the Orient house. He used his binoculars again and again, looking in every direction. Whenever he heard a bird's song, he pointed the field glasses toward the sound. Sometimes he remained motionless for a minute or more, "watching a bird do something special." He put on a real bird watcher act.

When he reached the area where he spent most of his time observing the house, he saw definite signs the area had been searched. But the recent rain had washed away the human scent and the dog was unable to follow it.

The OCI agents moved farther from the house and used more long-range binoculars and lenses on their cameras.

40. Where Did He Go All Night?

Nebraska

Daniel drove to the motel room in Alliance to call in a report to Rena. He arrived back at the ranch after midnight. Troy Hunter greeted him with some strange news.

"Little Horse took off about 1500. He hasn't returned yet."

"That's late. For the most part, he takes off much earlier. No idea where he went?"

"Nope."

"All right. Who's watching the ranch now?"

"Amos and Ken."

"How long they been out there?"

"Since 2345. We time our watches like the Navy."

Daniel heaved a big sigh. He was now in charge of this group. "Let's get some sleep. The three of us." He named Wes as the third person. "Wes, consider yourself the novice under training. Then we can relieve Amos and Ken at 0345. Where's Ray?"

"I'm right here, Daniel."

"Do a favor for me. Tell Amos and Ken to let me know the instant Little Horse returns. And we'll be there to relieve them at a quarter to four."

Ray took off for the observation post. Daniel turned to the other two. "I'll set my travel alarm. Let's get some shut-eye."

The alarm rang at oh-three-thirty. Daniel got up right away and woke up the other two men. They took the morning watch and waited. Little Horse returned an hour after sunrise. He landed and taxied to the barn, then dragged himself

232

into the ranch house.

"Where the hell did he go for the whole night?" Daniel wondered.

After grabbing a few hours sleep, Daniel and Wes made the trip to Alliance. They called Rena to report Little Horse's activities.

"So that's who that unmarked plane belonged to!" she exclaimed.

"What? You already knew about his flight?" Daniel asked.

"Not exactly," Rena said. "We had people watching a number of airports around the Midwest, and…."

"What triggered that?"

"My intuition," she replied. "I don't know why the idea popped into my mind. But about two weeks ago, I thought it might be important. Because you guys were out there watching this man. I don't know. Anyway, our agent in Saint Louis saw an unmarked Cessna land. She didn't think much of it until he took off. The FAA let us know about him leaving. In fact they put out an all points bulletin on his departure."

"Why?" Daniel asked.

"Because he took off without clearing with the tower first. Then he flew below the radars. None of them were able to pick him up."

"So, it looks like Little Horse's overnight trip was to Saint Louis."

"Yes it does. And from my end, it's a very important connection. We were guessing that Little Horse was taking photos of the ICBM silos. Now we can be pretty sure of it, and that he gave them to the Russians."

"That fits with him having a KGB officer here on the ranch."

"I agree," Skye said. "It also fits with people nosing around the Polaris submarines in New London."

"What's going on?" Daniel wondered.

"I'm sure we've stumbled onto a spy ring trying to get all the information they can about our intercontinental missile power."

*   *   *   *

Daniel wondered if Little Horse had still more photos of ICBM silos or if he had passed all of them on. He couldn't stop wondering about this. He waited until Little Horse and the housekeeper were both gone again, then entered the house. This time he would spend much less time inside it; he knew where to look and what to look for. He headed straight for the safe.

He found no photos or callouts of the missile silos. None. The safe was empty. Everything was gone. Were the items he saw before elsewhere in the house? Or did Little Horse take them all to Saint Louis on his overnight jaunt?

He locked everything, left things the way they were, and returned to the OCI observation point.

* * * *

Daniel Han and Chaské's friends continued to watch the Little Horse ranch. They took photos of and documented everything that happened. Every movement they could see. Every flight. Everything.

As they watched, Han and the Indians talked.

"Good white men try hard," Ray Takini said quietly. "But there are two concepts that are almost in conflict."

Daniel grinned. "Let's see if they're the same for Indian people. What are they?"

"First, we want them to respect us as people, as fellow human beings. But we also want them to… not only realize…, but also to understand our culture and how different it is from mainstream America."

"Same with us. Best we can do is to keep trying to teach. And keep helping to stop even worse people from taking over here."

"Exactly" Ray agreed. "And that leads to a desire for the public to admit how much we did for this country, how much we still to do."

"Yes. Same for our people."

"Yeah, all of us have helped America fight its wars. Indians guaranteed secret communications in both world wars. Choctaws started the so-called code talkers in World War I. And Navajo, Lakota, almost any Indian tribe with lots of native speakers were used in World War II. No codes to break. It's a language. And if you did happen to learn it, I'd guarantee a native speaker could detect the improper accent and be warned by it. Totally foolproof."

They lapsed into silence. But there was a feeling of being closer than before. They'd shared history together.

41. Waves In Saint Louis

Saint Louis

Each of the Waves went to Saint Louis by themselves. Laura drove her car. So did Jennie, with Tango in the back seat. Ruth travelled by bus. Merry took a train.

All were ready to get to work the next night. Rachel Johnson (Ruth), Linda Martin (Laura) and Marcia Linner (Merry) all visited separate clubs. Ruth danced, drank, and got propositioned, but turned down all proposals. Laura, playing coy and bashful, met a guy she liked. She left the club with him. Merry danced and had a good time but turned down a number of invitations to go home with men she met.

Jennie kept an eye on them as best she could from her car.

*   *   *   *

Ruth, Laura and Merry sat around a table in the Izbiza Bar, nursing their drinks and watching the crowd. They spoke carefully, trying to remember to use their aliases. They had to speak over the band, which was playing "The Lion Sleeps Tonight" by The Tokens.

"You know…, Rachel, I bet there are twice as many men as women in this crowd," Merry said.

"That's a good thing, Marcia, for the gals who want to meet guys." Ruth replied.

Laura didn't say anything. She continued examining the men in the club.

A soft male voice interrupted their observations. "Hello, beautiful ladies."

The three women looked up from their drinks. The man who stood next to their table was about twenty-five years old. He had blond hair, blue eyes, and fine features. He said: "Would you like some company?"

The band slid into a new tune, Chubby Checkers' "The Twist."

"Sure," Merry shouted over the music and gestured toward an empty chair. "Sit down."

He did so. "My name is Alex. What are your names?"

Ruth pointed as she introduced the women. "Marcia. Linda. And I'm Rachel."

"Do you live around here?" Alex asked.

"No," Ruth/Rachel answered. "We live in Illinois."

"Where in Illinois?" He shouted, moments after the band stopped playing. He was a little embarrassed as people looked at him curiously.

Ruth had to think fast. Then the band started playing Gene Chandler's great song, "Duke of Earl," quite loudly. The volume gave her a chance to think about an answer. She didn't want to tell her real birthplace. When undercover, she felt it was best to not give accurate personal information.... But she had to remember the information she did give. She thought of Rena's hometown. "We come from Rockford."

Alex paused until the band put away their instruments to take a break.

"So what are you doing here in Saint Louis?"

"We are looking for colleges to go to next year."

"What colleges are you visiting?"

"As many as we can. Washington University, even though it's expensive. Saint Louis University. Harris-Stowe State University. Maryville University. Stephens University."

"Are you Roman Catholic? You know a couple of those schools are Catholic."

"Marcia is close. She's Orthodox. The other two of us aren't Catholic. But those schools take in people of other religions."

Alex nodded. "Have you found one that you would want to attend?"

"No, not yet."

"What do the three of you want to study?"

"American History," Ruth said.

"Nursing," Laura/Linda said, looking down her nose. "Then I will go on to become a doctor."

"And I want to study Arabic and Hebrew. I already speak Russian, Hungarian and English," Merry/Marcia said.

"Are you Russian?" he asked. "Marcia is not a Russian name...."

236

"I am Hungarian, like my parents" said Merry. "We spoke both Hungarian and Russian at home."

"What are you doing here? At the Izbiza Bar?"

Ruth grinned. "Looking for guys," she said. "We heard there were some nice guys here. And handsome ones, too."

"Of course. We are Russians. Always handsome men." He pointed to Ruth's cocktail. "What are you drinking?"

"Orange juice and vodka," she replied.

"You call this a 'screwdriver,' right?"

"Yes."

"Why? Where does that name come from?"

"I don't know. I think it's always been called a 'screwdriver,' but I don't know why."

The band began to play some rapid Russian music. A number of men and women rushed to the dance floor. The men performed a very acrobatic dance with flips in mid-air and alternate leg extensions while squatting.

"What kind of dance is that?" Ruth/Rachel asked.

"It is called kazatsky, which means Cossack. It is a very old Russian folk dance. And very vigorous."

"I can see. Does it take a lot of practice to learn?"

"Oh, yes. One almost must grow up with it."

"Can you do this dance?"

"Yes. But I am not as good as those guys."

They watched in fascination until the dance ended. They had a few more drinks. Ruth felt like they'd made a good friend. *But*, she thought, *is Alex one of the spy network or is he in fact an immigrant from Russia. I guess only time will tell.*

The band returned from its break. They started playing Connie Francis' newest song, "Don't Break the Heart That Loves You."

* * * *

The next night Ruth returned to the Izbiza Bar. Alex was there again. He approached her. "Rachel, would you dance with me?"

"Not that Russian dance.... The kazah... whatever?" she asked.

"The kazatsky? No. The next dance will be rock and roll dancing."

They danced to the next few songs, including a slow one Ruth didn't know. Alex was a polite young man. He held her at a very proper distance. Then came a few more fast dance songs.

When they sat down again Ruth adjusted the barrette in her hair. Alex pulled out a handkerchief to wipe the sweat from his brow. It had a "C" monogram on it.

"Alex, I don't even know your last name," Ruth said.

"It is Ponomarev. P-O-N-O-M-A-R-E-V."

"So what does the 'C' on your handkerchief mean?"

"'See?'" He pulled out the handkerchief again. "Oh, that's not 'C'. That's the Cyrillic letter, the Russian letter, 'ess.' My mother gave me this handkerchief for my birthday a couple years ago. That is the first letter of my mother's sweet diminutive name for me. She calls me 'Sashka,' which means 'Little Sasha'."

"Sasha?"

"Yes. It's a nickname for Alexander."

Ruth nodded, wondering if this gentle person killed the two truck drivers in south-central Illinois. Such thoughts kept whirling through her head as they spent the night dancing and drinking. A few minutes before the bar closed for the night, she heard Alex ask a question.

"…with me tonight?"

"Pardon me?" Ruth came back to the present moment with a start. "What did you say?"

He looked down to the floor. "I'm sorry. I don't know what came over me."

"No, no. What did you ask me?"

"I asked if you would like to come home with me tonight. I enjoy your company very much. Would you spend the night with me?"

Ruth reached out and caressed his cheek. "I'm sorry, Alex. But I've had too much to drink tonight. I wouldn't be very good company. I'm afraid I'd fall asleep. And really, all I want now is companionship."

"All right, then," he smiled. "May I be your companion?"

*　　*　　*　　*

Merry chose a different club at random. There were only two Russians in the place. She overheard their conversation. They were talking about their jobs, some kind of technical work at a radio station. She didn't understand anything about it.

A couple men asked her to dance, but she didn't want to. She didn't want to connect with anyone. She certainly did not want to go home with a guy.

She left for home early.

* * * *

Laura found another Russian bar, Club Viktor. She met a man who chose her good looks and ignored her arrogance. She went home with him.

* * * *

Jennie Powers tried to keep track of all three of the operatives. But it was almost an impossible task. Having the walkie-talkies helped somewhat, but most of the time they sat stored in car trunks for fear that the wrong people would see them and realize the women were military personnel of some sort.

If the other women forgot to notify her over their walkie-talkies when changing locations, or if they were with someone and *couldn't* make a report, the best Jennie could do was watch the people going in and out of the clubs' front doors, one location at a time.

Tango sat in the back seat of Jennie's car as she ran around town to visit the various nightclubs. She was rarely permitted inside, so she had to be satisfied with sitting in her car within view of the establishments' entrances, crouched down to present the least possible profile to passersby.

This job was tedious and terribly boring. She tried to keep alert by taking numerous sips of strong coffee from a thermos. Then she had to go to the bathroom. The attendant at the nearest gas station wouldn't let her use the rest room there.

"You'll have to go to a gas station in the Negro part of town," he said apologetically. "You know, I'd let you, but my boss…. You know how it is, don't you?"

"Yeah. I know. Been here, done this before."

* * * *

Ruth, Laura and Merry met for lunch with Jennie. They sat in a small suburban café to talk over recent events.

"Not much action so far," Merry opened the conversation over a hamburger and French fries.

"I don't know," Laura said, biting into her chicken salad sandwich. "I met a nice guy."

"Where?"

"At a place called Club Viktor."

"What's his name?"

"Sam. Sam Balk."

"I met a very nice guy, too," Ruth said. "A Russian guy. Willing to talk. And after he invited me to spend the night with him and I refused, he still agreed to be a friend. Simple companionship. But I also met some creeps."

Merry shrugged. "I met a bunch of normal guys who didn't seem like the ones we need to find."

"I have one thing I want to emphasize when you are running around with your guys," Jennie said. "You simply must remember to report your movements. If you don't, you might find yourself in trouble and I'll be waiting for you to come out of a club in a different part of town. So be absolutely sure to report your movements."

"What if we're with someone and can't make a report?" Ruth asked. "If one of these guys saw us reporting on a Navy walkie-talkie, that would blow our cover, sure as hell."

Jennie thought silently for a long moment. "Let's try this. Make an excuse to check something in your trunk. Call me, but at the very beginning of your call say the words 'I sure hope everything is okay here.' I won't respond, so you won't have any sound coming from the walkie-talkie. Then add something like 'I don't want to go to Club Viktor,' or wherever, 'with a problem back here.'"

"Think that'll work?" Laura asked.

"I don't know," Jennie replied. "But we have to try something…."

As the meeting progressed, Ruth felt something was wrong. She looked from one woman to the other. Then it hit her. She, alone, wore the special barrette Rena gave them. She wondered why….

*   *   *   *

The meeting didn't last very long after lunch was done. Each of the three women went their own way. Merry visited her parents, who lived in Saint Louis. She still had her key to their apartment so she unlocked the door and went in. "Van itthon valaki?" she called out in Hungarian. "Is anybody home?"

Her mother came into the living room from the kitchen and hugged her. "Meredith! It is so nice to see you, my dear!"

"Where's Papa?"

"He's taking a nap. His health is not the best, you know. What are you doing here in Saint Louis?"

"Watching some Russian people here in town."

"This is for work with your OCI?"

240

"Yes."

"Do be careful, dear. You watch out. There are good immigrant Russian people here. And there are some very bad Russians in this city, too."

Merry laughed. "And how do you know this, Mama?"

"I just do. I watch and I listen. These are things we learned from living in Hungary. We came here to escape the Communists, but I still carry some of the habits from our life back there. So I know some people from Russia are here. And they talk very much like the secret police back in Hungary. They are very arrogant and think there is nobody here to understand them when they speak Russian. I think they might be here to spy on the Americans."

"I'll be careful, Mama." She swallowed hard, pausing for a moment. "When I got this job I said I would be willing to do almost anything. Now I'm in a situation where I'm kind of expected to go out with some of these people. Even sleep with them."

"Oh, no!"

"It was stupid of me to agree to do this for the job. I wish I hadn't. Now all I want to do is go home to Anton."

"See, there are good Russians around," her mother smiled. "So why don't you quit the OCI and go home?"

"That's what I want to do." Tears came to her eyes. "But I don't know how to approach my boss and tell her. I'm here on the job and she's back at Great Lakes."

"Is there no one you can talk to here about this?"

Merry nodded. "Yes, there may be. But she's a tough lady. I'll have to gather all my courage to tell her...."

42. Increased Curiosity

Long Island

Morgan Delano was on watch at the Orient house. He'd been on his feet for hours. He'd watched the sun come up through the budding foliage of the trees. Nothing was happening except his back was starting to hurt.

A Ford Galaxie 500/XL with New York plates drove into the driveway and halfway around the curve. It stopped in front of the house's main door. One of the guards stepped out of the house. He raised his hand in greeting.

The driver got out and started speaking Russian. "Здравствуйте, товарищ!"

The guard scowled. "Outside we must speak English, you fool. Others might hear us out here."

"What others? There's nobody else here! Who's going to hear way out here?"

"Those are the orders. You are part of this business. You know there are listening devices. Microphones with amplifiers. It is all right to speak Russian inside."

The visitor stayed a short two hours. There was no way to tell what the meeting was about.

*   *   *   *

Rena gave me another trip over a weekend. I got to see how Stolichek and Delano were doing and to support them on the very tough job that surveillance is. Basically, they gave me the same tour they gave Rena when she was out there. Then we stood in the woods for a few hours, watching and waiting.

Stakeout activities. Boring.

The real entertainment came from Pavio, the watchdog. He was kept chained up. He continued to try to get to our position in the woods. So we varied our watch location. The dog still picked up our scent, every time the wind blew from us to the house.

Two guards came out with the supposed owner. Del identified each of the Russians as they spoke, Stanislov, Maks, and later Mr. Glazov.

"Pavio acts like he smells something in woods," Maks said.

"Sniffing and barking," Stanislav added.

"And trying to go into woods."

"Where does he try to go?" the owner asked.

"Over there, Mister Glazov. And there."

"And...," the other guard tried to say.

"Yes, Maks?"

"And over there some number of times," Maks said.

"Does he growl?" Glazov asked.

"Little bit. Not often," Maks answered.

The owner scratched his chin. "He did not show that there was danger?"

"No," Stanislov said. "Most of the time he acts like he is curious."

"Did you let him loose?"

"Yes, sir. Sometimes. Sometimes he acts normal, playful. Other times he barks and tries to break chain."

"But no growling...."

"No."

"What was different in the times he played like usual and the times he tried to go into the woods?" Glazov asked.

Stanislov shrugged his shoulders. "I do not know."

"I think wind," Maks said. "I remember little bit of wind blowing when he wants to go into woods."

"Were the winds blowing in the same direction all these times?"

"No, I do not think so. From different directions," Stanislov answered.

"Yes!" Maks. "From out there to the house."

"So it carried the scent of whatever was in the woods? And the other times he did not pay attention to the woods. Correct?"

Both guards nodded.

Glazov stood thinking and looking around. "So he could be trying to get to animals out there. Maybe rabbits."

"Or bears," Maks said.

"There are no bears here," Stanislov sneered. "Woods are too small. But there are foxes...."

"And squirrels or deers," the other guard added.

"Enough," Glazov said. "Next time, go and look."

"Take dog with?" Stanislov asked.

"Whatever you think is best. Go and look. See what you can there. But be ready in case somebody is out there."

Stanislov waited until late at night before he leashed Pavio and checked out our location.

Thanks to moving around often, the we weren't anywhere near the spot they inspected. Furthermore, Stolichek had come up with a deterrent: a couple squirts of skunk essence on the spot they'd used would eliminate the human smell there.

But the guard and his dog did come looking for us in the woods, which made us extra cautious. We used our long-range binoculars and telescopic camera lenses much more often than we had before. But we still had to be sure we had a decent line of sight to the house.

After a day and a half, I returned back to Great Lakes, exhausted.

*   *   *   *

The leaves on the trees were filling out nicely. The OCI guys were more comfortable each day since the increasing foliage made it more difficult for people in the house to see them.

Even so, Stolichek was jumpy. He glanced at the time. It was close to noon. His watch was almost over. Breathing a sigh of relief, he let his guard down slightly.

Until he heard the leaves rustle right behind him.

As he jumped around to look, his mind flashed simultaneous thoughts. *Did someone find me? Is someone standing there now?*

43. The Sports Car

Saint Louis

Ruth glanced at the clock as she walked into the Izbiza Bar. It was a little after seven p.m. Even so, there were quite a few people in the establishment. The band wasn't scheduled to start for another fifteen minutes. She found a table and sat down alone. When the waitress came over, she ordered a screwdriver. She took a sip of her drink when she heard Alex's soft voice behind her.

"Hello, companion!"

"Oh, hi Alex! I didn't see you when I came in."

"Then it is a good thing I saw you! You are here early tonight."

"Yeah. I collected some information about the local colleges and dropped the papers off where I'm staying. I started to watch some television, but I got tired of staring at the walls of my motel room."

"Where are you staying here in Saint Louis?" Alex asked.

"It's a small motel up near the Poplar Street Bridge."

"I know of a nice boarding house with clean rooms. My mother runs it."

"So you want me to move in with you?" Ruth grinned. "What kind of a girl do you think I am?"

Alex turned bright red. "No, no! She does run a real boarding house. With a proper license and everything. It is a respectable place."

"How much does she charge?"

"Two-fifty each night. Three-fifty with supper."

"Does she allow pets?"

"Sure. What do you have, a cat?"

"I may be taking care of a dog for a while. A Saint Bernard."

"Oh, I don't know about that. We'll have to ask her."

The band was set up. It began playing with a raucous version of "The Peppermint Twist."

Ruth thought about refusing to even go to Alex's house. But then she thought it might be important to find out his address and report it to Rena. "All right. Let's talk to her tomorrow about getting me a room."

Alex looked around the bar. "It's dead here tonight."

"Most bars are kind of dead on Mondays. If they're even open at all."

He shook his head. "Not Russian places. They are open and busy all the time. Would you like to go to another place?"

"Which one?"

"A place called Club Viktor. Many Russians go there."

"Sure. Let's see what's going on there. It has to be livelier than this."

They walked outside. Ruth went to her car and opened it up. "Do you need a ride?"

"No, thank you," Alex replied. "I have my old jalopy parked right around the corner."

"Don't you have a sports car?"

He looked bewildered. He shook his head. "No. My friend, Sam, has one, but he won't let me drive it. I only have an old car. I can't afford anything better."

He told Ruth how to get to Club Viktor. Then he walked around the corner. Ruth sat in her vehicle for a while, calculating how long it would take for him to get moving. Then he rounded the corner and waved at her as he drove off.

Ruth went to her trunk, reported the change of nightclubs to Jennie, then drove off to Club Viktor.

They met there a short time later. This place had about three times as many people as there were at Izbiza. Ruth ordered another screwdriver and Alex ordered a shot of straight vodka. He drank it the same way as most of the other men in the bar. He placed his hand and the shot glass in front of his chin, then threw his head and hand back together. The vodka flew into his open mouth and he gulped it down. He slammed the shot glass down on the table that Ruth was afraid he would smash it into pieces, but it didn't break.

"Ahhh! Good vodka!" he said, eyes watering a little bit.

The band was playing all Russian music.

He had three shots, well spaced, before he looked around the nightclub. "This is a strange group here. The ones who are here all the time. They seem very much within themselves. They keep aloof. I think they permit me to be here sometimes only because I am Russian. But I think there is very much going on within their group that they do not let others know about."

"Like what?" Ruth asked quietly.

Alex shrugged his shoulders and shook his head. "I do not know."

*   *   *   *

Ruth and Alex visited Club Viktor the next couple nights. Alex perked up when a man walked in. "Ah, my friend Sam Balk is here."

"Aren't you going to go and greet him?"

"No. We'll let him settle in and have some vodka. Then we can go over."

"We?"

"Sure. You should meet this guy."

"Why?"

"He's famous in the Russian community here. He knows everyone. He's flashy. Drives a sports car. And he's in a play."

Ruth examined the newcomer in short glances. He looked familiar. Like someone she'd seen in a history book or on the news. He was short, no more than five feet six inches. Full face. Bushy mustache. Hair combed straight back without a part. Balk slammed back a couple shots of vodka. When the Russian band took a break, Alex stood up and motioned for Ruth to come with him. She stood up, straightened her skirt and the barrette in her hair, and followed Alex.

"Hi, Sam."

"Hello Alex. How are you?"

"I'm fine. I hope you are well also."

"Yes, I am. Спасибо."

"Let me introduce my friend. Sam, this is Rachel Johnson. Rachel, Sam Balk."

Balk stood and bowed. "I am happy to meet you, beautiful lady."

"I'm happy to meet you, too, Mr. Balk."

"Please, call me Sam. You are new to this city? Or at least you did not grow up here."

"Why, yes. How could you tell?"

"Your accent is different from the people here. Are you visiting or looking for work?"

"I'm looking for colleges I may want to attend."

"Yes. There are some very good ones here. Good luck in your search."

"Sam," Alex said, "what are you doing these days?"

"Oh, I go driving around the countryside."

"Yes, it must be fun with that sports car you have."

"Yes it is. And on the weekends, I still act in the play."

"Which play are you in now?"

"It is called *Winston, Franklin and Joe*. You should come to see it. It's about the three Allied leaders during World War Two. The first act is about the Tehran Conference and the second act is about the Yalta Conference."

"We will have to go see it."

"Let me know when. Then come to my house to pick up two tickets."

"Thank you very much, Sam."

He waved his hand in the air. "It is nothing, my friend."

They talked a little longer, then Alex and Ruth returned to their table.

Some time later, they left for Alex's home. Ruth examined the room Alex's mother was renting. She said she would think about taking it. When she left the Ponomarev house, Ruth stopped at a pay phone to call Jennie. They arranged to meet at an all night restaurant.

They settled in and ordered some post-midnight snacks and coffee. Jennie looked around. "I wonder where Merry is? She wanted to meet with me, too." She looked around again. "Oh, well. What do you have for me, Ruth?"

Ruth gave Alex's address to Jennie so she could send it on to Rena. She described Sam Balk and her meeting with him.

"You met this man face to face?" Jennie asked.

"Yes. He looked very familiar. Like someone out of a history book."

"Like who?"

"I can't remember. But I do remember seeing the face before."

"It may be important. If you do recall who he looks like, let me know."

When Merry showed up. Jennie and Ruth greeted her, but she just nodded in response. Jennie turned to Ruth. "All right. Get me that other information as soon as you can."

She nodded. "I'll call when I have something."

"Okay. See you later." Ruth departed. Jennie turned to Merry. "You called me for a meeting. What's happening with you? You have any new information for me?"

"No...."

"How have you been spending your time?"

"I've been to a few uninteresting clubs. And also visiting my parents."

"Have you connected with any of the Russians?" Jennie asked.

Merry stammered and stuttered. She began to speak a couple times before any words came out. "I... I can't continue with this assignment."

The other woman's face turned hard. She remembered Ruth's dilemma in Norfolk, when she wanted to quit. "Why not?"

"I know now it was a big mistake to tell Major Skye I would be willing to do anything for the cause."

"And what's the problem now?"

"I think I'm expected to sleep with some of these guys to get in with them. To gather information. But I can't do it." She started to cry.

"Why not, Merry?" Jennie asked softly.

"I can't cheat on my husband. I'll quit before I let that happen."

"I didn't know you were married." Jennie sat back and stared at the sobbing woman. Finally, she reached out and patted Merry's hand. "All right. We can't to force you to do something morally wrong. But I may have other jobs for you to do."

"Like what?"

"I don't know yet. Messenger activities, looking things up, those kinds of jobs."

"Thank you, Jennie," the younger woman whispered.

*   *   *   *

Alex and Ruth walked along the mighty Mississippi. It was drizzling, so they stayed under their umbrellas. They watched the river traffic and marveled at how the tugs seemed to be able to control the barges without any effort. At one point, a number of tugs sounded their horns one after the other. Each had its own distinctive pitch. "Sounds like a concert," Ruth quipped. "The Tugboat Concerto."

"Speaking of concerts," Alex said. "There is one tonight."

"A concert? What kind of music?"

"Classical music. An all Russian program."

"Whose music are they playing?" she asked.

"Some of the greatest. Tchaikovsky. Borodin. Mussorgsky." He smiled and looked down at his feet. Then he looked up at Ruth. "Would you like to go with me, Rachel?"

"Sure. How do we get there? Your car or mine?"

"You have a nicer car than I do, believe me.... Can we use yours? I'll pay for parking," Alex offered.

Ruth drove them to the concert.

The music was very good. She'd heard some of the selections before but not all. The program began with Borodin's "Polovtsian Dances," then came Mussorgsky's "Pictures at an Exhibition," followed by Tchaikovsky's "Orchestral Suite #3 in G-major." After the intermission, the orchestra played Tchaikovsky's "Symphony #6 in E-minor," named "The Pathétique."

That night, Ruth called Jennie and asked her to pass on the information that Alex Ponomarev, also known as Sashka, was not the Russian with the sports car, but it seemed that Sam Balk might be.

*   *   *   *

The next day was Friday. Alex smiled at Ruth as he asked: "Hey, Rachel, we can go to see Sam's play tonight, if you want."

"Oh, I'd like that, Alex," she said.

"All right, then. We must go to his house to pick up the tickets."

When they got there, Sam showed them around his house with proud grace. Besides being an actor, he was also a gardener. He even had a small hothouse behind his home. His specialty was growing beautiful roses.

Alex began to sneeze and couldn't stop.

"Are you allergic to roses?" Ruth asked.

"I don't know. I've haven't been around so many of them before."

"Ever start sneezing when there are only one or two roses around? Maybe a couple sneezes?"

"I never noticed, because if I was around roses, it wasn't for very long. I hope the car will soon be far enough away and I will stop sneezing. If I don't, then I might be allergic to something else." He put the theater tickets in his shirt pocket. "I'll wait for you at the car."

Sam showed off his beautiful flowers. He grew more than red and white roses. Some flowers had different combinations of colors, but the most exotic were the black roses and purple roses. Ruth especially liked his red and yellow combination.

As Sam and Ruth moved around the hothouse, she bumped into a wooden shelf that wasn't anchored to anything. It rocked a bit. One of the jars looked like it might fall off. Sam began to reach for a handkerchief to isolate his hand from the jar as he steadied it. But he quickly thought better of it, stuffed the handkerchief back into his shirt pocket and grabbed for a small garden rake to stabilize the jar. Once it was stable, he took a rubber glove from the shelf below the jar and pulled it on. He repositioned the jar. Pushed it farther back on the shelf. "You must be careful. That is nicotine solution I use for insecticide. It is very poisonous. So much that I cannot even use it full strength on the roses. That is why I used a rubber glove."

"What do you mean?"

"My first thought was to use my handkerchief, but poison would soak through and get on my skin," he said as he pulled on the glove and put it back on its shelf. "That is why I put on a glove to move it back."

Ruth pointed to the jar on the shelf. "It's that poisonous? Even if you get a little bit on your skin? You need to protect yourself even to touch the jar?"

"Oh, yes. It is very, very strong. I must wear rubber gloves whenever I use it. Skin soaks up nicotine very easy. Very easy. But it is good insecticide. It keeps bugs away from my flowers." Ruth paid special attention as he folded the handkerchief and moved it to his pants pocket. She noticed it had a "C" embroidered on one corner. She assumed that stood for the first letter of his Russian name, whatever name "Sam" was short for. "So, I can put my handkerchief back in my pocket. Poison did not get on it. I will not need to throw it away."

"Why would you throw it away?"

"If it gets any poison on it, I will take no chance for it to get onto my skin."

That evening, Alex and Ruth watched the play Sam was in. As they entered the theater, Ruth noticed Sam's name wasn't on the playbill at the front of the theater. "Alex? I thought your friend Sam Balk was in this play. What part does he play?"

"He's in it. He's one of the stars. He plays the part of Stalin."

"So why isn't his name on the playbill?"

"Oh! He uses a stage name. Arkady Badurov."

Ruth made a mental note to let Rena know of Sam's stage name.

The emcee welcomed the audience. "Good evening. I hope you enjoy tonight's presentation of *Winston, Franklin and Joe*. I'm sorry to say that one of our main actors, Donald Jennings, is no longer with our theater company. He was the actor who played Winston Churchill. His long-time understudy, Lionel Thompson, will take his place. Thank you and enjoy the play."

The play was quite good. The acting was exceptional for community theater. Sam played his part with great skill. He made it easy to believe Stalin was very concerned about the liberation of people from the Nazis and their welfare afterwards.

When the play was over, Ruth and Alex wanted to walk along the river, gazing at the tiny sliver of a moon, but it was drizzling and they decided to go for a drink.

When Ruth later returned home, she called Jennie. "I saw the play tonight, *Winston, Franklin and Joe*. Earlier I met the man who plays the part of Stalin. This guy is Russian, and has handkerchiefs with a monogrammed 'C' on them."

"What's his name?"

"Balk. Sam Balk. But his stage name is Arkady Badurov."

"Badurov? That's the name Steven Montaigne found for us. But it's a stage name? No wonder we couldn't find anything about Badurov! We should find more information about him now. And what's his home address?" Ruth gave it to her. "All right. I'll let Rena know right away." Then Jennie played a hunch. "By the way, does he drive a sports car?"

"Yes, he does."

"Get some pictures, Ruth. We need photos of the tires or the tire prints."

"I'll do my best."

"Make it a certainty. We have to get that information. But be very careful. This man is extremely dangerous." Jennie paused for a moment. "In fact, let me know when you go to see the car. I want to be close enough to help if you need me. Wear your pin with the bug in it."

*　　*　　*　　*

Alex and Ruth sat on a T-shaped pier extending into the Mississippi River. There was a drizzling rain. They watched the roiling fog from under their umbrellas. They both liked to watch the river. The afternoon temperature was almost eighty, but the rain and fog was a bit chilly.

Ruth used her 35mm camera to get some photos of the fog over the river. She made sure to put the cover back on the lens after each shot.

"You like photography?" Alex asked.

"Yeah. It's one of my hobbies. I love to get pictures of weather. You know, lightning. And pictures of the fog are best when it's rolling around like this. And if I'm ever near a tornado, I'd love to get a picture of that."

"That would be dangerous, wouldn't it?"

"Oh, I'd try to get the photo and duck for cover."

They sat side by side without speaking for a few minutes.

"You know, Rachel, I don't know why the United States and Russia are enemies," Alex said. "We fought Hitler together. We should still work together."

"That would be nice," Ruth agreed. She sat for a while, staring into the fog and drizzle. She wrapped her arms around herself to keep out the chill. "Alex, I'm getting cold out here. Can we go inside somewhere?"

"Certainly, Rachel. What if we go see what Sasha is up to?"

"Sasha? Who is Sasha?"

"Sam Balk. His nickname is Sasha, like my mother calls me Sashka. Same thing. So, do you want to go see what he's up to?"

"Yeah…. Yeah, let's pay him a visit."

Ruth didn't have a chance to report her movement to Jennie.

They found Sam washing and waxing his sports car in a carport. He had moved it under the carport a short time ago. Muddy tire prints were on the concrete behind the vehicle.

Ruth put on an act worthy of the theater. She ogled the little car. "Oooh, that's so nice! What kind is it?"

"It is a Moretti Sports Coupe," Sam replied.

"I never heard of that kind of car before."

"It is a very good little Italian car, but not very expensive."

Ruth examined the inside of the vehicle. "How fast can it go?"

"I do not know for sure. I have driven it over ninety miles per hour. It felt like it could go faster. Tachometer was not near highest part of the gauge. But I did not want to get a speeding ticket so I slowed down."

"That must have been exhilarating!"

"Yes. How do you say? A real rush." It was clear all the attention pleased Sam. After all, that was why he spent the money on this car, to get the attention of pretty women.

"Can I take a picture of you standing next to it?"

"Sure, I guess so."

Ruth uncapped the lens of her camera. She looked through the viewfinder and noticed that the wheels were turned the right direction for her to clearly see the tire tread. "Sam, why don't you lean on the car, there?"

"All right," he said, resting his body against the side of the vehicle, just behind the wheel well.

Ruth took one step left a bit, making sure she not only got Sam in the picture but also a good view of the front tire. She took one shot of him there, then carefully changed to camera to get a close up of the tires. Sam seemed to sense the difference of the camera position.

"I think you have enough pictures now…."

"Rachel," Alex interrupted, "remember we were planning on seeing a movie. We should go."

"Oh, yeah. I'm sorry, Alex. I forgot all about the movie. Can we still make the showing we want?"

"Yes, I think so. If we hurry."

"Okay. Well, Sam, I'll see you later. Thanks for the neat photos!"

"You are more than welcome, Rachel," Sam grinned, basking in the attention he was getting. "More than welcome."

After the movie, when Ruth got home, she called Jennie and told her of the pictures she'd taken.

"That's great. Roll the film back into the canister and bring it to my place. I'll air mail the film to Rena tonight."

"Another thing, let Rena know that Sam Balk is also called Sasha. So I'd guess his given name is Alexander."

44. The End of Orient

Long Island

Stolichek heard something rustling leaves right behind him. Heart pounding, he jumped around to look who was behind him. He pointed his skunk essence spray where the noise had come from.

Nobody was there.

He heard more insistent rustling. Lower. On the ground. He moved to get a better view. He caught the flash of a fox as the startled animal ran away. A mouse's tail stuck out of its mouth.

Again, like after the incident with the watchdog, he had to catch his breath. Compose himself. Breathe normally. *I must be a hundred-percent city person,* he thought, *when a little animal scares me so badly. Or else we are way overworked.*

But Stolichek's nervousness was justified. If the wind was blowing right, the chained up dog tried to get to wherever the watchers were. Even when they varied their location. Pavio picked up their scent every time the wind blew from them to the house. The guards got more and more suspicious.

*   *   *   *

Delano watched the Cadillac Coupe de Ville pull up to the Orient house again. It arrived around ten-hundred. He had to tell Stolichek, who was at the apartment. But it would take too long to walk there. So he made his way to the shore of Long Island Sound at the far corner of the woods. He activated the

255

walkie-talkie they had set up for such emergencies.

"George, they're back, ya know?"

"Who's back, Del?"

"The guy in the Cadillac, o' course."

"Is he alone or are any other people with him?" Stolichek asked.

"This time he's alone."

"Hmmm, interesting. I wonder what he's up to."

"Ain't he the guy Rena had the FBI track down?"

"Yeah. He works in New York City. At the United Nations. And he has diplomatic immunity," Stolichek explained. "Anyway, any idea what's happening over there?"

"No. They were speakin' Russian as he walked inta the house 'n' tha other guys, tha guys who live there, ya know? They didn't seem too happy."

"Come on back to the apartment, Del. I'm going to try to get someone here who understands their language. We'll see if Rena can help us." He hung up and dialed the operator to set up the long distance call to his team leader at Great Lakes.

"Major Skye."

"George here. We need help as soon as possible. We…."

"Slow down, George. Losing another couple minutes won't hurt your job. Take a deep breath, then tell me what's going on, and then tell me what you think you need."

Stolichek forced himself to calm down. He explained the situation. "And we think this guy's reason for being here tonight isn't visiting old friends. We need someone here who can speak Russian. ASAP."

"You're in luck. We have a contact in New York City. Her name is Senny Rusakova. We have already used her to translate some coded directions these guys sent out to their agents in Port Hueneme."

"How soon can she be here?"

"We'll get her there as fast as we can. Give me directions to Del's apartment so she can meet you there." He did so. "Okay, thanks," she said. "I'll stay at the office until I hear back from you."

"It might be quite late by the time we get back here to call you, Rena."

"I'll wait. We need to break this thing open."

"I agree. I'll call soon as I can. Later."

Skye called Commander Charlie Skripps, who was in charge of OCI at the Brooklyn Navy Yard. "Can we get Senny again? We need a Russian speaker ASAP. On the far eastern end of Long Island. Tonight. With stethoscope and nightclothes. We need to listen to a visitor in a house full of Russians."

Stolichek and Delano waited for Rusakova. After a few minutes, Del stood up. "I'm gonna go back an' watch the house. Just ta keep an eye on it."

"Okay," George said. "Give me a call on the walkie-talkie if anything happens."

Del nodded his agreement.

Rusakova arrived two hours before sunset. She and Stolichek dressed in black. She pulled a stethoscope from her purse and placed the earpieces around her neck.

They walked out to meet Delano. They sat in the woods until it was dark enough to approach the house. Del cautioned them. "Wait a while. Tha puppy hasn't been out for his twalette yet."

"Del, we can't wait all night. They could be saying something important already," Stolichek said.

"Yeah," Del replied. "I know. They been waitin' fer us ta arrive all day before they start sayin' important stuff, ya know?"

"Good point. I'll go around to the other side of the house. I'll draw their attention if they come out and look like they detected you. See you later."

Rusakova smiled and waved good-bye. Holding up the stethoscope diaphragm, she smiled and whispered to Del: "I will go to the window of a room where they are located and listen with these. I will go alone. You stay here to watch out for me."

She ran, stooped over, to the house. Del had a hard time seeing her, even though he knew right where she was. She snuck up to a window. Looked in. Walked to another window, more toward the front of the house.

The guard and the dog came outside. Through the front door.

*   *   *   *

Senny heard the guard and the dog come outside. She squatted as low as she could get.

Stolichek was in the woods on the other side of the house. He heard and saw the guard and the dog. He got his essence of skunk ready. Rustled some leaves. Did it again.

The dog barked and ran toward him, almost howling. It approached Stolichek and began snarling.

The guard commanded it to return: "Pavio! Come here! Heel!"

But it was an exercise in futility.

Stolichek waited until the animal was very close. Then he sprayed him with skunk oil. Right in the face.

The dog howled and ran back to the guard. The guard hit him. Grabbed his collar. Cursed in Russian as he dragged the animal around to the back and chained him up outside. "Now, you stupid dog," he shouted in English. "Now you stay here all night. You like skunk, you smell him until I am ready to clean you."

The guard went back inside. Rusakova made her way to the next window. Del could see people inside the house, on the other side of the window that Rusakova now targeted. She stayed well below the windowsill. She squatted down and pushed the stethoscope diaphragm against the lowest part of the glass. She stayed in that position for a long time.

Del marveled at how she could maintain her crouched position for so long. After a long time motionless, she moved a little, putting one foot away from her a bit. Some time later she returned that leg to its original position and extended the other foot. Del was reminded of the kazatsky, the traditional Russian folk dance, in extreme slow motion.

She returned to Delano's location in the woods after forty-five minutes.

"Didja hear sumthin' interestin'?" he asked.

"I will tell you when we are back in your apartment. You can listen when I talk to Maychor Skye. Can you let your partner know we are coming back?"

Del nodded. They walked to the edge of the woods as far from the house as possible. He called Stolichek on the walkie-talkie. When he disconnected, he turned to Rusakova. "Okay. George said we can go. He's gonna keep on watching the house, ya know?"

"I know," the woman smiled. "We can go now?"

Del nodded, tapped her on the shoulder and pointed in the direction they should use to return to the apartment.

A short time later, Skye answered her phone.

"Rena, this is Senny. I have some news for you."

"I'm ready to write. What did you hear?"

Rusakova chuckled. "Much of the conversation was about the dog Chorch sprayed with his skunk smell. They were very irritated because the dog found, as they thought, another skunk. But it soon became evident they were already irritated and this made their mood worse."

"What was bothering them?"

"They discussed not finding out anything about testing missiles from submarines based in New London. They are now convinced Cape Canaveral does the testing. Then one of them asked 'Do you think we should tell Loki?' Rena, who is this Loki?"

"We think he's their team leader for this spy team. We've had other indications of him."

"All right, then, he is no mystery to you. It also seems they are working through some import company in Chicago. They are not working through New York or their embassy in Washington. DC."

"We suspected as much. We can concentrate on the people close to us. And perhaps not all of them have diplomatic immunity. That's very good to know. Did you find anything else out?"

"Yes. Evidently, the visitor here believes their house in Florida was compromised. From what I could understand from the conversation at this end, Loki thought they might not have to worry about it, since a man named Voight moved out of the area. Loki also ordered a man named Dobbins to leave Florida."

"I suppose the cabin cruiser named *Mermaid II* will also disappear."

"I heard nothing about a boat. Also, it seems that Loki is worried that you had photos to identify his people who worked in Florida. He ordered that if any of their people ever returned to that state, they will have orders not to take the chance and to eliminate the people watching them. In any way possible."

"I'll have to warn Ford," Skye said. "And have him warn all the rest of our people there. But I won't pull them out. They'll have to be more careful and keep their guard up. Was there anything else?"

"No. But I think it is worth my trip up here from New York City."

"Oh, I agree. I have your address from our last job together. I will send you a check in the mail."

"No! Please do not," Senny said. "I will give my claim to Commander Skripps. That way we keep my name away from prying eyes."

"Do you think these people are watching you?"

"I have seen no such indication. But I know how to play this game. I want to stay invisible as much as is possible."

"All right. Commander Skripps and I will settle the financial accounts between us, then. Thank you, Senny. Thank you very much."

"Any time, Rena. If you need me again, chust let Commander Skripps know. I will be glad to help."

*   *   *   *

It became obvious the Russian guards at the Orient house had become much more observant. They investigated the woods every night. Within a couple days, two more guards arrived to reinforce the ones already there. They began to stake out the woods on a regular basis.

On one such sweep, the guards surprised Stolichek. He scarcely had enough time to climb a nearby tree with large low branches. He paused for a second to spray some of the essence of skunk onto the tree trunk below him. He continued to climb higher. He got out of sight, hidden by foliage, moments before the guards arrived. The dog took one whiff of the skunk smell and backed off. The guards followed the animal example.

Stolichek hugged the trunk to made it more difficult for anyone to see him. He limited his movements to the times the breeze blew the branches and leaves around. He spent what seemed like ages there, holding so still he hurt. His muscles tied up in knots. His legs fell asleep. They were so numb he felt nothing in them, not even the pain. He maintained his position by holding on tighter, arms wrapped around the trunk.

A half hour later, the guards left.

Stolichek gave them some time so he wouldn't get caught if they returned quickly. It took a long time to work the knots out of his legs. Then the sleeping-limb prickliness flooded through his extremities. It was all he could do to stop himself from screaming. He worked his way back to ground level. Painfully. Branch by branch. Even though he got blood to flow again, when he touched the ground his legs buckled under him like they were made of rubber. He tried to work the stiffness and pain out. It was quite a while before he could move away from the area.

He sat on the edge of the woods, looking out over Long Island Sound. Got up and walked his muscles back to normal. That took a good half hour.

He heard the buzz of a plane. Looked up. Followed it on a track to the small landing field a quarter of a mile in front of him. He moved back into the woods and continued to watch.

The plane taxied to the side of the landing field closest to the path through the woods. A short time later, Vladimir Glazov, the "owner" of the Orient house, came into view. He was accompanied by Arkady, the guard, and Pavio, the dog. As soon as all three climbed into the aircraft, it taxied around and took off.

That afternoon, a moving van arrived. Movers packed up everything from the house and carted it away. Gana Glazov went with it.

The next day, a real estate agent came to the house and put up a "For Sale" sign.

45. The End of the Cape Watch

Cape Canaveral

Ford happened to be out at his hiding place on the Cape early. At 2100, he was treated to a successful Air Force Minuteman launch from Launch Complex 32B, located almost all the way up the cape itself. It rumbled. The blast noise grew louder. Ford had to cover his ears with his hands. He was happy because the breeze blew the smoke and chemical residue away from him. The missile slowly lifted on its pillar of fire. Gradually its trajectory tilted and the missile headed downrange.

Ford looked around. Nobody else was in his area. He grinned and thought: *Gee, that's too bad, Dobbins. You missed a good show.*

* * * *

"Allen Dobbins" and the *Mermaid II* disappeared a week after "Douglas Voight" caught his train. They showed up at the Orient house.

* * * *

Len Ford continued to make courtesy visits with Special Agent Tramora at the Air Force base's security office.

"Well, Len, do you have any new information for me?"

"It's slow and boring," he said. "We're watching the two guys I told you about before. The diver, Allen Dobbins, seems to have disappeared. And we've lost track of his cabin cruiser, the *Mermaid II*. When his contact, Douglas

Voight left for Chicago, the FBI followed him. We are now working hand in hand with the FBI. Otherwise, there's nothing new."

"Thanks for the update," Tramora said. "Did you hear about our recent shot yesterday?"

"No. What happened?" He prepared himself for more bad news on the American missile front.

"Yesterday morning, at 0745, the Air Force shot up a Mercury Atlas from Launch Complex 14. The liftoff was spectacular."

"The test was a success?"

Tramora laughed softly. "It was a success but it wasn't a success. The Atlas carried a very special cargo. They shot astronaut Scott Carpenter up in a spacecraft named the Aurora 7. It made three orbits around the Earth. The flight lasted five hours."

"So, Carpenter is the second American to go into space, right? And everything worked perfectly?"

"The missile did. However the Aurora 7 spacecraft had a few problems. Carpenter had to use the manual controls of the craft in order to splash down safely."

"He did it manually?"

"Yes. And in the process, he proved one thing beyond a doubt: a human could be a successful back up to all the automatic equipment. He pulled a rabbit out of the hat to complete a successful space mission."

Ford grinned. "Wow! Maybe we *will* be able to meet the president's goal to get a man on the moon by the end of the decade."

"Maybe, maybe not," Tramora said. "But in my mind, the biggest problem with this mission is that the NASA powers-that-be see Carpenter as a failure. I've heard some criticism about him not paying enough attention to his instruments. But it seems they were malfunctioning and the astronaut turned to manual controls to bring the Apollo back safely. I think he did a magnificent job. But he has to live with his bosses...."

*   *   *   *

On 2 June 1961, the Navy had two successful Polaris launches from the USS *Thomas A. Edison*, one a little past two in the afternoon and the other around five-thirty in the evening. Two days later they had a Polaris Launch failure from the launch complex next to the one where Ford had rested at his lookout station.

But the OCI team was gone. The members of the Cape Canaveral OCI group had been called back to their home offices.

*   *   *   *

Long Island

Two days after Glazov, his wife, and the Russian guards left the Orient house on Long Island, OCI special agents, Coast Guardsmen, and FBI agents took over the grounds of the yacht owner. They photographed everything, identified everyone who had been there, determined every entry and exit. Everyone else did all the work, but they kept Stolichek around to identify items or verify their assumptions.

Stolichek was bored. He was ready to return to his home base.

The FBI tracked down the Glazov families and arrested them. But since they worked for the Russian ambassador to the United Nations, they had diplomatic immunity. All the American authorities could do was to send them home with orders to never return.

And they were on the pier waiting for Eduard Pletner, the diver, when the *Mermaid II* tied up again; nobody had notified him of the pullout. The FBI arrested him for being in the restricted waters of the New London Submarine Base.

"Not me!" Pletner said. "I was not anywhere near there."

"We have photos." The FBI agent in charge showed them to him.

"You can't see my face there. I tell you, I was never anywhere near those submarines."

The agent snapped down one photo after another, as he spoke. "Here you are getting in the cabin cruiser. Here you are dropping anchor in the Thames. Here you are getting into your wet suit, tanks and mask. Here you are getting into the water from the cabin cruiser and nobody else was with you. OCI agents even went onto the cabin cruiser while you were gone. Here you are under water at the sub base's piers. Note the equipment there. It's the same as what the photos show when you were getting ready to go into the water. Here you are climbing out of the water and back onto your boat. Same equipment. Here you are leaving the craft at the pier of this property on Long Island. We have witnesses who can testify against you. And finally, we have recordings of your conversations with Vladimir Glazov. We have a solid case against you." The special agent turned to his subordinate agents. "Take him away. Put him in solitary until we get all his superiors in this case."

46. Take Him Down

Nebraska

Han made the call from Alliance, Nebraska. Rena had some new information that Chaské discovered about Little Horse.

"Chaské found this information yesterday," she said. "He got clarification on why Little Horse is using a name like that. The meanings of Czech names translate into Indian sounding names. They all have sensible and descriptive meanings."

"Like Little Horse?"

"Yes. His name in the Czech language is Jan Konichek."

"I suppose 'Yahn' is their pronunciation of John, right?"

"Yep."

"So how did Chaské dig this out?"

"We asked Commander Fasano here to run a check, no pun intended, on Little Horse. One of the Commander's aides is a man named Jacob Skala. He happened to overhear Fasano making some calls and asked about them. 'Isn't that an American Indian name?' he asked. Fasano replied that it sounded like one but our guys insisted he wasn't Indian. 'All right,' said Skala, 'then run an identification check on people named Konichek. He may be Czechoslovakian.' Then it was easy to get his ID."

"I'm curious. What does Jacob Skala's name mean?"

"It means 'strong as a rock'. Other typical translated names are 'man who hurries,' 'he slept standing,' and 'he makes a fool of someone'."

"So if Little Horse was so easy to find, did he have a criminal record?"

"As a matter of fact, yes. And it fits into your situation. This guy is the son of immigrants who swam down a river to Austria and freedom. But it was one big fake. They are all agents for the Russians. His record is a string of flying into prohibited areas. It didn't surprise anyone to hear he was also flying a plane with no identification number on it."

"So what do we do now? Take him down?"

"You know Commander Blount is our commanding officer, and Fasano is our temporary boss because he's right here. When I let Blount know what Chaské found out about Konichek, he said to go get him."

"Aren't we in danger of alerting his people in St. Louis?"

"No," Rena replied. "We'll put out a news release about him being charged with flying into prohibited areas. So go get him out of there."

As soon as Han returned to the camp, he provided three others with handcuffs. Most of the men already had weapons, both pistols and rifles. Han had the whole group surround the house and the barn. He banged on the front door.

"Open up! Federal officers!"

Little Horse tried to run out the back door. Troy knocked him to the ground. Handcuffed him. After searching the house, they found undeveloped photos of missile silos on his person.

Han and Troy took the prisoner to Ellsworth. Han flew with him to Glenview where Skye and some local agents picked him up and took him to Great Lakes.

When interrogated, he showed his citizenship papers, but refused to say anything other than his name and a request for a lawyer. They promised him a lawyer well before his trial. Then they put him in solitary confinement, where they planned to keep him until they took the whole spy ring down. Then they would put him on trial.

47. Orders to Kill

Saint Louis

It was raining again. Ruth and Alex sat protected in a gazebo in the middle of a park. They talked for quite a while. Then Alex was silent.

"What are you thinking about?" Ruth asked.

"I love cowboy movies," Alex said.

"Cowboys and Indians?"

"No. Cowboy movies where the sheriff tracks down outlaws, bank robbers, killers, those kinds of guys. Gunslingers."

"So you like the shoot 'em up movies."

"Yeah. And horses. I love horses. I want to learn to ride a horse."

"But you wouldn't want to ride in the rain and the thunder. Loud noises can spook a horse, and if you are new to handling the animal, you can find yourself on the ground, fast."

"Well, Rachel, then we shouldn't go horse riding today."

Ruth laughed. "I will find out where we can go to visit a stable and ride horses."

"Really? When can we do it?"

"I'm getting tired of all this rain. It's dreary. We can go out there on the next clear day."

"I can't wait!" Alex exulted. "I'll get to ride a horse!"

*　　*　　*　　*

"Loki," his aide, Leonid Mazursky, said. "They arrested Konichek."

"On what charges?" Loki asked.

"Flying over restricted areas."

"Is that the only thing of which they accuse him?"

"That is all the news release mentioned."

"Nothing about espionage?"

"No."

"Very good. Be sure he doesn't crack and tell anyone anything else," Loki commanded. "But I am much more concerned about the big picture, as they say. What is happening to our people? First California, then Gyorgi disappears in Nebraska, and now this. Has someone found out about us? I want you to check with our OCI insider and find out."

*   *   *   *

There was thunder but no rain. Alex and Ruth walked along the river. They sat on the T-shaped pier and talked. When they parted, Ruth called Jennie to check in.

"I'm glad you called," Jennie said. "I wanted to thank you for getting the photos of Sam Balk's sports car. Rena is having them evaluated right now. I think they point to this guy, Sam Balk, and take the suspicion away from your friend Ponomarev."

"I hope so. Alex has some attitudes I don't especially like. But he's a naïve young man, not a killer."

"You may be right. And OCI Lakes is researching some other questions."

"Like what?"

"Rena and Chaské are trying to identify this Sam Balk, whose nickname is Sasha," Jennie answered. "And since Sasha is a nickname for Alexander, they're also searching for an Alexander Balk. And for anyone with those first names and a last name 'Balk' could be derived from."

"Sounds like quite a job. Wish them luck for me."

"Will do. Meantime, you stay as far away from these guys as possible without raising any suspicions. I'm trying to get Rena to pull all of us out of this city, for safety's sake."

"I'll be very careful," Ruth promised.

"Also, can we meet tonight some time?"

"Sure. Why?"

"I'd feel you were a lot safer if you had Tango with you. Let's meet so you can pick him up."

"You think I need to?"

"Yes. This is an order," Jennie insisted. "Something is whispering a warning inside me. God, are we all becoming intuitive like Rena?"

"I don't think so. I'm not getting any such messages."

"Anyway, I want you to take Tango with you."

Ruth met with Jennie an hour later. She climbed into the latter's car to be greeted by slobbering kisses from the Saint Bernard. She tried to wipe herself dry. "Thanks, Tango. Now I'm convinced you really love me."

"So, do you think Ponomarev is even one of the spies?" Jennie asked.

"I don't know. He doesn't impress me as the type. But I agree that Sam Balk, also called Sasha, may very well be our killer."

"I concur. I got to look at the photos and reports you took. Balk looks like Stalin. He's in the play *Winston, Franklin and Joe*. And he has the sports car that left the tire tracks at the murder scene. So be very, very careful for the rest of the time you're there. And stay away from Balk."

"Yes ma'am. I will," Ruth said.

"What are you planning for tomorrow?"

"We've all been drinking too much lately. So Alex and I are going out for a walk along the river tonight. And he's always wanted to ride a horse, so I made reservations to take him out to a stable in a couple days."

"Okay. Take Tango with you," Jennie said.

Ruth turned to the Saint Bernard. "Okay with you, boy?" The big dog put his front paws on the floor. This gave him enough room to wag his tail while he tried to give more kisses.

"Okay," Ruth laughed. "You can come with me."

*　*　*　*

"Loki, you remember Ponomarev?

"Of course. What about him?"

"He and a young woman named Rachel showed up at my house. She got all excited about my car, and took photos of it with me standing next to it."

"Why did you let this happen?" Loki demanded.

"She was cute. And all gushy over me and the beautiful sports car."

"Gushy? What is gushy?" Balk said it in Russian. "Oh. Gushy…. Hmf!"

"I stopped her after a few photographs. But I think if I made a big protest about it, she may have become suspicious…."

"Why should she?" Loki demanded. "Is she police or government agent, maybe?"

"Oh, I do not think so. But I wanted to be safe, so I ended it. But she was very cute."

"You are a fool, Sasha. Sometimes you think with your penis instead of your brain. Get out of my sight. Go on. Go away."

* * * *

Loki's aide approached him.

"Too many events are happening," Leonid said.

"What are you talking about?"

"Our man in California had to run to Canada. One man in Nebraska disappeared, and another was arrested for flying in restricted areas. We had to pull out of Long Island. And now our agents in Florida…."

"What are you trying to say?" Loki demanded.

"Maybe it is time to end this. As they say, close shop. Pull out. Leave."

"Not yet. We still have work to do. There is a delivery to make. And there are other tasks to do…. No, not yet, Leonid. But soon. Perhaps."

* * * *

"There is a very small Russian community here," Alex explained to Ruth. "There are really only three places where we can spend time with other Russians in a Russian atmosphere. There's the Izbiza Bar, Club Viktor and a small Russian Culture Center."

"I've been to the first two but not the Cultural Center. Where is it?"

"It's on DeMenil Road, the same street as a bunch of old mansions. It's kind of close to the famous Chatillon DeMenil House."

"It sounds kind of swanky. Not the sort of place one would associate with new immigrants."

"The owner of the house is very rich. He works with imports and exports. He makes a lot of money in his business. All the Americans want things from other countries. Greg, the owner of the house, lives on the top floors and lets us use his main floor as the Russian Culture Center for dining, drinking and dancing. Would you like to see it, Rachel?"

"I guess so. When can we go there?"

"How about this evening?"

The place was impressive. In the parlor, there were museum pieces placed on numerous shelves: nested matryoshka dolls, games and artwork.

The living room had been converted into a small dance floor with a bar off to one side. This was located across the room from three large mirrors. The woodwork was made of rich mahogany with northern white ash highlights. On either side of the mirrors there were built-in bookshelves made in the same style as the woodwork. Ruth looked over their contents. Most were in Russian, though there were some classics in translation.

She sat down at a table while Alex bought drinks. Laura Jaf came over to the table. "Ru... uh Rachel, let me introduce my new friend, Sam Balk. Sam, this is my friend from my hometown. Her name is...."

"Rachel... uh ... Johnson, is it not?" Sam smiled through his bushy mustache.

"Yes," Ruth replied. She turned to Laura. "Linda, we've already met. Alex took me to Sam's house to pick up tickets to his play. It looks like you made a good friend here. Congratulations!"

Laura and Sam looked at each other with amusement. Ruth wondered about that. *Well*, she thought, *maybe it's an indication they're happy to be together*.

Alex returned with another man. "Greg, I would like you to meet my friend, Rachel Johnson. Rachel, this is Greg Ekk, the owner of this place."

Ruth looked up at the man. He was average height with short brown hair, clean shaven. His angular face radiated a look of extreme confidence. His body was muscular, well developed. He held a vodka martini in his left hand and stroked the red and yellow rose in his lapel with his right. Then he stopped fondling the flower and reached out, took Ruth's hand and bowed slightly. "We are lucky, indeed, to have such a beautiful young woman in our center. Welcome, my dear Rachel. Welcome."

They talked for a few minutes before Ekk excused himself to take care of some business.

Ruth later went home and reported in to Jennie. She reviewed the three Russian clubs in town, where the "Russian Cultural Center" was located, and it's owner, someone named Greg Ekk or whatever Greg would be in Russian.

Jennie was silent for a moment, then she asked: "Was Tango with you?"

"No. I had to leave him in my car."

Jennie sighed. "I really want you to stay away from these guys. It's getting to be too dangerous."

"At least I was able to get you some more important information."

"Yes. We'll check this Greg out. His full name would be Gregory or something similar. This whole thing kind of makes sense. They're part of the community. Putting on plays. Hiding in the open. No one suspects anything because it all seems open and honorable. We know there are other cells hiding in New York City, Chicago, Boston, Los Angeles. And I think it's smart to hide where there are very few other people like you and still live openly. These

Russians aren't dumb. We need to keep an eye on them somehow. But a wary eye. I think these folks are very dangerous. You be careful, Ruth. Don't take any unnecessary chances. Stay clear of any place Sam Balk might be."

"Yes, ma'am."

*   *   *   *

There was another party at the Russian Culture Center. Ruth ignored Jennie's orders. She left Tango alone in her apartment so she could go to the party with Alex.

Loki sat in his dark office watching the crowd through the two-way mirrors. There was enough light on the other side to let Loki see out but not let the others see in.

A woman stood alongside him. When Ruth appeared she leaned over and whispered in Loki's ear. He looked up sharply, questioningly. "Are you certain?"

"Absolutely. She is part of OCI, investigating the murder of those two truck drivers."

"You should have let me know this the very first time she came here," Loki said. "We may already be too damaged to recover. Get Sasha in here now." The woman left in a hurry, but she mixed with the crowd in a normal relaxed manner.

Balk entered the office a few minutes later. "You wanted to see me?"

"Yes," Loki hissed. He pointed to Ruth on the other side of the two-way mirrors. "See that woman there?"

"You mean Rachel?"

"The one who calls herself Rachel. It is not her true name."

"Oh? What do you want me to do?"

"I want her dead. As soon as possible."

48. Firethorn Discovered

Great Lakes

"Hi, Rena," Chaské said when they met at the coffee pot.

"Hi! What's new?" she asked.

"I can't find any indication of Sam Balk being 'Sasha.' In fact I can't find anything on Sam Balk at all. There's no data, no ID, no driver's license. Nothing."

"Nuts." She took a sip of hot coffee. "Any good news?"

"Yes, as a matter of fact. Alex Ponomarev is the child of legal hardworking immigrant parents. His father was from Russia. His mother is a native-born US citizen."

"But the tire prints seem to point to Sam Balk's car.... And Ruth found out Alex's mother's nickname for *him* is Sashka. But he's not the killer." She sipped her coffee again. "Sam Balk is the Sasha we're is looking for. I'm sure of it. But we have to find proof."

"This might help. We know 'Sasha' is a nickname for Alexander. I'm already running a search on 'Alexander Balk.' We'll see what pops up."

"Thanks, Chaské. There has to be information on this guy somewhere."

*   *   *   *

Time continued to drag along on this unproductive morning. The afternoon turned out to be better. The phone rang about 1230. "Major Skye here."

"Major, this is Jack Barstow in the OCI lab. I have a bunch of photos the Waves in Saint Louis sent us. We've completed an analysis of some of them for you. Can I come up with them?"

"Definitely. I'm very anxious to see this information."

When Barstow arrived at Rena's desk he laid out the photos for her. "These," he said, "are the tire prints of the car the ladies saw."

"Those tracks look pretty close to the ones from the crime scene."

"They're identical. Who does the car belong to?"

"A guy named Sam Balk. We know who he is. Now we know he's the killer...."

Barstow rubbed his chin. "Well, I think so...."

"Why the uncertainty?"

"A vehicle can be borrowed from another person, an immigrant friend or a parent.... This car was at the murder scene. But we don't know who was driving it."

"Oh, crap. That fits with the way my whole day has been going so far."

"Sorry I can't be more help."

"No problem. You did your job and I have more data than I had an hour ago. Thanks." She paused. "By the way, did they send in other photos from Saint Louis?"

"Yes, they're in this envelope. Here, take it and put it in your files."

"Thanks."

"And if I find any new information, I'll contact you right away."

Barstow wasn't even out of sight when Rena started going through the pile of photos. She pulled one of them out. Went over to Chaské's desk. Handed him the picture. "This might help you somewhere along the line."

"Who's this?"

"Sam Balk. This is one of the photos Ruth took in Saint Louis. Thought it might come in handy for you."

Later that day, Chaské appeared at Rena's desk again. She looked up. He was smiling.

"You find something good?" she asked.

He nodded. "I think this might be our lucky day."

"Oh?"

"My search for 'Alexander Balk' paid off. There's an Alexander Balykin on the lists of the Soviet Embassy staff in DC. He's the son of a member of the embassy's technical staff. Which means he and his parents all have diplomatic immunity."

"Are you sure Balk and Balykin are the same person?"

"Absolutely. That photo Ruth sent you of the people in Saint Louis proved it. I got the official identification photo for Balykin from the State Department. No doubt about it, it's the same guy."

274

"So 'Sam' or 'Sasha' will be expelled from the U. S. back to the Soviet Union," Chaské commented. "Basically, he will be able to get away with murder. What're we going to do about him?"

"I don't know. Have to think about that."

* * * *

Chaské appeared at Rena's desk again. She looked up. "Yes?"

"I found out who owns the St. Louis house." He paused.

"Let me guess. New Horizon Imports."

"Close. The owner of record is Great River Medical Manufacturing Corporation. Which is another subsidiary of New Horizon."

"Interesting," she smiled. "New Horizon seems to be everywhere, doesn't it? But they won't own anything in a short time. Have you confirmed the ownership of the Little Horse ranch?"

"Not yet. That's next."

"Okay. Thanks, Chaské."

* * * *

The next afternoon, Commander Fasano called Rena into his office.

"Close the door." He pointed to a sideboard along one wall. "Get a drink."

"Uh-oh. Something pretty bad must have happened. But I don't want a drink this early." She sat down.

"All right. But remember where that bottle is," Fasano sighed. "We got this through various channels from our mole in the USSR."

Rena frowned. She took the paper the Commander held out. She read it, got up and poured a stiff shot of the offered scotch. After she returned to her chair, she said: "I assume this is for real or you wouldn't have shown it to me."

"You're right. This is the result of a top secret report from some of their field agents. They discovered a counter-espionage effort called Operation Firethorn, which is trying to infiltrate the Soviet spy network to either feed it false information or to put it out of existence."

"Operation Firethorn. That even identifies the traitor. I gave each of them a different operational name."

"I remember. And I remember you had different doubts about each of them. No more than three people used the term 'Operation Firethorn.' You, me, and that one operative."

"So what do we do now? If we arrest her, the spy ring knows OCI is on to

275

them. If we don't arrest her, she gets away." She paused. "I sure wish I could call and warn the others, but I don't dare. If they reacted in the wrong manner, they could tip our hand."

"From your report yesterday, I know we've found out who Sasha is. We've identified the tire prints."

"And some time ago, we solved the crossword puzzle and the message in blood," Rena added. "What we thought was '6-oh-c' was actually the beginning of "6 DOWN," in capital letters. We mistook the 'D' for an 'O' and the beginning of the 'O' for a 'C.' The trucker tried to write '6 DOWN' in his own blood. The clue for that part of the crossword was 'Soviet leader at Yalta.' That's the role Sasha or Sam Balk plays. Balk knew the trucker so he had to kill him. Then he took every bit of his identification to try to keep our suspicion as far away as possible from the killer."

"Call the ladies home, Major. We can take care of the spy once they're all back here safely. One of them is a traitor who is endangering the others. Call them home. Now. That's an order."

"Aye, aye, sir. I will contact Jennie right away. I'll have her round them up and bring them back." She returned to her desk, very worried. Her heart pounded. She called Jennie's apartment in Saint Louis. It rang over and over. "Come on, Jennie," she muttered. "Be home. Answer your phone."

She let the phone ring twenty times before hanging up.

Rena tried calling four more times, with the same results.

"What, are they out on the town or something?" she muttered as she tried calling yet again.

49. Death of an Agent

Saint Louis

Again, Saint Louis had thunder but the threat of rain didn't materialize. Ruth and Alex walked along their favorite spot of the Mississippi River. Tango trotted alongside, tongue hanging out, begging for another stick to chase. Once again Ruth threw the stick in her hand, as far down the road as she could.

"I have a surprise for you, Alex," Ruth said.

"What is it?"

"I made reservations at a stable for us to go horseback riding. Tomorrow at two in the afternoon. At last you get to ride a horse."

"That is a good time. I will be back from church."

"You're religious?"

"Yes. I was raised Orthodox and have kept it up."

Ruth nodded. *Is he really?* she thought. *Or is he just saying that. If he is religious I'd bet he's not a member of the Communist Party. Therefore not one of the spy ring.*

Tango returned with the stick.

"Enough with the stick, Rachel. Tango already has plenty of exercise. Try this." He reached down and picked up a flat stone. He inspected it approvingly. "We did this with such rocks at home." He threw the rock with a whiplash side-arm pitch. It sailed out over the water.

Ruth hung onto Alex's other arm and watched the stone skip across the water as far out as the darkness let them see. They looked like most young couples who walked along the riverfront together.

Jennie Powers remained in her car well behind them, watching. She

277

checked the time. It was 2030.

Ruth threw the stick again for the dog. She threw it out their favorite T-shaped pier. Tango ran after it. He picked it up in his mouth, held it and sat on the pier. The couple followed him onto the pier.

Alex and Ruth heard footsteps behind them. They turned. Sam Balk stood where the pier met land. He held a revolver in his hand. He pointed it at the couple. Alex gestured toward his friend. "Sasha, what are you doing?"

"First, we get rid of the traitor among us."

Alex misunderstood Balk's comment. He thought Ruth was in terrible danger. He shoved her toward the edge of the pier in hopes of pushing her to safety in the water. But Ruth's instincts won out. She teetered on the edge of the pier, keeping herself from falling into the river.

Sasha aimed at Alex and pulled the trigger. The bullet slammed into the center of the young man's chest. Ponomarev crumpled to the pier. The shooter turned to Ruth, who had regained her balance.

What should I do now? Thoughts raced through her head.

Sasha continued: "A reliable source told us you are a United States police officer. So...."

Ruth saw his hand squeeze the pistol as he pulled the trigger slowly. She dove behind some crates on the pier. The shot zipped right through the thin wood. It hit her on her left front side, below her breast. The bulletproof vest worked but the impact of the shot broke a rib. Ruth staggered back. She stumbled and fell into the water. As she fell, she pulled the hollow barrette off her head. Put one end in her mouth. Hit the water. Tried to float face down on surface as if she were dead.

Balk ran to the edge of the pier. He fired more shots at the woman, who floated semi-submerged with the current. One shot went through Ruth's left arm but missed the bone. She took a deep breath, as if gasping. Sasha fired another shot. This one broke her hipbone. She shuddered. Forced herself to go limp. Let out her breath and sank.

Tango growled deep in his throat. He jumped up on his hind legs. Pushed Sasha into the water. Looked over the pier to watch Sam flail for a few seconds. Then he ran back to land looking for Ruth. He ran around from spot to spot but couldn't find her.

Sasha swam to shore. He came out grumbling and shaking the water from his pistol. "Now I will kill dog, too."

He shot at the Saint Bernard but missed. Tango ran into the darkness of a nearby alley.

Merry was with Jennie in the car. She wanted to get out and shoot Balk.

"What would you use to shoot him with?" Jennie asked.

"Rena gave us two-shot zip guns."

"It wouldn't work, Merry. You have to get real close for those to be effective. Zip guns are for close-in protection, not this kind of situation."

Jennie's first instinct had also been to open the car door and run to help Ruth. *No, it would take too long for me to get there*, she thought. *And then what could I do? He'd shoot me, too, and then I wouldn't be able to help at all. Best to wait until he leaves then do what I can.* So she watched in horror from the car.

*　*　*　*

Ruth floated half submerged. She knew she was hurt badly. Hit at least in three places. She moved slowly, hoping beyond hope that Sasha would not hear her purposeful movements. She slowly propelled herself through the water. She took a long slow breath, doing her best not to swallow any of the river water. Yard by yard, she made her way toward a string of doubled up barges a short distance downstream. But she was too weak to get up onto them.

She prayed that somehow she would be able to get back onto solid land, but she wasn't sure that she had the strength to get out of the water, let alone do anything if she could. She knew she would need someone's help.

But she had no idea where anyone else was. Alex was probably dead. She didn't know where Jennie was. And she had no idea where Tango was. Maybe he'd run off to safety.

Sasha reloaded his gun.

Jennie watched with bated breath for half an hour as the Russian searched. He made his way to the barges. Jumped onto them. Looked down into the water searching for his prey.

Tango ran around the block and returned to Jennie's car. She saw him coming toward her. Opened the car door as quietly as she could. The dog jumped in, whining. The woman closed the door most of the way and shushed the animal. "We can't do anything yet, boy. So we stay here and watch. And pray...."

Ruth heard Sasha's footsteps on the barge above her. She controlled her fear enough to realize there were a series of ropes hanging from the barge deck into the water. She used them to pull herself around to the front of the barge. Her heart pounded in terror every time she made the least bit of noise. At last she turned a corner and found herself under the barge's overhanging bow. She hung on to another dangling rope. She held on for dear life. But she was exhausted and weak from loss of blood. She could feel herself losing strength. Gradually, her hold on the rope loosened and she began to sink. She wrapped the line around her wrist in what seemed like slow motion. But now she was able to stop sinking.

Jennie watched from her darkened car for more then a half an hour. Watched the killer searching. Felt her body shaking with the fear that she might be too late when she finally reached Ruth. She prayed intensely between sobs. When Sasha finally left, the dog tried to get out of the car. Fearing he'd break a window, Jennie held onto the scruff of his neck. "Not yet, Tango. Give him time to get far enough away."

She opened the car window and listened intently. A few minutes later a car started. Then the sound of its motor grew louder. The sports car zipped out of a side street in front of Jennie's car. Turned to her direction.

"Merry, Tango, get down on the floor! Now!" She pushed the dog down and leaned over on top of him. She could hear Sasha's car slow down. Sense that he was checking out her car.

Tango, don't breathe, she thought. *And you damn well better not bark.*

At last the car revved up and sped off.

Jennie stayed put a moment longer. She whispered: "God, I hope he's gone for good...."

After a few moments, she sat up straight. Tango climbed back onto the seat. Jennie opened the door. The dog jumped across her lap and made a mad dash down the street and across the barges, barking softly.

Jennie drove up the street to where the barges were tied before she stepped out.

Tango found Ruth and whined.

"Tango," Ruth murmured. "Help me...." The dog grabbed the rope she held. He pulled her up. But Ruth didn't have the strength to climb onto the barge. She fell back. Hung on as best she could, but her hands slipped. She tried to tighten her hold on the rope but slipped again. Tango yelped and let go of the rope.

Ruth heard a click, like a gun being cocked. She felt a hand on her wrist. Her spirits plummeted. "Oh, no! He's found me...."

*   *   *   *

Sasha stood before Loki and Leonid. "The woman is dead."

"It is now one-thirty. What took so long?" Loki asked.

"I had to search all over. But still I could not find her body."

"So, then, she is not dead...."

"I swear she is! I know I hit her at least three times. I saw blood. Saw her floating face down with the current for ten minutes."

"So where is her body?"

"I told you, I could not find it. I searched for twenty minutes. Believe me, she drowned and sank beneath the water. She is dead. Do not worry."

"Well, we shall wait and see. I want to be certain about this. She can identify us, Sasha. We must have her dead. Watch the obituaries and the stories in the newspapers. Be sure she is dead."

*   *   *   *

Jennie was on her knees. She reached down with one hand and pulled on Ruth's wrist. She grabbed Ruth's hair with her other hand. Then she pulled Ruth out of the water. The wounded woman was almost unable to move. She rolled her head, eyes wild with fear. She saw Jennie but it took her a while to recognize her friend.

In her delirium, Ruth mumbled: "Alex.... Poor Alex...."

Then, with a sigh, she passed out.

"Come on, you poor girl. Let's get you some help," Jennie whispered. She lifted Ruth with a fireman's carry. She started for the car. Tango trotted ahead, watching for strangers. Jennie placed Ruth onto the back seat where Merry tried to make her more comfortable. She raced to a hospital she'd seen a couple days earlier. Pulled into the entrance to the emergency room, jumped out and ran in. She flashed her U. S. Government identification, shouting: "I have a wounded law officer in my car. Take care of her now!"

Ruth was soon in emergency surgery under the care of a Dr. Masters. A nurse took down all the pertinent information. Then Jennie waited. And waited. Two hours later, the doctor came out. "They're still working on Miss Gardner," he told Jennie, "but she's going to pull through. She was very lucky. There were no internal organs or arteries hit. That makeshift bullet-proof vest saved her life."

Jennie showed him her OCI identification. "We want her shipped to the U.S. Naval Hospital at Great Lakes as soon as possible."

The doctor shook his head. "I can't. She'll die if she's moved too soon."

"As soon as possible, then. Meanwhile, do not let anyone in to see her. Not a single person except me. And if anybody asks about her, tell them she's dead. This must be kept secret or they'll try to kill her again."

"Who is 'they'?"

"Some enemies of the United States. Leave it at that."

"I understand. We'll keep her presence secret."

"Furthermore, to be sure we stop the people trying to kill her, I need a death certificate for Ruth."

Dr. Masters shook his head again. "Why?"

"I need to get a death notice put in the newspapers. To persuade the would-be killers they did their job. Then they'll quit looking for her."

"You don't need a death certificate to buy an obituary notice in the newspaper."

*   *   *   *

Jennie banged on the door of the Saint Louis Globe-Democrat. After pounding for over ten minutes, a man opened the door. "Will ya quit beating on the door? We got work to do, lady."

Jennie flashed her federal identification. "I need to see the person in charge here."

"Person in charge is the night editor. He's busy. And so am I...." He started to swing the door shut.

Jennie stuck her foot in the way. "I'm a federal law officer, and I...."

"Lemme see your ID again." He looked at it closely. "What's O-C-I? I never heard of it before."

"It's the Office of Criminal Investigation. The special police force of the United States Navy." The janitor didn't quite know what to do. Powers continued: "Check with your night editor. Let him make the decision whether or not to see me. But tell him this is a mater of life or death."

"Life or death, huh?" He scratched the back of his head. "Stay right there. I'll be back whether the boss wants to see ya or not." He shut the door.

Ten minutes later the night editor opened the door. "Hello. My name is Roger. May I see your identification?" Jennie showed it to him. He examined it closely. "Come on in, sit down and tell me what you want me to do. I'll see if I can help you."

Jennie explained the situation. "We're on a case and got a person inside a criminal ring. They discovered who she was and tried to kill her. We want them to think they succeeded. Can you print an obituary in the morning paper?"

"I should be able to move some items around and make room, if your piece isn't too long.... Write it up for me." He slid a pencil and paper over to her.

Jennie wrote: "Ruth Emily Gardner, 26, died of gunshot wounds while being robbed on Zepp Street. No known family survives her. Gardner was a Wave serving at the Great Lakes Naval Station. Her body will be released to the U. S. Navy for disposition."

The obituary appeared in the newspaper the next morning. Laura saw it and showed it to Sam. "You got her!"

They took the paper in to show Loki.

*   *   *   *

Skye's phone rang. "Major Rena...."

"This is Jennie ...."

"Where the hell have you been?" Skye shouted. "I've been trying to reach you for a day and a half!" Then she noticed the sobbing in her friend's voice. "Jennie, what's wrong?"

"Ruth was shot...."

"Oh, God. How bad...?"

"Pretty bad. They did almost three hours of surgery on her. She's out now and recovering. But...."

"How soon can you get her back here?" Rena asked.

"The doctor said at least a week...."

"No. Not good enough. You have to get her home sooner."

"I know. I'm trying. I was very worried the Russians would find out they didn't kill her and come after her again. But I was able to get a false obituary printed in the local newspaper. It got in this morning's issue. I did everything I...."

"Slow down, Jennie. Come up for air." Rena could hear Jennie taking a few deep breaths. "All right. Is Ruth in a secure place?"

"Yes."

"I'm sending Chaské down there. Armed. To protect her."

"Good."

"I want you to send the other Waves back here right now. You come, too, as soon as Chaské gets there. You understand?"

"Aye, aye, ma'am."

50. The End in Nebraska

Nebraska

Han and his Lakota friends continued to watch the Little Horse ranch. Even though Jan Konichek was no longer there, they still took photos and documented every move the other people made. It was dull and boring work, but they had their orders. There were always volunteers to go into Alliance, make the regular telephone report and go shopping for food. Anything to relieve the boredom.

A few days later the FBI showed up and took all the people at the ranch into custody.

The OCI team finally got orders to shut down their operation.

51. Back at Great Lakes

Saint Louis

Chaské reached Saint Louis during the night. He visited Ruth's room, but she was sleeping. Somehow he found the strength not to wake her up. He left her and stood outside her room. None of the hospital staff knew he carried a .22 caliber pistol in the pocket of his baggy pants.

Two days later the Navy was able to take Ruth out of Saint Louis. They sent a plane in with a "stokes stretcher," a metal tube and wire mesh device with which the Navy carried wounded sailors around a ship without causing more damage than had already been sustained. They put Ruth in the stretcher, put the stretcher on a gurney and covered both with a sheet. Rolled the gurney to an ambulance. Whisked the supposed cadaver away to the airport where the Navy plane waited. In a matter of hours Ruth was delivered to "Hospitalside" at Great Lakes.

*   *   *   *

Gardner was put in a private room at the U. S. Naval Hospital at Great Lakes. Two OCI guards stood outside her door. Skye presented her identification.

"Yes, ma'am. We know who you are. You have permission to visit this patient any time you desire."

"Thanks. Who else can get in to see her?" Rena asked.

"The medical personnel whose photos we have for comparison. Commander Fasano of the OCI office here at Great Lakes. A Commander Blount, if he comes in from Norfolk. And you, Major. Those are the people we

285

can allow to enter this room. Oh, yes, four of your operatives, Cobbe, Ford, Hunter, and Stolichek, can enter to guard her from the inside. Orders of the commanding officer of Hospitalside."

"Good. Thank you. May I go in now?"

"Yes, ma'am," one of the guards said as he opened the door for her.

Cobbe was the guard inside the room. As Rena entered, he asked: "Want me to leave, Major?"

"No, you can stay."

"Yes, ma'am."

Ruth had a heavy cast around her hip and a large bandage on her left arm. Her other cast was under her gown. She was awake.

"Hi, Ruth! They taking good care of you here?" Rena asked.

"Yes." Ruth tried to sit up straighter. She gasped in pain. Her hand flew to her left side and held it as she took rapid and shallow breaths.

Rena frowned. "Were you hit in the chest, too?"

"Yes and no," Ruth said between clenched teeth. "The first shot hit the bullet-proof vest. It protected me but it hit me like a sledge hammer and broke a rib."

"So don't try to sit up. Lay there and rest." Rena pulled a chair around so she could sit facing her operative.

"Where's everyone else?" Ruth asked. "I was sure Chaské would visit me as soon as he could."

"He was the one who brought you back under guard from Saint Louis. He's resting right now. You can see him in due time. But first, tell me everything you remember about the night you were shot."

"Don't remember all of it," she murmured.

"Tell me what you can."

Ruth spoke haltingly. She related everything she could, sometimes going back to fill in the details. Rena listened carefully. She finished: "I can't believe he could do this. How could he? Someone who grows such beautiful flowers?"

Rena decided to keep Gardner's whereabouts secret. And to be sure it stayed secret, she decided to tell all of the other operatives she'd been killed. Other than the guards at Hospitalside, only two people in her office, Chaské and Jennie, knew the truth about Ruth's situation.

Rena called her group in for a meeting. Merry had returned days ago, after Jennie sent her back. Rena had reassigned Merry to another operation where she wouldn't be required to do undercover work.

Rena met with the others in the group's staff meeting room. Chaské, Jennie, Laura, and everyone else of the special OCI undercover unit who were at Great

Lakes were required to attend. "I'm afraid I have some bad news." She paused for effect. "Lt(j-g) Ruth Gardner is dead."

Laura cried out like she'd lost a sister. She began wailing. She couldn't stop sobbing. Tears flowed down her cheeks.

She is one hell of a good actress, thought Rena.

Chaské and Jennie sat and watched. They didn't want to interfere with what Rena was doing or with Laura's display. Each was able to put a look of disbelief on his face, just for show.

Chaské swallowed hard. "How do we know this?"

"I saw the report in the Saint Louis newspaper," Laura said between sobs.

Skye continued: "We believe she was killed by the same man who killed the truck drivers."

"Where is her body?" Chaské asked quietly. "The last time I saw her was when we got back and some medical people were rolling away a covered gurney."

"She's in the morgue," Skye lied. "We're performing an autopsy and trying to determine the exact cause of death. When we're done, when the case is over, we'll have her funeral at Arlington National Cemetery. Like we did with Brandon Lunch."

Chaské lowered his head and looked up through narrowed eyes. Rena was glad that he was also a very good actor.

Laura continued sobbing loudly.

I should arrest Jaf right now and throw her into the brig, Skye thought. *But then I'd still have to get enough on her to convict her. I think the best bet would be to give her enough rope to hang herself.*

When the meeting was over, Skye turned to go back to her desk. Chaské stepped up alongside her. He held her arm, stopping her from leaving. "Let's talk." Chaské shut the door then, confronted her. "I just want to know how Ruth really is."

"As far as the others, everyone except you and Jennie are concerned, she's dead, Chaské."

He stared at her. His eyes bored into her. "And in reality? I haven't tried to visit her. Like I said, I last saw a covered gurney being rolled into the hospital. But she wasn't dead when I flew with her from Saint Louis."

Rena placed her hand on his arm. "She's at Hospitalside. Under protective guard, recuperating," she said quietly. "She's going to live. Go home now and rest. I'll talk to you tomorrow."

"Can't I go to see her?"

"You are on the permitted list. But I want you to stay away for a while.

We…. Chaské, we have a mole in our group…."

"Ah, so that's why Laura put on such a show. She's trying to take the suspicion away from herself."

"We're sure she's the mole. But we need absolute proof. So we're saying Ruth died because we're trying to flush out the spy in our midst. Make her incriminate herself. Just keep on acting like the news you heard in the meeting is true in order to help me do this."

"I'm so glad Ruth's going to recover," he murmured.

"So am I. Tell the others you're going home to mourn."

Chaské nodded. Stood up. Tears filled his eyes, but both he and Rena knew they were tears of relief. He opened the door and left.

When Skye returned to her desk there was a note from the lab waiting for her: *We recovered enough of two bullets from Ruth Gardner's wounds to compare them to the bullets from the truckers' murders. From the rifling, it looks like they both came from the same gun.*

Skye turned when she heard a noise behind her. Laura Jaf stood there.

"When will Ruth's funeral be?"

"After we're all done with this case, like I said in the meeting."

"Why not earlier?"

"Because we bury our dead when the case is over so everyone can be there."

Laura's eyes held a look of doubt. Suspicion. Uncertainty. Skye's intuition kicked in full-time. She could almost read Laura's mind. *She remembers the bullet-proof vest and the hollow barrette I gave her. I'll bet she's wondering if Ruth also had one. If Ruth could swim underwater for a while. If there were others, like Jennie, nearby who could help her. If Ruth is already dead or if she'll have to complete the job herself….*

*   *   *   *

Skye knocked on Commander Fasano's door. He looked up. "Come on in, Major. What can I do for you?"

"I'm not sure if you can do anything, Commander. But I'd like you to try contacting your connection in Switzerland. We have proof Hansard is part of the spy ring. We're holding him prisoner, but he's not saying a thing except asking for a lawyer. His Swiss accounts showed a lot of variation in the deposits. I'd like to check if all of the variations were due to money made in investments or if some of that came from being paid to spy on us."

"That makes sense to me. But I don't know how well it will go over in

Switzerland or how we could tell that he was also being paid to spy on us."
Skye's shoulders drooped at this. "However," Fasano continued. "I will try to
get what information I can, on the basis that it may change international legal
proceedings. I'll see what my contact can do for us."

A couple days later Fasano reported his Swiss contact had indeed found two
types of deposits in Hansard's account. There were some deposits of the same
amount every month from sources other than the investments.

*　*　*　*

"When will I get out of here?" Jan Konichek asked the guard outside his
solitary cell. "I am going, how do you call it, stir crazy."

The guard taunted the prisoner. "Looks like your friends don't want to quit.
We could get you on another charge. Attempted murder, accessory to murder,
of a federal officer."

Konichek sighed deeply. Shook his head. "Get for me the O-C-I people."

"Why?"

"I want to give them information."

The guard called Major Skye from his station phone. She sent Chaské
Hunter to the brig. When he got there he stood in front of the cell.

"You wanted to talk to us?"

"Yes...." Chaské waited. Konichek swallowed hard before he spoke again.
"You are part of this O-C-I?"

"Yes. Here's my identification." Chaské showed his ID card.

"Do you know who Sam Balk is?"

Chaské nodded. "Yes. The son of a technician in the Soviet Embassy in
Washington, DC."

"That is correct. Therefore he has diplomatic immunity."

"We already figured that out. Tell us something new."

"He is an assassin," Konichek said nervously. "He killed your truck
drivers. I am sure he has killed other people, too. And he will kill me if they
ever find out I told you this information."

"We'll protect you." Chaské turned to go.

"There is something else." Konichek swallowed hard. "You have a spy for
the Russians hiding in your organization."

"Who is that?"

"Laura Jaf. I heard about her when I visited Saint Louis once. They were
very proud that they accomplished her placement in your OCI."

"Thank you for verifying our suspicions. We will act on it in the proper manner. Will you be willing to testify at her court martial?"

"I... I do not know. I would be in much danger...."

"What if we simply asked you to write up that information and sign it. We could warn the court martial personnel not to speak your name out loud. It will go better for you if we legally have your help."

Konichek thought for a moment then nodded. "Yes, I will write this information for you."

*   *   *   *

First thing the next morning, Chaské returned to Skye's desk. "What's next?"

Rena nodded toward the meeting room. When the door was shut, Chaské continued. "Can you fill me in on where the operation is now?"

Rena told him everything she knew about the Waves' activities in Saint Louis and the shooting. "Also, the other day I got the report from the lab. The bullets in Ruth matched the ones that killed the truck driver. Ruth is now over at Hospitalside. Cobbe, Ford, and Stolichek are guarding her in her hospital room. And we have OCI guards at her door."

"Isn't she safe, even here?"

"We don't know. We're doing our best to keep her safe."

"By the way, when I talked with Jan Konichek, he admitted that Laura Jaf was one of their agents. And he is willing to sign an affidavit to that effect, but he doesn't want to publicly appear as a witness."

"That's good news. I'd prefer a witness, but the affidavit should work."

"So what's our next step? Remember, Sasha is the son of an embassy technician. He and his parents all have diplomatic immunity. We can get 'Sam' or 'Sasha,' or whatever his name really is, we can get him expelled from the U.S. back to the Soviet Union. But that's about it, legally."

"In which case, he gets away with murder," Rena said.

Chaské threw himself into a chair and growled. "I don't suppose there's any way we can kidnap him and bring charges against him...."

"Dream on." Rena paused for a long time. "But there is something else we can do...."

Chaské frowned. "All I can think of is...."

Rena nodded.

"You can't be serious," he said. "You just can't be serious."

Rena gave the order: "Kill Sasha."

Chaské shook his head. Images of Korea flooded his head. Hundreds of bodies. Wading in blood to go and kill more North Korean soldiers. He shook his head and sighed. "I've done enough killing for a lifetime. Korea saturated me with death. And this would be face to face. I don't know if I can do it."

"All I can say is remember this guy killed two innocent and helpless truck drivers and tried to kill Ruth. And we don't know how many others he killed. If we don't get him, he goes home free and clear."

Chaské sat for a while, chewing on his lip. He sighed and whispered: "I guess I have to do it."

"Ruth told me that when she visited him at his greenhouse, she bumped into a wooden shelf that wobbled a bit. Sasha very quickly grabbed a rubber glove to protect his hand when he reached out to keep a jar from falling. He explained that the jar held a nicotine solution that he used for insecticide and that it is extremely poisonous. You might be able to find some way to use his insecticide on him. Make it look like an accident."

"I have to think about how to get this done. I have to think. I'll be back later."

"Keep in mind he tried to kill Ruth...."

52. Chaské Collects Information

Great Lakes

Rena had Laura arrested and imprisoned in a high security block. She interviewed the prisoner in her cell with guards outside the door. "Why? Why did you sell us out?"

The other woman shook her head. "I didn't sell you out."

"We know you did. And we know you leaked our operation to your Russian friends."

"And how do you know that?" Laura smirked.

"When I sent you three women to St. Louis, I gave each of you different code names. We got a report from one of our agents in the USSR that the Russians had found out about Operation Firethorn. You were the only one using that name."

"Oh, and the others didn't know all the code names?"

"Did you know the others' code names?"

"Sure. Uh…."

Rena waited until it was obvious Laura didn't know any of the other names. She shook her head. "Silverbell? Thunderbush? Did you know about those names?"

Laura swallowed hard. "No."

"So you had to be the one who told them."

Laura scowled. "Prove it."

"Oh, we can. We will. And when we do, you will spend the rest of your life in the most uncomfortable prison cell I can find." Rena smiled. "That's a promise."

"Go to hell."

"And until then, we'll store you in a secure psychiatric ward."

"Psych ward? Why?"

"Because it's the safest place I can think of to put you until we're ready to court martial you."

"Fuck you," Laura snarled.

Rena walked to the door and motioned for the guard to open the door. He did so. Rena nodded toward Laura. "Shackle her. Take her to Hospitalside. Make her secure in the Psych Ward."

"Aye, aye, Major."

"You can't do this!" Laura shouted.

Rena nodded to the guard and walked out, saying: "Lock her up."

* * * *

Chaské returned to Rena's office. "You said I should use the nicotine insecticide to kill Sasha. Any idea how to do that? Am I supposed to inject him with it or what?"

"It's cleaner than shooting, strangling or using a typical poison. And if you do it right, it can even look natural."

"How?"

"Nicotine is absorbed by the skin very easily."

"So I pour it over his head? Soak is feet in it? What?"

"Ruth mentioned that he keeps a large jar of it on a shelf. Go down to Saint Louis and scout out the landscape. Then figure out how to do the job."

"Okay. Now, I have to get a pretty complete descriptions of the area. Take me to see Ruth."

"Oh, yes," Rena said. "There's one other thing I'd like you to try to do."

"What?"

"Bring back the stolen manuals on the Super-Terrier and Super-Talos."

He nodded. "I'll do my best to get them away from those people."

* * * *

Evan Dawes called Rena. "This is a call to prepare you for some possible emergency activity. We've had agents working for the cleaning company at the building where New Horizon has its main offices. We discovered a secret room behind a bookcase. It didn't have any sensitive material in it, but it did have safes, a darkroom, film development chemicals and microfilm equipment."

"Did you get into the safes?" Rena asked.

"Of course. They were both empty."

"So, Evan, why the call? What kind of warning? What are you expecting?"

"The Russians have all the equipment here in Chicago to make strips of microfilm. Now, I'm playing a hunch. You guys are missing some materials from the murder of those truck drivers, right?"

"Yes," Rena replied.

"And you've been investigating illegal picture-taking at some ICBM missile silos, around the submarine base at New London, and around Cape Canaveral, right?"

"Yes."

"So I suspect these guys are going to put it all on microfilm and somehow get it back to the Soviet Union. Do you have any idea where those materials are being stored in the meantime?"

"We're watching a location on the south side of Saint Louis. So, what is the possible emergency activity you spoke of?"

"If, and we don't know if this is true or not, but if this secret room is where they're going to create the microfilm to send back, you might like the opportunity to create some alternate microfilm of unclassified materials which could fool the casual observer. Then we could substitute your unclassified material for the classified info."

"So we could try to get a head start by collecting the material we could use now."

"Yeah. Legal pictures of missile silos, if there are any. Unclassified materials having to do with anti-aircraft missiles. Electronic circuits. Those kinds of items."

"All right. And come the time you need this on film, will you be able to see how they've arranged the materials so we can duplicate their film?"

"We will try." Dawes promised.

"We'll be waiting."

"By the way, I don't know if this will help your case or not, but we've followed some of their people around the city. They ride in class. In a '62 white Cadillac with a black top."

Rena gasped. "Evan, would you repeat that?" He did so. "That doesn't help much but it definitely connects that office in Chicago to a damning conversation that Eric Matthews overheard at the Red Arrow, a jazz club in Chicago...."

"Yeah, I know the place. What was the conversation about?"

"Two guys came into the men's head while Eric was in a stall. They were talking in Russian, which he understands. They mentioned a truck leaving Saint Louis and somebody named Sasha quote—doing the job—end quote. It was obviously a reference to the murders of the truck drivers in central Illinois. They also referred to something we would never suspect was missing. I think they were talking about the plans for a new missile the Navy is developing and which we discovered had been compromised in California."

"How does the Caddy enter the picture?" Dawes asked.

"Eric tried to identify these guys as soon as he could get out of the head. He saw two men leaving and rushed outside. That's when he saw the Cadillac leaving the parking lot."

"Sounds like coincidence to me."

"It may be," Rena agreed. "But the timing was intriguing, especially since the music was still being played and Eric didn't see any other people leaving the club. I think it's one more little clue to piecing this whole thing together."

"You may be right. If nothing else, it *is* an interesting coincidence."

*   *   *   *

"Hiya, babe! How you doin'?" Chaské greeted as he entered Ruth's hospital room.

Ruth grinned back at him. "Perhaps better than you'd be doing with a hole in your arm, a broken rib and a busted up hip bone."

"Well, you haven't lost your attitude. Oh, should I say, sense of humor?"

"Sense of humor sounds better." He leaned over and kissed her. "Mmmm," she said. "You want to climb into this bed with me?"

Chaské looked around. "Nah. There are too many people watchin' us. I prefer makin' love without an audience. Besides, there's no way I'd want to be charged with causin' you to re-break any bones."

Ruth shook her head and sighed. "I just can't win, can I?"

He stood by her bedside holding hands with her. "We'll make up for it later. Meanwhile, I need to get some information from you. Sam Balk has diplomatic immunity. I'm goin' to exact punishment from him anyway. He's not goin' to get away with the murders and attempted murders."

"How can I help, Chaské?"

"I need to know as many details about 'im and his residence as you can remember. Where does he live, what's the layout of his house, where's the hothouse with the insecticide, are there other things I should know about?"

Ruth told him the layout of Balk's house. "And you might want to start out at Club Viktor. I'd bet you'll meet Balk there. Let him take you to their so-called 'Russian Culture Center.'" She paused for a moment. "Oh, yes," she said with a knowing smile. "Stay away from the piers and barges on the riverfront."

"No, you definitely have not lost your sense of humor."

"I didn't mean to be funny. I want you to come back alive."

* * * *

Chaské entered Ruth's hospital room to say good-bye before he left for Saint Louis. There were no guards at her door. As he entered her room, he noticed Ruth make a sudden motion. He watched her as he closed the door behind him. She yanked her hand out from under her pillow.

"Where are your guards?"

"Nobody's out there? I guess the OCI guys were pulled because I was so close to being released. But one of our three, Cobbe, Ford, or Stolichek, should still be around. I bet they were standing by the nurses' station and saw you. Recognized you...."

"I didn't see any of them, but you could be right." He paused. Stared at Ruth with an accusatory look on his face. "What're you hidin'?"

She shrugged her shoulders. "Nothing! Why would I be hiding anything?"

"Don' know. But I'm curious." He reached under her pillow. "Nothing there."

He watched Ruth for a long moment. Her eyes shifted all over the place. She looked guilty. But, she looked a lot better than when she first arrived at the hospital. Then she'd been pale, ashen from loss of blood. Since then, she regained a more normal color and she moved much more easily. But she was still missing her radiant smile.

Her eyes darted a couple times to the drawer in the table next to her bed and turned back almost instantly. Chaské thoroughly searched the drawer. "Again, nothing. Why're you actin' so nervous?" He paused. An idea popped into his head. "Are hiding a syringe and needle somewhere?"

"No." She looked around the room as if she were searching for the best way to say something. "I... I tried to keep one from the shots they were giving me, but couldn't manage it." Ruth began to cry. "Where are they keeping her?"

"Who?"

"Uh...."

"Who, Ruth?"

"Laura," she whispered.

"What are you plannin' on doin'? Ruth?"

"I… I wanted to inject Laura with something."

"Why?"

"She identified me to them and they tried to kill me."

"You do that and you'll be put away for decades. I need you too much to let you do that."

She broke down completely. Tears streamed from her eyes.

"I want justice," she wailed.

"Rena will get it for you. If you want to help, think of this. Rena already has everything she needs to convict Laura. Even a witness's testimony."

"If nothing else, I could inject her with air in her veins," Ruth said.

Chaské shook his head. He reached out and grabbed her by the shoulders. Shook her softly. "Ruth! Stop this! Let Rena do it right. Laura won't ever walk the streets again as a free woman."

She sobbed uncontrollably. Chaské sat on the edge of her bed. Took her in his arms. Hugged her softly and held her lovingly. He knew she needed more sessions in the sweat lodge. Those had helped her get over the deaths of the two men she thought she'd killed on the last case. "Shh," he comforted. "You're not Laura and murder isn't your thing. Besides, there's been enough killin' with this case. And revenge isn't the Indian way."

"I'm not Indian," she sniffed.

"Huh!" he laughed. "You don' know how close you are…."

Chaské hugged Ruth and held her for a long time before he walked into the hall and searched out his fellow operatives who were supposed to be guarding Ruth. "You guys better stay right at her door. Or better yet, inside the room when you can."

"Why? What happened?"

"She was talkin' about huntin' down Laura and killin' her."

53 Staking Out Saint Louis

Great Lakes

Today I graduated from the Mark 37 Gunfire Control System Class C School. The toughest part of the school was the old monstrosity, the Mark 1A Fire Control Computer.

They assigned me Temporary Additional Duty to the FTA school at Great Lakes, as an instructor's aide. It seems they had no specific reason for me to return to the fleet yet, so they kept me here. I'm not complaining. I'm still with Rena.

*   *   *   *

Saint Louis

The first thing Chaské did when he arrived in St. Louis was to find all the places Ruth told him about: Club Viktor, The Russian Culture Center, Sam Balk's home. He tried to devise a feasible plan.

He decided to take Ruth's advice and start at Club Viktor. He ordered a shot of vodka. He sat there and sipped it. A man plopped down in a chair across the table from him. Chaské recognized Balk from his photos.

"You can not be Russian. Not the way you drink your vodka. This is a Russian club. Who are you? What are you doing here?"

"How am I supposed to drink this?"

"Like so." He lifted his own shot glass to his lips and threw the liquid down his throat in one smooth motion. "Now, what are you doing here?"

Chaské downed his shot in the Russian manner. "Actually, my grandmother was Russian."

Sam looked doubtful.

"It's true. She lived in Alaska, which was once Russian territory. She was even Orthodox religion and still spoke the language. Russian merchants and fur traders came there without wives. They took Eskimo and Indian women. My ancestor who 'married' a Russian was a Tahltan Indian. So I'm part Russian, kind of. Anyway, I heard about this club and thought I'd stop in and see some of what my grandmother used to talk about."

The Russian stared at him, thinking. Chaské noticed his hand inside his jacket, as if he were checking his gun. Chaské had already noticed the bulge.

"So, will you drink vodka with me?"

Chaské was prepared for this. He'd been "practicing" since he got the assignment, drinking a little more each night. "Sure, I'll drink with you."

"Good." Sam ordered two shots of vodka, one for each of them. Chaské had five shots in the next forty-five minutes.

* * * *

In another part of town, Leonid Mazursky reported to Loki. "Blaine is dead. He killed himself. Villand also. And the Canadian authorities captured Hansard and turned him over to the American Navy."

Loki seemed utterly disinterested.

"Loki, did you hear me?"

Loki looked up. "It makes no difference. None at all."

"What? Why?"

"We are done with them. This saves us the trouble of killing them."

* * * *

Balk had told him he was welcome, so the next night, Chaské returned to Club Viktor. The Russian was there again. When Chaské mentioned he'd been in Korea, they sat and talked war stories. Balk didn't claim to be in the war, but he said he had served in the army.

"I do not trust those Chinese," the Russian said. "They have too many people and they are too powerful. I hear the Russians have border skirmishes with them all the time."

They talked late into the night. When the club started to close, Balk asked: "Do you want to come to my place and have another drink or two?"

"Sure," Chaské replied. He wondered how he was going to handle being in the enemy's territory and already half snokkered. These guys could drink him under the table without even trying. Balk could be trying to get him drunk and talkative enough to slip up. The man may have been suspicious of this stranger's arrival so soon after shooting Ruth. But Chaské rode with Balk to his home anyway. He wanted to get the layout of the man's house.

On the fourth or fifth shot, Chaské tossed back his head to down the shot, missed his mouth and threw the booze all over his shoulder. "Oh, man. I gotta go home," he said. "I'm not used to drinkin' the way you guysh do any more."

"Can I give you a ride?"

"No, thanks. I'm stayin' at a friend's house not too far from here, and the walk in the fresh air will do me some good."

"Tomorrow, if you want, we will go to our local private place," Sam said. "We call it our Russian Culture Center. Would you like to go there?"

"Yeh. Shounsh good. See yuh tamorrah."

Chaské left the house. When he got around the corner, he headed for the alley, and made himself vomit up as much of the alcohol as possible. He heard someone walking.

Are they following me? he wondered. He needed to be sure he was safe, so he walked about ten blocks, stumbling, zigzagging. He saw someone enter an apartment building. The stranger didn't need a key to the front door. Chaské sat on the curb and dozed for a while, then he got up and entered the apartment building. He stumbled up to the third floor, rattled the keys he had in his pocket, and ducked into a janitor's closet. He sat there, still and quiet.

He heard footsteps back and forth a couple times. Then nothing. He played it safe, resting his head on his arms supported by his knees. Fifteen minutes later, he heard the same footsteps. The man in the hall walked back and forth a number of times. At last he went back down the stairs. Chaské waited until 0500 before leaving, very carefully. He didn't see anybody outside, so he headed for his hotel.

54. Firethorn Loose

Great Lakes

It was late. We felt pretty good about our odds of taking down the spy ring. We'd had a few drinks to celebrate. Rena and I had barely gotten into bed when the phone rang. Rena's smile quickly disappeared from her face. The call was short.

"What's the matter?" I asked.

"The head nurse at the hospital notified me that Laura Jaf knocked out a Wave hospital corpsman in the psychiatric ward who was coming to sedate her about oh-two-hundred. Laura took the corpsman's uniform, then knocked out the room guard and left the hospital. It took the staff almost fifteen minutes to realize the corpsman hadn't returned to the nurses' station. They have no idea where Laura disappeared to."

"How'd she knock out a guard? Karate?"

"I don't know, but I'll have someone's head for this," Rena said. She made a couple quick calls to get more people over to Hospitalside to protect Ruth. She wanted at least three guards there at all times with reliefs there every four hours."

*   *   *   *

Saint Louis

Chaské met Balk at Club Viktor. They had a couple drinks, then headed over to the Russian Culture Center. Chaské drank little, on the excuse that he was still hung over from the previous night. He wasn't obvious about it, but he noticed the big windows and identified them as two-way mirrors, so he knew there was another room there. He wondered if it was an office.

He got a small glass of vodka and sat in an easy chair near the two-way mirrors. He could almost make out some of Loki's conversation. It was loud and clear when he shouted at the caller.

Chaské had a couple more drinks before he begged out. "Thanks for your hospitality. But I'm still feeling the drinks from last night and I don't want to make myself sick. I can't drink like I used to. But I like this place. May I return?"

"Sure, sure," Sam Balk nodded. "You're one of us, no? Come back any time."

Chaské smiled as he left. *Come back any time. I think I will.*

He returned to his hotel in a roundabout way. Then he phoned Rena. "Laura called the Russian Culture Center," he reported. "The call made a man there very angry. I had a hard time makin' out more than a word or two until he shouted 'A public phone, Laura? I cannot believe you are so stupid. As of this instant, you are out in the cold!' I thought she was bein' held in a secure facility."

"She escaped. Thanks for this report, Chaské," Skye said.

Then there was silence on the line for a long enough time that Chaské asked: "You still there, Rena?"

"Yeah. My intuition is working overtime. I think I'll check the base telephone records."

"Check the public phones, too," he suggested. "Meanwhile, I still have work to do here."

*   *   *   *

Great Lakes

Skye was about to call Base Communications when her phone rang. The voice of the caller came before she could finish identifying herself.

"Major Skye? Brownleigh here, at Base Communications. We have some information for you."

"What did you find?"

"We picked up a call from the public phone outside the gedunk a couple blocks west of the FT School building. Know where that is?"

302

"Yes."

"The caller phoned someone in Saint Louis."

"Who made the call?"

"We couldn't bug the phone without a court order. We don't know."

"So who did they call?"

"Don't know that either. But they had a 771 exchange." He told her the last four digits of the phone number. "You might get more information about it from Ma Bell in Saint Louis."

"All right. Thanks for your help."

"You want me to keep monitoring these phones?"

"If you would. For another couple weeks."

"Will do. I'll call you if we find anything else."

"Okay. Thanks."

Rena hung up the phone. She placed her elbows on her desk. Held the palms of her hands open, facing her, and dropped her forehead onto them. "Well," she mumbled, "that information is on the wrong end of the call. I wanted most to find out who and where the caller would be. We're lucky that the guy in Saint Louis got so angry. 'A public phone, Laura?' Thank you so much, Chaské." She took a deep breath. "Well, back to work."

She called as many of her operatives as she could. Assigned them to cover all the gates through which a person could leave the base.

Laura flitted from shadow to shadow, staying as clear of the barracks as she could because she knew they had sentries outside. She tried to stay invisible, wondering what to do next, crying constantly. Finally she decided to try to get to the New Horizon Imports office in Chicago. After she killed Ruth. But she had to hide until morning. She found an unlocked car in the student parking lot, across the street from the FT barracks and spent the night sleeping in the back seat.

55. *Bad Data to Russia*

Great Lakes

Evan Dawes called Rena in the middle of the night.

"Hi, Rena!"

She recognized the voice immediately. "Hi, Evan," she said, still half asleep. "What's going on?"

"Remember me telling you the FBI tapped the phone on the New Horizon offices?"

"Of course I remember," she mumbled. She was a bit irritated at this call. "Why the reminder at this hour?"

She could hear the laughter in his voice when he answered.

"We may have struck it rich. We got a tip from our wiretap. Boris Dikau, the head of New Horizon, called Loki from Chicago. They arranged for a courier to go to Saint Louis, pick up a package and bring it back immediately."

Rena woke up instantly. "Great! Do you need any help covering this?"

"No. We have it covered. The FBI will follow the courier. This was a courtesy call. And a reminder. If they bring back your classified materials to make into microfilm, you folks are going to have a pile of work to do. And I'd guess it will have to be done overnight."

"We're ready," Rena said. "We've collected a lot of material that might be appropriate for whatever they included. You're right. This could be the delivery of the missile manuals we're missing. Thank you very much Evan. Let us know what they have and when you need the replacement film."

"We will do so."

*   *   *   *

Dawes called again in the middle of the following night. I half woke up, to the point where I almost heard the FBI agent telling Rena what they'd found. But not quite.

She set out to finish the job of re-introducing me to full consciousness. She shook me. Vigorously. About three times as hard as she needed to, all the time calling out: "Eric, damn it! Wake up! Now! We have work to do!"

"I've been awake for quite a while," I mumbled, but she'd already returned to her phone conversation. "Okay, what do you want us to do?"

She listened for a long time. She replied to Evan in cursory half-sentences a number of times, listening at the other times.

When she hung up, she said: "Evan Dawes called again."

"Yeah, I got that part of it."

"The New Horizon office has received the missing missile manuals and the microfilm photos of North Dakota and Cape Canaveral. They're in Chicago right now...."

"Okay, yeah...."

"Evan wants us to gather a bunch of official Navy electronics books and microfilm them. Also, to include cutaway views of unclassified surface-to-air missiles, you know, weapons we don't care they know about. Also include schematics of any unclassified computer circuits. Put it all on microfilm. And he wants us to create two film rolls of the scenery, one of the South Dakota missile silo country and one of unclassified missile shots from Canaveral."

I nodded. "In other words, anything that may seem meaningful with a cursory glance but is useless to them."

"Right. As far as the new Super-Terrier and Super-Talos are concerned, he wants two arrangements of microfilm, a one- and also a two-roll version. Both ways."

"Why?" I asked.

"Because he doesn't yet know how many rolls they're going to put those manuals on. And...."

"Good point. We do need to substitute the same number of microfilm rolls they prepare, so they can send them home without suspicion."

"Yes. And we should have them down to Dawes real soon. As he put it, 'yesterday if possible'."

Then she explained what we needed to do to get the fake materials down to Chicago.

I got a micro spy camera from the OCI office. I met up with the office's microfilm expert. Together we took the camera to the FT school. I inhabited an unused closet with a Radar Special Circuits book I'd studied from. Took a lot of photos from it, minus pages with critical classified circuits. We also gathered the most complex unclassified materials from the Electricity and Electronics Preparatory or E&EP School and the electronic materials from the earliest weeks of the FT school. I also found a basic book on transistorized calculating and computer circuits. Basic items. Unclassified. And we took a lot of photos. Arranged it under the headings of "Super-Terrier" and "Super-Talos." We got all that onto two rolls of microfilm.

Someone else at the OCI office searched through the photographic files and pulled out missile books. He extracted pictures similar to what Evan had described to Rena. Still another person found a pile of photos from the South Dakota countryside, photographs from Army, Navy and Air Force reports on the new missile silos. And a bunch of unclassified military pictures of missile shots from Cape Canaveral and other missile-testing grounds. Anyone in the world would be permitted to view everything they collected and put on the microfilm. They made two copies, one copy on a single roll and another on two rolls, like Dawes had asked for. And they provided copies of all the paperwork, punched to fit three-ring binders.

We had to finish doing all this by noon. It was a very hurried job, but we were able to do it. Almost. We handed over our materials to Rena at 1210. She sent them by special courier to Evan in Chicago.

*   *   *   *

In the middle of the night, the FBI agents were back in the secret room at New Horizon, a supposedly totally secure area. It looked like they were just in time. The illegal pictures and reports were on a shelf near a camera that could take microfilm photos. A pair of shoes lay on top of the cabinet, topside down. The heels were separated from the main part of the shoe. Each shoe had a hollow heel able to hold two rolls of microfilm.

Dawes made sure he knew which of the original rolls held what information. He replaced each roll with the film we sent, placing the ones with the same data in the same location and with the same orientation. He put the New Horizon rolls in his pocket.

Then he pulled out a sheaf of papers with three-ring holes punched in them. He opened the stolen missile books and replaced their pages. He stuffed the stolen materials back into his shirt, thinking: *I do hope they don't look at these manuals before they send their courier back to Russia. That could blow our*

whole operation wide open....
Then they closed up the secret room and got out of there.

56. Assassination

Saint Louis

It was early in the morning. Oh-two-hundred. Chaské snuck into Sam Balk's greenhouse, which was attached to the side of the Russian's home. There was a wooden shelf in there, not anchored to anything, crowded with gardening tools and pesticides. In one corner there was an axe with a split handle. A replacement handle stood next to it.

Balk was a heavy smoker of very strong European cigarettes. It would take a large dose of nicotine-based insecticide to kill him.

Chaské took a pair of rubber gloves from a shelf, took a syringe out of his shirt pocket and filled it with the nicotine pesticide. He capped it and returned it to his pocket. Picked up an empty glass jar in one hand and the spare axe handle in the other. Now he was ready.

He stood in the darkness to one side of the door to the house. Threw the empty jar into a corner near the house, onto the concrete floor. It made quite a loud noise in the night as it shattered. Sasha soon came out to investigate. Chaské let him take a couple steps into the greenhouse, then hit him on the back of his head with the axe handle. He caught Balk as he fell and moved him next to shelf full of pesticide. He laid him down on his back. Positioned him as if he had tripped in the darkness and fallen next to the shelf. Made it look like he hit the back of his head when he fell.

Chaské looked at the unconscious man. A string of thoughts flashed through his mind. *I do not want to kill anymore. But I swore an oath. Indian people live and die by their promises, by their good word. And I swore to not let you get away with murder. I gave my word.... Also, there were other ways to smuggle those photos and plans out but you didn't use 'em. You killed innocent drivers, Sasha. And if I kill you I'd be executin' someone who would otherwise get away with murder. Someone who would be executed if you stood trial for murder in the U.S. Yeah, I've had too much killin' already. But I can't go back on my oath. And I can't let you get away with cold-blooded murder. I'm sorry.*

Chaské reached down and took off Sasha's shoe. He injected the murderer with pesticide. Between the toes as if he'd tried heroin. He put the shoe back on and tied the shoelace. He took a huge jar of pesticide and set it aside. Then made sure he was far enough from possible splashing and pushed the shelf over. It made a nice mess, but this had to look like Sasha fell and tried to grab the shelf to stop the fall. Like he was poisoned by the resulting breakage.

Done, he thought. *Now to cover my tracks.*

Chaské picked up the jar of insecticide he'd earlier set aside and broke it next to Sasha, being sure the killer was lying in the liquid. He took off his rubber gloves and threw them where they would have fallen off the self when it fell over. With tears in his eyes, he wiped the axe handle clean, then turned and headed for the culture center.

❋   ❋   ❋   ❋

Chaské got to the Russian Culture Center at 0330. He picked the lock to get inside. He was very careful and very quiet. He didn't know who was still here. And he suspected someone lived here, too. Carefully, silently, he moved around the walls of the main room, checking for a safe behind the pictures. There wasn't one. He scouted out the hallways leading from the main room. Found a door that looked like it led to the room behind the two-way mirrors. He opened it carefully. Nobody was in there. He entered the room and closed the door behind him. Checked behind the pictures here. Nothing.

He stood wondering where they would have put the items Rena wanted him to retrieve. He picked the lock to the big desk and searched through the drawers. He found aerial photos of the truck murder scene, the Illinois troopers and Rena. But there was no trace of the manuals or the South Dakota missile silos. He headed back to the door. He was about to open it when he heard a dog growl outside.

Chaské looked around. There were no windows in the room.

But if this was a secret room, he thought, *there must be another way out in case of an emergency.*

He noticed two walls with drapes. There was only a blank wall behind the closest one. He checked behind the other drape. Again nothing.

He was puzzled. He looked through the desk again but there didn't seem to be any secret latches or buttons. And he could lift up desk legs a quarter inch without anything happening; there were no wires connected to the legs.

He turned to the bookshelves on the fourth wall. They all seemed solid. Starting with books closest to the drapes, he pulled books back so he could look behind them. One couldn't be pulled out, but it tilted. There was a soft click and a whoosh behind the adjacent curtain. He pulled the curtain back. A door stood ajar. He noted which book activated the secret door, in case he needed to use it again. Then he stepped through the door.

He found himself in a small secret room. It was full of shelves, but they were all empty. However, there was a small safe on the floor in a corner. Chaské sat down next to it, doubled himself over so he could put an ear against the safe, and began slowly turning the knob. After ten minutes fiddling with it, he began to recognize the sound of the tumblers falling into place. He soon entered the combination. The safe held a three-ring binder with pages describing the Super-Terrier and Super-Talos missiles, the copied files from the missile development office in Port Hueneme. He placed the binder under his arm. Closed the safe. Stood up.

Next to the shelves was a door. It opened to a flight of stairs going down to the basement. He went downstairs. The cellar was dark, except for the light shed by a street lamp in line with a basement window. The bottom of the stairs was near a door to the pen yard but it was locked from the outside. He turned to the dirty basement window, which measured about two-and-a-half feet wide by one-and-a-half feet tall. He could see the streetlight through the dirt on the glass.

Chaské pulled a box over from under a workbench. Examined the window. Its lock and the hinges were rusted. He returned to the workbench, where he found a large screwdriver. Once again he stood on the box. Began working at prying the window lock loose. After a half hour, he succeeded. He pulled on the window. It came loose with a loud creak. He froze. Stood there for five minutes. There was no movement upstairs. He pulled it more open. He worked until he could fit through. He was outside in the free night air by 0430.

57. Firethorn Stalking

Great Lakes

Laura chose a hospital floor Ruth was not on. The morning after she escaped from the Psychiatric Ward, she made a dry run dressed in the corpsman's uniform she'd stolen. She walked through the hospital like she was on an errand. She stepped into a room. Patients were in both beds.

"Good morning! Are you two comfortable?"

Both patients smiled and nodded.

"That's good. Do you need anything?"

"No. I'm fine."

"So am I. Thanks."

"So the staff here is taking good care of you?"

Both men nodded.

"Great," she smiled. She turned and exited the room. Continued down the hall, passing a number of other corpsmen. She was dressed like a nurse. She looked like a nurse. She acted like a nurse. None of the staff questioned her.

Encouraged, she moved on to the floor where Ruth was. Looked over the charts. The Wave corpsman behind the desk was looking at her quizzically. "I don't recognize you. What's your name and where do you work?"

"I'm Linda Martin. I work at the Special Communicable Diseases Lab."

"Where is that?"

"Washington, DC. I have to take a blood sample for a test on a Wave, a Ruth Gardner."

"There's nobody here by that name."

"But my supervisor told me she was here.... Oh, she might be here under

311

her operative's name? Rachel Johnson?"

"Yes. She's in room 214," the corpsman pointed. "Down the hall there."

Before Laura was even out of sight, the Wave called Major Skye to let her know about this visitor. Rena, in turn, called Ruth's room.

*   *   *   *

Laura snuck into Ruth's room. The patient was asleep. Laura lifted a syringe from her apron pocket. She moved closer to inject the patient. She grabbed Ruth's arm with her left hand. Got the needle an inch from her vein on the inside of her elbow.

Ruth's guards, Hunter, Cobbe, Fladeboe, and Stolichek came out of hiding from behind the drapes and the door to the head. Cobbe reached Laura first. Grabbed her wrist and twisted. Laura winced. Dropped the syringe onto the bed.

Then Ruth was wide awake. She used a corner of the sheet to pick up the syringe and hand it to the closest OCI agent. "Here Chaské. Here's the evidence for another criminal charge." She looked at her attacker. "Gotcha, Laura. We were warned by the desk corpsman. We were waiting for you. I don't think you'll ever have to pay room and board another day of your life."

"Come on," Everett growled. "We'll get you quarters somewhat more secure than the Psych Ward this time." He nodded to Stolichek. "Let's get her out of here, George."

*   *   *   *

Rena visited Laura Jaf in her new high-security brig cell. "So now, you tried to murder one of our agents again."

"What? I had nothing to do with shooting Ruth."

"That's not what I'm talking about, Laura. And you know it. We analyzed the liquid in the syringe we caught you with. And we have witnesses. You were about to inject Ruth with it. Potassium chloride in the blood veins would have killed her. Why did you turn on your country?"

"It was never my country. My grandparents came from Eastern Europe. My mother's parents believed in the Revolution. They worked for it quietly in America since before the Great Red Scare of 1919. My parents weren't joiners so they never left any record of their political beliefs, but they were influenced enough by my grandparents that they raised me to work for our victory."

"How did you get through security in the Navy?" Rena asked.

"I never needed any secret clearance or anything like that. And confidential clearance is granted by one's commanding officer. And my grandparents were far enough from me that no flags were ever raised. So I was in good shape."

Rena nodded. "Well, right now, your situation is pretty desperate. Cooperate and we'll talk about your future."

"And if I don't?"

"You won't have a future," Rena replied.

"Fuck you. You'll get nothing from me."

"You know, your situation is hopeless. You won't ever see your victory. When we put you on trial, you'll be in prison for the rest of your life. Or you'll be executed."

"That's the way it goes," Laura said defiantly.

"Your choice, Laura. I offered to help you and in your arrogance, you refused. Have a good life locked up 'til you die."

*   *   *   *

Later that day, the FBI began rounding up the whole spy network. Rena had expressed concern that OCI and the FBI needed to verify that the Russian carrying the microfilm got on a flight heading for home. So Evan Dawes asked her to come to Chicago and "work" at the airport. She helped take tickets from passengers boarding a flight to London with connections to Paris, Budapest Rome and numerous other locations.

The courier this time was none other than Grigori Ekk of Saint Louis. "Loki." The FBI followed him on his flight from Saint Louis to Chicago. They followed his taxi to the office of New Horizon. The cab waited for him while he made a quick trip inside and picked up the microfilm. They could tell he did that because he exited the building wearing the shoes seen in the secret room, the ones already prepared with the microfilm in the hollowed out heels. He got back into the taxi, which took him to O'Hare Airport.

Rena smiled as Ekk approached the walkway to the airliner. She would be able to observe him entering the plane, watch the doors close, and see the plane take off. The Russian was calm, almost self-satisfied, as he waited in the boarding line.

Rena thought to herself: *I would love to be with you at delivery time, when your superiors see what's on that film.* Her smile at the thought looked like she truly meant what she said to him: "We hope you have a wonderful flight, Mr. Ekk."

Ekk smiled and boarded the Boeing 707 for his flight heading home.

58. The End of Firethorn

Great Lakes

On 29 June 1962, Laura Jaf, Hospital Corpsman 3rd Class, United States Navy, was court martialed. It was an open and shut case. She was found guilty of treason, espionage and attempted murder as charged. She was sentenced to life imprisonment at the Navy Brig at Portsmouth, New Hampshire.

On the night after her conviction, Laura worked a spring loose from her prison cell bunk. She dug the sharp wire end into her wrist three times. Ripped apart the veins and arteries there. The next morning the guards found her dead on the floor, lying in a large pool of her own blood.

* * * *

I spent the day interviewing people to fill in all the details of this operation. Even Leonid Mazursky agreed to spend a fair chunk of time with me to let me know what happened inside the so-called Russian Culture Center in Saint Louis.

That afternoon, Commanders Blount and Fasano called a special meeting at the OCI office in Great Lakes. Major Rena Skye missed the beginning of it because she was making sure Grigori Ekk made his flight in Chicago. Everyone else was in attendance.

Blount stood up. Rubbed the back of his neck. Looked at Fasano with a silly grin. Waved one hand at the gathering of people. "I came here to tell you how unsuccessful we were on this case. I was ready to say that it was all for naught. However, you did get the killer of the truck drivers and eliminated a double agent." Rena entered the room at that moment. She stood in the back of the room and listened. "But, I was going to say, even though you accomplished those two objectives, our operation was not successful. We thought we ought to stay out of the espionage business and stick with the police work we're trained for. I believed OCI was at a dead end. We should stay away from trying to catch spies. The FBI and the CIA can do their own dirty work. We're a police force."

Rena raised her hand. ""Pardon me, Commander. Can we talk, the two of us, in private?"

"No, Major Skye, we'll stay right here." He paused with a sheepish grin on his face. "They say it takes a big man to admit he was wrong. I don't know, perhaps it does. I do know it knocks a guy down a peg or two. I was wrong about you folks. Commander Fasano brought me up to date on what you were able to accomplish. That's why I won't go running to a private meeting with you, Major Skye.

"I'm eating a healthy serving of crow, and I'm doing it publicly. I want all of you to realize I can make mistakes. I admit it. If you catch me being wrong, let me know. But do it as politely as you would to any full Commander in the U. S. Navy." This brought a laugh from the crew. "And I'm glad to report that the FBI has arrested or deported all of the Russian agents you've been watching.

"Now, Major Skye, Commander Fasano has told me about the events of the past few days. Please fill in the whole group on what you, and your Chicago and Saint Louis contingents accomplished?"

"Certainly, Commander. Some of the new information concerns why I was late to this meeting, sir. We did intercept the missile information. We did recover the classified manuals for the Super-Terrier and Super-Talos missiles. The Russians got all of that information on microfilm, but we were able to swap their film with our film having no classified information whatsoever on it. But it still looked like real missile data. Sir, the Russians did not get anything damaging to our missile development effort."

"Are you certain it made it's way to Moscow?"

"It's on the way right now, sir. Not long ago, I returned from bidding Grigori Ekk bon voyage as he carried our faked film in his shoes onto a flight to Moscow. Also sir, as far as working a spy case, I'd like to mention that when this whole thing started, we had no idea we would be breaking up a spy ring. We kind of slipped into it, not knowing what was happening."

"I realize that, Major."

"Finally, sir, I want to thank the team for working this case with their whole heart and soul. You folks did a tremendous job. And I thank you for your dedication and your effort."

"There are some specific people I want to acknowledge" Blount said. "First, will Lieutenant Eric Matthews please step up here?" I did so, wondering what this was all about. "Eric, I have the honor to present you with these new collar devices. Take those old insignia off." I broke into a big grin as I took off my old collar devices. Commander Blount continued. "Let me pin these on for you. Lieutenant Commander Eric Michael Matthews, I congratulate you on your advancement."

"Thank you Commander." I said as I saluted him.

"The biggest regret I have is you won't be able to wear these in public while you're in the field as an under-cover operative. But we will remember." He held out his hand to shake mine. "And," he laughed, "You are once again the same rank as Major Skye."

I grinned. "Thank you sir."

"All right," Blount said. "Now, will Rodney Hunter please step forward?" Chaské did so, a quizzical look on his face. "It pleases me to no end, Chaské, to notify you that you have been advanced to the civilian pay grade of GS-3, with a nice pay raise. Congratulations."

"Thank you, sir," Chaské said as they shook hands.

"Finally, I need to see Matthews and Skye in private. Everyone else gets two weeks leave. Go now and enjoy yourselves."

Our private meeting was to let us know that I had one week of leave instead of two. I also had to report to the USS *Ricketts* (DD-891) in Key West, Florida, at the end of that week. Sigh. No rest for the wicked…, uh-uh…, no rest for the good guys.

*   *   *   *

Commanders Fasano and Blount hosted a party for us at the former's home. I sat cuddled next to Rena and listened to all the conversations. Nobody mentioned Laura Jaf. It seemed that all of us simply wanted to believe she never existed. But from the thoughts racing through my head, I knew we couldn't. A foreign spy had worked her way into our group and we couldn't help but wonder how.

"Chaské," Rena said. "When are you and Ruth going back to South Dakota?"

"We leave tomorrow. We both have to heal."

"When will you return?"

"I don' know," Chaské replied. "I might not ever return to this."

"What would you do to make a living if you left us?"

"I do have a degree in sociological research. I can go to work in Pierre, Rapid City, Bismarck, Fargo, Sioux City, Des Moines, Minneapolis, Saint Paul...."

"All right, all right." Skye nodded. "But remember, Chaské, you're on contract. We can suspend it for a while. I'll list you as on a leave of absence. Let me know if and when you want to return. I realize I asked you to do a very difficult thing. And you did. Go home and heal. I'm sorry I had to force you to do what I did.... And think about this, Chaské: I won't ever ask you to do anything like this again. Never. I promise."

He swallowed hard. "Yeah. I've been thinking about what happened. We *are* a military outfit. And I didn't have to look him in the eye. His eyes were shut after I knocked him out...."

"Keep that sense of humor. It'll help."

"Yeah, but I'll need quite a few sweats to finalize this. For me this was a murder, not soldiering. I don't know how long it will take...."

"I know you were given two weeks leave, but take as long as you need. Keep in regular contact and let me know how it's going. Take all the time you need."

Chaské nodded.

"And Ruth, you're in the Navy and can't take off on a whim. But I'll push the papers through for a month's recuperation leave. I'll mail you the official papers. Now, both of you go on and heal yourselves. Call me and let me know when you're ready to return."

Chaské paused before he said. "I won't kill any more."

Rena nodded. "I know. Like I said, I won't ask you to."

Across the room I heard Stolichek ask: "Len, you going back to New Hampshire?"

"For a while, to see *ma mère*."

"You going to run the Appalachian Trail again?"

"No, I don't think so. Not this time. After I visit my family for a while, I'll be off to Miccosukee land in Florida."

Rena and I heard this and both of us frowned, as did Stolichek. But everyone in the Florida crew grinned and nodded knowingly. Cobbe asked: "Going to go see a certain pretty woman you met at the Royal Baby's Bar and Grill?"

"Yep. We seemed to hit it off pretty well. You even said you thought I hit a home run with her. So I'm going to visit her at her homeland."

Rena smiled. "A woman! Perhaps the one reason he'd ever go someplace other than the White Mountains." Then she turned to Jennie and Glenn who were, of course, sitting quite close to each other. "And you two, what're you going to do for two weeks?"

"We're goin' down to Chicago," Glenn replied. "Listen to some great jazz."

"Yes. And make love three times a day," Jennie added with a big smile. "We've even mentioned the 'M' word."

"What's the 'M' word?" I asked.

Jennie shook her head. "You men. So, you don't know everything." She grinned. "For the ignorant among us, the 'M' word is 'marriage'."

Rena was ecstatic. "Are you kidding me? When you going to …?"

"Hold yer horses," Glenn grumbled. "We only mentioned it. We don' have any plans yet ta speak of. Don' get the cart ahead o' the horse."

Jennie took a big breath as she looked at Rena and me. "And what about you two lovebirds?"

"We'll go down to Key West or some place nearby," Rena said.

"I didn' know there was any place near Key West." Glenn said.

"They're sending me down there to pick up a ship in a week, I said."

"New assignment already?"

"Yep. OCI got word of a missing officer down there. I'm going back undercover."

Glossary

This glossary is for people who are unfamiliar with some of the Navy terminology in this story.

NOTE: Naval terms in the body of an entry may also have their own entries, indicated by being underlined, so you can look for more detail there. This is a general glossary and some entries may not have been used in this novel.

ASAP (AY-sapp). Abbreviation for "As Soon As Possible." Pronounced as a word, never spelled out.

A School. A basic school to train a sailor in one specific rating: Fire Control Technician, Electronics Technician, Gunner's Mate, Boilerman, Quartermaster, etc.

Aye, aye. A naval affirmation meaning three simultaneous things: I heard, I understand, I will obey.

B School. A school for advanced training for one specific rating. Often considered the equivalent of "college." The FT B School began with six weeks of mathematics starting with basic algebra and going on to differential and integral calculus.

BuPers (byew-perz, evenly stressed). Another term for NavPers.

caliber. The size of a gun. The destroyers of this period had a main battery of 5"/38 caliber guns. This means that each barrel was five inches wide in the inside (i.e., it fired a five-inch diameter shell), and 5x38 (190) inches long. Newer destroyers of this period had 5"/54 caliber guns.

Cape Canaveral. A cape about halfway down the eastern (Atlantic) coast of

Florida. The center of the American space program. After the assassination of John F. Kennedy, the name of the facility and the cape was renamed to Kennedy Space Center and Cape Kennedy. The name of the cape has since been changed back to Cape Canaveral, which holds the Cape Canaveral Air Force Station. The Kennedy Space Center kept its name in honor of the assassinated president.

civvies. Civilian clothes.

CO (see-oh). Commanding Officer.

court martial. The Navy equivalent of a court trial, except there is a court of some number of officers instead of a jury. The three levels of courts martial are: Summary - a trial by one officer; Special - a trial by three or more officers; and General - a trial involving a law officer and at least five other officers. If requested by an enlisted person, other enlisted persons may be named to a Special or a General. Only a General may impose the death penalty, dishonorable discharge, imprisonment of over six months or hard labor for more than three months, loss of over 2/3 or for more than six months.

C School. A school to train A School and B School graduates to learn how to maintain the equipment on a particular system. The major system in the 1960s was the Mark 37 Gunfire Control System (GFCS Mk. 37).

deck. The floor.

director, gun director. A box-like unit, in which two to six men are stationed during battle. The director holds telescopes, radar equipment, and often a rangefinder. These are all pieces of equipment used to find, lock on and track targets. Thus, the director sends signals to direct the rest of the fire control equipment to calculate where the guns should be pointed to shoot down an enemy target.

dungarees (DUNG-guh-REEZ). From a Hindi word for blue denim cloth. Dungarees were the working uniform of Navy enlisted men below chief petty officer. The uniform consists of denim trousers, chambray (a lighter weight blue material) shirt, and blue baseball cap. The shirt may be long or short sleeved. In tropical climates, the work uniform may dispense with the shirt altogether, permitting sailors to work in their white tee-shirts. Civilians generally call the dungarees "jeans" or "bluejeans."

E&EP School. Electricity and Electronics Preparatory school. A six weeks long school that taught people going into numerous technical ratings. Subject matter was Direct Current (electrons, resistors, etc.), Alternating Current (inductors, capacitors, transformers, etc.), and Motors and Generators. Each of these segments lasted two weeks.

FT. Fire Control Technician, the rating that maintained the equipment used to control the shooting of shipboard guns and missiles. FTs were further designated as FTG for gunfire control or FTM for missile fire control. This job rating (category) is now known as Fire Controlman (FC).

Great Lakes Naval Station. A multi-command U.S. Navy base, east of North Chicago and on the shore of Lake Michigan, approximately twenty miles north of downtown Chicago. In the 1960s it was the home of three major commands. The Recruit Training Center (RTC) was a major boot camp, though not the Navy's only one at the time. It was on the west side of the base. The southern side was nicknamed "Hospitalside," and was a major Naval Hospital. The northern side of the base was the home of the schools command, where many ratings had their major or only training schools.

gun director. See director.

gunwale (GUHN-l). The very top edge of the side of a ship or a boat.

helo. A helicopter. The term "chopper" was generally not used in the Navy. That was more of an Army term.

Hospitalside. The command that is part of the Great Lakes Naval Base which includes the U. S. Naval Hospital.

HQ. Headquarters.

Hueneme, Port (wye-NEE-mee). A coast town in California, surrounded by Oxnard and about halfway between Santa Barbara and Los Angeles. Home of a Construction Battalion (CB or SeaBee) Center. In the 1960s there was a missile facility at Hueneme.

leave. A period of time that can be considered the Navy's version of "vacation." The government gives active military people 30 days of leave each year, which can be carried over from year to year. Compare with liberty.

liberty. Time off from one's duties lasting some set period of time. On weeknights, it is generally overnight. On weekends it is Saturday and Sunday ("48-hour liberty" or "a 48") if one has the duty on Friday, or Friday night, Saturday and Sunday ("72-hour liberty" or "a 72") if one does not have the duty on any of those days. Over a holiday weekend, it might be possible to get a standby to have "a 96."

listening mode. A method of using a ship's sonar to listen for noises underwater. The sonar is not allowed to "ping" (transmit a sound), so other vessels cannot hear it and no echo is returned. Listening mode is strictly a passive sonar technique.

Mainside. In the 1960s, Norfolk Naval Base had two major pier areas, The D & S Piers (q.v.) was a smaller area a short distance and separate from the remainder of the base, which was called "Mainside." This was the location of the cruiser, carrier and supply ship piers, recreational clubs, administrative buildings, supply centers, etc. At Great Lakes Naval Base, Mainside was the portion that was not part of Hospitalside. This is where the training commands and administrative offices were.

Mayport. A naval base on the coast, east of Jacksonville, Florida.

Mugu, Point (muh-GOO). An area in California, south of Oxnard and southeast of Port Hueneme. Point Mugu is the site of a Naval Air Station (NAS).

NAS. Naval Air Station.

NavPers (navv-perz). The Bureau of Naval Personnel, which makes sure that ships are manned at their proper level, among other duties.

Navy Exchange. The Navy's equivalent of the Army PX (Post Exchange). Basically a small department store, where sailors could buy all-important items and many luxuries.

New London. A city on the eastern end of Connecticut. It is the location of the major U. S. submarine base on the east coast.

NS. Naval Station.

OCI or Office of Criminal Investigation. Fictional crime fighting service of the U.S. Navy. In reality, this was the Criminal Investigation Division (CID) of the Office of Naval Investigation (ONI). The actual CID later became NIS or Naval Investigative Service, and later NCIS, the Naval Criminal Investigative Service.

overhead. The ceiling.

passive sonar. Using sonar in listening mode.

Point Mugu. See Mugu.

police one's brass. Ammunition cartridges are made of lead bullets and brass shells or casings, which hold the gunpowder that propels the bullet. After a weapon is fired, a revolver continues to hold the shell in its rotating cylinder, but an automatic weapon ejects the brass casing out of the way so it can load another cartridge. If a shooter cleans up after him/herself, picking up the shells to keep the area neat, to save the shells or to keep them from becoming evidence, this is called "policing one's brass."

port. There are two definitions for this term: 1. The left side of a ship or boat. 2. A harbor or a city on the ocean where ships may visit.

Port Hueneme. See Hueneme.

R and R. Rest and Recreation. Free time off from one's duties. Generally a good excuse for special liberty.

rack. A bunk.

rank. The levels of commissioned officers. "Commissioned" means that they get their position and authority from Congress. Note, there have been changes in the name and possibly the duties of "Commodore" in the late 1900s. From lowest to highest, the naval officer ranks are:

Ensign (Ens), pay grade O-1. Wears one one-inch stripe on the sleeve, single gold bar on the collar.

Lieutenant junior grade (Ltjg), pay grade O-2. Wears one one-inch stripe below a half-inch stripe on the sleeve, gold double bar on the collar. In conversation, this rank is often shortened to "j-g."

Lieutenant senior grade (Lt), pay grade O-3. Wears two one-inch stripes on the sleeve, silver double bar on the collar.

Lieutenant Commander (LCdr), pay grade O-4. Wears two one-inch stripes on the sleeve with a half-inch stripe between them, gold oak leaf on the collar. This is the normal rank of a destroyer's Executive Officer, or a larger ship's department head.

Commander (Cdr), pay grade O-5. Wears three one-inch stripes on the sleeve, silver oak leaf on the collar. This is the normal rank of a destroyer's Commanding Officer (Captain) or of a larger ship's Executive Officer.

Captain (Capt), pay grade O-6. Wears four one-inch stripes on the sleeve, silver eagle on the collar. This is the normal rank of a larger ship's Commanding Officer (Captain). The Commanding Officer of any ship carries the title and honors of Captain.

Commodore (Comm), pay grade O-7. Wears one two inch stripe on the sleeve, one star on the collar. Wartime rank only. In peace time, senior Captains are named to the positions (and the honors of) Commodore when in charge of smaller collections of ships (divisions and squadrons). Now known as Rear Admiral (lower half).

Rear Admiral (RAdm), pay grade O-8. Wears one two-inch stripe below a single one-inch stripe on the sleeve, two stars on the collar side by side. Now known as Rear Admiral (upper half),

Vice Admiral (VAdm), pay grade O-9. Wears a two-inch stripe below two one-inch stripes on the sleeve, three stars on the collar in a straight line.

Admiral (Adm), pay grade O-10. Wears a two-inch stripe below three one-inch stripes on the sleeve, four stars on the collar in a straight line.

Fleet Admiral (FltAdm), pay grade O-11. Wears a two inch stripe below four one-inch stripes on the sleeve, five stars on the collar in an octagon. Extremely rare. Like a Five-Star General. Nimitz held this rank during World War II, equal to Eisenhower and MacArthur.

rate. The level of Navy enlister personnel. Similar to what "rank" means for officers..

rating. The occupational specialty of an enlisted person. Each rating has a two-letter abbreviation, and sometimes a third letter for a subspecialty. Thus a fire control technician is an FT. If in a rate lower than the chiefs, FTs have a subspecialty of "G" for gunnery or "M" for missiles. Thus a second class gunnery Fire Control Technician would be abbreviated FTG2. Some other common abbreviations are: bos'n's mate (BM), gunner's mate (GM), hospital corpsman (HM), signalman (SM), sonarman (ST, for sonar technician), radarman (RD), and electronics technician (ET).

sand dollar. A species of round burrowing sea urchin that is extremely flat.

ship. An ocean going vessel too large to be placed on another ship, except for a submarine, which is called a boat.

Shoot the shit. To talk informally, gab, gossip.

Stokes stretcher. A stretcher made out of metal tubing, with heavy wire mesh shaped to be form fitting for the human body. It was designed to move strapped-in wounded people up and down ladders and companionways without exacerbating their injuries.

time, telling military time. Each hour has its number, and is put in terms of hundreds. The hours in the second half of the day use the numbers thirteen through twenty-four. Thus, 7:00am is 0700, pronounced "oh-seven-hundred." A half hour later is 0730, "oh-seven-thirty." Noon is 1200, "twelve hundred." In the evening, 8:00pm is 2000, "twenty hundred." When designating watches, the time is often abbreviated: the afternoon watch can be called the 12-1600 or "twelve-to-sixteen hundred." Midnight can be either 0000 (not spoken often) or 2400 ("twenty-four hundred").

Notes

1. OCI:

The Office of Criminal Investigation (OCI) is my invention. It is very loosely based on the Office of Naval Intelligence, Criminal Investigation Division. I don't know if ONI CID used the racial and gender diversity that I use in my fictional organization. I only saw ONI and CID operatives work from the outside.

I decided to use the wide variety of people I did for two reasons. First, it simply makes sense (to me) for this kind of operation. It would help placing agents in better locations and make collecting the necessary data/evidence easier. Second, other agencies, such as the various spy networks, certainly did use more than white males as operatives. Therefore, I integrated the Office of Criminal Investigation and added women as appropriate.

As a side note, the CID of ONI was later separated into the Naval Investigative service (NIS) which later became the Naval Criminal Investigative Service (NCIS).

2. NUCLEAR WEAPONS PERSPECTIVE:

The concept of nuclear winter had not yet been developed in 1962. Everyone thought that whichever side got in a massive nuclear attack first, without any enemy response, was an automatic win. The story in *Operation Firethorn* reflects that thinking.

Richard Bergeron

About The Author

(Photo © 2012, Barry Kleider)

Richard Bergeron grew up all over the U.S.A., but primarily in Rock Island, Illinois. In 1960, he joined the Navy at age 19 and stayed for ten years.

He served five and a half years on sea duty, mostly on destroyers. His final assignment was as a weapons control electronics repair and maintenance instructor in Newport, Rhode Island.

Bergeron moved to Minnesota in late 1969, where he worked at Control Data Corporation (CDC), the Red School House in Saint Paul, Minnesota Educational Computing Corporation (MECC, the "Oregon Trail" people) and August Technology Corporation. He served two years in AmeriCorps with the Minnesota Department of Human Rights and a year as VISTA Leader with the Minneapolis Public School system.

He married his wife Barbara in 1968. They have three sons.

Bergeron earned a Bachelor's degree *summa cum laude* (1978) with an American History major and an American Indian Studies minor. As a result of his association with Indian people, a Dakota family adopted him.

He and Barbara worked for eleven years with the Minneapolis Juneteenth Committee to put on a major celebration of the end of African American Slavery.

Now retired, Bergeron is able to do two things he's wanted to do for many years: teach American Indian Studies in the Minneapolis Schools' Community Education Program, and write books.

Bergeron's novel, *Needle on the Haystack*, was his first published fiction. This book, *Operation Firethorn*, is book two in his OCI series. He has also published a book of poetry, *Where Did The Sunrise Go?*

His website is richard-bergeron.weebly.com. Among other things there, you can find photographs and miscellaneous information relating to his writing.

www.ingramcontent.com/pod-product-compliance
Lightning Source LLC
Chambersburg PA
CBHW062037170626
46813CB00001B/355